RAVES FOR
JAMES PATTERSON

"Patterson knows where our deepest fears are buried... There's no stopping his imagination."
— *New York Times Book Review*

"James Patterson writes his thrillers as if he were building roller coasters." — Associated Press

"No one gets this big without natural storytelling talent—which is what James Patterson has, in spades."
— Lee Child, #1 *New York Times* bestselling author of the Jack Reacher series

"James Patterson knows how to sell thrills and suspense in clear, unwavering prose." — *People*

"Patterson boils a scene down to a single, telling detail, the element that defines a character or moves a plot along. It's what fires off the movie projector in the reader's mind." — Michael Connelly

"James Patterson is the boss. End of."
— Ian Rankin, *New York Times* bestselling author of the Inspector Rebus series

CAJUN JUSTICE

For a complete list of books, visit
JamesPatterson.com.

CAJUN JUSTICE

JAMES PATTERSON

PATTERSON

AND TUCKER AXUM

GRAND CENTRAL
PUBLISHING

NEW YORK   BOSTON

Copyright © 2020 by James Patterson
Preview of *The President's Daughter* copyright © 2021 by James Patterson and William Jefferson Clinton

Hachette Book Group supports the right to free expression and the value of copyright. The purpose of copyright is to encourage writers and artists to produce the creative works that enrich our culture.

The scanning, uploading, and distribution of this book without permission is a theft of the author's intellectual property. If you would like permission to use material from the book (other than for review purposes), please contact permissions@hbgusa.com. Thank you for your support of the author's rights.

Grand Central Publishing
Hachette Book Group
1290 Avenue of the Americas, New York, NY 10104
grandcentralpublishing.com
twitter.com/grandcentralpub

Originally published in trade paperback and ebook in July 2020
First oversize mass market edition: May 2021

Grand Central Publishing is a division of Hachette Book Group, Inc. The Grand Central Publishing name and logo is a trademark of Hachette Book Group, Inc.

The publisher is not responsible for websites (or their content) that are not owned by the publisher.

The Hachette Speakers Bureau provides a wide range of authors for speaking events. To find out more, go to hachettespeakersbureau.com or call (866) 376-6591.

ISBNs: 978-1-5387-5234-0 (oversize mass market), 978-0-5387-5238-8 (ebook)

Printed in the United States of America

OPM

10 9 8 7 6 5 4 3 2 1

For my beautiful wife, Heidi, who put her life on hold to move around the world because of my career. You are my treasure.

—Tucker

CAJUN JUSTICE

PART ONE

NO GOOD DEED GOES UNPUNISHED

CHAPTER 1

"ABRA LA PUERTA!" she screamed.

Secret Service agent Cain Lemaire shot up in bed. He left behind the recurring nightmare loop he had already experienced too many times, awakening to the high-pitched shouts of a woman.

"Open the damn door!" she repeated in a thick accent. These were not cries for help but the sounds of an angry woman demanding attention, pounding on a door down the corridor from his room.

Cain blinked his eyes several times, struggling to read his watch in the darkness. The curtains were half open, but the sun was not yet out. He flipped on the bedside lamp and saw it was barely five thirty.

Who is she? he wondered. *And why is she banging on a door at this hour?*

She continued making a commotion in the hallway. He rolled out of bed and threw on a hotel robe he took from the closet. He grabbed his cell phone and government-issue SIG Sauer .357 off the nightstand, concealing the pistol in the outside pocket. The fully loaded gun was heavy, like a brick. It pulled noticeably on the robe.

He cracked open the door but didn't see anyone. He

opened the door wider, making sure to scan the hallway. He peeked to his left and right. A strong perfume permeated the air. The source was surely the scantily dressed brunette a few doors down. She had a large purse slung over her shoulder. When she turned to look his way, her gaudy oversize hoop earrings swung wildly. Cain recognized her. She was striking enough to have caught his attention the previous night. She had been sipping a cocktail by herself in the hotel bar when he'd passed by on his way to his room.

"Your friend kicked me out without paying me!" she cried out. She marched toward Cain in her shiny leather high heels.

"Tranquila," he said as he raised his palms to her, in an effort to slow her momentum. *"Tranquila. No es un problema."* He knew her theatrics would draw unwanted attention. "Relax. I will fix this. Trust me."

"I don't trust you! I don't trust *any* of you! That *maricón* agreed to pay me. He owes me six hundred dollars!" She pointed down the hall without taking her eyes off Cain. She had deep brown eyes that matched her hair, which cascaded all the way to her lower back.

Cain assumed she was pointing to Special Agent Tom "Tomcat" Jackson's room. Tomcat was married with two daughters but known within the Secret Service as a playboy. His ego was as large and developed as his physique, and this was just the kind of woman he'd pick to experience a *different* side of the country.

"Six hundred dollars?" Cain asked incredulously.

"Yes!" She nodded. "Six hundred. This was not a date; it was a business deal."

Drawn to the disturbance, a uniformed security guard approached carefully. His wrinkled face projected alarm. Cain got the feeling the sleepy security guard rarely encountered problems at the five-star resort.

"Señor," the guard said. "Is there a problem?" He spoke in English, but it seemed limited.

"No hay problema. Todo está bien. Voy a arreglar esta situación," Cain rattled off, perfectly trilling the r's, the way his Spanish teacher had taught him. *Señora Lana would be proud,* he thought. *She always told me my Spanish would come in handy someday, but she probably never imagined it would be to calm an angry prostitute.*

Cain's conversational Spanish had also come in handy as a naval officer flying P-3 airplanes for counter-drug operations after 9/11. That was a time when the American government was waging war on narco-terrorism throughout Central and South America. He'd grown up speaking Cajun French with his parents, but Spanish was a lot more useful these days.

The woman continued arguing with Cain, switching back to Spanish for the security guard's benefit. *"No! No está bien. Ese cabrón me debe dinero."*

Watching them interact, Cain sensed that the security guard knew the señorita. Cain overheard her mentioning the president, and that's when he interjected. He *had* to.

"I already told you: I will take care of this." He walked toward Tom's room and knocked on the door. There was no answer. He knocked louder.

"He's a liar! *Mentiroso!* I know he's in there," she yelled.

Cain reached into his pocket. *Wrong pocket,* he thought as he felt the steel of the SIG Sauer pistol. He fished for his BlackBerry in the other pocket. When he found it, he thumbed his password and telephoned his partner. He even placed his ear to the door, and could hear the faint tune of Tom's "Smooth Latin" ringtone. Tom had changed it during their flight down. Tom didn't pick up, and eventually the call went to voicemail. Cain tried to turn the door handle, but it was locked.

He looked at the upset woman and the security guard. He shrugged his shoulders. "I'm sorry, but nobody answered."

The prostitute became more enraged. "*Voy a llamar la policía. La policía!* Police!" she threatened. "I want to file a police report. Now!"

The guard was sympathetic to the señorita's threats to involve the police—he was muttering something about how the American officials invaded the hotel like locusts and acted as if they owned the place. They were speaking Spanish faster than Cain could follow, but he picked up key words and understood their body language. The guard unclipped his radio from his belt and keyed the mic. "*Necesito el gerente. Ahora por favor.*" The security guard had urgently requested the hotel manager.

It wasn't the first time this manager had been called because of an agent's actions. *How's he gonna respond this time?* Cain wondered.

CHAPTER 2

THE HOTEL MANAGER, with every strand of his jet-black hair perfectly in place, rounded the corner and approached in his charcoal suit. Two additional security guards flanked him. *Tomcat ain't skating out of this one.* Cain returned to Tom's door. He knocked much louder this time. No response from inside the room. He redialed his colleague, but still no answer. *I've gotta do something before this blows up and the police are called. This situation is escalating quickly and is about to get way out of hand.*

Cain knew he would have to deal with Tom later. It wasn't the first time he had covered for his partner during an overseas trip. Tomcat's antics were an annoyance and distraction from the real reason they were here: to provide maximum protection for the American president.

The manager extended his hand, which Cain shook. "This lady is very distraught. She claims your friend owes her six hundred dollars."

"Sir, I have no idea what happened between her and my colleague."

"She would like to file a police report," he added.

Cain grimaced. Prostitution was legal and regulated

here, but this was still poor PR. "I know this much: it won't look good for the hotel *or* the Secret Service if we involve the police."

The manager signaled his agreement with a slow nod.

"I don't have six hundred dollars," Cain said, "but I will pay the lady what I have." He looked past the manager and directly at her. *"No es un problema. Yo te pago."*

He walked into his room and toward a pair of slacks strewn over the chair in the corner. He picked them up and caught the sweet scent of a Rocky Patel cigar—a reminder of his time the previous night at a chill jazz club near the hotel. Rummaging through the front pocket, he retrieved his leather money clip—a wedding gift from his father. It was engraved with the initials CML, and below that was the inscription *Micah 6:8.* In his money clip were a Virginia driver's license, a government-issue travel card, a personal Visa card, and roughly three hundred bucks in a mixture of American dollars and pesos.

He walked back into the hallway, where they were eagerly waiting. He stripped the money from his clip and showed her his limited funds.

She pointed to his wrist. *"El reloj,"* she requested.

"Absolutely not," he replied.

"Give me your watch," she demanded. "Or all six hundred dollars."

"This watch was a gift from my wife. *De mi esposa!*" he said in forceful Spanish, now losing his patience with the prostitute. *There's no way in hell she's getting the Omega Seamaster Claire gave me!*

"Este o nada." He raised the cash again in a non-verbal take-it-or-leave-it. "A little bit of something

is better than a whole lot of nothing. *Algo es mejor que nada.*"

She snatched the money out of his hand.

The manager had witnessed him pay the woman, and then instructed the guards to escort her from the hotel in a discreet manner. He turned to Cain. "Mr. Lemaire, this is a five-star hotel—"

"Yes, it is," Cain interjected before the manager could finish his sentence. "You run a beautiful hotel."

The manager smiled at the compliment. "And we have many VIPs staying here. Everyone's safety and comfort are my primary concerns."

"Mine as well. Second to the president, of course."

"No more problems, please." The manager's words were more like a demand than a request.

"You have my word," Cain replied. "But tell your security guards to keep her far away from us this week. She's a bomb ready to explode, and we don't wanna be anywhere near her when she does."

Cain went back into his room, closed the door, and glanced at his watch. It was almost six. Early sunrays poured into the room. He was still tired from staying up late to finish all his paperwork for this presidential visit. The security assessment had to be sent to the intelligence unit in DC for final approval. *Had it not been for Tom Jackson, I might've gotten another hour or two of much-needed sleep.*

He stood at the window and looked out at the ocean. Palm trees were lightly blowing in the wind, and in the greater distance, fishermen were casting traditional rope nets. *With the exception of that señorita, this port city seems like a peaceful place,* he thought. He closed the curtains and grabbed his encrypted Dell laptop. He fired up the computer and reviewed the president's classified schedule. The Summit of the

Americas was a high-profile international conference, and protecting the president took its toll on the agents. A medical researcher commissioned by Congress had concluded that for every year an agent was on presidential protection duty, he aged two years. Cain's sandy hair had no signs of gray, but he was still always struck by how much older he looked than others in their late thirties. It was genetics, he reasoned—the crow's feet surrounding his light-green eyes—coupled with a career as a naval officer and a Secret Service lifestyle that required endless travel, too little rest, and the stress associated with the dread that you could miss the one attack that would throw the free world into chaos. An assassin had to be lucky only once, but agents had to be prepared *all* the time. They were willing to trade their lives for the president's.

Cain had thought the navy was bureaucratic, but the Secret Service was even worse. It was a draconian agency with strict rules and unwritten guidelines. Cain didn't like the administrative BS or the office politics, but he didn't mind the rigorous schedule. He enjoyed seeing new places and found comfort in belonging to a warrior family, even if it was at times described as "dysfunctional."

As Cain read the notes emailed back to him from the intelligence unit, he heard a knock at his door. He suspected it was the señorita again. He slammed the laptop shut and tossed it under a sheet on his bed. He opened the door, but it wasn't the señorita. It was a face he recognized all too well.

CHAPTER 3

"THANKS, CAIN. I owe you one." The brawny agent invited himself in. Tomcat was wearing swim trunks and a T-shirt that advertised the Ohio State Buckeyes. Ohio State was his alma mater.

"You coward!" Cain exclaimed. "You were hiding in your room."

"Nah, man. I swear. I was taking a shower."

"Bullshit! I didn't hear the shower. Besides, if you weren't in there, you wouldn't *know* that you owe me one. And it's not just one, Jackson. It's three hundred."

"Tell me you didn't pay that whore three hundred!"

"Do me a favor. As long as I'm footing the bill, don't call her a whore."

Tom rolled his eyes. "Always the gentleman."

"Quite frankly," Cain continued, "I'm surprised she'd sleep with you for so little."

Tom laughed defensively while lifting his shirt. "Have you seen my abs? Women pay *me*."

"Pull your shirt down. The entire service has seen your six-pack. Plus, your pasty skin's blinding me without my sunglasses." Cain wasn't ready to let him off the hook so easily. "Why the hell weren't you answering your phone? What if I had needed you for real?"

"I told you, man. I was in the shower. I couldn't go to breakfast smelling like sex, especially in this nice hotel."

"The manager came up here with two security guards. They escorted your date out of here. I swear, I'm done covering for you. This was worse than Itaewon—"

Tom smiled. "Korea was a blast."

"How would you even know? You were so wasted I had to carry you all the way back to the hotel."

Tom laughed. "You remember too much shit!"

"It's a blessing and a curse. With you, it seems to be more of the latter."

"Come join me," his partner suggested. "They serve great Bloody Marys at the poolside bar, and I've got two complimentary vouchers."

"POTUS is wheels down in less than twenty-four hours. You can't drink."

"Twenty-four hours? That's plenty of time to sober up. Get dressed. Come on. They might even have some grits and those French doughnuts you like."

"I'm skipping breakfast, and certainly the pool. The local police are coming, and I've gotta address some security concerns before POTUS arrives. You're free to join me and do your job."

"Nah, I'm good. You've got this covered," Tom said. He turned around and left Cain's room.

CHAPTER 4

CAIN REOPENED THE CURTAINS and lifted the window. The hot, humid air poured into the room, reminding him of home in Louisiana—except for the saltwater smell. Seagulls squawked as they floated over the beach. It was still early—no beach-goers, just a few dedicated joggers. He wished he were out there running, but his normal schedule had been altered unexpectedly. Just the thought of Tom having a Bloody Mary at the pool angered him. *Thousands of people apply each month for the Secret Service, and this ungrateful asshole is taking up a spot—making over a hundred thousand dollars per year and traveling the world on the government's dime!*

Cain placed his pistol on the vanity table and sat down. He focused on his government-issue weapon. He was proficient with all firearms, but he preferred the Italian-made Beretta 92FS. That's what the navy had issued him as an aviator. That said, if he were ever shot down, he'd be better off with a comfortable pair of running shoes instead of a pistol. Better to flee from captors than battle them with a lone pistol. But now, as the president's bodyguard, his duty required running *toward* the sound of gunfire—the opposite of the body's natural instincts. It had required months of intense training at the Secret Service academy in Beltsville, Maryland.

He unsheathed his duty pistol from its tan-colored Prince Gun Leather holster. He released the magazine and racked the slide, ejecting a bullet from the chamber. He caught the hollow-point bullet midair and neatly placed it on the table. He double-checked to ensure that his SIG was empty. He fieldstripped the weapon and laid out each part carefully, inspecting every piece as if his life depended on its reliability—because it did. And so did POTUS's. Cain and his fellow team members trusted one another to shoot straight when the time called for it.

He cleaned and lubricated as necessary before reassembly. He function-checked the SIG Sauer .357, and pulled the trigger and dry-fired it several times. He hoped that squeezing the trigger repeatedly would slip into his subconscious and help with one of his recurring nightmares.

Other agents had described nightmares of being chased, or their teeth falling out, but not Cain. He had two recurring nightmares: one was personal, and the other always involved an assassin attacking the president. Cain would always draw his weapon and try to put two bullets into the attacker's center mass, but his trigger would not budge. He hoped that dry-firing his service pistol several times a day would transfer into his dreams and end that hellish loop.

He slapped a loaded magazine into the SIG and racked the slide. He released the magazine and inserted one extra hollow-point, bringing the total number of bullets to fourteen. He was always prepared for battle, and he wanted to make sure he had every round possible.

He wiped off the excess oil and holstered his SIG. It fit snugly, a testament to the craftsmanship of the artist who had molded the sheath from a single piece of high-quality cowhide. He looked upon the tools of his trade—gold-plated five-star badge, pistol, two extra magazines, pair of stainless-steel handcuffs, handheld radio and custom-molded earpiece, expandable steel baton, colored lapel pin—and inhaled the strong odor of gun oil. *If I can figure out how to turn this smell into men's cologne, I would make my millions and retire,* he thought. *But where would I go? I'm dedicated to the Service. Working in the Presidential Protection Division is exactly where I want to be.* He was an actor on the stage the Secret Service informally referred to as "the show," and it consumed his life. The Service had taken him in. They were his adopted family, and they were a tight-knit group.

His room phone rang.

"Señor Lemaire?"

"*Sí.*" He recognized the slow, heavily accented voice. It was Carlos, a retired midlevel police supervisor, now the hotel's chief of security. They had been working together for this presidential visit.

"I know you are busy, but it's very important that—"

Noise in the hallway prevented Cain from hearing Carlos.

"I'm sorry," Cain replied. "Please say that again."

The chatter in the hallway grew louder.

"*Un momento, por favor,*" he said before placing the phone down and opening the door.

Several agents, wearing shorts and with beach towels draped around their necks, were discussing their exploits from the previous night, bits of profanity mixed into their conversations.

"Guys! Tone it down. I'm on the phone. It's important."

"It's not even eight o'clock yet," one of the agents said.

"Quit screwing off," Cain replied. "We've got work to do."

"Plenty of time for that. We're all heading to the pool."

Cain shook his head in annoyance and returned to the phone.

"I apologize for the interruption," Cain offered, and inhaled deeply to calm himself.

"That's why I'm calling, Señor Lemaire. We need to talk. I'll be waiting for you in the lobby."

"Can we discuss it over the phone?"

"No," he said. "This is best discussed in person."

"I need a minute to get dressed."

"Of course, but please hurry."

The dial tone echoed in Cain's ear.

CHAPTER 5

THE LUXURY HOTEL bustled with guests, but not tourists. Most were American government officials. Secret Service agents occupied an entire floor, including the rooms above and below the president's suite. Other rooms were used by military advisors, a communications team, political aides, and other straphangers who always accompanied every VIP entourage. *If the American taxpayer only knew how much money was spent for such presidential visits...* Cain thought.

Angel was the Secret Service code word for Air Force One, and it was landing in less than twenty-four hours. Because there was still a great deal of advance security preparation to be done, Cain anxiously stood in the lobby, waiting to meet with Carlos. The hotel's head of security seemed to always be running late. Cain had learned from his travels, which had taken him to more than one hundred countries on six continents, that only a few cultures had an obsession with punctuality. Americans and Germans certainly fit the stereotype, and from what he had heard from his twin sister, Bonnie, the Japanese were also mindful of being on time. By comparison, South America as a whole seemed much more laissez-faire.

While impatiently waiting in the lobby, Cain marveled at the building's architecture. It was nothing like the cookie-cutter hotels back home. This hotel had a colonial feel to it, with magnificent wooden columns and high ceilings that supported elaborate glass chandeliers.

His focus was interrupted by the immaculately dressed Carlos, whose tailored suit fit snugly on his large frame and was accented by a Rolex watch and gold rings. Cain wondered if the man had amassed his fortune as a captain with the police force or as head of the hotel's security department.

"Señor Lemaire. Let us sit down over here"— Carlos gestured with an open palm—"where it's more private." He looked around the lobby as one might at an ATM in a sketchy neighborhood. "I heard about what happened this morning. We're used to these things here. And quite frankly, we think it's only human nature. Man has been chasing woman since the beginning of time. But we may have a problem. I received a phone call from our national newspaper. They were asking questions. I think the woman has talked to the press."

"What?"

"It appears so, señor."

"Well, there's no story here. I'm sure the press will realize that, and it'll be old news by the time Air Force One arrives. That beautiful Boeing 747 has a way of stealing the limelight when it lands."

"Señor. You don't know Latin women like I do. I've been married to four of them, divorced from three. This *puta* is not going away."

Cain's BlackBerry vibrated on his hip, opposite side from where he carried his concealed pistol. He never wanted to accidentally grab his phone when he intended to draw his gun. While on duty, he also always made sure his ringer was switched to Vibrate, especially after a colleague forgot to do so during a speech by former president Carter. Deacon (the Secret Service code name for the thirty-ninth president) had been in the middle of delivering a speech when the agent's phone rang, and President Carter fixed the agent with a look. The agent was so mortified he'd offered to resign the following day.

Cain grabbed his phone from its holster on his belt and rested it on his thigh while Carlos continued talking. He flipped it over and glanced at the screen. There was a high-priority notification. Next to the message was a red exclamation mark. The email was from Supervisory Special Agent LeRoy Hayes.

"Please pardon me for one second, señor. This is my boss trying to reach me from Washington. He's usually hands-off, so it's unusual."

"Claro." Carlos waved his hand in the air as if swatting a fly.

Cain read the short email. "Reports of excessive drinking and good-time girls. Embassy is aware. Return to DC tomorrow, 0855 hours United flight. Your relief is already en route. EOD."

Cain was stunned. He knew that EOD meant "end of discussion," but it was a forceful way to state it. He suddenly felt sick to his stomach.

"Are you okay?" Carlos asked. "You look ill."

Cain scrolled to the top of the email to see who else was on the distribution. Tom Jackson and ten other agents. All twelve had been out the night before, just blowing off steam in their typical fashion while globe-trotting on behalf of Uncle Sam, forging camaraderie among men who daily put their lives in one another's hands. Few people understood the stresses placed on

them or their families' sacrifices. One agent had retired abruptly upon returning from an overseas trip.
He noticed a drawing on the refrigerator that his
son had made at school. The Secret Service agent
noticed Mom, the daughter, the son, and their dog.
Confused, he asked where he was in the picture. "At
the White House, where you always are, Daddy," the
boy answered.

Cain's phone buzzed. It was Tomcat calling. "Are
you already doing the security assessment?"

"I should be, but I'm not. I'm still trying to tie up
your loose ends!"

"Where are you?"

"I'm in the lobby."

"Stay put. I'll meet you there. Coming now."

Cain looked at Carlos. "You weren't joking about
Latin women."

"I never joke when it comes to women *or* money."

"Judging by your jewelry, you've done much better
with money than you have with women."

Carlos smiled, and Cain continued. "But what I
need help with right now is figuring out how to
manage this rogue-woman situation."

"She reminds me of my second wife. You cannot
manage this. Nobody can. This is going to be painful
and expensive."

CHAPTER 6

TOM JACKSON WAS now wearing flip-flops, swim shorts, and a muscle shirt. A thick pool towel was dangling over his right shoulder as he rushed up to Cain, who was finishing his conversation with Carlos.

"You're leaving a trail of water drops in this nice lobby," Cain pointed out, annoyed.

"That's the least of my concerns right now! What do you think this is about?"

"You know exactly what this is about! It's about you being reckless. Cheap. Irresponsible. And selfish!"

"Selfish?"

"Yeah, you heard me right. You were only thinking about yourself. I don't care about what you and that woman did last night. But your selfish actions this morning are interfering with a lot of other people."

"Well, I'm going to call Hayes. Flying back to DC before the president gets here is stupid. They've already spent the money on us being here. I can make an economic argument on the matter."

"An economic argument?" Cain was in disbelief. "Like the one you made a few hours ago with the woman who stormed out of this hotel with all *my* money?"

Tom said nothing. He used his towel to continue drying off.

Cain went on. "Since when does Uncle Sam give a damn about how much money is spent on these trips? If you're going to call Hayes, make sure to get your story straight first. You're not going to get one over the King." That was Cain's nickname for their boss, LeRoy Hayes. In Cajun French, LeRoy meant "the king."

"There's nothing to get straight. This is all bullshit. You know it, and he knows it."

"It's *not* bullshit," Cain insisted. "If you're gonna buy flesh, then you gotta pay—in more ways than one."

"What's that supposed to mean?"

"Some things you just gotta learn on your own, Jackson. But I'm pretty sure I'm not alone on this one. The King is gonna think this is bullshit, too, but not in the way you think."

"You're always putting LeRoy on a pedestal. He's a has-been. Been with the agency over ten years and he'll never rise any higher than SSA."

"Perhaps. But the King was a beat cop and a street agent before he became a pencil pusher. If you go after him, he's going to counterattack like a bobcat that just got his tail pulled."

"I'm the one who's getting my tail pulled," Tom lamented. While still standing in the lobby, he phoned their supervisor and put the call on speaker. "You busy, boss?"

"Yes, I am," LeRoy Hayes replied.

"Okay," Tom said, oblivious to LeRoy's answer, "I'll keep it short."

"You got thirty seconds, because I've got an emergency meeting with the special agent in charge."

"An emergency meeting with the special agent in charge?" Tom asked.

"Am I talking to a parrot?" LeRoy asked.

"No, sir."

"The SAC wants some answers. *Imagine that,*" LeRoy said.

"I wanted to talk about your email telling us to end mission and report back to DC."

"Tom Jackson, I can't believe you are calling me to discuss this over an unsecured line in a foreign country. Actually, I *can* believe it. Nothing you do surprises me anymore."

"Sir, is there any flexibility on that order?"

"Negative. Bottom line: make sure your ass is on that flight in the morning."

"The others, too, right? Not just me?"

"Until I can get the facts ironed out, *all* twelve of you who were on my email," he said before hanging up.

Tom looked at the phone to make sure it wasn't connected any longer. He turned to Cain and began to vent. "I'm so sick and tired of this agency. Everyone walks around like—"

Cain interrupted. "Pipe down, man. People can see and hear us. We're in the lobby of a five-star hotel, for Christ's sake."

"I don't care where we are! I'm not going down over some bullshit like this."

"Neither am I," Cain replied. "I promise you that."

"What do you suggest, then?"

"Start planning damage control. Triage. Stop the bleeding."

Three men in breathable short-sleeve button-down shirts and khaki cargo pants entered through the lobby doors. They made eye contact with Cain. Plainclothes police officers. Although he had never met them before, Cain had worked with lots of cops throughout the world. He knew how to detect them in a crowd. Cops carried themselves differently.

"I'm going back to the pool," Tom said. "After all, according to Hayes, it's my last night here."

"Jackson, it's just one more night. Maintain a low profile for the rest of this trip. Got it?"

Tom smirked and started to walk off but turned around to make one last comment. "Don't work too hard today. You're on the same flight as me in the a.m."

Cain felt his anger surfacing. *Put it aside—for now. You've got a job to do.*

CHAPTER 7

THE THREE PLAINCLOTHES policemen approached Cain.

"Are you Cain Lemaire?"

"Who's asking?" He was always on guard, but even more so when working in a foreign country.

The oldest officer reached into his back pocket. "I'm Detective Rojas," he said as he opened his wallet and showed his badge. "My office was told the Secret Service wanted to do another security assessment before the president arrived."

"Yes," Cain answered with relief. He thought they might have been there because of the prostitute. "That's right. I knew we were meeting today, but I guess the time got away from me. I've been handling a bunch of other stuff this morning."

"That's all right," Detective Rojas said. "We are here to help you." He extended his hand.

"Mucho gusto." Cain shook the detective's sweaty hand. "You gentlemen walked here?"

"Yes. Parking is prohibited because of the international conference."

"But you're a cop. Like Kojak and Columbo. You can park anywhere."

Cain smiled, but he got the impression that the officers didn't get the American references. He understood his job was not all operational; it was also diplomatic in nature. He represented the American president, and he needed the assistance of the local police for such momentous visits. "Well, I certainly appreciate all your help to make this mission go well. Your support is why these presidential trips are successful."

"We are happy to help you. We enjoy the overtime."

Cain propped his tactical backpack on the floor and unzipped it. "*Compañeros,* I brought some gifts for you." He reached into the black canvas to retrieve various pieces of Secret Service swag. He had baseball caps, patches, shot glasses, coffee mugs, and challenge coins.

The officers graciously accepted. But while they liked the gifts, they seemed more impressed with Cain's boots. He wore a pair of rust-colored alligator boots with his navy-blue suit, sans tie.

"You *Americanos* are cowboys," said Rojas, scratching his salt-and-pepper goatee. "Like President Bush."

Cain chuckled. This was the first time he was working with these officers, but he knew American politics often came up in conversation. Perhaps sensing a moment of awkwardness, another officer asked, "Where can I get boots like these?"

"My old friend, goes by the nickname Prince, makes these at his camp on the bayou."

"*Donde?*"

"*Mi casa en Louisiana.* It's a town two hours from New Orleans. He makes boots, belts, and holsters out of leather, alligator, and lizard. Let me know what you want, and I'll make sure to bring it on my next trip."

"Okay." The officer smiled. "Hopefully they are comfortable, because with so much vehicle traffic today, we must walk to the conference."

"*Bueno*. A walk sounds"—Cain paused only long enough to inhale deeply—"nice after the morning I just had. I can use some fresh air."

Cain and the officers headed to the main door. The bellman, wearing a button-down jacket and white gloves, opened it. A burst of heat rushed into the lobby. "Have a good day, Mr. Lemaire," he said.

"*Igualmente,*" Cain replied. "*Hasta luego.*"

The sun shone brightly and not a cloud was present. Cain retrieved a pair of sunglasses from his inner jacket pocket.

"Where shall we start?" one of the officers asked.

"From the beginning," Cain said. "Let's walk the entire path. I wanna know this place so well that locals would pay me to give tours."

As they walked, Cain mentioned several security concerns he had. "This morning, I saw boats not too far in the distance, over there." He pointed toward the ocean, which was only a hundred yards or so away.

"*Sí,*" the third officer replied. "Many of our people fish to feed their families."

"I understand," Cain said. "Growing up in Louisiana, I did the same thing. Fried catfish was a staple for us."

"A staple?" the officer asked.

"Yeah, um…" Cain searched for a definition. "Like a main dish. We ate it often."

The officer nodded his head.

"I'd like to have at least two police boats out on the water," said Cain. "I'll give you two Secret Service agents to put on the boats."

As they continued walking the route toward the conference building, Cain pointed out additional areas of concern. "I would like to put a countersniper on that tall building there, and also on top of that white building over there. We'll have a team on the roof of the hotel where the president is staying, so this gives us a triangle of protection."

"This is no problem. Our military snipers have been informed you may request this."

"Thank you very much. We'll place a member of my team with each of your military snipers. The Secret Service agent will serve as a scout."

"A scout? They aren't bringing their *own* rifles?"

"Yes, they are. But overseas, we prefer to be scouts. If somebody does get shot, it's always more politically correct when the local police or military kills one of their own, as opposed to us."

"Here"—Detective Rojas stroked his beard—"we don't give a damn about political correctness. A dead asshole is just a dead asshole."

Everyone laughed. It was a nice distraction for Cain. If only for a brief moment, it got his anger toward Tomcat out of his mind.

They had passed a few shops when Rojas pointed out an ATM. "This is a safe place to get pesos," he said. "If you need to get money—say, three hundred dollars—this would be the place I recommend."

Speaking of assholes, Cain thought. The amount quoted was too specific. Cain was naturally easygoing, but he didn't like being the punch line of a joke. "Are you messing with me?"

"Cain," Detective Rojas said, "this is *my* town. Nothing happens without *me* knowing about it."

"I'm listening," Cain replied.

"She came into the station wanting to file a report this morning. The desk officer referred her to me."

"Why you?" Cain asked.

"I run the special investigations unit."

"What did she tell you?"

"It does not matter," he said.

"It matters to me." The edge on Cain's words was sharp.

"What matters is what I told her."

"And what was that?"

"Salte de mi oficina ahora! Puta!"

"Good, because I already paid her, and she was not even with me."

"She doesn't want money," Detective Rojas said.

"I'm starting to gather that. Sounds like she wants revenge."

"Hopefully she was worth it," the youngest officer said to the laughter of everyone except Cain.

"Not for me. I was just trying to put out a fire, and now I'm getting burned."

"Burned?" Rojas asked curiously.

"I guess you don't know *everything* that goes on in your town."

"What do you mean?"

"I've been recalled back to DC. I fly back tomorrow. Hell, practically the whole team flies back tomorrow."

"But the president arrives tomorrow."

"I know. They've already sent agents to relieve us. I'm just out here with you guys to try to do as much as I can before I leave."

"I like America," Detective Rojas said. "I do. But sometimes I don't understand your country. Holly-wood produces movies like this all the time. My wife loves *Pretty Woman*."

Cain smiled. "Well, that woman from last night got a huge disappointment. Tom Jackson is no Richard Gere."

"I can't understand this. Your government sends you all back because of one prostitute's complaint? This woman is a troublemaker. Plain and simple. I kicked her out of the station. I took care of this for you."

"I wish it were that easy," Cain said. "But the truth is my boss and his bosses see this whole thing differently than you and me. The Secret Service is embarrassed by this because they were notified after the American embassy was informed. The Service doesn't like surprises. Surprises are bad — really bad — in this line of work. They'll see it as a black eye on our agency."

"Since you are leaving tomorrow, do you still want to continue working now?"

"Absolutely," Cain said. "And I'd better use that ATM. I need some quick cash. There's still enough time for my partner to get into more trouble."

Detective Rojas nodded. "I've been a police officer for twenty-eight years. I know what it's like to have shitty partners."

"It's nice to have things in common," Cain said. "But I wish that wasn't it."

Several hours later, after conducting the advance security preparations and host-nation liaison, Cain returned to the hotel. The same bellman was on duty. He always seemed eager to practice his English. "Mr. Lemaire, you look like you had a lot of sun today."

"Yeah." Cain dragged out the word. "I guess you could say I got burned today — in more than one way."

"Are you finished now?" the bellhop asked.

"Sure am. It was a long day, but I'm glad it's finally winding down now. How was yours?"

"Very busy, too. Many guests today. I mailed that package to Japan for you."

"Perfecto! Muchas gracias." Cain handed him a generous tip before he continued toward the elevator. As was his habit, he automatically scanned the lobby for anything out of place. He stopped when he recognized the acne-scarred man walking toward him.

CHAPTER 8

"GOOD TO SEE YOU AGAIN, brother!" Cain's academy classmate, now an agent from the Atlanta office, bear-hugged him.

"It sure is, Teddy! Just wish it were under different circumstances."

"You're telling me! I was this close"—he signaled with his thumb and index finger—"from busting a counterfeit ring. Got a group of Nigerians putting out the best hundred-dollar bills I've seen in my career."

"Ah, man. I'm sorry. I can't believe they'd pull you from that case to come down here for this."

"I'm *not* surprised. Nobody in our agency cares about investigations. If you want to get promoted in the Service, you have to be on the president or vice president's detail. Otherwise, before you know it, you're fifteen years in and still guarding a garbage can in a hotel alley. I've become best friends with Oscar the Grouch."

"Well, the Service is overreacting on this one. I'm hoping it will blow over as soon as they get the full details," Cain replied.

"Tomcat and some of the others, I can see. But you? I'm not judging. I was just surprised to see your name."

"It's not what it appears," Cain said. "When a skunk sprays, a lot of bystanders have to deal with the smell, too."

As Cain talked with Teddy in the lobby, he noticed other agents hauling suitcases and coordinating room requests with the receptionist. The hotel had been booked completely, so getting the exiting agents checked out and their bookings replaced with the new agents was causing a logistical nightmare.

"Cain, you're one of the few on the president's detail who I actually like," Teddy told him. "You don't have an ego the size of Air Force One. So, I don't want you blindsided on this one. This is gaining more traction than you probably expected. The SAC in Atlanta is referring to your team as the Dirty Dozen. And apparently the White House is concerned that if the media gets ahold of this, it will overshadow the president's participation at the Summit of the Americas. The Service's PR guy is already talking to the White House in case they need to issue a press release."

"A press release? Are you yanking my chain?"

"Afraid not, brother. I don't want you getting burned over this."

Cain chuckled. "If today had a theme, it'd be *getting burned*."

"Just watch your back."

"I'll deal with management as soon as I get back. Don't worry about me. You just stay focused on keeping the president safe here. You've been out doing field investigations for so long you've probably forgotten how to do protection."

"I had to knock the wax off my earpiece," Teddy joked.

"That's disgusting."

They laughed together. Cain described the security

assessment and explained the primary and secondary routes and safe havens. He handed his colleague business cards and contact numbers for key personnel he had interacted with.

"Sounds like you've done all the work for me," Teddy noted. "I would have expected nothing less. Any other agent would have quit as soon as he learned he was being pulled from this trip. But not you."

"I've double-checked all the routes with the local police. I know I don't have to tell you this, but don't let your guard down. These international conferences are publicized well in advance, and always make me nervous. The manager has another route you can take the president tomorrow to escort him to his room. He'll show it to you tomorrow morning when he's back on the clock. That way you can avoid going through the kitchen. I always have a bad feeling about that."

"Remember Bobby Kennedy," Teddy said, referring to the senator's assassination in the kitchen of the Ambassador Hotel. "We must have seen that video clip a hundred times in the academy."

Cain nodded. "At least a hundred. Should you run into any hiccups or have any questions, just shoot me an email or give me a call. My flight isn't until eight in the morning. And I'd rather talk to you than Jackson."

"Who wouldn't?"

Cain smiled. "Good luck with the visit."

As Cain started toward the elevator, the agent's eyes were diverted downward. "Those gators waterproof?"

"Of course."

"Good."

"Why?"

"They'll need to be to wade through the shit you're about to trudge through in DC."

CHAPTER 9

CAIN RETURNED TO his hotel room and welcomed the cool air blowing from the AC unit. He felt sticky, and his suit was soiled with sweat. He couldn't wait to disrobe and take a cold shower. While in the shower, he kept replaying the events from that morning. *Should I have paid her, or just let the police get involved?* Neither scenario was ideal, but he concluded that he had made the right decision.

He hurried to meet up with Tom Jackson in the hotel's lobby. While waiting, Cain noticed the woman he'd paid off, sipping a cocktail at the hotel bar. *So much for the security guard's promise to keep her away. He's probably getting a kickback.*

"Where we going tonight?" Tom asked.

Cain maneuvered his body to block Tom's view of the hotel bar. "Definitely away from here. I know just the place. Saw it today while doing the security advance with the locals."

"That's what I'm talking about. Local cops always know where to go to have a good time."

"It's a British pub."

"Let's go to a club, not a British pub."

"Absolutely not. It's nearby, and I'm starving for some fish-and-chips. It'll be a chill spot for us to strategize about the way forward. We *need* to. That's the most important task ahead of us."

Cain asked the bellhop to hail a taxi. When they jumped in, Tom began running his mouth a thousand miles an hour.

"Not here," Cain interrupted him. "We'll be at the pub shortly. Let's discuss it then."

"This cabby probably don't even speak English," Tom commented.

"Regardless, Jackson, you've embarrassed me enough today."

"All right," he conceded. "I'll wait till we get to the pub."

The pub was heavily accented with thick, dark wood. It was shaped like a rectangle, and British memorabilia—photographs and artifacts—adorned the walls. It was empty, not including the English expat in his sixties who said he was the owner. "What are you blokes drinking?"

"Two whiskeys," Tom answered.

"And fish-and-chips," Cain added. "Make the chips extra crispy, please." He grabbed a matchbook from the bar and continued toward the back corner. He absentmindedly rubbed the matchbook in his left hand—between his fingers. He and Tom sat down at a table. "I wasn't expecting *this*," Cain said flatly, referencing the fact that the soundtrack to *Grease* was playing in the background from two speakers mounted on the wall.

The owner brought them their drinks.

"Must be some serious discussions going on tonight."

"How do you reckon?" Cain asked. He caught himself feeling more suspicious than usual.

"Fellas, this place is almost empty. Yet you chose this corner. You don't look like businessmen—too athletic for that—so I figured you're here for the Summit of the Americas and are probably going to discuss politics or security—maybe both."

"Good eye," Cain said.

"I wasn't always a bartender," the man said. "Name's McMillan. Call me Mac. Used to be navy intelligence. For Her Majesty, of course. I should've stayed in, but I fell in love with a local woman."

"So much for being intelligent," Tom quipped.

Cain turned to Tom. "Like you have any room to judge." He then turned back to Mac. "I hear they're hard to resist."

Mac chuckled. "Yes, they are. So, I moved here and opened up this pub."

"It's a nice place you have," Cain said. "And it's a pleasure to meet you."

"It's not fancy, but I'm proud of it." Mac used the dead air to excuse himself. "Well, I'll leave you fellas to it. Your fish-and-chips will be out shortly."

The pub offered enough privacy for Cain and Tom to talk openly. They discussed the events that had transpired and predicted what would happen.

"The Service has a long history of partying and screwing around. We're no different from the politicians we swore to take a bullet for," Tom commented before gulping his drink.

"You know we're not held to the same standard as politicians," Cain said. "They can be as crooked as a dog's back leg, but we carry gold badges. The public demands more from us. It doesn't matter if you were a Secret Service agent for only a month ten years ago. If you were arrested for DUI, the headline would read 'Ex–Secret Service Agent Arrested for Driving

Drunk.' We have to think strategically here if we're gonna get out of this mess."

"What do you mean? What are you thinking?"

"Well, for starters, did she ever tell you what she did for a living?"

"Nah. I just thought she was a local who wanted to party with someone on the president's security detail. Relax, bro. We did nothing wrong. We'll be fine."

Cain became angrier. "*We* did nothing wrong? *We?*"

"Yeah, *we* did nothing wrong."

"If *we* did nothing wrong, then why am *I* leaving before this mission is complete?" Cain continued, raising his voice. "Hell, the whole team has told you over and over to maintain a low profile. Don't draw so much attention to the Service. You know we operate in the background, but you always find a way to put us in the spotlight."

"*You* like to operate in the background. *You* don't mind being a shadow." Tom puffed out his chest and pointed to it with both index fingers. "But I'm different. I'm in the show, baby. As you like to quote, 'To thine own self be true.' I'm just being true to myself."

"And to your wife and kids back home? Are you being true to them?"

"Don't go there, bro! I love my family and provide for all their needs. They have a roof over their head and food on the table. I take care of *my* family."

"What about your family *here*? Your Secret Service family?"

Before Tom could answer, their attention was drawn to the bar's entrance. Three other Secret Service agents stumbled into the pub. It was apparent that this was not their first stop of the evening. Upon seeing Cain and Tom, one of them pointed and shouted in a slurred voice, "It's the other members of the Dirty Dozen."

With his large arm, Tom motioned for them to come toward the back. "Welcome, men!"

"Don't call 'em over here," Cain urged. "We still have business to discuss."

"Plenty of time for that. We got a long flight tomorrow." Tom turned his attention to his colleagues who had just poured in. "I was just about to challenge Cain to a game of darts. Right, Cain?"

"I'm not playing darts with you," he said flatly. He then looked straight into Tom's eyes. "This conversation ain't over."

The five agents gathered around a dartboard, but Cain didn't play. He was too ticked off to enjoy the pastime. The other agents tossed darts and continued discussing the injustices of being recalled from their mission.

"Recalled?" Cain said. "That's a nice way of saying kicked out, or booted."

One of the agents was an old-timer nearing retirement. "I'm divorced, thanks to the Service. They can't do squat to me. And they're seriously mistaken if they think my enjoying the warmth of a lady is going to stop my retirement."

A sudden bright flash lit up the dim and smoky establishment. Cain turned toward the cause: a woman clutching a professional-looking camera with an expensive zoom lens.

"Get that bitch!" one of the agents shouted.

Tom bolted from the dartboard and rushed toward the woman as she tried to exit the bar, grabbing her sleeve and preventing her escape.

"Soy reportera para El Tiempo," the startled camerawoman shouted. *"Dejame ir."*

"Give me that camera!" Tom demanded.

Mac intervened, placing himself between Tom and the frightened woman. "It's okay. She's just a local reporter."

"No, it's not okay," Cain said, having rushed toward the altercation. "Jackson's right. She's got a picture of us drinking in a bar. We want that film."

"Or she'll have trouble sitting down when I shove that camera up her ass!" Tom said.

"Knock that shit off!" Mac said, siding with the reporter. "She's welcome in here just like you fellas. And if you blokes don't calm down, I'm going to ring the police. This is *my* bar!"

Tom gripped the camera and yanked it out of the reporter's hands.

"Dame la cámara!" the reporter yelled.

"Fuck you!" Tom shouted back.

With one quick movement, Mac struck Tom's throat with an open palm. Tom fell backward and dropped the camera. It crashed onto the floor and smashed into several pieces.

The other agents rushed to Tom's aid as he gasped for air. They were about to fight Mac when Cain shielded the bar owner and pulled him aside. "Naval intelligence my ass! That strike looked more like a technique taught to the British SAS."

The camerawoman quickly recovered her broken camera and fled. The inebriated agents attempted to chase her, but gave up after a few seconds because she was too quick.

"I understand this is *your* business," Cain said, "but please understand *our* concern. We're United States Secret Service agents. We don't need this reporter posting our photos all over the place. You know what I mean—OPSEC. We try to fly under the radar. The word *secret* is in our name."

"Really?" Mac belly-laughed. "If you boys are trying to stay secret, you've done a bang-up job since you arrived in this country. Besides, it's just one photo. What can it hurt?"

CHAPTER 10

THE AGENTS RETURNED to the hotel that morning with just enough time to pack their bags, check out, and catch their ride to the airport. They used their diplomatic passports and a courier bag to bring their weapons on board.

"I'm in seat 14A. What seat are you in?" Tom asked Cain.

"Thankfully, not one near you."

"Ah, man, don't be like that."

"Enjoy the flight, Jackson," Cain answered with a sarcastic tone. "We're on it *because* of you."

"At least it's a free flight back home," Tom said. "You'll be sleeping in your own bed tonight."

"On that note, I'm gonna catch some z's. So, don't bother me on this flight."

Cain settled into his seat and peered out the window. They departed northbound and he could see farmland off to the right. When the pilot banked left, Cain marveled at the sea and the sailboats until they vanished in the distance. The sea was no stranger to him, yet it always seemed mysterious—a duality of giving life and taking it.

He took a sip of his black coffee. He always thought

the beverage tasted better at higher altitudes. Plus, it forever reminded him of his navy days, when he had depended on coffee to stay awake for the thousands of hours he spent flying his P-3 over the oceans, searching for Russian submarines or South American drug runners.

Next to him sat an elegantly dressed woman who appeared to be in her early forties. She seemed interested in what Cain was busy scribbling in his black Moleskine journal.

"Are you writing a book?" she asked.

He looked up. "Maybe someday, but not today. This is just a collection of my notes—work things, restaurants, names of people and hotels."

"I get motion sickness easily," she said. "So I try to disconnect from the world when I'm on a flight."

"Normally, I'd try to watch one of the new releases, but I'm collecting some thoughts for an important interview tomorrow."

"Job interview?"

"Something like that. I have a boss who's gonna ask me a lot of questions about my trip down here."

"How did you like your visit?"

"Wish I could've stayed longer."

"Oh, I know what you mean," she said.

You have no idea *what I mean,* he thought. He had a dull headache forming, a combination of lack of sleep, alcohol, cabin pressure, and the stress of being recalled from a mission, which had never happened to him before. He retrieved a bottle of Tylenol PM from the bag resting at his feet and swallowed two pills.

"You can always come back," the woman said.

He nodded in agreement.

She continued. "I was there to meet with the

CEO of a large jewelry company. My business is in diamonds."

"And where are you from?"

"I'm from Thailand. Have you ever been? We call it the Land of a Thousand Smiles."

Cain lowered his head. Before he could respond, the flight attendant approached. "Sir, the gentleman in seat 14A ordered this for you." She presented him with a Jack Daniel's on the rocks.

"You're too kind," Cain said.

"It's my job," she said, and smiled.

Cain winked playfully. "I meant calling him a gentleman."

She grinned even wider.

"Thank you, but please take it back to him. Tell him I'm already asleep."

Cain looked at the passenger next to him. "It's been nice talking with you. I've got a long travel day ahead of me, so I'm gonna close my eyes for a bit. I hope you find a good movie to watch."

"Do you have any recommendations?"

"You've Got Mail."

She tilted her head and raised her eyebrows. "You like *You've Got Mail*?"

"What can I say?" He smiled. "I'm a sucker for romantic comedies. And Tom Hanks is a great actor."

"I agree with you. It's one of my favorites. That and *When Harry Met Sally…*"

"You'll find 'em under the Classics category. Enjoy the movie." He jotted a few last-minute notes in his journal before nodding off.

After landing in DC, Cain collected his luggage and walked out of the airport. The sun's rays aggravated his migraine. He rummaged through his backpack for a pair of aviators to shield him from the brightness.

He found his government car, parked at long-term parking. *Had I known this mission was going to be cut short, I would have splurged for short-term parking.* He cranked the sedan, rolled the window down, and hit I-66 eastbound.

Most people complained about DC's traffic, but not him. He recognized the trade-off: being able to experience the history and museums. He saw a road sign advertising the Smithsonian's National Air and Space Museum at the Steven F. Udvar-Hazy Center, one of his favorite places to visit when he wasn't working. It always brought back good childhood memories of his dad, Claude, teaching him and Bonnie how to fly. Claude still owned and operated a small crop-dusting business near Lafayette, Louisiana.

Cain pulled curbside in front of his two-bedroom town house. The American flag above his porch blew lightly in the wind. He noticed two packages by his door. He grabbed them on his way inside the house. Although he had moved to DC two years prior, most of his belongings were still packed in cardboard boxes. He weaved through the maze of unopened boxes and headed straight to the kitchen.

He was parched. He grabbed a bottle of water and looked at his packages. One had a customs form and Japanese characters. He found himself feeling cheerful for the first time in days at the sight of her handwriting. It was a gift, and he knew who had sent it. He ripped open the parcel.

CHAPTER 11

CAIN'S NIGHTMARE ENGULFED HIM. He twitched in his sleep and was relieved when his cell phone buzzed on his hip, waking him. He saw that he was still sitting in the recliner, still wearing yesterday's clothes. *I must have been more tired than I thought.*

"Hello?" he answered groggily.

There was no reply. He cleared his throat. "Hello?"

"Happy birthday to you. Happy birthday to you. Happy birthday to the best twin brother in the world."

Cain smiled and joined in on the last line of the chorus: *"Happy birthday to you!"*

They both laughed a similar chuckle.

"How's my favorite brother?" Bonnie asked.

"Better now that I'm talking to you. How's life in Tokyo?"

"It's busy! It's five thirty in the afternoon and I'm still at work. Picking up *another* shift. But I couldn't not call my favorite brother on our birthday."

"Well, I'm glad you called. Even if it is three thirty in the morning here."

"The time difference is horrible!"

"Half the time my body doesn't even know what

time zone it's in. But I was so excited to see your gift yesterday. The Japanese instrumental CD is perfect. It worked as advertised. I listened to it for a bit and it helped me fall asleep."

"You're home? I thought you were in South America."

"It's a long story."

"I always have time for your long stories."

"Well, I *was,* but a bunch of us got recalled. Some colleagues enjoyed the company of some local women, and one agent in particular kicked his date out in the morning without paying her. She—"

"Without paying her? So, you mean a prostitute?"

"Anyway," Cain continued. "She started a scene, so I paid her what I had before the police got involved."

"Ooh, this sounds good. Who was it?"

"I'll give you three guesses, but you're probably only going to need one."

"If I get it right on the first try, will you come out to Japan?"

"Ha!"

"I bet it was Tomcat. He's such a *cochon.*"

"Bingo!" *Cochon* means "pig" in French. "We got back yesterday. We have to answer to management later on today."

"What's the worst that can happen to you?"

"They could fire me."

"Fire you?" She scoffed. "Nobody is going to fire you."

"I'm probably being a little dramatic, but it's a possibility."

"Well, you have always had a little flair for the dramatic. You'll be fine, brother. You're a dedicated agent. They're lucky to have you. With your experience, you could easily be a private investigator or a pilot. You could make so much more money in the private sector."

"Maybe. But you know how I feel about money as a motivating factor. I'm more interested in service to country."

"I know. I'm just saying there are other options out there besides the government. But you'll be just fine once you explain that you were trying to avoid embarrassing the Service."

"They might give me a few days' suspension without pay."

"Then you can come visit me in Japan! We can hang out together on the beach in Zushi. We'll spend *my* money. I can also introduce you to some of my cute Japanese coworkers. I've told them all about you. They'd love to meet an American gentleman like you."

Cain laughed. "I'd love to visit you, but that flight would be brutal. What's it—about fourteen hours?"

"I'll use my family perks and get you upgraded to business class."

"That sounds nice, but like you said, I'm sure everything will work out once I explain what happened. Then I'll be back on the president's schedule soon."

"Sucks for me. I was looking forward to hosting you on this side of the world, especially before summertime. Vacation season picks up and all our flights are booked. I'm already having to cover extra routes."

"That must be why Pops said he couldn't reach you last week."

"Yeah, probably. I was flying to either Seoul, Guam, Hong Kong, or Singapore. We're trying to compete with the Asian airlines. It's tough! They're paying their flight attendants peanuts."

He laughed.

"What's so funny?"

"Nothing."

"No, really. What was so funny?"

"When you serve your customers peanuts, expect to be paid in peanuts."

"That's domestic! Not international."

"Just don't fly yourself to death," Cain said. "I read an article that the Japanese are dealing with a crisis: employees are working themselves to death. There was a photo of Japanese men sleeping at their cubicles."

"Sometimes I get the impression that Japan's national motto is Work Harder, Not Smarter. But I like my job as a flight attendant, and I like it here in Tokyo. I feel really safe." Bonnie changed the subject. "Have you talked to Mom and Pops lately?"

"Not since before I left. You?"

"It's been about two weeks. It was so funny watching them try to use Skype. Pops can fly an airplane but can't operate a smartphone."

Cain and Bonnie laughed together.

"Well, in all fairness," he said, "his airplane is older than us!"

"And with the way he cares for it, it'll probably outlive us all." She laughed. "Did he send you the usual birthday present?"

"Yup, a box of Community Coffee's dark roast with chicory."

"I don't know how the Lemaire men can drink that nasty crap. Way too strong for me."

"It'll certainly put some hair on your chest."

She laughed. "That's *not* the look I'm going for. Just make sure not to drink too much of it, or you'll never get any sleep."

"Okay, Mom."

"Hey! I'm just concerned. You told me you were still having nightmares."

"You can't have nightmares if you aren't sleeping."

"That's why I sent you the CD! Have you talked to the Secret Service psychologist?"

"God, no! They claim to be confidential, but if the Service is paying their salary, that's who they're loyal to."

"Have you considered talking to a priest?"

He paused before responding. "I haven't been to a church in years. You know that."

"Well, I'm here for you, brother. I know this sounds bad, but I hope they suspend you."

"What?"

"You need a vacation, and I'd love to see you in Japan."

"I don't need a vacation."

"You're just like Pops. You'll work till the day you're dead."

"Sounds like you, too. Hey, keep your eyes open. I sent your birthday gift with some extra things, too, so you can share it with your colleagues."

"I can't wait! You're always so thoughtful."

"You, too, sis. Well, I better sign off. Gotta get ready for my meeting."

"You have a meeting on a Saturday?"

"This investigation is kicking into overdrive. LeRoy wants to know my side of what happened, and nobody cares whether it's Saturday or Sunday."

"Good luck with the King!" she said. "Call to update me right after. Love you."

CHAPTER 12

CAIN ENJOYED COOKING, but he hadn't shopped since his trip. He opened the refrigerator and saw it was empty, except for leftover Chinese, a bottle of mustard, some salsa, eggs, and a few bottles of Coke—the ones made in Mexico with the real sugarcane instead of the fructose corn syrup. He grabbed two eggs and placed them in a pot of water. While they boiled, he brewed a batch of Community Coffee. He flipped through a stack of mail while he sipped the chicory coffee his dad had sent him. *Mm. This is good. Feel the life coming back to me.*

During the commute to the office, his mind naturally went to his interview. *What should I say? Should I be forthcoming about Tomcat?* He eventually settled on a plan to discuss only things he had firsthand knowledge about. He wouldn't speculate about rumors or side conversations he'd had with Tom Jackson and the other agents.

Cain was so deep in thought that he was surprised at how quickly he arrived at the White House. He grabbed his wallet from his back pocket and flashed the uniformed Secret Service officer his credentials, which displayed his official photograph and the US code that delineated his authority and jurisdiction.

"Welcome back, Agent Lemaire," the officer said. "I heard it was quite the party trip." The cocky officer smirked.

What a jerk! Cain thought. But he understood the conflict between the uniformed division and the agent corps. The agents knew that the officers wanted to be agents, and the officers complained that agents were egotistical prima donnas who thought they were God's gift to federal law enforcement.

"For an agency with 'Secret' in its name, it's troubling how fast gossip travels," Cain replied, not trying to hide his annoyance. "For someone of your tenure, I would have expected better."

"Is it gossip when there's a picture of you and a few others out drinking the night before the president arrives?"

Cain's head rocked back. "What are you talking about?"

"It hasn't made the American news yet, but our intelligence branch showed us a photo this morning during roll call. It shows you, Agent Jackson, and a few others throwing darts with beers in your hands."

Cain was blindsided. "Open the gate!" he demanded. He stomped on the throttle and skidded his government sedan into one of the first come, first served parking spots. Sunrise was still an hour away, so there were still plenty of spots. His plan had been to work out in the office gym before employees started trickling into the building. *That'll have to wait. I gotta track down this photo.*

Instead of using the normal door to his office, he went straight to another entrance. The uniformed officer allowed him to pass. Cain strode through the hallway adorned with portraits of past presidents. The red carpet beneath his feet was about an inch thick. He made a left turn and went toward some downward stairs. A chain blocked the entrance and a sign said RESTRICTED ACCESS. He unhooked the chain and proceeded to the intelligence branch, which occupied a secure command center in the basement of the White House. They monitored everything from CCTV cameras: the airspace around the White House, even the air quality the president breathed.

The analyst was managing two computer screens on her desk.

"The officer outside told me you had a picture of agents out drinking."

"Good morning to you, too, Agent Lemaire."

"I'm sorry, Annie. I just got the news dumped on me from the guard outside."

"Bad news travels fast."

"You're telling me."

"Give me a second and I'll pull it up on the big screen."

"Oh, no! Don't do that. Just pull it up on your computer. I'll look at it here with you."

For the first time, Cain saw the picture the reporter had taken while they were at the British pub. "I was off duty and off the protective detail by that point," he muttered under his breath. Regardless, he knew the perception would not be good. "How'd you get this picture?"

"The State Department received it from our embassy. The photo was broadcast on a news story."

"Oh, God," Cain said as he buried his head in his hand. "How can we squash this from spreading?"

"Cain"—she looked at him sympathetically—"you know I'd help you if I could. But it's too late."

"What do you mean it's too late?"

"This picture came in last night when I wasn't on shift. It was forwarded to the director. He has it now."

"The director? What did he say about it?"

"He said he would take care of it. Whatever that means."

"That means it ain't good. I should've snagged that camera myself and shoved it up Tomcat's ass."

CHAPTER 13

SUPERVISORY SPECIAL AGENT LeRoy "the King" Hayes grew up in Harlem and had worked as a beat officer with NYPD before getting hired by the Secret Service during the Clinton administration. He liked the status that came with being a special agent but was unhappy with the agency. He believed his skin color kept him from getting promoted any higher in the organization. "The only color this agency recognizes is white," he would often say.

"My day is just starting, and I'm having to deal with this buffoonery," LeRoy said now in an agitated tone. A flashy dresser, he prided himself on his fancy suits and silk ties, designer ones he'd get his academy classmate, now stationed at the US embassy in Rome, to ship him. Cain's well-manicured supervisor had a thin mustache and a bald head, and he puffed on a purple e-cigarette with gold leaf clusters. "Tell me what happened, and don't lie to me."

"I wouldn't lie to you, and you know that," Cain fired back.

"Hell, I *know*. But those bastards in the ivory tower are crawling up my ass. The brass wants blood on this one. It's bad."

"You can't get blood from a turnip, or from me, on this one," Cain said, wondering if that was true.

"Just explain the situation and leave all that Southern talk out of it."

Cain looked beyond LeRoy's mahogany desk and at the wall displaying a black-and-white photo of Dr. King giving his famous "I Have a Dream" speech. Next to it was LeRoy's Columbia University degree. Despite his resentment of the perceived racism in the Service, LeRoy never forgot how far he had come in life. "From the slums to the show," he would remark proudly. Cain knew of LeRoy's sacrifices and had a great deal of respect for his life journey.

Cain was describing his security preparations in very specific terms and being very thorough when LeRoy cut him off.

"I get all that. I'd expect nothing less from you. Get to the fucked-up part—the *real* reason we're sitting here staring at each other."

As he had promised LeRoy and himself, Cain didn't lie. He spoke only about the events he experienced firsthand, and he was rather broad in his explanations. He concluded, "I don't even know her name. But I gave her some money so she'd leave the hotel and not cause any problems for POTUS's visit."

"That's where you went off the rails," the King barked. "You are a good agent, but God, you're blind. You paid a prostitute you didn't even fornicate with. If this weren't so asinine, dragging this agency through a scandal, I might be laughing."

"This isn't a scandal," Cain said defensively.

"The police notified the American embassy. Twelve agents had to be recalled to DC, and the president—don't even get me started on that issue. He's at an international summit, having to defend those entrusted to defend *him*. That is what we, a collective society of like-minded people, call a scandal. Even your kin in Mississippi would agree."

"Louisiana," Cain interjected. He had worked for LeRoy for a year and knew his boss liked to tease him about his Southern roots.

"Same difference! Listen up! Bottom line is you're on paid leave pending the outcome of this investigation."

"You're suspending me?"

"You get the best of both worlds. You get to suckle off the government's teat, and you don't have to stand duty."

"I don't mind the duty, though. You know I'm passionate about my work," Cain said.

"Don't piss on my leg and tell me it's raining. I like my job, too. But I'd rather be at home watching *Judge Judy* and getting paid for it."

Hold your tongue, Cain. Don't make this worse.

"Also, you've got a meeting with the doc tomorrow at nine."

"I already knocked out my physical for the year," Cain said. "Scored excellent in every category except flexibility."

"I'm talking about Dr. Anna Spencer, the Service's psychologist. She's been ordered by the director to meet with each of the Dirty Dozen to determine your suitability for this line of work."

"You gotta be kidding me." Cain knew he was raising his voice. "Sometimes I think I'm the only sane one here."

LeRoy tilted his head and widened his eyes. "Go home. Get some rest. Just be prepared for tomorrow."

"Yes, sir." Cain stood and turned to leave.

"Slow your roll."

Cain stopped midstep.

"Because you're on administrative leave pending the outcome of this investigation, I'm going to need to hold on to your badge and gun."

"Boss!" Cain exclaimed. "You can't take my badge and gun. This is just an administrative inquiry."

"My hands are tied," the King replied apologetically. "This is coming down from higher up."

"How high?"

"Nosebleed high," LeRoy replied.

Cain reluctantly handed over the tools of his trade. His identity was tied up in his job. He searched for a loophole. "DC is a violent place. You leave me nothing to defend myself with."

"Don't flatter yourself. Nobody is desperate enough to rob a man in a Sears suit and a Walmart tie."

"Hey! This might not be a hundred-dollar tie like yours, but it's nice. My sister sent this from Japan."

"Let's not waste time talking about Japanese fashion. I got more knuckleheads to deal with. Now, don't forget. Tomorrow at zero nine hundred. Answer her questions right so I can get you back on POTUS's detail."

"Gladly," Cain replied.

"And one last thing. Your keys. Turn 'em over. You can't drive a government car while you're on administrative leave pending a"—the King used air quotes—"'management-directed inquiry.'"

"A management-directed inquiry?" Cain repeated in disbelief. "Sounds more like a witch hunt. And history showed us how that ended."

"Then you better get rid of your broom and black hat, because they're getting the matches and piling up the straw."

CHAPTER 14

THE DAY PASSED SLOWLY. Cain's family called to wish him a happy birthday, but it didn't *feel* like his birthday. There was no cause for celebration. His thoughts had huddled around his psychological evaluation. *If I can just get this test over with, I'll be reinstated,* he reasoned.

The next morning he faced the bathroom mirror. The sunlight peered through the window, brightening the small room. "Let's go with the half Windsor knot," he said aloud. "Gotta look extra sharp today."

Cain exited his house. He felt the crisp, cool morning air. He loved Arlington in April. He intended to get into his sedan, and then remembered that he had been ordered to leave it at the office. *That's embarrassing,* he thought, regarding his lapse in memory. *Maybe my work life is becoming as muddled as my personal life*.

Given that he was clad in a suit and tie, he had to rethink his commute to the shrink's office. It had been several months since he had ridden his motorcycle, but he put the question of whether he had lost any of his riding skills out of his mind. His concern was the inch of dust on the cover. It may have been waterproof, but it wasn't dustproof.

Last time he rode the motorcycle was in winter. When he'd yanked off the cover, the neighbor's cat, which had been sleeping on his seat, snarled and darted off. *Tigger probably scared me more than I scared him,* Cain recalled. "All right, let's see if Tigger is underneath. Here, kitty kitty." He carefully removed the cover to give Tigger enough notice and so that the dust wouldn't dirty his suit. Second by second, the shiny Harley-Davidson with lots of chrome came into view. *It still looks as beautiful as the day you gave it to me, Claire Bear.* It was a Road King from 2003—the year Harley celebrated its hundredth anniversary— and his wife, with financial help from her father, had gifted it to him to commemorate his service in the United States Navy. Claire had wanted to buy it in fire truck red, but her father, a prominent defense attorney in New Orleans, had persuaded her to pick blue to symbolize the oceans that the navy sails. Cain loved the classic look of the motorcycle, with its leather saddlebags and whitewall tires. He was beyond thankful for the gift and never held it against his father-in-law that he defended the same types of drug criminals that Cain helped put behind bars as a counter-narcotics pilot.

The Harley hemmed and hawed as it cranked and spit out bluish-gray smoke from its exhaust before finally settling into a rhythmic rumble. The entire motorcycle gyrated, and Cain rolled the throttle a few times to warm it up. He threw on his brown aviator jacket, put on a pair of riding glasses, snapped the button on his low-profile helmet, donned his leather gloves, and cruised toward the White House.

The wind blew past his ears and the cold stung his face. His feet shifted the gears as his hands pressed the clutch. He and the motorcycle operated as one—man and machine linked together. When he arrived at the shrink's office, he noticed a fancy BMW with vanity plates but no other motorcycles in the lot. *You never see a bike outside a shrink's office,* he observed. *I don't need a shrink; I just need to ride more.*

He walked into the lobby and checked in with the receptionist.

"You're all checked in. Please help yourself to one of our magazines and the doctor will see you as soon as she can."

Cain looked at his Omega Seamaster. "I had an appointment for nine."

"Yes, sir. I see that. Dr. Spencer is usually really great about time, but today she seems to be going a bit over with her eight o'clock patient."

"Who is that?"

"Oh, I'm sorry. I can't disclose that. You know: patient privacy rules and laws."

"I understand that. I just thought I might know the person."

"It's certainly possible. Your agency has kept us very busy lately."

Cain nodded before he took a seat and perused a few magazines on the coffee table. He skipped the celebrity news and went straight to a *Time* magazine. The cover's headline caught his attention: TEN IDEAS THAT ARE CHANGING YOUR LIFE. Above that, in smaller print, was a caption about Japan's unity after disaster. He tried to follow Japanese current events so he could have a better understanding of his sister's life in the Far East.

He flipped open the magazine and started reading about Japan. The article was about the extraordinary resilience and unity of the Japanese people; it allowed them to cope with the previous year's 9.0 magnitude earthquake, tsunami waves, and breakdown of the nuclear reactors. Seeing the devastating pictures and reading the traumatic story of how twenty thousand people perished caused his heart to pump faster. The words and pictures made him feel as though he was there—right in the middle of it all. He heard their screams. Sweat beaded on his forehead, and drops started plopping on the pages as he thought of the rushing waves of water.

A door creaked as it opened. One of his colleagues was walking out of the psychologist's office.

"Mike," Cain said, "you look like you've seen a ghost."

"She's good, Cain. Really good," Mike said in an exhausted tone. "You're going into the lion's den. Be careful."

Before Cain could respond, Dr. Anna Spencer appeared at the doorway. Her pale-blue eyes pierced right into Cain's.

"You must be my next victim," she said with a disarming smile.

CHAPTER 15

SHE LOOKS AS THOUGH she's in her late thirties, at most forty. Cain began creating a baseline profile of Dr. Spencer. *She's single—no ring. Attractive, keeps herself in great shape. Not surprising: one of the unwritten rules of the Secret Service is to hire only pretty women and athletic men.* The Service knew that politicians were always concerned about who surrounded them, and how that would impact their public image. The agents groaned and, with self-deprecating humor, referred to themselves as "window dressing" and "expensive chauffeurs."

"If I'm one of your victims," Cain replied with a smile, "I'm a victim of circumstances."

"Oh." Dr. Spencer smiled back. "I like you already. We're going to have a lot of work to accomplish in a short amount of time. Please, come in." She invited Cain into her office with a wave of her palm.

"It's just what I would have imagined a shrink's office to look like," Cain said once he was inside and she'd shut the door.

"Please explain," she said. He detected a faint European accent, possibly German.

"Everything's black leather—the chair and couch. Probably faux, but still leatherlike. In that corner is a healthy spathiphyllum plant that stretches toward the ceiling. That's very relaxing, and I'm sure the oxygen it produces helps aerate this room when it gets stuffy." He smiled again. "And I'm sure a lot of hot air gets blown around in here."

She listened but didn't reply.

"The only thing missing," he continued, "is a mini-bar. *In vino veritas.*"

"Yes! In wine there is truth," she said. "But I'd probably lose my license if I gave alcohol to my clients."

"The irony," he said. "You might lose your license, but you'd probably help some of your patients."

She glanced at the clock on the wall. "Oh, we better get started. We're already behind schedule. Your time is important, so I apologize for that, Mr. Le Mayor." Cain winced as she mispronounced his surname. "But I'm glad you came."

He cleared his throat. "I had no choice, doctor. My boss ordered me here. But I'm quite confident you'll quickly determine that I'm perfectly fine and not in need of any further psychological evaluations."

"You'd be amazed at how many of my clients tell me that," she said, and smiled that disarming smile again. "Nevertheless, I think you will find *some* benefit in our session, Mr. Le Mayor."

"It's actually pronounced *Le Mare,*" Cain said with a smile.

"Pardon?" she said.

"It's French," he replied. "It means 'the sea.' But I'm pretty informal. You can just call me Cain if you'd like."

"Perfect. I prefer being on a first-name basis with my clients."

Cain chuckled nervously. "Well, I'm not really a client. I'm just in here for this one session, and once you sign me off as capable of protecting the president, I'll be back to work."

"You seem very confident you'll pass my evaluation," she said.

"My colleague, who just left sweating bullets, said you are really good. I'm trusting his confidence in your skills."

She smiled, obviously pleased at the compliment. "Your accent—I've been trying to place it as you speak. I'm pretty sure it's from the South, but I'm not quite sure where."

"I'll give you a hint," Cain said. "Thank God for Mississippi."

She put her pen to her mouth, still thinking.

"How about, 'We're not all drunk Cajuns'?"

"Louisiana?" She grinned and wagged her pen at him.

"You got it, doctor."

"I must confess that I haven't visited yet, but it's on my list," she said. "The food, the music, and the people all seem so interesting. How long has your family been there?"

"Several generations, for sure. I've never done any type of research, but I know my ancestors came from Nova Scotia in the late seventeen hundreds."

"I find family history and their dynamics fascinating—from a social and clinical perspective. *Where* we are born shapes so much of our lives."

Cain laughed. "Well then, I can't wait to hear your analysis on this one. The story goes that my mother was at home making one of her delicious chicken and sausage gumbos when her water broke. My aunt Elmer Lee was at the house, too. They jumped— well, waddled is probably more accurate—into the pickup and rushed to get my pops, who was out inspecting a nearby sugarcane field. In hindsight, my mother and aunt should have just gone straight to the hospital. But I wasn't going to wait any longer. I popped out right there in the cane field. A field hand experienced in delivering farm animals served as my momma's makeshift ob-gyn. A few moments later, my sister came out, too."

"That's an incredible story. So, you're a twin, then?"

"Yes. My sister is Bonnie."

"That doesn't sound very Cajun. Right?"

"My dad has a weird obsession with everything having to be symbolic, especially when it comes to names. Since sugarcane is sweet, he wanted something that represented sweetness. *Bonbon* is the French word for candy. So he came up with Bonnie, and we called her Bonbon when she was a child. And Cain is for sugarcane, though my very Catholic mother chose the biblical spelling. And of course they named our younger brother Seth."

"Like the biblical story?"

"Yes. But there's no rivalry between us."

"Are you close to your brother?"

"My *sister* and I are the closest, of course. It comes from being twins. If she stubs her toe, I can feel it. If she is in some type of danger, I can sense it." *I can't believe how open I've been with this shrink.* "I'm normally a much more private person, and here I've been just flapping my jaws."

"No, not at all. You're a great storyteller," she noted.

He looked around the room for a second before asking, "So, am I cleared to report back to duty?"

She laughed softly. "Not so fast. We're getting closer, but we still have some work to do."

"What *else* do you wanna know, doc?"

Dr. Spencer put down her pen and looked directly at him. "Tell me about your nightmares."

CHAPTER 16

CAIN'S HEART THUMPED in his chest. He could feel the rush of blood expanding his veins and arteries. Even if the psychologist was dangerously good at her job, there was no way she could know about the nightmares that plagued him. Cain had never shared them with anyone except Bonnie.

Stall for time! Stall her! His session was scheduled for only an hour, and he figured he could run down the clock. "Doctor, could you please repeat the question?"

"Nightmares, Cain. Tell me about yours."

"Um." He fumbled for an answer.

"Everyone has them," she said with a clinical demeanor.

He let out a huge sigh of relief. *She doesn't know. She's just fishing.* "I don't have any."

"Ah, come on, Cain. Even tough guys have nightmares," she replied. "It's just the unconscious talking to us. We can learn from it."

Don't trust her! his mind shouted. *Talk about something safe—an old nightmare.* "When I was a pilot in the navy, I'd sometimes dream that I was flying over the ocean. It would start getting pitch-black and I wouldn't be able to see the horizon. The stars would be reflecting off the water and my instruments would become too blurry for me to read. I'd lose all reference to up and down. Alarms would start sounding in the cockpit and then my propellers would stop spinning. Everything would go quiet. The silence was eerie. All I would hear was my team pleading, 'Hurricane, save us.' But I couldn't see anything—I was flying in the blind."

"What would happen?" Dr. Spencer asked.

"I'd crash. The plunge into the ocean was always violent enough to jar me awake."

"That's scary, indeed," she said. "I can't imagine being in such a terrifying situation. But nightmares teach us something about ourselves."

Cain remained silent for a beat. "This nightmare pushed me to become better. I read more books, trained harder, and flew more missions. I trained for emergencies until they ceased to be emergencies. Making sure my crew felt safe with me was my obsession."

"I find it interesting that your nightmare is not a monster per se, but rather a scenario."

"Why is that interesting, doc?"

"Well, we choose our careers. And your history shows a pattern."

Cain found himself being drawn into her line of questioning. *Mike was right. I better be careful. She's good, and I don't know where she is leading me.*

"You are attracted to dangerous jobs."

"I guess you could say to dangerous hobbies, too. Like flying and riding a motorcycle. Or maybe I just took too many punches to the head when I boxed in high school."

Cain saw that his official personnel file sat open on

her lap. She riffled through the pages. "Or perhaps your boxing experience has helped your on-the-job ratings. I see you have excellent marks in physical fitness."

"I don't hit the bag as much as I'd like to anymore, but I still remember the techniques—jab, cross, hook, uppercut. I was a freshman in high school when an old Cajun hired me to help him build a boxing gym. As part of my labor, he gave me a key to the gym and I practiced every day after school. When he saw that I was committed to the sport, he started training me."

She continued thumbing through his paperwork. "You also have excellent ratings in shooting."

"Been shooting a gun since I was three. Comes with the territory of being born in South Louisiana, the Sportsman's Paradise."

"Oh, my," she said. "That doesn't sound safe."

"I think it's safer when you have a respect for it, rather than a fear."

"One of your supervisors described you as 'fiercely loyal and married to the job.'"

Cain liked the compliment but was embarrassed by all the praise. "This ain't just a job. It's a vocation. This profession called me. I know this probably sounds cliché, but I wanted to serve my country at the highest level. Protecting the president allows me to do that."

"Your Secret Service file is thicker than most I see," she observed.

"That's probably because it contains my military records as well," Cain said.

"It shows assignments all over the world—many that would give a normal person a case of adrenal fatigue or PTSD. Do you feel like you've experienced any symptoms of the illness?"

"Is that what the experts call PTSD nowadays? An illness? Like catching the flu?"

"PTSD affects everyone differently. Some become more aggressive, while others become more withdrawn. Many of my clients are veterans returning from Iraq or Afghanistan."

"I appreciate your trying to help them," Cain said. "We are quick to send people to war, yet slow to treat them when they come back. It's a real shame."

She nodded in agreement.

An awkward silence followed. "You asked earlier about my brother," Cain finally said. "He's not the younger brother I remember growing up. Operation Iraqi Freedom changed him. He's a different person now. He can barely hold down a steady job. He lives with our parents. Farmwork seems to be helping him with his anxiety."

As he spoke, Cain had been studying Dr. Spencer's Stanford University degree, hanging on the wall behind her desk. *Why would such an educated woman choose the bureaucracy of government employment instead of private practice? Fear of failing at private practice?*

"Mind if *I* ask a question, doc?"

"That's not normally how my sessions go, but sure. I'm flexible."

"Why did you spend hundreds of thousands of dollars to graduate from the number one college in psychology, only to end up becoming a government functionary like myself?"

"I'm actually in private practice. I contract with the Secret Service on a limited basis. They find it cheaper to hire me case by case instead of full-time."

Cain chuckled. "I'm a patriot. I love my country. But the government trying to save money is something I rarely see—if ever."

"Economics is tied to behavior. Some risky, some conservative. But a decision is always required. You made an assumption—a snap judgment—based on a degree hanging on my wall. Am I correct?"

"Yeah," Cain replied. "I'll give you that. In my line of work, I have to make judgments, or people get killed. When I see a crowd clapping for their favorite politician but one man is not, it catches my attention. When I see people out wearing T-shirts and shorts yet one is in a heavy jacket, it catches my eye. So, yes, I make judgments based on my observations. It comes with the job."

She continued probing. "Do you think you have good judgment?"

"In some things. In others, probably not. If you ask my supervisor, I have poor judgment in clothes, because my style is more subdued." Cain chuckled. "The Service is peculiar in that regard: they'll judge your value to the team based on the quality of your tie or cuff links."

"What about judgment in your friendships?"

"I'm loyal to a fault."

She looked up from scribbling notes on her yellow legal pad. "Please explain."

"I try to give everyone the benefit of the doubt. I don't always succeed, but I *try* to see the good in people."

"Loyalty is usually an admirable trait. But many people don't realize there is a dangerous subcategory of loyalty. We refer to it as toxic loyalty. For example, those who were loyal to the Nazi regime."

"Doctor, I work for the Secret Service, not the gestapo. You don't have to lecture me on toxic loyalty. I've walked the grounds at Dachau. It made me sick to my stomach."

"I didn't mean to upset you, Cain."

"You didn't upset me," Cain replied flatly, masking his spike in blood pressure.

"I'd like to transition from friendships to relationships. Many of my clients struggle with relationships. As you know, the Secret Service has a 70 percent divorce rate. I notice you're wearing a wedding ring, but your file says nothing about your being married—except to the job."

A flood of emotions—a mixture of anger and guilt—suddenly overcame him. He still wasn't ready to confront it. "I still wear my wedding ring to honor my wife, Claire. She and our baby boy, Christopher, are dead. My file doesn't mention them because I joined the Secret Service afterward."

"Would you like to talk about it?"

"No," Cain said. "It's got nothing to do with my job performance, or my ability to protect the president."

He looked at his watch. "My hour is up, doctor. I wouldn't want Uncle Sam having to pay for any extra services that aren't necessary, just so you can make the payments on your BMW X5."

Her mouth opened in shock. "How did you know I drive a BMW?"

"I told you, doc. I read people for a living. Your accent is German, and I saw a BMW parked outside with personalized plates. The Service *never* authorizes personalized plates. It's a security issue."

"Ah," she said with a tinge of relief. "Good observation. I guess I should change those?"

"Only if you're concerned for your safety. I'm sure you deal with a lot of crazies in here, but I'm not one of them. I believe I've demonstrated that I'm capable of carrying out the duties of a Secret Service agent."

"Yes. My report will give my blessing for you to continue your service."

"Thank you, doc." Cain stood to leave.

"One last bit of advice, if I may, Cain." She phrased it in such a way that he knew the advice was coming whether he wanted it or not.

"Don't let loyalty be your downfall."

CHAPTER 17

CAIN WALKED OUT the office door and took a deep breath. It was midmorning, and while the sun was out, dark clouds were moving in from the east. *Thank God that's over.*

He straddled his Harley and cruised the short distance to Old Ebbitt Grill, a favorite hangout of Secret Service agents. The establishment teemed with energy and political history. Former presidents had played dominos there while discussing policy, but Hollywood made it even more famous when Clint Eastwood played the piano there during a scene in *In the Line of Fire*.

Cain pushed through the rotating door and grabbed a pack of matches from the hostess table. He knew the restaurant well and sat himself at the bar. Cain removed his tie and folded it before placing it in his suit's inner pocket. He plopped his heavy elbows onto the thick wooden bar. He looked around the place, studying the stuffed animal heads mounted on the wall.

"Your usual, Mr. Cain?" the freckle-faced bartender, clad in the uniform issue of suspenders and a bow tie, asked from behind the bar. Bill was a young college student working to pay for his political science degree at nearby George Washington University.

"Not today, pal. Make it a sweet tea. Craving a taste of home." Cain then mumbled under his breath, "Sometimes this city reminds you just how far from the farm you are."

"One sweet tea coming up," Bill said.

"Could you also put an order in for the shrimp and grits?"

"Absolutely, sir." Bill punched the lunch order into his computer and then hurried to make the drink.

When it arrived, Cain squeezed the sliced lemon into his tea. He used the straw to stir the drink before tossing the straw onto the bar. He took a large sip. *That hits the spot.*

As Cain continued gazing around the room, the flat-screen television in the corner caught his attention. Normally a sporting event played, but today something much more important was broadcasting. The volume was too low for him to hear, but the caption read SECRET SERVICE PROSTITUTION SCANDAL. Then the photo of Cain, Tomcat, and the others playing darts with drinks in their hands at the British pub flashed on the big screen.

Cain pushed the tea aside. "Bill, I *will* have my usual."

Bill looked confused. "Was it not any good, Mr. Cain? I can make you another."

Cain was still staring at the screen.

"Hey, Mr. Cain. Isn't that you and Mr. Tom?"

"Looks like it, doesn't it?" Cain replied, too angry to be embarrassed.

Bill poured a double Jack Daniel's on the rocks for Cain. "This one's on the house, Mr. Cain."

Cain pounded back the drink. *Strong. Just like I*

like 'em. He didn't enjoy drinking out of bitterness or anger, but the alcoholic drink was familiar to him. It was comforting, and he hoped it would help calm the anger boiling to the surface.

"Make me another, will you?" Cain asked.

"No judgment from me, Mr. Cain."

Tom Jackson arrived shortly afterward and grasped Cain's shoulder. "I love this place—for the scenery, if nothing else." Tomcat gazed upon a group of young professional women sitting at a table about ten feet away. They were enjoying cocktails, and giggled and looked away when Tomcat made eye contact with them.

Cain pointed at the empty stool next to him. "Sit down, Jackson. Be serious for once in your life."

His face reddened. "I am being serious." Tom then motioned to the bartender. "Billy, get me a beer."

"His name is Bill. Why do you call him Billy?" Cain snapped.

"What's got you so pissed off?" Tom asked.

"His name is Bill. Not Billy."

"He's wet behind the ears. Probably still a virgin. When he grows up, then I'll call him Bill. But forget about him. How did that meeting go with LeRoy? You didn't call me afterward."

"I didn't call *anyone* afterward."

"Yeah, but I told you to call me right afterward."

Cain scoffed. "When are you going to get it, Jackson? It's not always about you."

"*You're* complaining when it's me they're looking to fire, man?"

"I'm telling you the truth," Cain replied. "Which is something you need to start doing."

"The truth, huh? How about this for truth? I hear they're going to make you and me take polygraphs."

Cain shook his head and exhaled deeply. "The King didn't mention anything about a polygraph, only a psych eval."

"So, what else did the King say, man? Is he on our side?" Tom asked.

"On *our* side? Of course not. You know the King. Think of the position you've put him in, and—"

"Hey, it wasn't just me, pal. There was a bunch of guys screwing off down there."

"Yeah, maybe. But the others paid their debts." Before Tom could open his mouth to reply, Cain lifted his finger to Tom's face. "Let me finish. He's *also* pissed because they're squeezing him hard on this one. Management is not going to sweep this one under the rug."

"Management? What a joke! With all the stuff they used to pull, now they're the moral authority?"

Cain finished his second Jack on the rocks with three swigs, just as Bill brought out his shrimp and grits. The plate was sizzling and smelled delicious, but Cain had lost his appetite. "Bill, Mr. Tom Jackson will cover my tab. He still owes me several hundred."

"You know I'm good for it. I'll get your money. Payday is next week."

"I'm not going to hold my breath. You squeeze a quarter so tight the eagle screams."

"Ah, come on, now. My wife and kids bleed me dry."

"You don't give a shit about your family!" Cain shouted.

"At least I have one," Tom said without thinking.

Cain clenched his fist and launched it at Tom's face. It connected with a thud, and Tom knocked over two barstools as he fell to the floor.

"This *is* all your fault," Cain barked at Tom.

"You're fucking with *my* life and career, and you don't even give a shit."

"I think you broke my nose," Tom exclaimed as blood trickled out his nostrils.

"You're lucky to still have teeth in that head of yours," Cain said between angered breaths.

"I've got nobody on my side, Cain. Not even you anymore."

"Own it. You made your bed. Now lie in it," Cain said before turning and heading toward the exit.

Tom yelled out, "We were all off duty! The media is blowing this out of proportion."

"It's always someone else's fault with you. Clean up your mess!"

CHAPTER 18

CAIN STORMED OUT of Old Ebbitt Grill and paused on the wide sidewalk. His blood was pumping, and his hands were trembling. His head swam with frenzy and he felt the effects of his drinks. He looked left and right. Traffic was picking up. He looked skyward and saw several dark clouds hovering overhead. A downpour was threatening. He had completely lost his cool and punched his partner, something he thought would never happen.

He swung his leg over his motorcycle. He dropped it into gear, rolled the throttle, and sped away. He navigated the windy streets and impatiently paused for a group of Asian tourists in the crosswalk at the Lincoln Memorial. There were at least fifty of them, and they were not in a hurry. They were snapping photos and talking with one another. Cain twisted the throttle several times and the Harley-Davidson's engine roared, frightening the tourists. He then sped right through a narrow opening in the crowd.

He was cranky and full of rage. *I'm not supposed to be dodging pedestrians on my bike! I'm supposed to be protecting the president. He relies on me, and I've let him down.*

He skidded to a halt in his driveway, running into the wall and putting a softball-size hole in the drywall. He flipped down the kickstand and killed the engine. He threw the cover over the Harley and went inside to treat the migraine that was pounding his head like a jackhammer. He wanted to see a doctor about them—they seemed to be increasing in frequency—but he hadn't made the time yet.

He slung his leather bomber jacket over a kitchen stool, grabbed a glass, and filled it with some water from the tap. He put the glass down and started rubbing his temples to ease the pressure. *I need a Tylenol PM.*

As he headed to the bathroom, he accidentally kicked over a box. Framed pictures spilled out onto the living room floor. One was a wedding picture—*his* wedding picture.

He grabbed the picture and marveled at it. In the photo, he wore his naval service dress whites, and Claire beamed with angelic beauty in her lace wedding dress. They were staged in front of St. Louis Cathedral, across from Jackson Square in the French Quarter of New Orleans. He and Claire had been hugging and flirting, to the frustration of the cameraman trying to capture their perfect moments.

I remember that day like it was yesterday. Claire Bear told me it was bad luck to see the bride on her wedding day, but I convinced her that was antiquated foolishness. He closed his eyes and immediately went back to that occasion.

They had secretly met up that morning right before sunrise at Café du Monde, which was open for business twenty-four hours a day. Foghorns blasted through the air as ships navigated the Mississippi River. They heard the chatter and footsteps of a few nearby tourists making their way back to hotels after staying up all night exploring the dark side of New Orleans. They took in the aroma of coffee percolating and the smell of sugar. They snacked on beignets— fresh ones right out of the fryer and doused with powdered sugar. When Claire laughed, her hair blew in the wind, and he'd catch a hint of her shampoo. They had dreams. Dreams to start a family and grow old together.

"I hope I can fit into my wedding dress after eating these little devils," Claire had joked.

He had kissed her comfortably. "I will always love you." He was completely in love with her—and had been, from the moment Bonnie first introduced them.

"Promise?"

"To the day I die, and beyond."

Cain opened his eyes. He found one of the boxes on the floor, the one labeled MUSIC, and pulled out his old record player. When he plugged it in, a light turned on. *Great! It still works.* He returned to the box and rummaged through the records. He grabbed one of their favorites. He slid the record out of its protective sheath and gently placed it on the player.

A few seconds later, the bass-baritone voice of Johnny Cash singing "You Are My Sunshine" sounded throughout his home.

Cain found himself singing the words and slowly moving to the beat. He went into the kitchen and fetched bowls from the cabinet.

I should have done this a long time ago. He started making shortcut beignets and brewing chicory coffee. Whenever the song reached its end, he'd go back and start it over again. He never grew tired of that song.

He picked the beignets out of the fryer and placed them on a plate, then sprinkled powdered sugar on them. He was supposed to let them cool for a few minutes, but he couldn't wait any longer. He quickly devoured his beignets, even burning his tongue on the hot doughy sweetness.

He was recovering from his sugar rush and sipping on his black coffee when his cell phone rang. The caller ID said it was Jill, an agent he'd known for just over a year. She worked on the vice president's security detail. Cain figured he should take the call.

"Hello, friend. It's good to hear your voice," she said.

"Yours, too."

"The rumors are flying around the office."

"I'm sure they are. Nothing we do is secret, apparently."

"Surely not even *you* would think that getting into a fight at a Secret Service hangout was going to stay quiet?"

"I lost my composure today. Tom brought out the worst in me."

"He brings out the worst in anyone within ten feet of him. He's completely toxic. All that creep thinks about is himself."

"Thanks for calling, Jill. But I'm not in the mood to talk about Tom."

"I want to help, Cain. Let me help you."

"There's nothing you can do."

"Would you like to at least talk about it?"

Cain chuckled. "Now you sound like the agency's shrink."

"I could cook you dinner. When was the last time you had a home-cooked meal?"

Cain felt a smile forming. "You're always so thoughtful, Jill. But I'm all set for tonight—I just swallowed a bunch of beignets."

"Beignets? What's that?"

"A New Orleans doughnut sprinkled with enough powdered sugar to make you forget your worries. They were just what the doctor ordered. They hit the spot."

"They sound delicious. Maybe you can make *me* some sometime."

There was a slight pause as Cain stumbled to find a response. He'd never even considered sharing beignets with anyone since Claire. "Sure," he replied.

"How about a run tomorrow?" Jill asked. "You can burn off those doughnuts, and I can—"

"It's supposed to rain tomorrow."

"I've never known you to be afraid of anything, especially a little rain."

"I'm worried about it messing up my hair."

Jill laughed. Cain never put product in his hair.

"But I'm game if you are," he said.

"Great! It's a date," she said.

"I'll see you at the mall at six."

"I look forward to seeing you," Jill said.

"Have a good night," Cain said.

"Sweet dreams," Jill said softly before hanging up.

CHAPTER 19

UNDER A GRAY canopy of clouds, early-morning runners had already started their exercise around the National Mall. The landscaped park was full of joggers, people playing soccer, and others throwing Frisbees. Unlike Cain's native Louisiana, this place seemed to prioritize fitness. He always chalked that up to the stress of the jobs in the nation's capital, as well as all the ambitious interns and type A personalities that were attracted to high-paced jobs for government movers and shakers. His hometown embraced the Big Easy lifestyle, where everything took on a slower pace and centered around good food and cold drinks.

It didn't take long for Cain to spot Jill's blond hair in the distance. She was stretching. Flexibility came naturally to her. She had gone to college on a soccer scholarship and had been hired by the Secret Service right after graduate school.

"It's great to see you, Cain," she said, and gave him a big hug. She held the embrace a few seconds longer than Cain thought was usual. "It's just not the same running without you."

Cain caught a whiff of her freshly shampooed hair.

"You, too! You must be staying busy. I haven't seen you in a while."

"Me? You're the busy one!"

"Well, you know how it is. It never seems to slow down."

She nodded in agreement.

"Shall we?" he suggested.

"Let's do it," she said. "You think you'll be able to keep up with me this time?"

Cain laughed. "I can keep up! When I'm running behind you, it's because I've *chosen* to." He smiled.

She smiled at his remark, and the two began running along the path. They passed art galleries, memorials, and his favorite: several Smithsonian museums. Recent events weighed heavily on Cain's mind, but he didn't want to bring them up. He placated Jill with mostly small talk during the run, and after about thirty minutes, they turned onto the road toward Arlington National Cemetery. Their small talk had come to an end.

"How much longer will you be on admin leave while they finish up their silly investigation?" Jill asked.

"I thought you were enjoying running with me. Now you're ready to send me back to work?" Cain teased.

"Everyone knows this has Tomcat written all over it."

"Is it that obvious?"

"Yeah, it is. At least for us smart ones, and anyone who has ever met Tomcat."

They continued running for a beat before Jill went on. "I trust you, Cain. You know that. I've told you things I've never told anyone else. That's why I'm telling you this."

"Okay," Cain said, pacing his breathing. He knew

Jill could outrun him by several more miles—even though he'd never admit it.

"I'm leaving the Secret Service."

Cain stopped running and began a slow walk. "You're leaving? No. No. No. Please don't tell me that. We need good people like you."

"I'm sick and tired of the macho, sexist culture. I can't take it any longer."

"If this is about how some of the guys are treating you, I'll talk to them. I'll set 'em straight."

"No, Cain. It's deeper than just one or two agents. Tomcat is a dime a dozen in the Service. Until they get a female director, *nothing* is going to change."

"Where are you going to go?"

"I'm transferring to NCIS. You know, the Naval Criminal Investigative Service. I'll lose a little pay in the beginning, but it'll be worth it in the end. There are a lot more women in that agency."

Cain shook his head in disbelief. "I'm sad to hear you're leaving us."

"You make it sound like I'm leaving law enforcement. I'll still be an agent." And then, pleading: "Come with me, Cain. It's a more stable life at NCIS."

"No. I'm not leaving the Service. And I wish you wouldn't, either."

He turned left and started walking toward the gates at Arlington National Cemetery. Jill followed a step behind him. Cain waved at the security guard, who waved back at them. The three knew one another. The president and vice president, along with their Secret Service details, often visited the cemetery for official functions throughout the year. Cain and Jill had coordinated security logistics many times with the security guards.

The sky was still overcast—hiding the sun. The

roar of jet engines departing Ronald Reagan airport could be heard overhead. The dew glistened off the sea of white crosses, and the magnolia trees were in full blossom. Birds chirped to one another as they dashed from tree to tree. Cain found the sacred grounds especially peaceful that morning—even majestic.

He started to cool down, just as they arrived at JFK's grave site. His thoughts were lost in the eternal flame dancing in the wind. *Loss is the one constant in life,* he thought. He felt deep sadness. He hadn't even been born when Kennedy visited Dallas that fateful November day in 1963, but he felt a bond with the charismatic president. Cain had spent weeks at the academy studying the assassination and watching the video repeatedly. Unlike investigations in which you knew you were successful when you arrested the suspect and he confessed to the allegation, you never knew what disaster you may have prevented in protection. Presidents Lincoln, Garfield, McKinley, Kennedy, and Reagan served as stark reminders of what had *not* been prevented. *Their stories serve as a reminder for me to always be ready. And they also remind me why the Service needs sharp agents like Jill.*

Jill spoke up. "Just because I'm transferring to NCIS, it won't change anything between us."

Cain locked eyes with hers. Before he could respond, his phone rang. He looked down and saw that his supervisor was calling. He had been expecting this call.

"You're up early, boss," Cain said quietly, out of respect for the cemetery's rules.

"Why are you whispering?" LeRoy asked.

"I'm at Arlington," Cain replied.

"You spend your mornings at a cemetery? That's awkward."

Cain started to explain but was cut off.

"No judgment from me, and no explanation necessary. Let's just hope it's not a sign of things to come."

"What?" Cain asked.

"I've got some good news and some bad news. Which do you want first?"

"I need some good news."

"Your polygraph is today. At fourteen hundred."

"*My* polygraph? You never mentioned anything about a poly."

"Just tell the truth and you'll be fine."

"You know how I hate those things."

"Everyone does."

"If that's the good news, what's the bad news?"

"The examiner is Cynthia Gorst."

Cain exhaled. "That's not such bad news. She's a nice lady—very professional." Cynthia had conducted his agent applicant exam to determine his eligibility for a top secret security clearance.

"Things have changed since your last polygraph to get hired with us. Cynthia is now divorced. I heard it was a nasty split. Husband was cheating on her with her best friend."

"Ouch," Cain said.

"Yup. Ever since then, she's been tougher. Good luck."

Jill put her arm on Cain's shoulder. "They're putting you on the box?"

"Appears so. It's ironic, huh? They trust me to stand next to the president with a gun, but they don't trust my statement."

"Cain, you're the most honest guy I know." She reached up and touched his face. "I like this new stubble look on you, but I'd shave before your poly. You know the Service is all about appearances, and they'll judge your honesty on something as superficial as how you look."

CHAPTER 20

THE POLYGRAPH ROOM was spartan, like an isolation cell in a psychiatric ward. The walls were bright white and devoid of any pictures. The ceiling had a small air-conditioning vent and a long rectangular fluorescent light fixture. *What is with the government and their fluorescent lights?* Cain wondered. The room was strategically designed that way; the focal point, after all, was the large black leather chair with straps and buckles. *That looks just like Gruesome Gertie,* Cain thought. *I'll never forget seeing that electric chair at Angola.* Professor Foster, his criminal justice teacher, had taken the class on a field trip to the legendary penitentiary.

Cain instantly recognized the short woman with blond curly hair that stopped at her shoulders. Cynthia looked the same, he thought, with the exception of a few gray streaks in her hair and perhaps a few extra pounds that naturally came with age and a sedentary government position. She wore black suit pants and a loosely fitted red blouse, which she had covered up with a black sweater jacket.

Cynthia was a special agent like Cain but had been with the polygraph division for years. Many of Cain's colleagues on the president's protective detail referred to agents in the technical services division as desk jockeys or, collectively, the rubber gun squad. But Cain tried to shy away from that kind of talk about others. *I have enough faults of my own,* he figured.

"Hi, Cynthia. It's nice to see you again."

"Good afternoon, Agent Lemaire," the examiner said in a matter-of-fact tone.

Cain shook her hand and found it to be unnaturally cold. "Wow! You must be freezing in here."

"I keep it cold in this room so that I get better readings on my equipment. Plus, if I see you start sweating, I'll know something is amiss." She seemed more formal than usual, certainly more so than she'd been during Cain's initial polygraph many years before.

"Well," Cain said with a natural smile, "I don't plan on sweating. But if anybody could make me sweat, it'd be you."

His joke was lost on her. *She seems to have lost her joy,* he observed. *Maybe the divorce?* He ran a few other possibilities in his mind. *Burnout from the job? Government bureaucracy could beat down almost anyone.*

"Before we start," the examiner said, "I have to hook several of these instruments to your body. They will monitor your heart rate, perspiration, and pupil dilation."

Cain sat down, and as she connected the gadgets to his body and the cable to her laptop, he tried to break her hard exterior. "Your perfume smells nice."

"I'm not wearing any perfume," she replied.

"Huh," he remarked. "Must be your natural scent, then. It's very pleasant."

There was an awkward silence for a moment before she answered. "I just had mixed vegetable masala from the Taj Mahal Indian restaurant near the office. Maybe you're smelling that on my fingers."

Without skipping a beat, Cain nodded and replied, "It's a pleasant fragrance. I've always liked the smell of coriander with a hint of paprika and butter."

"The food was good, but I must confess, I don't have the most refined palate. I'll eat anything. My ex-husband—"

"Ex-husband?" Cain interjected, feigning ignorance.

"It's no secret."

"I stay out of the gossip. But I'm sorry to hear. It's certainly his loss."

She gave a half smile—enough for Cain to think he might be able to win her over after all.

"My ex and I were once vacationing in the Jewish quarter of Kraków. It was a quaint neighborhood with that old-world charm. The lovely waitress had placed a basket of bread and a plate of cheese on the table for us. I was devouring what I thought was the best cheese I had ever had. I mean, I can't express how delicious this cheese was. I pushed the plate over and told him he had to try it. He took one bite and started dry heaving. I thought he was about to throw up right there on the table. He yelled out, 'That's not cheese! It's butter!'"

Cain laughed heartily. "Well, I gotta put butter on everything—even my vegetables. I'm from the South. At least I'm not as bad as the Georgians who run the chow hall at FLETC—they consider mac and cheese a vegetable!"

Cynthia laughed until she seemed to remember that the exam was being recorded. At that moment, she quickly returned to her stoic and professional demeanor.

She grabbed a checklist. "Okay, Agent Lemaire. The Secret Service considers this an administrative inquiry, not a criminal matter. Therefore, I will not be reading your Miranda rights. However, I will be providing you with your Kalkines warning and then asking you a series of test questions to establish a baseline. Just answer them with a simple yes or no. Do you understand?"

"Yes."

"Is your name Cain Michael Lemaire?"

"Yes."

"Are you currently employed as a United States Secret Service special agent?"

"Yes."

"Have you ever dived with sharks?"

"Yes."

She looked up from monitoring her machine to study Cain. She appeared surprised by his answer. "Are you serious?"

"Yes."

"For pleasure?"

"I thought it would be." He gave an impish smile.

"Have you ever climbed Mount Everest?"

"No."

"Okay. Now that I've established a baseline, we'll move on to the specific questions that are for the purposes of this examination," Cynthia said. "Have your actions in a professional capacity ever made you vulnerable to blackmail?"

"No."

"Have your actions in a personal capacity ever made you vulnerable to blackmail?"

"No."

"Have you ever paid a prostitute?"

"Not for sex."

"Agent Lemaire, please answer the question with just a yes or a no."

"It's not that simple of a question. I didn't pay for sex, and I didn't know she was a prostitute."

Cynthia inhaled and exhaled deeply. "Agent Lemaire, have you ever given money to a woman who could have been a prostitute?"

"Yes."

"Did you give her that money to cover the cost of a sexual exchange?"

"I didn't have sex with her."

"Agent Lemaire, again, this is a yes or no question. Did you pay a prostitute to cover the cost of a sexual exchange?"

"I have no information about any sexual exchange."

"I'll rephrase my question. Yes or no answer only. Did you give money to a woman who you believed was receiving money for sexual activity?"

"Yes."

"Thank you, Agent Lemaire. This concludes the scope of this polygraph examination."

"That was the quickest poly ever," Cain said in frustration. "That was completely politically motivated."

Cynthia unhooked the instruments dangling off Cain and provided him with a list of instructions.

"This is an ongoing internal investigation. You are not allowed to discuss this with any other agents. Supervisory Special Agent LeRoy Hayes will be in touch with you regarding the outcome of this investigation."

"Can I talk with my supervisor about this test?"

"Yes, but only your management team."

"How long do you think the results will take? When do you think I'll be reinstated to return to work?"

"Agent Lemaire, neither I nor the test detected any signs of deception from you. However, that doesn't *necessarily* mean you are clear. My results will be evaluated by another examiner, and the Service will have your results by close of business today."

Cain stood and shook her hand. "Thank you for your time today. Wish I had seen you under different circumstances."

He went to the bathroom in the hall and splashed cold water on his face. He might not have sweated, but he had certainly started warming up in there despite the cold. He wiped the water off his face with a brown paper towel. It felt like wiping his face with sandpaper. The government spared no expense on many things, but creature comforts like toilet paper and napkins were not among them.

He exited the bathroom and saw the King leaning against the wall with his arms folded. Using just his back and shoulder muscles, he pushed himself off the wall and quickly approached Cain. "Lots to discuss. Walk with me."

CHAPTER 21

CAIN AND LEROY walked through the government hall toward the exit, busting through the double doors and outside to the parking lot. It was still drizzling, so they remained under the overhang. LeRoy pulled out a pack of Kool cigarettes and offered Cain one.

"No, thanks. I thought you quit—isn't that why you vape with that purple thing now?"

"I'm not a quitter! I just can't smoke these in the office."

Cain scoffed. "You know vaping ain't allowed in the government building, either, right?"

"Cain, the day I take policy advice from you is the day I'll turn in *my* badge and gun."

Cain handed LeRoy a matchbook from his pocket. It was the one he had taken from the British pub.

LeRoy studied the matchbook. "Ain't *that* some shit. Don't try to rope me into this boondoggle."

"You already are."

"Touché," LeRoy replied, and then lit his cigarette. He took a deep drag. He slowly exhaled puffs of smoke into the air. Cain could smell the menthol. "Look," LeRoy said, "the SAC called me into his office a little while ago. He wants *me* to ask if you'd be interested in something."

"Why wouldn't the SAC just ask me, then?"

"He thinks you and I get along well."

"We do—for the most part," Cain replied.

"He knows that you and I see eye to eye on most things with the Service. That's why he reached out to me. He was hoping I could"—LeRoy paused—"*convince* you, was the actual word he used."

"I'm listening," Cain said, eager to hear what LeRoy was going to say next.

"The SAC wants *this* to be over as quickly as possible."

"Me, too," Cain replied. "The SAC and I have that in common."

"He's getting a lot of heat from the director, because now the director's job is on thin ice."

"So, what's the SAC proposing?"

"He'd like for you to wear a wire and get confessions from the other agents."

"Absolutely not," Cain protested. "I'm not a rat."

"Relax," LeRoy said. He took another drag from his cigarette. "I told him you'd never go for that. But I came up with a solution."

"It can't be any worse than *his* solution." Cain's anger was palpable.

"I told the SAC that you knew only about Jackson's affair. Let's concentrate on that one. You are in a unique position to help the Service get rid of him."

"By *get rid of,* you mean *fire*."

"Yeah. Tom Jackson's an asshole. The world's full of 'em. He'll be right at home in the private sector."

"Firing Tomcat is your job, not mine. All you have

to do is make him take the same poly you made me take today."

"We did," LeRoy said, and turned his head away—toward the parking lot.

"Aaaand?" Cain dragged out the question. "And?" he repeated when he didn't get an immediate response. "For Christ's sake, what are you not telling me?"

"He passed it."

"Bullshit."

"It's true. I saw the report."

"The final report, maybe, but not the results."

"I'll deny this if I'm ever asked." LeRoy pointed his cigarette at Cain's face to emphasize the importance of what he was about to say. "This is just between you and me. But the report showed what he purported—that he had consensual sex with a woman and never paid her."

"What about adultery?"

"It's not a crime. The Service will just handle that with an administrative infraction."

"It's like I'm living in a twilight zone."

"I hear you. That's why I think there is more to it."

"Like what? Of course there is more to it."

"Cynthia was busy polygraphing other agents, so he ended up with a different examiner. They had worked some missions before, several years ago. Jackson might've had some dirt on him."

Cain shook his head in bewilderment. "Unbelievable. I swear, Tomcat has nine fuckin' lives."

"And you have one. Remember that." The King flicked his cigarette into a nearby water puddle. He watched the water extinguish the ashes and then opened the door to walk back into the building.

"Oh," he said, turning back. "One last thing. The

SAC wants to see you in his office at zero eight three zero tomorrow."

"That can't be good," Cain replied.

"You know the SAC's reputation: he's a hard-ass with a vindictive streak. Make sure to have a solution, since you didn't like mine or his."

CHAPTER 22

CAIN RETRIEVED HIS personal cell from his suit pocket. He flipped through his contact list and thumbed his favorite. The phone started dialing the international number.

"Hey, twin brother! I've been waiting for your call. What's the word?"

"I just finished my polygraph exam. I'm pretty sure I passed it. I was honest and the examiner said she detected no deception."

"I don't think that matters, though."

"What do you mean?" Cain inquired.

"I saw the picture of you, Tomcat, and the others drinking at the pub. Plus, I saw the prostitute on television. She was giving a damn interview, destroying any credibility you guys have. The government will do what it always does: it'll find a scapegoat. Looks like the media brought it to them on a silver platter."

"She's going to milk this cash cow for as much money as she can," Cain said as it dawned on him.

"You think you'll be mentioned?" Bonnie asked.

"God, I hope not."

"Prostitution wouldn't even be mentioned in the Japanese news," she said. "Nobody cares about that kind of stuff here. One of my clients is the CEO of one of the largest auto companies in—"

"One of your clients?" Cain interrupted.

"Yeah, one of my students," Bonnie clarified. "I teach English to a few business executives to make a little extra money."

"I didn't know that."

"Well, I don't tell you *all* my secrets."

"That's probably the best news I've heard all day!"

Cain and Bonnie laughed together.

"Anyway, as I was saying, I've been telling one of my clients about your situation."

"Sis, please don't do that."

"He can help, Cain. This is exactly what you need. He runs one of the largest auto companies in Tokyo, and he is looking for a bodyguard."

"A bodyguard?" Cain said with disgust.

"I know. You guys hate that word."

"We're not bullet catchers. We use our brains, too."

"Some more than others." Bonnie giggled. "The work here would be easy lifting and the pay would be good. Plus, it gets you closer to me. Maybe then Mom and Pops would come out here to visit. You know they're never going to travel this far unless we're both here."

"They're homebodies. They'll never leave the farm. Plus, they wouldn't leave Seth by himself, and he ain't gonna fly that far." Cain paused a beat. "Thanks for thinking of me. But I'm going to settle this tomorrow morning at my meeting with the SAC."

"Fine. If they do end up giving you a few days off work, go down to the farm. Mom would love to see you, and there is plenty of stuff you could do to help out Pops. It'll be good for your soul to get back south for a bit, too."

"Maybe so."

"Give 'em hell, brother. With what you've been through in life, this ain't no hill for a mountain climber."

"I can always count on you to be my biggest cheerleader."

"We're family," Bonnie said, taking on a more serious tone. "We'll always have each other. No matter what."

CHAPTER 23

CAIN HAD BEEN UP for hours. His sleep was restless. After he lost count of how many times he tossed and turned, he got up and sat at the dining table. The rain and gray clouds from the night gave way to a morning that dawned into a brilliant blue sky from horizon to horizon.

I hope this is a sign of positive things to come, Cain thought as he finished his third cup of coffee. *Time to get ready for the SAC.*

He went to his closet and picked out his sharpest suit—a tailored navy blue with pinstripes. He had custom ordered it for when he was on assignment in Seoul. The president had attended a nuclear security summit and greeted American troops deployed at the demilitarized zone, or DMZ, as they called it. Security had been extra tight and Cain vividly recalled constantly scanning the large expanse of land, hills, and forests for snipers. *Had just one North Korean soldier fired upon the president, World War III would have erupted.*

Cain donned a starched white shirt, a blue-and-yellow-striped tie, and a pair of caramel leather boots. He was impeccably dressed. *Jill was right—the Service judges you on how you look.*

As he left his bedroom and headed toward the door, he saw the framed picture on the dining table. He kissed two of his fingers and placed them on Claire's face. "Thank you for talking me through this, Claire Bear. We have a plan, and I promise I'll stick to it."

CHAPTER 24

THE WHITE HOUSE MEETING began promptly at 0830. LeRoy ushered Cain into the office of the special agent in charge. Unlike the director, who oversaw the entire mission of the Secret Service, the SAC was responsible for overseeing all facets specifically related to the safety of the First Family. His walls were full of framed and autographed pictures of himself with presidents, world leaders, and members of various royal families. The SAC was in his midfifties and still physically fit. He chalked that up to a life without alcohol, living by Mormon principles, and good physical fitness habits he cultivated while playing high school and college basketball. He was clean-shaven and seemed especially proud of his full head of salt-and-pepper hair. He held every strand in place with some type of shiny styling product.

"Thank you for coming today, Agent Lemaire," the SAC said with a calm and welcoming demeanor.

"Thank you for calling this meeting," Cain replied. "I'm hopeful we can put this behind us so I can get off admin leave and come back to work."

"I understand how difficult this last week has been for you," the SAC said. "Quite frankly, it's been challenging for *all* of us. You've done a great job protecting our nation's leaders, Agent Lemaire. You've kept yourself in shape, you've been reliable, and you were honest during your polygraph exam yesterday."

"Would you have expected anything less from me, sir?"

"No." His hands came together under his chin, propped up by his elbows on the desk. "I don't have a lot of time, so let me just cut to the chase. A proverbial line has been drawn in the sand. This has come straight from the director. Because *you* paid the prostitute— regardless of whether you had sex with her or not— you're in hot water. It's like the childhood game of Duck, Duck, Goose. Remember that game?"

"It's been a while, but yes."

"Well, you're it. And the only way for you not to be it is for you to work with our internal affairs investigators and get confessions from the other agents. If I'm going to identify and extract this cancer from our organization, I've got to know how malignant and widespread it goes."

Tomcat—you son of a bitch! What I wouldn't do to roll back the clock and not pay that woman. I should throw your ass under the bus...

"Permission to speak freely?" Cain asked.

"Of course," the SAC replied.

"Sir, if I did as you requested, I would never be trusted by my colleagues for the *rest* of my career. And as you know, trust is paramount in law enforcement. Nobody would ever work with me again, and I would be an outcast. I would be ineffective in my role to protect POTUS. I don't think our Service is plagued with this cancer you speak of. I think it's just a very few members who made some very poor decisions."

"It's more than a poor decision. They compromised national security! They had foreign nationals in the same room as US government devices."

That's quite a stretch, Cain thought. Besides, those devices were encrypted—set to erase themselves if the wrong password were entered three times.

"So, what's it going to be? Are you going to play ball with us?" the SAC demanded. "My instructions from the top were clear, Agent Lemaire. If you're not going to assist us, then you are allowed to resign."

Hearing the demands—practically an ultimatum—from the SAC felt like a sucker punch to the solar plexus. Cain felt numb, but anger tingled deep inside his core.

"Assist you?" Cain asked. "That's exactly what I did. My actions most likely prevented this from spiraling out of control. Had I not paid that woman"— Cain paused—"*on behalf* of the Secret Service, the police would have gotten involved and this would have likely resulted in arrests."

"This is not personal," the SAC continued. "It's just business—a business that requires the highest levels of integrity, patriotism, and the trust of the American people and the officials we took an oath to protect with our very bodies, if necessary. There are already members of Congress trying to strip away our mission to protect the president and give it to the damn FBI!" The all-American SAC was starting to lose his patience.

"They always threaten that, sir." Cain looked to LeRoy, who sat there without saying a word. *Why don't you say something instead of just sitting there?* "Congress threatened it after Kennedy was killed, after Reagan was shot, and even after that couple crashed the White House dinner."

The SAC stood and pounded his desk. "I offered

you an opportunity to resign and keep your security clearance—and your honor! I swear—"

Cain interjected, "There's no honor in resigning this way."

"Your other choice is getting fired. There's certainly no honor in *that*. You'd lose your top secret clearance, and you'd never be accepted in a law enforcement position again!" The vein on the side of the SAC's temple was now pulsating. He snatched a piece of paper off his desk and tossed it to Cain. "Read it, you arrogant asshole!"

Cain looked at the letter. *It has been an honor serving alongside my friends with the United States Secret Service, but after long and careful consideration, I feel my resignation will allow me the stability to pursue my personal aspirations,* it read. Cain couldn't believe they already had a resignation letter typed and prepared for his signature.

"Personal aspirations," he said aloud. He then looked from the SAC to LeRoy. "What does that even mean? You and everyone else in this building know I have no personal aspirations."

LeRoy continued to remain quiet. The SAC's hand was shaking from the confrontation, but he used it to provide Cain with a pen. It was one of those expensive, heavy pens that a CEO would use to sign business deals.

"You can shove that pen up your ass, *sir!*"

"Get the hell out of my office," the SAC demanded. He motioned to LeRoy. "Get this ungrateful man out of my office."

"Gladly," Cain replied.

Once they were in the hallway, Cain turned to the King. "You could have warned me, LeRoy!"

"Since when do you call me LeRoy?"

"Since you're no longer my boss, you cowardly son of a bitch. That's when!" LeRoy looked shocked at Cain's response. "I walked right into a firestorm and you just sat there like a frog on a stump."

"Agent Lemaire, my office, now!" LeRoy shouted as Cain turned to walk away. Something in his tone made Cain look back.

CHAPTER 25

LEROY NODDED TOWARD his office door. Cain went in and LeRoy quietly closed the door behind him. He motioned for Cain to have a seat, but he shook his head in defiance. "I'll stand," he said.

"Please, take a seat," LeRoy said as he moved behind his desk and plopped down into his nice executive chair. He clasped his hands and laid them down on his immaculate desk. He calmly looked at Cain, who had no idea what to expect.

He's probably about to give me some type of half-assed apology, Cain thought. *I'm not interested in listening to anything like that.*

He couldn't have been more wrong.

"Don't you *ever* call me a cowardly son of a bitch again," LeRoy said.

Cain felt his eyes bulge as he searched for his response.

"You don't have a clue how far I stuck my neck out for you," LeRoy continued. "The White House is so embarrassed by what happened that the SAC was promising the chief of staff that he'd fire your ass personally. But I convinced him to go through the steps—hoping you'd get enough ammunition to save your job. Your meeting with the SAC went down pretty much like I had imagined, except for the part where you told him to shove that pen up his ass." Cain thought he perceived a slight smile on the King's lips. "I respect your decision, but I'm not sure I would have done the same thing."

"'To thine own self be true,'" Cain said. "'Thou canst not then be false to any man.' At the end of the day, I gotta stay true to myself."

"Man, you can quote Shakespeare all day, but I told you heads were gonna roll, and mine was damn sure not going to be one of 'em. I've worked too long and too damned hard to get where I'm at. And I'm not going to trade my career for yours, that piece of shit Jackson, or for the others. There aren't many agencies looking for an old black cop these days. This is all I got." He leaned back in his chair and folded his arms.

Cain's demeanor softened. He didn't agree with what happened at all, but he understood LeRoy's position a little better. "I'm sorry about the cowardly son of a bitch remark."

LeRoy dismissed it with a wave of his hand. "You're a damn good agent, and it's a shame we're losing you. I just wanted you to know that."

Cain shook LeRoy's hand.

LeRoy smiled. "Now take your sorry ass back to Alabama."

"Louisiana," Cain replied.

"Same difference." LeRoy smiled even bigger. "Good luck to you, Cain. You'll be just fine."

"Long live the King," Cain muttered under his breath as he left LeRoy's office and headed toward his own to box up his belongings.

CHAPTER 26

CAIN'S OFFICE WAS a large open bay with about fifteen desks separated by five-foot dividers. *Never in my wildest dreams could I have envisioned how this day would end up. I knew I'd retire someday and have to box up my things, but I thought it would be after a long and distinguished career. There would be cake and punch and everyone gathered around. They'd tell exaggerated stories and roast me. I'd be the butt of jokes, at least a few.* This day was different. There was no fanfare. No cake. No punch.

He headed straight to the supply room. While he gathered a few cardboard boxes, Jill quietly walked into the cramped room.

"How did it go?" she asked. She was now wearing a gray suit and carrying her pistol on her hip.

"I kind of resigned."

"*Kind of?*" she said. "Is that even a thing? Sounds like *kind of* being pregnant. You either did or you didn't."

"Well, that hypocrite gave me *his* pen to sign *my* resignation letter that *he* had already typed up."

Jill looked on wide-eyed.

"I told him to shove that pen where the sun don't shine."

"Oh, God." She gasped and covered her mouth with her hand. "Yeah." She nodded. "Yup. I'd say you resigned, all right."

He looked straight into her blue eyes. "They don't deserve you, either. You were right to decide to leave."

She hugged him. "These assholes don't deserve *you*. It's shit like that—that's why it's getting easier and easier for me to leave the Service."

"Let's talk later," Cain suggested. "When it's more private. Rumors fly around this place."

"Yes, they do."

Cain headed to his desk. Colleagues circled around him as he opened the drawers and started going through his things. More than one apologized. "It's a witch hunt, brother. I'm sorry." Cain flipped through a few loose papers with notes on them. "Don't need these anymore." He tossed them into a trash can. He riffled through some business cards, discarding most of them but keeping a few he thought might be helpful later. He grabbed the challenge coins he had received from VIPs he had protected. He put those and a few other personal items he had collected from his travels into a box. He found the drawings and thank-you cards some children had given him when he and Tom had been tasked with participating in a local school's career day. He placed the keepsakes in the box.

His desk phone rang. He instinctively reached out and grabbed the handset but paused.

"Maybe it's POTUS calling—granting you a stay," one agent remarked.

Jill leaned in, and Cain strained to hear her over the noise of everyone jeering and telling him what he should do. "Don't answer it, Cain. You're a free man now," she whispered in his ear.

Cain took his hand off the handset. "I guess you're right."

He was walking toward the exit when Tom Jackson appeared.

"I'm sorry it all ended like this, Cain. Maybe this is a blessing in disguise."

Cain scoffed. "For you or for me?"

"Let's go, Cain," Jill said.

Tom looked at Jill. "Hey, the men are talking here."

"You're such a sexist pig," she said with disgust in her voice.

"She's right, Tom," Cain said. "We have a saying back home. *On récolte ce que l'on sème.*"

"What's that mean?" Tom asked.

"You reap what you sow, and your storm is a-coming."

"Oh, yeah? We'll see about that. I won't hold my breath for your Cajun voodoo to curse me."

Cain looked around the room, and at the items he had placed in the box. "You know what? I don't need this shit." He turned the box upside down and dumped the contents into the trash can. He tossed the box on the floor and kicked it. It went flying through the open-bay office. Jill trailed him as he headed toward the exit. "Call me later," she said. "Please."

CHAPTER 27

THE TOWN HOUSE was only fifteen hundred square feet, but the moving company was expensive.

"If you can just wait about a week, I can give you a 15 percent discount," the sales representative had said.

"No. I've gotta get outta here. I'll pay your premium price."

When the movers had finished boxing everything up, Cain walked through the house one last time. He wanted to make sure he had left nothing behind.

"No reason for me to ever come back," he said aloud.

"Never say never." The reply startled him. Jill had shown up unannounced.

"What are you doing here?"

"I came over to cheer you up. But more importantly, where are *you* going, mister?"

"Home."

"You just resigned yesterday."

"It's been a long time coming, I guess."

Jill stood there. "Were you going to tell me?"

Cain looked at her. He paused long enough to exhale. "I don't know. Perhaps if things had been different."

"Things are different now. I'm leaving. You're leaving. This is a fresh start for the both of us."

"You deserve better than me."

"Can't I be the judge of that?" she asked.

Cain smiled, but for only a brief moment. "I've neglected my family long enough. And right now, they feel more important to me than ever. I'm gonna head to the bayou."

"Can I convince you to stay?"

"You know me too well. Once my mind is set on something, there's no changing it."

"I guess," she replied, nodding her head. "The least I can do is give you a ride to the airport."

"I'm not flying, Jill. I'm taking that." He pointed out the window to his Harley-Davidson.

"All the way to Louisiana?" she asked in disbelief. "How long will that take?"

"Long enough for me to clear my mind."

She hugged Cain, collapsing into his arms. After holding the embrace for quite some time, he pulled her arms off him.

"You take care of yourself," he said as he straddled his Harley.

"What do I have to lose?" she said, and rushed in for a kiss. It was their first. "And it's not good-bye," she said. "It's 'see you soon.'"

He fired up the Harley, eased out of the driveway, and rolled the throttle until he disappeared down the street.

It would never have worked, he told himself.

CHAPTER 28

CAIN RODE HIS HARLEY south on the I-85. To break up the long travel by motorcycle, he stopped overnight in Atlanta, and then rested at an old friend's wildlife rehabilitation farm in Pass Christian, Mississippi. On the third day, before sunrise, he picked up the I-10 west and rolled into the New Orleans French Quarter. It had been years since Hurricane Katrina stormed through the Crescent City with a vengeance, but to Cain it still looked the same. New Orleans had been resilient, and he was impressed by how the city had kept its spirit and culture alive. *If New Orleans can bounce back, so can I.*

He parked the motorcycle near Toulouse Station and peeled himself from the handlebars and leather seat. His body ached all over and his muscles were stiff from holding the same position for days. He walked along Decatur Street and stopped at the Café du Monde he and Claire had visited on the day of their wedding. Just as then, cargo ships blasted their foghorns to alert others as they sailed with their goods. Docked in the Mississippi River was the *Natchez,* the legendary steamboat. In just a couple of hours, it would be transporting tourists back in time to an era more akin to the Civil War. Filling the Vieux Carré with its melodious tunes, the steam calliope would be playing something like "Paddlin' Madelin' Home."

Cain could smell the yeast and the sugar being fried as he took a seat at one of the round tables under an outdoor ceiling fan.

"What can I getcha, sugar?" the kind-faced black waitress asked. She wore a white shirt, a white cap, and a white apron stained with powdered sugar.

"The usual." He smiled, feeling the strain on his windblown face.

"Sure," the server replied without even writing it down. Anyone who asked for "the usual" was a local.

Two minutes later, she returned with chicory coffee and a plate of freshly fried beignets coated with powdered sugar. Cain sipped his coffee and ate his beignets. His body was still stiff from the long road trip from Arlington, but the bold coffee felt like medicine as it lubricated his joints. From his table, he watched pigeons walking around, pecking at crumbs. Farther in the distance, across the square, he saw the three spires of St. Louis Cathedral. Claire had been far more religious than he was, and it had meant a great deal to her to get married at the oldest cathedral in the United States. Their wedding was not the huge spectacle it could have been, but, stepping out into the square when the ceremony was over, Cain thought the whole world was open to them. He had never been happier.

It's been years since I've stepped foot in that church, he thought. He placed a ten-dollar bill on the table and secured it with his now empty mug. He stood and meandered along the sidewalk, through a gathering of artists and street vendors now setting up for the day, and arrived at the front steps of the cathedral.

He looked skyward. The cathedral towered into the heavens. He walked up the stairs and pushed the heavy, solid-wood doors open. The church was lit by the early-morning sun shining through the stained-glass windows. A row of flags adorned the second-story balcony. Although it was an American church, it looked as though it had been transplanted straight from a village in France.

Cain spotted the confessional in the corner. He pushed the curtain aside and entered. He kneeled and made the sign of the cross. "Bless me, Father, for I have sinned. It's been eight years since my last confession."

A creaking sound echoed in the chamber as the old priest shifted his position. "May the God of all mercies help you make a good confession. Proceed, my son."

Cain took a deep breath and slowly let it out. "I killed my wife and son."

CHAPTER 29

CAIN PUSHED THROUGH the church doors. The outside light blinded him. The sun was shining over the Mississippi River, its rays reflecting off the downtown buildings like a prism. It was a typical Louisiana day: hot and muggy. He was pissed when he realized he had left his Ray-Ban sunglasses in the confessional, but he wasn't going back for them. He lifted his hand to shield the blaze.

He had done it. Finally. He had confessed. Yet he didn't feel any better. No weight had been lifted off his shoulders. That void deep in his heart still ached. The confession had managed only to bring up the past and stoke the fires of that trauma.

Cain hurried through the crowd of tourists that had grown. He was soaked in sweat. He climbed onto his Harley and navigated the busy, tight streets until he accelerated onto the on-ramp for I-10 westbound toward Baton Rouge. When he crossed the grated bridge and looked left toward LSU's football stadium, he knew he'd be home in no time. He kept pushing westward until he arrived in Lafayette—a thriving city that still felt like a small town.

Cruising old asphalt roads past South Louisiana's

rice fields brought back memories. Riding the bike allowed Cain to be part of the countryside, not just an observer. The thick air whipped past his helmet, and he smelled the familiar odors of mud and wetlands. Home was drawing near. Everywhere he looked, he saw flashes of his past—where he'd hunted ducks with his dad, where he'd ridden dirt bikes with Seth, and where he, Bonnie, and their friends would gather around the bonfire on Friday nights after school. He'd had the best of both worlds: he had grown up in the country, but the city life of Lafayette was close by.

At the end of the paved road, he turned right onto a dirt road and headed toward the lone house in the distance. The white paint was fading and chipping in certain parts of the early-1900s Acadian-style farmhouse. He found himself rolling on the throttle, eager to finally arrive home. His motorcycle kicked up a trail of dust that followed him like a shadow. When he came to a halt, it engulfed him.

The southern breeze carried the dust away, and Cain patted the remaining dirt off his clothes. His dad and younger brother were draining the oil on a bright-yellow crop duster in the barn, which served as a makeshift hangar. They stopped long enough to look up to see who had arrived.

Cain removed his helmet and hung it on the handlebar. Sunny, the golden retriever that the local American Legion had given Seth to help with his PTSD episodes, trotted toward Cain with his tail wagging.

"Hey, buddy," Cain said as he patted the top of the friendly dog's head. "You been taking care of my brother?"

Claude removed his glasses and rubbed his eyes

as if he couldn't believe what he was seeing. When he realized it was his older son, he dropped his tools and raced toward Cain. The two of them embraced, cheek to cheek. Cain almost collapsed into his arms, supported by his father.

"It's been way too long." Cain sighed.

"Stopping by to make your annual visit?" Seth said sarcastically as he casually strolled toward Cain, wiping grease off his hands with a rag.

"I'd come more if you weren't here," Cain joked. "Get over here and give me a hug. You're moving like an old man."

"Welcome home, son." Tears were forming in Claude's joyful eyes. "Are you jus' makin' a pit stop, or ees dis for good?"

"At least for a while," Cain replied.

"Dieu merci!" Claude said with excitement. "Dat's music to ma old ears."

Margaret, Cain's mother, saw the celebration from the living room window. She rushed outside and hugged Cain tightly as the men peppered him with questions.

"Let my boy take a breath for a moment. He's been on the road for no telling how long," she scolded.

"Thank you, Mom."

She stepped back and eyed Cain up and down. "You're looking so thin," she said. "You mus' be starvin'."

"I could eat."

"We all could," Claude said. *"Allons à la maison.* Me, I'm gonna prepare da bes' crawfish étouffée wit rice you ever had."

The family sat together at the wooden table in the kitchen while Claude rustled up dinner. "Seth, fetch me some green onions from da garden."

"Can't it wait? I'm interrogating Cain about why he's back home all of a sudden."

"He ain't goin' nowhere. You'll have plenty of time to git dem details. Go grab some okra, tomatoes, an' squash."

"I'll go get 'em," Cain said.

"Jus' sit an' relax, son. You been ridin' for days," Claude said. "Seth got two legs."

Cain laughed. "I hear that. But I need to stretch mine. I'll go help you, Seth."

The brothers walked outside and starting picking vegetables from the garden. They were practically shoulder to shoulder, but when Cain looked over at his brother, he saw Seth at about seven or eight years old. *Just like old times,* he thought. *Gathering vegetables for dinner. Except the innocence of that seven-year-old boy was left overseas in a combat zone.*

"I'm glad you're here to take care of Mom and Pops," Cain told his younger brother.

"The farm has a way of taking care of all of us. Glad you're back home, Cain."

They walked back into the house with a handful of the freshest vegetables. Cain was feeling nostalgic. He looked around the kitchen and noticed that nothing had changed in the last thirty-something years. The same wallpaper and old family pictures adorned the walls. It comforted him. The whole experience of being back home felt like being a bird returned to its nest. He exhaled deeply and then smiled. Here he could relax completely.

"Whatcha lookin' at, sweetie?" Margaret asked as she placed a soft hand on Cain's face.

"This kitchen looks the exact same as it did when I used to live here."

"So many memories created here," she said. "So

many meals together. I wouldn't change it for the world."

"Ma heart ees full tonight." Claude, a typical Cajun, wiped tears from his eyes. "I'm as happy as a tick on a fat dog."

Cain laughed. "That's just the onions making you cry."

"Non," he shot back, and shook his head. "I'm so glad to have ma family togeder. Da only way to make dis day any better ees eef Bonnie waz here wit us."

"I'll talk to her," Cain said. "Maybe she can dead-head this way soon."

"Good! Well, dinner ees done," Claude said with glee. He offered a blessing over the meal and then served his family. He made sure everyone put plenty of food on their plates. "Eef you go to bed hungry, eet's your fault."

"God, it smells heavenly," Cain said. "I can't remember the last time I had food like this." Cain took one bite and nodded in approval. *"Ça c'est bon!"*

Claude smiled and winked. "We have plenty of work here on da farm to keep you busy," he said. "An' we don't need no money. Dis house has been paid off since your grandfather waz kickin'."

Margaret smiled and placed her hand on top of Cain's, which was resting on top of the dining table. "I'm not goin' to let you go this time."

Cain took a second helping of corn bread and spread some butter on it with an old knife that had a fleur-de-lis on the handle. "I'm not planning to go anywhere. This is where I belong for now. *Si Dieu le veut.*"

CHAPTER 30

A CROWING SOUND pierced the silence, waking Cain from the most restful sleep he could remember. He peeled back the window's curtain and saw a haggard rooster balancing on top of the wooden fence around the barn. The sun was barely entering the day. *When did Pops get a rooster?* he wondered. *He hates that sound as much as I do.*

Cain lay back down on the mattress. It was the same bed that was his in high school. The springs were worn, and it no longer provided any back support. But his mom and dad came from the generation that didn't believe in getting rid of anything, so Cain's old room was practically the same as when he left for college, with the addition of a few "great deals" from yard sales that had accumulated in the corners. That's where Cain differed from his parents: he didn't like clutter and didn't hold on to things "just in case" he might need them someday. He had brought everything that was important to him to Louisiana: his motorcycle, his wedding ring, his wristwatch, his wedding picture, and a photo of his son, Christopher, sleeping on Cain's chest.

He slowly made his way out of bed and into the

kitchen, where Claude was already sitting at the table, working on a crossword puzzle.

"Asian mafia?" Claude asked.

"Um," Cain said. "Can I at least get some coffee first—to get my brain going?"

Claude put down his crossword puzzle and grabbed coffee beans from a brown paper bag in the fridge, where he stowed them to keep them safe from the humidity. He ground the whole beans and placed them in his French press, then opened the cupboard and grabbed two mugs. He poured each of them a cup.

"Chinese triads," Cain suggested.

"Not enough letters. Six letters an' has a *z* toward da end."

"Try *yakuza*," Cain said.

"Dat's eet! Hopefully Bonnie ain't messin' wit dem folks."

Cain laughed out loud. "She's so busy at work, I don't think she has time for a social life, much less time to hang out with the Japanese mafia."

"Well, you know your sister. She always liked dem bad-boy types."

Cain smirked. "How many of her boyfriends did you run off the front yard with a shotgun?"

Claude chuckled. "I quit countin' a lon' time ago."

The rooster crowed again.

"When did you get a rooster?" Cain asked.

"Dat's Mignon. He's ma li'l cutie. I rescued heem from an overcrowded chicken house. Da older roosters waz pulling out hees feders. Caused dat little fellow all kinds of stress. He's happy on da farm. Dem feders will grow back. I guarantee eet. We have a competition each mornin'—to see who wakes up firs'."

"Well, you're up before Mignon. That's impressive. How you sleeping?" Cain asked.

"*Bon. Très bon!* Happy you're back home, son."

"Me, too."

"How you slept?" Claude asked.

"Like the dead. I didn't toss once."

"You needed dat. You waz starting to look older dan las' time."

Cain chuckled. "I *am* older than last time. Plus, I've gotten some extra city miles on this body since last time you saw me."

"I hear dat. Give eet some time. Your feders will grow back, jus' like Mignon's."

"Besides that little competition with Mignon, why are you up and dressed so early? Aren't you retired by now?"

"Shhhhit. I'll be retired when dey bury me. Dem floods hit dis region hard. Damaged soybean fields. People's livelihood, son. I'm flyin' to Abbeville dis morning. Need to fertilize a few soybean an' rice fields."

"Is Seth able to help you with the business?"

"Eet comes an' goes. Sometimes I feel like I lost heem in Iraq, an' other times he's da old Seth we raised here on da farm. But havin' your bes' friend take hees last breath in your arms on da battlefield— eet's a tough ting to experience. It would change anybody."

"You have him flying any?"

"Nah. I can't risk eet. Can't have heem havin' an episode in da air. As long as he's on da ground wit Sunny, he's fine. He helps me wit da maintenance. Da boy can fix anyting. He even painted dat bird a few monts ago."

"Is that why it's bright yellow now?"

"Easy to spot in da sky," Claude replied, and winked.

They chitchatted in the kitchen for about ten more minutes and then Cain followed Claude to the barn. A light wind blew through the barn door, bringing the wind chimes to life.

Claude pointed to the corner of the dusty barn. "Eet's still dare. Your punchin' bag. Hittin' dat old ting ees still da best way to get rid of any stress you got."

"I can't believe it hasn't dry-rotted by now," Cain said as he walked toward it.

"I can," Claude said. "Eet's American made. Eet's built to take a beatin'. Jus' like dis Air Tractor 802." He pointed to his airplane. "Jus' like dat rooster. An' jus' like you an' me."

Cain helped his dad pull the airplane out of the barn.

"I'll be back soon," Claude said. He hopped into the cockpit. "Clear prop!"

Cain looked around to make sure it was safe. "Clear!" he yelled back so his dad could hear from inside the cockpit.

Claude flipped the switch and the propeller started spinning strong after initially rotating lazily a few times. A cloud of smoke blew out the exhaust, which was normal for its first flight of the day. He taxied onto the grass and took off into the sky. He rocked his wings before turning westbound and disappearing into the distance.

Cain walked over to the heavy bag. His boxing coach had long since passed away, but Cain could still hear him talking. "Sometimes a fight jus' comes a-looking for you. When dat happens, you finish eet."

The more Cain thought about Tomcat and the SAC, the angrier he became. He picked up his old gloves and studied them. They were marred with sweat and dried blood. Unlike with the heavy bag, the years of abuse and heat and humidity had dry-rotted them. He tossed them on a stack of hay. He started punching the bag with his bare fists. He continued punching the bag until he couldn't lift his arms anymore. They burned as if they were on fire, and his heart felt as if it was about to explode. His knuckles bled, and he was drenched in sweat. He took off his shirt to wipe away the sweat from his face and the blood from his hands. He plopped down on a bale of hay and watched squirrels play in the treetops as he tried to catch his breath and make his heart rate slow down. He remembered his navy training about how to combat-breathe to lower his heart rate. *Inhale through the nose. Hold it for four seconds. Exhale through the mouth. Hold it for four seconds.* He repeated this process several times.

His breathing had slowed enough for him to hear the faint sound of Claude's plane returning. Cain turned skyward and searched for his father. He saw the plane bank left and position for a landing on the grass strip. Cain had watched his father land at least a thousand times, but it never got old. He always marveled at what a great pilot Claude was. He swooped the plane over the grass in a slow and steady way and touched down like a butterfly with sore feet. He killed the engine about twenty yards from the barn and let the momentum carry him the rest of the way. When the prop stopped windmilling, he jumped out of the cockpit and onto the wing as if he was still a young man.

"You're still looking good, Pops."

Claude smiled, showing his teeth. "Ain't nuttin' to eet. Dat flying keeps me young. I'll keep at eet until I can't do eet anymore."

"You want me to refuel it?" Cain asked.

"Non. J'ai terminé."

"That's not bad—done with work and it's not even nine o'clock yet."

"Life's simpler out here. Not easy, jus' simpler."

From the distance, a pickup truck turned onto the long dirt road that led up to the house. After a few moments, it pulled into the driveway.

"Well, dat didn't take long. News still travels fas' out here in da country," Claude said with a smile.

"What are you talking about?"

"You'll see," Claude said as he walked toward the house, opened the screen door, and went inside.

Cain still didn't recognize the truck, but he recognized the lady who stepped out. She was wearing cowboy boots, tight jeans, and a smile that could light up a room.

CHAPTER 31

"WELL, WELL, WELL," she said. "Normally, you can't believe all the rumors you hear in a small town. But in this case..."

"Elise LeBlanc," Cain said with excitement. They had known each other since elementary school.

"In the flesh," she replied.

Cain rushed toward his high school sweetheart, and they embraced.

"Oh, you stink to high heaven! Mr. Lemaire working you to death already?"

"I was exercising. Had you told me you were coming, I would have fancied myself up a little bit."

They laughed together.

"You look amazing," Cain said.

"You, too. So, what's a gal gotta do around here to get a flight over the bayou?"

"Well, normally, I'd charge you full price. But I haven't flown in over a year, so if you're willing to trust me, I'll take you for free."

"Ain't nothing free in this world, honey, but I ain't scared to go up with you. It'll be just like old times."

"I'll be right back," Cain said. "Let me grab the keys and change my shirt—something less sweaty."

"And less bloody," she said.

"You've gotten more demanding over the years," Cain joked.

"I just know what I want," she replied.

The screen door slammed as he ran in and then out of the house, back toward Elise. They walked toward his dad's low-wing taildragger. Most agriculture planes were designed for only one pilot, but Claude owned the two-seat variant since teaching his children how to fly had been important to him.

Cain held Elise's hand to help her step onto the wing and into the open cockpit. He buckled her seat belt and handed her a headset.

"Aren't you going to give me your old scripted safety briefing?" She giggled. *"If you throw up,"* she mocked, *"then I'll throw up, because I'm a sympathetic puker. And if I start throwing up, then I'll have to declare an emergency."*

Cain smiled at the nostalgia. "Nah. I have a stronger stomach than I did in high school." He jumped in, buckled himself, and put on a headset. *This* is *just like old times.* He smiled even bigger than he had when she had gotten out of her truck.

"What kind of takeoff do you want?" he asked.

"Like the ones you used to do."

"Can you handle it?"

"I can handle anything you throw my way." She was clearly flirting.

"Roger that." Cain applied full throttle. The turboprop sprang to life and they catapulted into the sky at over 850 feet per minute. Cain leveled off at 1500 feet and they soared over the marshlands while catching up. They had shared many flights together over the bayous, but it had been so many years since they'd been together.

"I heard you got a divorce," Cain said.

"That's the thing about small towns. Can't do anything without everybody knowing your business."

"I didn't realize it was classified information."

"Last year I caught Scottie 'dating' a girl that worked at his nightclub in Lafayette, and it was the straw that broke this camel's back. But we share joint custody of Brandon. Every boy needs a father in his life."

"How old is Brandon now? Six? Seven?"

"Ten!"

"Wow. Time flies," Cain said in disbelief.

"It'll slow down for you now that you're back home."

"Well, I might only be here temporarily."

"What do you mean? You just got back."

"Bonnie calls practically every day, begging me to come out to Japan. She says there is a job waiting for me there if I want it."

"Well, do you?"

"Do I what?"

"Do you want to move to Japan?"

"Not really. I like it here. What they say is true: there's really no place like home. But it would be great to be closer to Bonnie."

"If you *were* to stay, you could run for sheriff. You'd win for sure."

Cain scoffed. "Oh, God. That's the last thing I'd want to do. Way too political. I'd just enjoy flying some fertilizer runs. And speaking of flying, we gotta head back. We're running low on fuel."

"Perfect timing. I have to pick up Brandon."

After Cain landed the plane, Elise exclaimed, "That was exhilarating! It brought back such great memories." Then she added, "I'm putting together a little picnic next weekend, just me and Brandon. We'd love for you to join us."

"That sounds nice. I'd like to be there. What can I bring?"

"Just yourself."

CHAPTER 32

BASKING IN THE RAYS of early-summer unemployment, Cain fell into an easy routine at home over the next few days. He was helping out his family around the house, and even flying some crop-dusting missions for his dad. Tending the garden, making house repairs, and tinkering on the airplane was tiring work, but it felt therapeutic to Cain. He was eating healthier and sleeping better than when he was on the president's whirlwind schedule.

On Sunday morning, as was custom, the family gathered around the kitchen table to enjoy breakfast together.

As they passed around the plate of buttermilk biscuits, Seth kept staring at his brother. "What's got you grinning like a Cheshire cat?" he asked.

Margaret and Claude laughed.

Cain spooned out some homemade mayhaw jelly from a glass jar and spread it on his biscuit before answering. "It's certainly not you."

The family laughed harder, and Claude even slapped his leg a few times while laughing. When the laughter subsided, Margaret spoke up. "Elise has invited him to a picnic today."

"Oh." Seth smirked and nodded his head. "Is that why you were out early this morning washing your motorcycle?"

"Nope," Cain replied.

"I'd wash my bike if I had a date with Elise," Seth said.

"My Harley needed it. It was a long road trip, and the bike's caked with bugs." He changed the subject. "Now that everyone knows what *I'm* doing today, what are you guys doing?"

"We're going to mass at ten," Margaret said. "Like we do every Sunday."

A typical Cajun family, the Lemaires were devoutly Catholic, and going to mass every week was expected. But Cain wasn't interested in going to mass, so he didn't reply. Instead, he just continued eating.

To break the awkward silence, Claude spoke. "I gotta fix dat fence post on da east side of da property dis afternoon."

"Pops, I'll fix that for you tomorrow," Cain said.

"Yeah," Seth interjected. "Cain and I can fix that tomorrow. It's Sunday. Just take it easy today."

Claude shook his head. "Nah, tomorrow will have eets own problems dat need fixin'."

After breakfast, Cain jumped on his Harley and rode out to Evangeline Oak Park, a small and peaceful patch of greenery near downtown St. Martinville. Elise had laid out a blanket on the grass, a perfect spot under the shade provided by the oak trees that lined the muddy waters of Bayou Teche. Brandon was nearby.

Cain thought about their lifelong friendship. He and Elise had been best friends throughout grade school. They had been inseparable and became high school sweethearts. They even kept dating for a little bit of his freshman year at USL. But Elise never went to college, nor did she desire to leave South Louisiana and explore the world like Cain.

"Twenty years and not much has changed in this old town," Cain said.

"I like the routine of it," Elise said. "It's comfortable."

"I'll have to get used to routine if I decide to stick around," he said.

"Well, maybe today's picnic will help you decide," she said.

"Maybe."

"But you're right," she said. "Being out here does bring back such great memories. If I could only go back in time."

"And do what differently?"

She smiled. "Make sure you didn't get away."

"I didn't get away. *You* couldn't make up your mind. So, I had to make up mine. Started hanging out more with Bonnie on the weekends in New Orleans, and then joined the navy right after college."

"Your sister never did like me very much."

Cain laughed. "Bonnie never approved of any of my girlfriends, at least not in the beginning."

"Except Claire," Elise said. Her voice showed that she had never really gotten over that.

"Well, Claire *was* her best friend, before she was mine."

"Mr. Cain," Brandon interrupted. "Can I check out your motorcycle?"

"You betcha." Cain stood and walked over to the motorcycle with Brandon. "Are you going to ride a motorcycle when you get your license?"

"Yeah," Brandon said proudly. "But mine is going to be green like the Incredible Hulk's."

"That's cool," Cain said.

"Can I sit on it?" he asked.

"Brandon, don't bother Mr. Cain," said Elise.

"Oh, no. It's no bother," Cain said. "Anyone who likes my motorcycle is a friend." He winked at Elise.

"Okay, then," she said. "Mr. Cain said it's fine."

Cain helped Brandon onto the bike and showed him some of the dials, levers, and instruments. "This is your speedometer."

"What's the fastest you've gone on this motorcycle?" Brandon asked.

"Fast as the bike can go. My face nearly blew off."

"That is so awesome," Brandon said. "Can we start it?"

"Sure. This green *N* light means the bike is in neutral. But to be safe, we still apply the brakes. Put your hand on the brake lever and squeeze it. Hold it. And now flip this switch."

The bike roared to life and rumbled. Brandon clenched his fists to hang on to the rattling handlebars.

"Slowly release the brake," Cain instructed. "It's okay. The bike's in neutral. Now roll back the throttle a little bit. Let the bike talk to you."

Brandon rolled the throttle and the bike gyrated more and rumbled louder. The ten-year-old boy's entire body shook. "This is so cool!" he shouted over the noise of the modified pipes.

"Oh, God!" Elise exclaimed loud enough for Cain to hear. He turned and saw her looking over at a nearby pickup.

"What's wrong?" he asked.

"It's Scottie," she said. "He kept texting me, but I ignored him. Now he's pulling up over there. We better go. I don't want any trouble."

"I'm not going to let him ruin my day," Cain said.

"He's been drinking again," Elise explained. "I can tell from his texts. He gets angry when he's drunk."

"I can identify," Cain said. "I've been angry for a while—even when I'm sober."

"This is different, Cain. He gets irrational—unpredictable."

Scottie slammed his truck door and marched toward them.

"Get away from my family!" he yelled at Cain. "Get off that motorcycle, Brandon!" he yelled again. "Get off that thing now!"

Elise ran toward Scottie to stop his advancement. Cain couldn't hear what she was saying, but it was clear that she was pleading with him to go away.

Scottie pushed her aside with his arm and moved toward Brandon. "I told you to get off that bike!"

"Cool it, man," Cain said. "Brandon couldn't hear you over the pipes."

"You don't tell me to cool it. And don't tell me what my son can and cannot hear." Scottie reached out and snatched Brandon's collar to rip him from the bike.

Cain saw red. He grabbed Scottie's shirt with both hands and shoved him to the ground. The impact of hitting the ground knocked the air out of Scottie's lungs. "You better cool it, Scottie, or I'm going to put you to sleep right here!"

Elise ran over to Cain and tried to pull him away from Scottie. Brandon pleaded with him. "Mr. Cain, please stop. You're hurting my dad."

When Cain heard Brandon's words, he released his grip. He couldn't believe how enraged he had gotten. Professionally, he was used to being in control of his actions. The navy and the Secret Service had once trusted him with the most important missions. But with his firing from the Secret Service, his personal life continued to spiral. He was like a wild dog without a pack.

Scottie coughed and gasped for air. "You think you can come into town and steal my family?"

"I'm not stealing anybody's family."

"You're drinking with my wife!"

"Ex-wife!" Elise interjected.

"And my son is on your motorcycle."

"I'm not stealing anything, *cochon*. I'm moving to Japan."

"Japan?" Elise asked. She looked disappointed. "I guess you've made up your mind. And it's all my fault again, you running off to Bonnie. Please stay."

"Let him leave, Elise," Scottie said, clearly embarrassed and still regaining his breath.

"Thanks for the picnic, Elise." Cain looked at Brandon. "You're a good kid. Listen to your momma." He turned to Scottie. "If you hurt either one of them, I'll come back and deal with you myself."

"You threatening me? I'll call the sheriff."

"It's not a threat. It's a promise." Cain swung his leg over his Harley and fired it up. He stomped on the gear and took off.

During the ride back to the family farm, Cain struggled to make sense of how things had gone down at the picnic. *Why did I say I was going to Japan? I don't even know if I want to go all the way over there. I'm finally back home, and I'm enjoying it, and then* this *shit happens. I thought I might be able to come back home and settle in. But it never works out for me.*

When he arrived home, Cain headed straight to the rotary phone on the kitchen wall. He dialed zero and an operator answered.

"I'd like to make a collect call."

"What's the number?" the operator asked.

"It's going to be an international number."

A few moments later, he heard Bonnie on the other end of the line. *"Moshi moshi."*

"Hey, sis."

"Hey, brother. It's really early here. Is everything okay?"

"Yeah, it was just my turn to wake you up."

She half giggled in her groggy state. "Are you still enjoying being back home?"

"I was."

She cleared her throat. *"Was?* What happened?" Her voice was suddenly much clearer, as if she had sat up in bed.

"I was at a picnic with Elise."

"Elise LeBlanc? She's got a lotta drama. You can do so much better than her."

"In all fairness, you've never liked any of my girlfriends."

"That's not true!" she fired back. "I loved Claire."

At that moment, Cain heard his cell phone ringing. Without even looking at who was calling, he hit the button to silence and send the call directly to voicemail. He figured it was Elise, and he wasn't interested in speaking with her right now. He went back to talking to his sister, and the phone started ringing again. "Hold on one sec, sis. Let me turn this damn thing off." He saw the caller ID. It was a Washington, DC, number: LeRoy Hayes. *Why the hell would he be calling me?* he thought. "Bonnie, can you hold on just one more second? It's LeRoy. Let me see what's so important he'd be calling me on a weekend."

Cain answered his cell. "I got Bonnie on the other line. It's an international call, so make this quick."

"Nice to hear from you, too," LeRoy said

sarcastically. "I just thought you'd like to know. Figured I owed you that much."

"Know what?"

"Who turned state's evidence and ratted on the other agents."

Cain wanted to say he didn't care, but that would have been a lie. "Indulge me."

"None other than Tom Jackson."

"You've gotta be shittin' me—he caused this whole storm, and then wore a wire to incriminate the others?"

"Yep."

"Unbelievable." Cain ended the cell call and put the handset back to his ear. "Bonnie, I'll take that job."

"Really? That's fantastic news! What changed your mind?"

"Surely my string of bad luck can't cross the ocean with me to Japan."

"You're going to love it here. Trust me: you won't regret it."

PART TWO

THE GAIJIN

CHAPTER 33

CAIN SLIPPED ON a pair of Bose headphones and closed his eyes to the sound of jazz music playing softly in his ears. The international flight afforded him plenty of time to think.

"You an' your sister are two peas in a pod," Claude had said as he drove Cain to the Lafayette municipal airport.

"We *are* twins," Cain said lightheartedly.

"Jus' when I got you back home—you're leavin' again."

"It'll be just for a while."

"Dat's what Bonnie said, too. An' now eet's been over a year."

"I'm going to go reconnect with Bonnie. Bring family a little closer to her until she can get transferred closer to home. Plus, it'll give me the time and distance I need to clear my mind and make a little money. Then I'll be back."

"I'm thankful you an' Bonnie are gonna be reunited. I jus' fear you gonna stay like her—maybe even find a family an' make Japan your new home."

"I ain't gonna stay there forever, Pops. And Bonnie ain't, either. Look at the bright side. She's doing really well with the airlines, and this keeps her far away from that ex-boyfriend of hers. You know: the one with that sketchy import-export business."

"I never liked dat New Awlins man," Claude said with a scowl. He sighed. "She had to git away from dat ol' boyfriend, an' I guess you gotta git away for a bit, too."

"I do," Cain said.

"I can tell someting's eatin' atcha. Fightin' a man at da park in front of hees kid ain't you."

"That's only half of it," Cain said. "But I don't feel like getting into it right now."

The ANA flight attendant gently placed her hand on Cain's shoulder. She was sharply dressed in a blue-and-gray suit, with a pink scarf loosely tied around her neck.

"I'm sorry to wake you," she said meekly.

"It's okay. I wasn't asleep. Just thinking."

"We are serving our in-flight meal now."

"Great! I'm starving."

"Would you like spicy octopus or freshwater eel?"

Cain was used to eating unusual things both abroad and at home in Louisiana, but these options did not sound appetizing. "Neither. I'll just have a sandwich, please."

"I'm so sorry. These are our only options on this flight."

"In that case, I'll skip dinner."

"Skip dinner?" His American idiom confused the porcelain-skinned flight attendant, whose jet-black hair was pulled tight in a ponytail.

"Nothing for me. Thank you."

"I'm worried you will be hungry. This is a long flight."

It must be a cultural thing, Cain thought. She seemed

genuinely concerned about him, but not enough to serve something palatable. "Don't worry about me. I'll survive, as long as you pour me a whiskey and turn the AC up. It's hot as hell on board."

She covered her mouth and giggled quietly. "Americans always complain about the temperature. But Japanese people get cold easily."

"Well, tell 'em to bundle up, because I can't disrobe." Cain's remark fell flat on the charming flight attendant.

"I'm just joking with you. But I am serious about the whiskey."

When the plane finally landed, Tokyo's Narita International Airport was bustling with travelers, tour groups, and uniformed volunteers directing passengers to various immigration and customs checkpoints. Cain stood out from the Japanese population, and not only because he wasn't Asian. He was taller than everyone else, and he wasn't wearing a white mask over his mouth like so many other travelers he saw. He immediately spotted Bonnie near his gate. She was wearing her sleeveless blue-and-black fitted flight attendant uniform and had used her airline credentials to bypass security and meet him upon arrival.

He hugged his sister tightly, lifting her a foot into the air. Although they were twins, he was six inches taller.

"It's so great to see you, brother! Welcome to Japan!"

"You look fantastic!" Cain was amazed at how Bonnie had flourished in Japan.

"Thank you. You look like shit!"

"Cut me some slack. I couldn't sleep. It was so freaking hot on that plane, and I'm starving. They offered me snake on board."

"You mean eel?" Bonnie laughed. "That's a delicacy

here. With all your worldly travels, I thought you would have known that."

"If I wanted to eat snake—or eel, for that matter—I could have stayed back in Louisiana. I need a good ol' cheeseburger."

"Only place nearby for that is McDonald's," Bonnie said.

"How about a coffee shop, then? I can grab a sandwich."

"That'll work. There's a Starbucks in Terminal One." She grabbed the handle of his rolling carry-on bag. "Where's the rest of your luggage?"

"This is it. That carry-on and this backpack."

"You travel light!"

"Don't need much," he said.

She looked down at his alligator boots. "Well, hopefully you don't need new shoes while you're here, because they won't have your size—or style!"

"What exotic place are you flying to today?"

"Guam. It's a popular vacation destination for the Japanese. Anyway, let's get you fed. I don't want Mom hearing you were hungry and I didn't do anything for her favorite son."

Cain laughed. "You and I both know Baby Seth is her favorite."

She smiled. "You mean the one who still lives at home?"

"I'm kind of glad he's home," Cain said. "He helps take care of Mom and Pops."

"You give him too much credit," she said. "Mom and Pops take care of *him*! But enough about home for now. You are finally in Japan. I can't believe it!" She reached an arm out and wrapped it around Cain's waist as they walked through the airport. "I'm so excited for you, being here. Give it a little time.

You're going to fall in love with this place, just like I have."

"I can't promise I'll fall in love, but I promise to keep an open mind."

"Good, because you'll need it here."

They exited the arrivals lobby and took the elevator to the airport mall. The Starbucks was busy, but they were able to find a small table after waiting a few minutes. Bonnie placed her purse on the table, put Cain's suitcase next to her chair, and got in line.

"You're kidding, right? You're leaving your purse on the table?" Cain said, shocked.

"It's completely safe here. This is how the Japanese reserve tables at Starbucks," Bonnie told him. "They put their things down, then they get in line."

Cain chose a grilled chicken wrap, a bottle of water, and a tall black coffee. He reached for his wallet, but Bonnie was faster. She gave the barista some yen.

"You're not gonna pay for your first meal in Japan," she said. "It's on me."

Cain smiled. "Okay. The next one's on me."

She smiled big. "I'll make sure to pick an expensive sushi restaurant with great reviews."

Cain laughed. "I'm sure this place is full of great sushi restaurants."

He noticed that his sister had upped her lifestyle here in Japan: expensive watch, designer purse, and styled hair. "I just can't get over how great you look," he said.

Bonnie's face turned red. "You're giving me a complex. Did I look that bad in the States?"

Cain laughed. "Not at all."

"What can I say? Japan's been good to me. It'll be good to you, too."

"You even lightened your hair. Do Japanese men prefer blondes?"

"Life is certainly easier here as a blonde." Bonnie grinned. "Most men don't notice such things, but you've always been very observant."

"The blond hair must help you get noticed around here—with all the dark clothing and brown hair I see, I feel like I'm attending a funeral."

Bonnie laughed. "Japan is changing. A little bit at a time. It's a very slow change, but they are letting more and more outside influences in."

They enjoyed catching up in person, but he was jet-lagged and exhausted from the travel. At one point Bonnie looked at her phone. "Tanaka just texted me. He's getting off the train and will be here in just a minute. He's a security guard at the company, and he's going to be your point of contact at your new job. I can't wait to introduce you."

"How's his English?"

"Really good. He studied aviation at Embry-Riddle in Florida for years."

"If he's a pilot, why's he working as a security guard at this automotive company?"

"He never finished his degree. He had to come back to Japan. He wasn't a pilot, but he knew enough about commercial aviation that he was able to get a job at United Airlines. That's how we met."

"What did he do for the airline?"

"He worked various jobs—mainly checking in passengers and sorting baggage issues. Anyway, his dad, who works for the Tokyo National Police, thought he could do better and helped him get the security job at the automotive company. You're going to like him; he's really cool. He's Japanese, but he's not, if you know what I mean."

Cain chuckled. "Nah, I don't really know what that means. At least not yet."

"Well," Bonnie said, "you'll see, the longer you're here."

"So why didn't they just hire a retired Japanese cop to protect this CEO? Somebody who knows the language, customs, and already has police training? Why did they go searching in America?"

"Japanese police don't have the experience that you do. This country is so safe. I don't even think the police carry guns—at least not the ones you normally see on patrol. The threats on this CEO are unusual. I think their executive team is panicking."

"The police don't carry guns? What do they do, carry sticks and knives to a gunfight?" Cain asked with a grin.

"I've never felt scared here. This isn't like New Orleans, where I carried my Mace with me everywhere I went."

"Sis, every place has its dark side."

Just then, a young Japanese man walked up to their table.

"Perfect timing, Tanaka," Bonnie said. To Cain, Tanaka looked like every other Japanese businessman in a dark suit, a dark tie, and a crisp white button-down shirt.

Cain stood to shake Tanaka's hand. "It looks like you stole my tie."

"I'm sorry?" Tanaka's face immediately projected worry. "Can you please say that again?"

"He's just joking, Tanaka-san," Bonnie said. "My brother likes to joke."

"I like to joke, too," Tanaka said. "But you seemed so serious."

Cain laughed. "That's my poker face. I've been working on it."

Tanaka smiled. "Okay. Because there are probably one hundred million ties like this in my country."

All three of them laughed. Cain grabbed a nearby chair and pulled it to their table so Tanaka could have a seat.

"Please don't judge me for being at Starbucks literally right after my flight," Cain said. "What can I get you? It's my treat."

"Thank you very much, but I have this," Tanaka said as he lifted a plastic bottle and showed Cain the label.

Cain looked at the green label and saw some English among the scattered Japanese characters. "'Japan's number one green tea brand,'" Cain read aloud. "I'll have to try that sometime."

"Tanaka, I was just giving my brother some backstory on Mr. Sato, the CEO," Bonnie said. Then, addressing Cain: "Mr. Sato is acting very counter to usual Japanese culture, both by refusing to step down in the midst of a PR scandal and by actually hiring you, an outsider, to protect him. This is a very rare opportunity for you."

I left one international scandal to be part of another? "Tell me more about this scandal," Cain said.

Bonnie continued. "The news is reporting that the auto company falsified emissions controls. This is a huge embarrassment, and Mr. Sato is worried that angry stockholders may attack him because they've lost so much money. And it's not just about money. The CEO has *shamed* these people—betrayed them."

"Shame is worse than death," Tanaka interjected. "Death comes to us all, but you *choose* to bring shame onto someone. In Japan, it is customary for a boss to resign when he has shamed the company. Sato-san, our CEO, refuses to resign. He is adamant that he has done nothing wrong. But there are many people who lost their jobs and their savings because of the news of this scandal."

"You'll see what we're talking about the longer you are here. The Japanese culture is like nothing I've seen anywhere else in the world," Bonnie said.

Cain took another swig of his water. "Do you think anyone will really attack this CEO?"

Tanaka said nothing; Bonnie filled the silence. "I'd be surprised if someone did. But I imagine Mr. Sato is scared. That's why he wanted a gaijin."

"A what?" Cain asked.

"You're going to hear that word a lot here. It means 'foreigner.' Right, Tanaka-san?"

"Yes. Today *gaijin* means 'foreigner.'"

"Today?" Cain asked, surprised. "What did it mean yesterday?"

Bonnie laughed. "You're going to stick out like a sore thumb here."

"It's an old word. It means 'barbarian.'"

Cain chuckled. "I've been called lots of things, but never a barbarian."

Bonnie continued. "Mr. Sato thinks an American will protect him the best since Americans will do anything for money. After all, most Japanese think Americans have no culture or honor. *Greed* is what motivates America. Ironically, it's most likely greed that got him into this mess anyway."

"What do you think, Tanaka?" Cain asked.

"We are honored to have you here. We are only a few security guards, but we are excited to work for you."

"When do I meet the big boss?"

"Sato-san?"

"Yes," Cain replied. "That's why I'm here."

"Tomorrow. First, I will take you to Yokohama. This is where everything is. Your apartment, our company. I would like to introduce you to the city a little bit before you start work tomorrow. Japan is very different from the United States."

"I can already see that," Cain said. "But I'm used to adapting. Plus, Louisiana can't be too much different from Japan."

Bonnie burst out laughing. "He's joking again, Tanaka-san. My brother can be sarcastic at times. You'll learn his sense of humor."

Tanaka smiled and nodded his head.

"Well," Bonnie said, "I've gotta check in for work."

Cain and Bonnie hugged each other tightly as they prepared to leave the Starbucks.

"See you soon," Cain said.

"Can't wait!" she exclaimed. "I'm still in shock you're here. Call me selfish, but I'm glad things worked out like this."

"Like what?" Cain asked.

"For the better. You're finally here!" She turned to Tanaka. "Take care of my brother."

"He looks like he can take care of himself," Tanaka said.

Bonnie laughed. "True, but trouble always seems to find him."

"That makes two of us. Two good people fleeing trouble back home only to end up in Japan," Cain said.

Bonnie smiled and then embraced her brother one more time.

Cain allowed himself to feel a surge of joy deep in his heart. *Maybe this will actually work out,* he thought.

"Safe flight!" he shouted to Bonnie as she headed back to Narita's departure lobby.

CHAPTER 34

"OUR COMPANY HAS ARRANGED for Black Cat to deliver your luggage to your apartment. It'll be there, waiting for you in a couple of hours," Tanaka said as they approached the Black Cat counter at Narita airport.

"That's cool," Cain said. "Is this popular?"

"Yes. It's cheap, too. Many Japanese use this company so they don't have to carry their luggage on the trains. As you will see, the trains are very crowded."

"Makes sense," Cain said. "And it's thoughtful. I'll hold on to my backpack, though."

After dropping off Cain's small suitcase, he and Tanaka took the escalators down to the basement floor of Narita International Airport, where Tanaka used a computer kiosk to purchase two tickets for the rapid train to Yokohama.

"I'm amazed," Cain said. "Everyone actually stands on the left-hand side to allow people to walk past on the right. That never works in America—even when there are signs."

"Yes. I know. America encourages the individual. Japan encourages harmony in the whole."

Tanaka showed Cain how to cross-reference his

ticket with the digital sign on the train. "This is our train. It departs in three minutes."

They boarded and took their assigned seats. The train was full.

"Tokyo is overrated, I think," Tanaka said. "I much prefer Yokohama."

"What's the difference?"

"Cain-san, to a gaijin, everything looks the same here. But to a Japanese person, we see the differences."

"If you and I are going to work together, we've gotta iron out a few things. First, just call me Cain. Plus, you and I look to be the same age. How old are you, anyway?"

"I'm thirty-five."

"Okay, so I'm just a few years older," Cain said. "And secondly, I want you to teach me to see these differences you talk about."

"Okay, Mr. Cain."

Cain chuckled. "Just Cain will be fine. We're operators. We're going to be working together. You're gonna be my second-in-command. We have to trust each other."

"Okay." Tanaka smiled. "You have my word."

"Talk's cheap, Tanaka. Let's shake on it."

They shook hands.

"I'm still amazed. This train is completely full. We're like sardines in a can, yet everyone is so polite. There's nobody talking, besides me." Cain chuckled lightly. "And when an elderly person gets on board, a younger person gives up their seat."

"There are over thirteen million people in Tokyo. A city this size could never exist if we weren't polite to each other," Tanaka reasoned.

"And so many people are reading—actually reading—a book! It's a dying hobby in America."

"Maybe that is because America makes the best movies," Tanaka said, and smiled. "I wanted to visit Hollywood when I was in college, but I never made the time. I can't wait to visit California someday."

About an hour later, they arrived in the city. From the train window, before it went into the station, Cain noticed flickering lights and a Ferris wheel in the background.

"Before we go to your apartment," Tanaka said, "I'd like to take you to my favorite *izakaya*."

"Gesundheit."

"What?" a confused Tanaka said.

"I thought you sneezed. What was that word you said? *Isa*—"

"*Izakaya*. It's the Japanese word for pub. I would like to buy you a drink at my favorite *izakaya*."

"*Now* you're talking, Tanaka-san. I can use a drink before sleeping like the dead tonight."

The *izakaya* was loud and boisterous. Through the thick fog of cigarette smoke, Cain could see that the place was packed with Japanese businessmen in suits. The men were yelling at one another to be heard over the buzz of the crowd.

"This seems like a complete contrast to the Japanese men I saw at the airport and on the train."

"Oh, yes. Society does not allow this in public. But in here, it's okay for salarymen to let off some steam. It's actually expected." Tanaka took off his tie and neatly folded it before placing it in his jacket pocket.

"Good to know," Cain said. "What are we drinking?"

"Sake!" Tanaka shouted in order to be heard.

"That'll work," Cain shouted back, and showed his approval with a thumbs-up.

The waitress brought two wooden boxes filled with sake.

"This is how we traditionally drink sake," Tanaka explained. "The sake is originally in barrels that are broken down into these smaller cups for us to drink from."

"That's neat," Cain said. He raised his small wooden box. "Cheers."

"Kanpai!" Tanaka raised his drink.

Cain and Tanaka drank several cups of sake; they lost count of how many exactly. Tanaka flagged down the server and ordered soba noodles.

"Do you want some soba noodles also?" Tanaka asked Cain.

"I'm good. The sandwich Bonnie bought me was enough."

A few moments later, the waitress brought the noodles in a large bowl.

"That looks like a horse trough," Cain said.

Tanaka smiled and grabbed a pair of wooden chopsticks. He started picking out the noodles and slurping the broth.

"My God," Cain said. "That slurping sound is like someone scraping their fingernails across a chalkboard. Do all Japanese slurp their noodles, or just the ones in this bar?"

"Slurping loudly is how we tell the chef that it's good."

"In my country, we let the chef know the food is good by eating *all* of it and returning an empty plate. How can you skinny fellas eat so much?" Cain asked.

"Noodles do not count as food. We Japanese have a separate place in our stomachs just for noodles." Tanaka laughed.

"Hey, you can make jokes, too. Let's *kanpai* to that."

"I miss American food so much," Tanaka said. "I love American things. The food, the music, the movies, and the big pickup trucks."

"What else?" Cain asked.

"American women."

Cain laughed and Tanaka joined in on the laughter for a second before explaining. "American women are much more forward than Japanese women. I had a girlfriend in Florida. She had blond hair and blue eyes—very American. She introduced me to a lot of different things."

"I bet she did," Cain said with a loud laugh. *"Kanpai!"* In unison they took another swig of the warm sake. "What does your wife think about that?"

Tanaka laughed. "I'm not married. I still live with my parents."

"Really? I left the house at eighteen."

"Yes, I know. That's very common in America. But in Japan, it's very expensive. Many Japanese stay at home until they get married."

"When's that?"

"First, I must find the right girl. And she's probably in America." Tanaka smiled.

"Kanpai!" Cain said, and they gulped another shot of sake.

Tanaka, now red-faced from drinking, had lowered his inhibitions. "I would have stayed in America had it not been for my father."

"What do you mean?"

"I miss America. It is the Wild West. Here in Japan, we have too many rules. Don't get me wrong. Tradition is nice, but adhering to tradition got in the way of my dreams."

"What dreams are you talking about?"

"I wanted to be an airline pilot. That's why I was in university in Florida, at Embry-Riddle in Daytona Beach."

"Yeah, I know it. I was stationed at JAX for

years with the United States Navy. We'd go down to Daytona for various events."

"Yes—so many things to do in Daytona. I had a lot of American friends. I was becoming too American, my father thought. I was at a party where there were drugs. The police came. I didn't take any of the drugs, of course, but I was in the house where they were. The police took us all to jail. My father is an inspector with the Tokyo National Police. He made me return to Japan immediately."

"I'm sorry to hear that." Cain sympathized with Tanaka.

"No, I'm the sorry one. I talked way too much tonight. The train is no longer running."

"It's only just after one o'clock."

"Yes, but in Japan, the trains stop at one. It's very inconvenient for us Japanese. But we must not say anything."

"You must not say anything?"

"We have a saying here: The nail that sticks out gets hammered down. Trust me; I get hammered down a lot."

"So you can take a beating? That's good. Means you're resilient."

Tanaka seemed to appreciate the compliment.

"Well, surely we're not the first people in Japan to close down a bar. So, what's the solution?"

"Japanese always have a solution. Tonight, we sleep in a hotel."

"That's fine. I've spent so many years in hotels that they're like second homes to me."

"I assure you, Cain. You have never stayed at a hotel like *this*."

CHAPTER 35

THEY WALKED THE tiny streets for just one block before they arrived at a hotel.

"What is this place?" Cain asked. "It looks like those pods from the movie *The Matrix*."

"This is a capsule hotel. It's cheap."

"Yeah." Cain scoffed as he looked around. "Herpes is cheap, too. Doesn't mean I want any."

Tanaka didn't seem to get Cain's joke. "This is very popular in Japan. It's our best option tonight. I'm so sorry. I should have looked at the clock so we didn't miss the train."

"Well," Cain said, "it's just for one night. Plus, one of the reasons I came to Japan was to try different things. I'm dead tired from the jet lag. I'll be asleep in no time."

Tanaka spoke with the clerk for a few moments, then used an automated vending machine to book rooms.

"This receipt has your password on it. You will need it to access your capsule. Also, we must take off our shoes and wear these slippers."

Cain tried on the largest pair they had, and even though they were backless, his heels still stuck out by about three inches.

Cain's "room" reminded him of something from a sci-fi movie: each was part of a row of stacked pods just big enough for a body. Inside was a thin mattress, a folded sheet, and a pillow.

Tanaka effortlessly climbed the ladder and slipped into the capsule. Cain, on the other hand, hit his head as he tried to enter the capsule.

"This was not made for Americans!" Cain exclaimed.

"See you in the morning," Tanaka said.

"It *is* the morning," Cain replied.

"Yes—you're right. I meant sleep well."

"There'll be no sleeping well in this thing, Tanaka. The only way I fit in this thing is to curl up in a ball. And the mattress is only about an inch thick to pad my two-hundred-pound body. After tonight, no more of these capsule hotels."

"It's a deal. I promise. I probably won't get very much sleep, either. It's exciting that you're finally here. I can't wait to introduce you to everyone later today."

Cain rested his head on his backpack and closed his eyes. After tossing and turning for a bit, he eventually drifted off into a deep sleep.

CHAPTER 36

CAIN OPENED HIS EYES but saw nothing. He was in complete darkness. He couldn't even see his hands in front of his face. Panic started to set in. He rubbed his hands over his face, feeling the outline of his jaw, mouth, nose, and eyes. Where am I? *The strong scent of pine wafted into his nostrils. He felt his heart against his chest, beating faster and stronger.* Where the hell is this? *He strained to remember.*

He stretched out his arms in each direction, mapping out his surroundings. My Zippo lighter, *he thought.* Yes! *He fished for it in his backpack. He retrieved it, flipped open the brass lid, and lit the wick. The warm glow of the dancing flame produced enough light for Cain to see where he was. He was trapped inside a wooden box—a coffin.*

His casket crackled and warped as the red-hot fire raged, consuming the wood like a colony of starving termites. Cain's body burned and the hair on his arms and face singed. "I'm burning alive!" *he shouted in terror. He heard the faint sound of monks chanting in a foreign language.* "Get me outta here!" *he yelled at the top of his lungs.* "I'm in here!" *He kicked and punched as hard as he could.*

The loud bang and the hallway light that poured into his small cell jolted him awake. He had busted open the capsule's door.

Cain crawled out as quickly as he could, gulping for fresh air. His heartbeat pulsated through his chest like a drum. Streams of sweat fell to the floor and puddled. He sighed. *It was only a nightmare. Combat-breathe,* he told himself. *It was only a nightmare,* he kept repeating. "I gotta get outta here," he mumbled under his breath.

Cain left his backpack in the capsule and traded his slippers for his boots. He tried to peek in Tanaka's capsule, but the privacy curtain was drawn across the tiny window. *How in the hell did Tanaka sleep through that?*

Cain dashed down the stairs to the ground-floor lobby. It was brightly lit. Everywhere he looked, fluorescent lights illuminated the hallways. It felt like a sterile hospital. The nightmare, coupled with the blinding lights, triggered another one of his stress-induced migraines. He rubbed his temples as he searched for the exit.

The automatic doors slid open as he approached. *This place just keeps getting weirder and weirder.* He crossed the narrow street and walked along the sidewalk. Mere hours earlier, the place had buzzed with pedestrians, cyclists, scooters, and cars—all in an orderly fashion, though. But now, at a little past three o'clock in the morning, the city resembled a ghost town whose people had evacuated and forgotten to turn off the lights. Neon lights flashed in every direction. *Who is paying the electric bill for an abandoned city?* Cain looked in every direction. He didn't see a single person walking. It was eerily quiet until the sound of a car rolling over loose gravel echoed between the buildings. The black Toyota sedan taxi cruised by slowly. The driver, clad in a white dress shirt and white gloves, gripped the steering wheel in a perfect three and nine position. He looked like a ghost passing in the night. He never even turned to look at Cain.

The railroad tracks lay to the left in the distance, but the trains were stopped and completely powered down. A cool breeze materialized from nowhere and blew lightly. It felt good against Cain's sweaty forehead. The early-morning wind jostled the red paper lanterns hanging outside various restaurants along the corridor of closed shops and boutiques.

Cain continued exploring this strange land. He approached the only business that appeared open. A wooden sign was propped up on the sidewalk, in front of the door. Cain couldn't read any of the Japanese, but a little of the writing was in English. The sign said SOAPLAND and had a picture of a geisha bathing a man who was sitting in a large wooden tub. Below it, in all capital letters: NO FOREIGNERS!

Cain peeked into the window of the glass door. A thin Asian woman was standing inside. She was dressed in a kimono and had her hair pulled up in a bun. She was escorting a Japanese man to one of the closed rooms in the back. "This ain't the place for me," Cain muttered under his breath, and continued walking.

I've traveled all over the world, yet this place feels the most alien—with its flashing lights, advertisements, strange food, difficult language, and a culture still gripping its origins. Despite Bonnie, Cain felt alone in Japan. *The irony,* he thought. *To be one person in a sea of many millions, but to still feel like an outsider.*

CHAPTER 37

HE WALKED BACK to the capsule hotel. Tanaka's curtain was still drawn. Cain knocked on his door, which looked like the door of an American washing machine. Cain pounded louder with the bottom of his fist until Tanaka finally answered.

"Is everything okay, Mr. Cain-san?" Tanaka asked, wiping the drool from his mouth.

"I'm fine. I'm just ready to start work."

Tanaka used his fingertips to wipe the crud out of his eyes and then studied his watch. "It's only four o'clock, sir. We can sleep for another two hours."

"Plenty of time to sleep when we're dead." Cain realized the irony as soon as he said that. "I was hired because we have a lot of work ahead of us. Lives are in danger. Let's get an early start today."

"Yes, sir."

Tanaka and Cain used the shower facilities at the hotel and then caught a series of connecting trains that eventually stopped near the automotive company's headquarters, which were in an industrial area of Yokohama—near the seaport. This location had been chosen for strategic purposes, and the company had been able to buy much more land for a cheaper price than what they could have purchased it for in Tokyo.

An overweight security guard in his fifties sprang to life when he realized that his new American boss had arrived. Cain extended his hand. "Good morning. My name is Cain Lemaire. It's a pleasure to meet you."

The security guard's face turned red. "Sorry. No English." He ceremonially bowed to Cain.

Cain turned to Tanaka. "Please tell him I said it's a pleasure to meet him, and I look forward to working with him. I'll have lots of questions for him, but later. I like to just observe things on the first day."

"Okay," Tanaka said, and spoke in Japanese for what seemed like a much longer time than necessary given what Tanaka was translating. Tanaka and the security guard continued a back-and-forth conversation. Cain looked on with slight suspicion—he was always a little skeptical during his world travels that his words and tone were being translated appropriately. Cain knew that Tanaka was the security guard's supervisor but was impressed by how much reverence the much younger Tanaka still showed his elder.

"Where do you keep your employee records?" Cain asked Tanaka as they left.

"Employee records?" Tanaka asked.

"Yes. You told me a lot of employees lost their jobs and their life savings. Each one of them is a potential threat to the CEO. Money and revenge are a motive to murder. I want to see each of their files."

"They'll be in Japanese."

"Have 'em translated. In the meantime, I'll look at their official photos. A picture is worth a thousand words. Also, are there any physical fitness requirements for security staff here?"

"Fitness is encouraged but not required."

"The first overweight Japanese person I've seen in this country, and he's on our security detail? He'll have a heart attack if he has to get into a fight."

Several hours later, when it was a more reasonable time for employees to start arriving for work, Tanaka approached Cain.

"Sato-san has arrived," Tanaka said. "I'll take you to his office."

"How does he get to work?" Cain asked.

"Morita-san is his driver."

"Is Morita-san part of our security detail?"

"No," Tanaka replied.

"He needs to be if he's going to drive our principal. I'll make sure he receives specialized training in counter-ambush driving."

When they entered the reception area of the CEO's office, Cain noticed a beautiful Japanese woman sitting behind a desk. He extended his hand and she stood.

"My name is Cain Lemaire."

"Hello, my name is Tamura."

"Is that your last name?" Cain asked.

"It is my family name. My given name is Umiko."

"U-mi-ko," he repeated slowly.

"Hai," she said.

"That's a beautiful name," Cain told her.

"Thank you." Her pale face showed a hint of a blush.

"What does it mean?"

"It means 'the sea.'"

"Are you pulling my leg?"

"I'm sorry?" She was confused by the American idiom.

"My name *also* means 'the sea,' but in French."

"I know." She smiled. "I studied French in high school."

"Enchanté," Cain said.

"Enchantée," she replied. "Monsieur Sato is expecting you." She opened the door to Mr. Sato's office and led Tanaka and Cain into the room. She stayed there to scribble notes on a legal pad.

"Welcome to Japan, Mr. Cain." As a prominent business leader of an international company, Koichi Sato was familiar with Western culture. He shook Cain's hand.

"Thank you, sir. It's an honor to be here. Thank you for this opportunity."

"It is *our* honor," Sato replied. "Bonnie-san was my English teacher, and she highly recommended you."

Cain chuckled. "She's done a great job, because your English is excellent."

Mr. Sato shook his head to show humility and dismiss the compliment.

"I'm serious, sir. Your English is fantastic, and you couldn't find a better English teacher than her. You're in good hands."

"That's funny," he said. "She said the exact same thing to me about you. That I'd be in good hands."

Cain smiled. "We don't look alike, but we're twins."

Mr. Sato looked around the room at his employees. "I'd like to talk to Cain-san privately, please."

Tanaka and Umiko looked caught off guard. They glanced at each other, stood, bowed, and then exited the room by walking backward.

Mr. Sato leaned forward, moving closer to Cain. "Now I can talk more openly about the threat I face."

"The threat *we* face," Cain said before Mr. Sato continued. "When I took this job, your threats became my threats. We're in this together."

CHAPTER 38

CAIN EXITED MR. SATO'S OFFICE about fifteen minutes later. Tanaka and Umiko were standing in the lobby, waiting impatiently.

Cain sighed. He had learned more in that meeting than he had anticipated. He turned to Umiko. "It was nice meeting you. I look forward to working with you more."

"Me, too," Umiko replied with a smile that showed off her perfect teeth. "Maybe my *Français* and English will get better." She giggled and placed her hand over her mouth.

Cain smiled. "Your English and French are better than mine."

"*Merci,*" she said.

"*De rien,*" he replied.

Cain and Tanaka left the CEO's office quarters and headed back to the security office.

From his desk's landline, Cain called Bonnie.

"How's your first day at the office going?" she asked.

"I can already tell I'm going to have to make some changes."

"What kind of changes?"

"I've got a lot more work ahead of me than I

originally thought. But I'm so jet-lagged right now I gotta be careful about making any major policy changes. Security here has been too complacent for *waaaay* too long. Security cameras are in black and white, one of my officers is retired on duty and on the verge of a heart attack, and there's another one who looks at cartoon porn all day!"

"*Hentai,*" Bonnie said.

"What?"

"*Hentai.* It's what the Japanese call anime porn. It's very popular here—you'll even see men reading it at the 7-Eleven."

"In the States, the police would get dispatched if a man was caught looking at pictures of a man having sex with a schoolgirl. Look, I understand there are cultural differences, and I'm trying to keep an open mind. But some things are just way too weird for me to accept."

"Like what else?"

"Like the fact that I can get a coffee, a bag of potato chips, an ice-cream cone, and a pair of ladies' underwear all from the same vending machine!"

Bonnie started laughing uncontrollably. "It is a little weird."

"A little? It's creepy!"

"Okay, I'll give you that one. We can talk more about some of these cultural differences over drinks."

"I look forward to that conversation. Anyway, I've called a mandatory meeting for tomorrow."

"That'll make their day. The Japanese *love* meetings."

"Well, they're not going to like this one," Cain said.

"Oh?"

"I'm going to lay down the law."

"Well, that's why Mr. Sato hired you and nobody else."

"Sounds like he hired me because of you," Cain said.

"What do you mean?"

"Doesn't sound like Mr. Sato needed any more English lessons."

"I teach more than just language. I also teach international cultural norms and other important things a leader who's doing business all over the world should know."

"I'd like to get together with you as soon as possible, though."

"You're already itching to buy my meal at the most expensive sushi restaurant in Yokohama?"

Cain chuckled. "Well, not the most expensive one. I haven't gotten my first paycheck yet. But I need to ask you about some things."

"Sounds serious. Is everything okay?"

"Let's talk in person."

"Okay. Let's meet at the Yokohama Station at six tonight. How about the west entrance, in front of Tully's coffee shop?"

"Tully's coffee shop. West entrance. Eighteen hundred. See you there."

Cain hung up the phone and called Tanaka into his office. "Please let the guys know we're going to have an all-hands tomorrow at oh seven hundred hours."

"All-hands?"

"It's a navy term. It's a meeting for everyone on the security detail."

"Okay, boss. What's the dress code?"

"Normal working attire."

"*Hai.* What would you like served at the meeting?"

"Huh?" Cain asked.

"Tea, water, Coca-Cola? Maybe something—"

"Tanaka-san, this is a work meeting, not a social gathering."

"Hai." Tanaka bowed. "But it is customary to—"

"I want everyone's mind focused on the business of protecting Sato-san and this company," Cain interrupted. "Not on what beverage is going to be served."

"Hai. I will let everyone know." Before Tanaka walked off, he asked, "Do you want Morita-san there?"

"Absolutely," Cain replied. "As the driver, he has a very important role."

"Okay, but he will be driving Sato-san during that time."

"Okay. Slide the meeting to the right one hour. Let's meet at eight."

For the rest of the day, Cain studied translated personnel records and walked around the complex to inspect security vulnerabilities. He looked at his watch. *Ah, I've lost track of time. I've gotta rush to meet Bonnie.*

He'd learned that the main Yokohama train station was the fifth busiest train station in the world. The compound was a massive labyrinth that accommodated over two million passengers per day with trains, buses, taxis, restaurants, and even high-end shopping. It was Cain's first time taking the Japanese train by himself, but thankfully the tourist signs were printed in English.

Cain spotted Bonnie with ease. She was a blonde and taller than the average Japanese person, but it also helped that she was wearing a red dress in a sea of black and gray clothing. She was standing in front of Tully's coffee shop, waiting for him.

Cain hugged Bonnie. "Sorry I'm late."

"It's six oh one. You better have a good excuse," she joked. "Because the trains are never late in Japan."

"This station is an absolute madhouse," Cain said.

"If you think this is bad, you should try Shinjuku Station at seven in the morning. It is a confusing maze, with millions of people going to work, and thousands of kids rushing to school. Sometimes the trains are so packed that people can fall asleep standing up!"

"Oh, hell no!" Cain replied. "I'm not ready for that."

Bonnie took Cain to one of her favorite sushi places. It was quaint and cozy inside the small restaurant.

"I still can't believe you are really here in Japan, about to eat sushi with me."

"Give me some credit. I would've eventually made it here."

"Not if you were still working for the Secret Service."

"It was hard to take any vacation with the demanding schedule," Cain admitted. "The president received at least five threats per day, and each one had to be thoroughly investigated."

"Is that normal, or is it just this president?" Bonnie asked.

"Nah, doesn't matter who's in office. The crazies are always looking to get themselves in the paper. Plus, we were always short-staffed. Lots of agents were jumping ship to other federal agencies. But I'm here now. How do we order?"

"I'll do all the translating, buddy," Bonnie said. "As the conveyor belt rotates, I'll let you know what's on the plate. If it sounds good, just grab it. At the end, they'll stack our plates up and charge us."

"You mean *me*?" Cain asked.

"Exactly!" she exclaimed.

Bonnie described the various sauces at the table and showed Cain how to use the chopsticks.

"They're called *hashi,* and the Japanese take eating

with them very seriously. As with most things Japanese, there are lots of rules regarding the use of *hashi*. For example, make sure to use the chopsticks holder. But don't cross the chopsticks when you put them on the holder."

"That sounds dangerous," Cain joked. "What happens if I do that?"

"It's a major faux pas. Also, don't stick your chopsticks in a bowl of rice, and don't pass food from *hashi* to *hashi*. It's all got to do with funeral rituals here."

"Got it," Cain said, and diverted his attention to the conveyor belt, which was on a continuous loop to provide the hungry customers with ever-present plates of fresh sushi. "I can recognize a few dishes," he said, and pointed at one. "That looks like tuna."

"Yes, it is. And they have a few different grades— depending on how much you want to spend. That's why the plates are different colors."

"My first time eating sushi in Japan—I want the best." Cain reached for the plate and used the wooden chopsticks to dip the tuna in a mixture of soy sauce and wasabi. "Ah, this is delicious! So fresh."

He and Bonnie took turns grabbing plates off the conveyor belt and together enjoyed their meal.

"Oh, you'll like this one," Bonnie said as she grabbed the red plate from the conveyor belt. "It's the chef's special, and he barbecued it. They use a special sauce that really brings out the flavor."

Cain was getting competent at using the *hashi*. He picked up the sushi, put it directly in his mouth, and slowly chewed. He closed his eyes and relished the moment. "You're right. This is *really* good."

"I knew you'd like it. It's a delicacy here."

"A delicacy? I've heard that word used before." He looked suspiciously at Bonnie.

"I told you eel was delicious!"

"I wish you hadn't told me what it was," Cain said. "I would have enjoyed it more."

"Eel *is* delicious!"

"Don't say that word again, sis." His stomach was churning. "You know what they say about payback."

She laughed. "You've always been good at payback!"

The conversation flowed naturally for a bit before turning to their family back home.

"Have you talked to Pops?" Cain asked.

"He and I talked yesterday. He asked about you, and I told him you had arrived safely and that you were doing just fine getting settled in."

"Thanks. We don't want him and Mom worrying. They still look good and healthy, but they're getting older."

"So, what was *so* important you couldn't wait to see me?" Bonnie asked.

"What can you tell me about the yakuza?" Cain asked.

Bonnie quickly looked left and right to see if anyone had heard Cain. "The Japanese don't even say that word in public. And I only know what I hear from some of my Japanese friends."

"Well, what do they say?"

"I guess they're like the Italian mob back in New Orleans. You know: they stick together, wear suits, and when somebody crosses them, they are dealt with by violence. Why? You're worrying me."

"I met Mr. Sato this morning."

"What does he have to do with the yakuza?"

"I'm about to tell you if you'll let me finish."

"Sorry," she said.

"Mr. Sato had everyone leave the room, and he

told me that he is most worried about the yakuza attacking him."

"Why would they go after him?"

"He said the yakuza had invested heavily in his company's emissions reduction technology, and now they're losing a lot of money. I mean *a lot*."

"I'm so sorry, Cain. I didn't mean to get you involved in this. I thought this would be an easy security job for you."

"Easy is boring," he said.

"The yakuza are outcasts here," she continued. "They're bad people. Killings are very rare here, but when somebody *does* get murdered, you can almost bet your life on it that it was the work of the yakuza."

"Do you know anybody I can talk to who would have more information?"

"What about Tanaka's dad? He's an inspector with the Tokyo police."

"I already thought about that. I've gotta tread lightly. I don't wanna put any more tension between Tanaka and his dad. You know: the whole thing about Tanaka being yanked out of America and brought back to Japan."

Bonnie nodded. "I met an American journalist several months back who knows a ton about Japanese culture and crime. He works for the military newspaper—the *American Flag* or something like that—"

"The *Stars and Stripes*?"

"Yes! That's it. He's also married to a Japanese woman and speaks really good Japanese."

"That's great," Cain said. "What's his name and number?"

"His name is Champ Albright the Third. I have his contact information somewhere at my apartment."

"It'd be nice to meet another American here."

"What are you gonna do?" she asked, looking very concerned.

"I took on this job knowing the risks. It's my problem to deal with, not yours."

"There's no dealing with the yakuza, Cain. You're a gaijin."

"That's right," he said, and grinned. "I'm a bar-barian."

"An *outsider*. And it's *not* funny." She pointed her finger at him and shook it. "They won't think twice about hurting you if you get in their way."

CHAPTER 39

THE SECURITY DEPARTMENT'S small break room had a coffee machine and a rice cooker on the countertop. One lone vending machine with flashy lights was situated in the corner. A calendar with a dozen pictures of Mount Fuji was tacked to the white wall.

Cain pulled Tanaka aside. "Can I count on you to translate for me?"

"I can, but they all speak English."

"They told me they spoke very little English."

"If a Japanese person cannot speak perfect English, they say they cannot speak it."

"English is my mother tongue and I don't speak it perfectly. I'm a product of the Louisiana public school system. Have a seat, Tanaka. I'll speak to everyone in English."

"Very well." Tanaka bowed his head and gathered the three security guards and the driver before he took his seat.

Cain began the meeting promptly at 8:00 a.m. "Gentlemen, what is our greatest threat?"

Cain watched the men look at one another. Tanaka spoke up. "An employee who was laid off by the company and is now angry."

"*Hai.*" The other guards agreed and nodded their heads in unison.

"That is certainly a threat," Cain said. "But our greatest threat is the unknown—the one thing we cannot predict. *That* is what we must train for."

"How do we train for the unknown?" Tanaka asked.

"Great question. My father had a good friend named Frank Rogers, who was an old crusty flight instructor. He was known for telling his students, '*In der Not frisst der Teufel Fliegen.*' That's German for 'In an emergency, even the Devil eats flies.' We are in an emergency situation. We are a global automotive company with over 135,000 employees. Our cars are sold in more than one hundred countries. Yet as a security staff, we are understaffed and undertrained. We're going to have to make some sacrifices until we get some backup. I'm increasing our shifts from eight to twelve hours."

Everyone looked on with great focus. Then one of the security guards raised his hand.

"Speak freely," Cain said.

"Will we get overtime for this?"

"I'm working on that. I just have to find the right person to discuss this with."

"That will be Umiko-san," Tanaka said. "She is the executive assistant to Sato-san. She can usually cut through a lot of typical Japanese bureaucracy."

Perfect! Cain thought. He had hoped to find an excuse to see Umiko again. "I'll talk to her as soon as this meeting is over." He turned his attention back to the entire group. "So, we're going to increase our work hours, and we'll need to find and hire three additional security guards."

The oldest security guard finally overcame what

seemed like hesitation to ask a question. "Cain-san, Japan is very safe. Why do we need more guards?"

"Because I'm adding Mr. Sato's house under our protection umbrella. Our team is going to start watching it, too."

"He lives in a very nice neighborhood. Very expensive. Very safe," the guard replied, clearly thinking the gaijin was overreacting.

Cain kept the yakuza threat to himself. He didn't want to spook his security guards until he had learned more. "We also need to update our equipment. No more black-and-white CCTVs. We need color cameras, and a pan-and-zoom feature. We need earpieces for our handheld radios." He looked one of the security guards directly in the eye. "And no more reading *hentai* on the job!"

The three security guards sat quietly in their chairs. "Are there any questions?"

Nobody said anything. "Now is the time to ask any questions, because we're about to stomp on the gas and go full speed ahead. We all need to be operating on the same eight cylinders. Or, in the case of Japan, on all four cylinders." Cain smiled but noticed that nobody got his joke. "Complacency kills, gentlemen. We're going to start asking ourselves every day: 'How would I attack Sato-san in this scenario?' And we're going to start training in self-defense. We're not talking about doing katas and swinging nunchucks here. I'm going to teach you the skills I learned at the Secret Service and in the navy. I'm talking about being able to put a suspect on the ground quickly while the other team members *cover* and *evacuate* our protectee. That's *cover* and *evacuate*. That will be our MO."

Tanaka looked around the room, then stood and bowed before he asked, "Boss, what is *MO?*"

"*Modus operandi.* How we will conduct the business of executive protection."

"*Arigato gozaimasu.*" Tanaka bowed.

"Okay, that's all I have for now. Let's get back to work." Cain clapped his hands in a gesture to motivate his team.

The security guards and the driver stood in unison and bowed. As they were exiting the room, Cain asked the driver to stay behind.

"Morita-san, how long have you been with the company?"

He strained his eyes as he thought. "Forty-seven years."

Cain's eyes widened and his mouth gaped open. "Wow! That's impressive."

Morita-san smiled and nodded his head with several short, quick bows.

"How long have you been driving for Sato-san?"

He held up two fingers.

"Ever since Sato-san became the CEO two years ago?" Cain asked.

"*Hai.*"

"Forgive me for asking this, but how old are you?"

"Sixty-seven," Morita-san replied.

"It's my pleasure meeting you." Cain bowed.

Morita left the security office and Cain approached Tanaka. "Are the guys always this quiet, or just in my meetings?"

"This is very typical of a Japanese meeting. We have two ears and one mouth, to listen twice as much as we talk."

Cain smiled.

"But they understand what is required," Tanaka said with confidence.

"What do you think about Morita-san?"

"He is very loyal, and very reliable."

"Yeah," Cain said. "But he's getting up in age. Can he see well? What are his reaction times like?"

"He drives very safe," Tanaka said. "He is very cautious."

"Wouldn't Sato-san want a younger driver who could probably see better and have faster reflexes?"

"Old age is relative in Japan. We have more centenarians than any other country. Plus, loyalty is very important to Sato-san. Morita-san has been with the company since he was twenty years old. He has no family. This job is his only family."

Cain understood what it was like for a man's job to be his only family. He took a deep breath and exhaled. "I'm heading over to Umiko's office to talk about some of these changes. Can you talk to your dad for me? See if he has some people he could recommend to add to our security staff? Maybe some recently retired cops who still want to work, or maybe some applicants who were qualified but didn't get hired by the police department?"

Tanaka inhaled air through his teeth with a slight head tilt. After a brief hesitation, he nodded his head.

"Good! Can you get right on that for me? We're about to apply full military power."

Tanaka nodded, but it looked to be more out of habit than out of understanding.

"That's a navy term," Cain said. "It means we're about to maximize our protection for Sato-san at a speed never seen here before."

Tanaka smiled and nodded his head. He was clearly excited to be working for Cain.

Cain started walking toward the exit. "Time for me to go grease the wheels with Umiko-san."

CHAPTER 40

CAIN WALKED ACROSS the parking lot, entered the main lobby, and took the stairs to the second floor. Umiko was sitting behind her desk, finishing up a phone call in Japanese. She wore a black fitted blazer with a white blouse. Her hair was pulled back, and she had sweeping bangs. When she finished her call, she stood and walked from behind her desk, now revealing her pencil skirt and heels.

She is so beautiful, Cain thought.

Umiko seamlessly switched from her native Japanese to English. "Cain-san, it's nice to see you."

"You, too, Ms. Umiko. Are you busy?"

"We have a lot of important meetings today. We have the press conference next week in downtown Tokyo."

"Where in Tokyo? I thought it was going to be here."

"We changed it at the last minute. It will be at the Tokyo International Forum. It has a beautiful glass atrium. All the Japanese press will be there and Sato-san will be talking directly to the news. Many people will be there. It's very exciting."

"I'm sure it is, but this event is a nightmare from

a security standpoint. It's televised, located at least an hour's drive from here, announced a week in advance, attended by the public, and I've only got three inexperienced security officers on the payroll. I don't like it at all. We're not ready for this type of event yet."

"The building is significant. It will symbolize Sato-san's courage and strength as he moves our company forward."

"I thought Sato-san was the one giving the statement, not the building," Cain quipped. "I was assured by Mr. Sato that I could make any security adjustments that were necessary. And considering the scope of this type of event, I will need to make some changes."

"Okay," she said. "Mr. Sato told me to give you anything you needed."

"We need to hire three more security professionals."

"Where will you find these people on such short notice?"

"I talked with Tanaka-san. His father is an inspector with the Tokyo police."

"I think the extra security will be good. I'm sure Sato-san will be pleased with your changes."

"Also, I need to update our equipment. We're going to need a drone. We'll use it for aerial surveillance and for crowd control. And we're going to update our security cameras to something more modern. I'm also going to have them installed at Mr. Sato's house."

"*Sugoi!*" she said, sounding amazed. "You are making lots of changes."

"I hope it's not a problem," he said.

"No. I think it's good that you are here."

He smiled. "I'm glad to be here."

"Please have Tanaka-san prepare and forward these requests to me. I will personally get them approved."

"*Merci beaucoup,* Umiko-san. And there's one last

request." He figured this one would be difficult for them to understand.

"Yes?" she said, and waited patiently.

"My team is not ready to provide the type of security needed for this large-scale event. It's a long drive, through a heavily populated city, with lots of choke points and ambush spots. My team is not used to operating in motorcades, and they're not familiar with all the potential safe havens. It is my strong recommendation that Sato-san and I take a helicopter to the event."

Umiko's eyes widened. "A helicopter?"

"It's the safest and the quickest way," he replied.

She breathed in through her teeth. "I will talk to Sato-san about this. I think it is possible."

Cain smiled. "Good. Thank you very much. This is very helpful."

"I'm happy to help you," she said.

Cain caught himself staring at the warmth of her smile and the kindness in her eyes. "I've gotta run now. I'm about to teach self-defense to my team."

"You know karate?"

"Well, it's not karate per se. It's more like American boxing."

"Do you like the martial arts?"

"Yes, I do. Very much."

"Me, too." Umiko's face seemed to brighten. "I take kendo lessons three times a week."

Cain was impressed. *She's beautiful, kind, speaks three languages, and can probably kick my ass!* he thought.

"Kendo is like sword fighting," she said, "but we don't use a sword. We use a *shinai*—a wooden bamboo stick that takes the place of the katana, the sword. Kendo is more popular with women than judo or karate."

"I'd love to watch one of your classes someday," Cain said.

"Would you like to come tonight? I have class at seven."

He was caught off guard by her forwardness. Most Japanese he had interacted with were very timid, but he appreciated her confidence. "I'd love that."

"Great! I will swing by your office at six," she said.

"As long as you ain't swinging a"—Cain paused to remember the word—"a *shinai* or katana at me."

She smiled. "We can take the train to my dojo. I hope you will like it."

He returned the smile. "I'm sure I will. I already do." He left her office and headed back to the security department with a spring in his step.

CHAPTER 41

CAIN LOOKED UP from his desk. Tanaka was standing at the doorway.

"May I come in, Cain-san?"

"Of course, Tanaka. I have an open-door policy. You don't have to ask for permission."

"Are you almost finished with work for the evening?"

"What's up?"

"I was planning to go to the Hard Rock Cafe. They have a live band tonight. It's a Journey cover band."

"I love Journey. Their new Filipino lead singer, Arnel, is fantastic!"

"The cover band is not as good as the real band—"

"They never are," Cain said.

"But they are good. And I love the American nachos at Hard Rock."

Cain laughed out loud—one of those boisterous laughs that come with being in a great mood.

"What's so funny?" Tanaka asked.

"I've never thought of nachos as *American,* but I guess they are in some weird way. I would love to join you, but—"

A soft knock at the open door interrupted his conversation with Tanaka. It was Umiko.

"But," Cain continued, "I'm going to kendo class tonight."

"I see," Tanaka said. "You really like Japanese culture, don't you?"

"More and more every day," Cain replied.

"*Eto,* I can't wait to hear all about it tomorrow morning," Tanaka said.

"It's a deal, and rain check on the American nachos."

"I'm going to have to really study English expressions to understand some things you say," Tanaka said.

"I know, buddy. I use a lot of slang." Cain sang *"Don't stop believin'"* in his best Steve Perry voice as he ushered Tanaka out of his office. Cain flipped the light switch, and he and Umiko headed to the station where they caught the train to the dojo.

"Umiko-san, I'm really excited to watch your kendo class tonight. Are you the best student?"

"Some are better than me," she humbly said.

"And I bet you're better than some—perhaps most," Cain replied. "How many students are in the class?"

"Ten."

"Just ten?"

"Martial arts used to be much more popular in Japan, but now everybody wants to play tennis, golf, or *especially* baseball."

"Baseball can be fun to play, but it's boring to watch. Second only to golf."

"American influence has really made baseball popular. And it's more of a team sport, whereas the martial arts are all about disciplining the individual's body and mind." She pointed to the sky. "And I cannot forget. My sensei always says kendo is also to cultivate a rigorous—no, that's not right—a *vigorous* spirit. A lot of sports focus on making the body strong. But fighting without discipline and rules is just violence. That's why the martial arts have tradition *and* religion."

"Good point," Cain noted. "It wasn't until I joined a boxing gym in high school that I learned how important the mind is in fighting. Control your fear and try to outsmart your opponent."

"We're here," she said with excitement as they approached a nondescript multilevel building.

"Well, that's convenient for everyone—to have the dojo so close to the train station."

"Hai."

"It's not what I expected," Cain said.

"Really? What were you expecting?"

"I guess I was expecting some type of traditional hut outside town—in a small village. Definitely someplace more remote than next to the train station."

Umiko giggled. "The martial arts are already dying in Japan. Imagine if the dojo was outside the city."

Cain followed Umiko through the doorway. They took the narrow stairs to the second floor. He knew immediately upon entering the large open-bay room that he was in a sacred place. The walls and floor were constructed of wood, and he could see martial arts equipment hanging on the walls. There was a small entryway with several cubbies and shelves filled with shoes. Umiko had slipped off her shoes and deposited them into an empty cubbyhole before Cain had even removed his first boot.

"I really need to get some slip-on shoes if I'm gonna stay in Japan," he said as he struggled to figure out how his boot would fit in one of the empty wooden cubbyholes.

Umiko giggled under her breath. "I like your boots. You should keep them," she said with a shy smile.

Umiko showed Cain where the visitors sat: in a loft just outside the training floor. The loft was designed to give spectators just enough distance away from students dangerously swinging their forty-two-inch *shinai* practice swords. There were eight wooden chairs in a line against the wall.

"Do you need anything?" Umiko asked. Cain was touched that she was paying extra attention to his comfort.

"Nah, I'm good."

"Great. I have to go change now. I'll be back soon."

The students started trickling out of the locker room wearing their kendo uniforms. The uniform consisted of a white pajama-like jacket, a pair of baggy black trousers that looked like a skirt, and plenty of protective equipment for the head, forearms, and chest. Some students were already wearing their head protection, while others were cradling it in the crook of their elbows.

An older man dressed in a worn martial arts *gi* started ceremonially beating a large drum in the corner. The beat echoed throughout the training hall. Cain could feel its vibrations. The drum seemed to represent the start of the class, since all the students uniformly got in line: three rows of three, and one row of one. The instructor, a small Japanese man who looked to be in his late sixties, approached the front of the class and yelled out something in Japanese. The students bowed to the instructor and then paired off.

For the next hour, students screamed and shouted *"Kia!"* as they swung their *shinai* at one another's heads and torsos. Their strikes were so fast that often

Cain couldn't even see the contact that had been made. When the class ended, the students removed their sweat-soaked protective face shields. The majority went to the locker room to change, but Umiko headed straight for Cain. Her hair was pulled up in a bun. The glistening sweat on her face, paired with her nimble prance, made her appear ethereal.

"I'm so thirsty," she said.

"I'm happy to get you some water. There are at least five million vending machines in this country."

She giggled. "How about an Asahi?"

"An adult beverage? Even better! I can use a cold one myself after watching you tonight. You are fierce!"

Umiko smiled with a slight bow. "*Arigato goza-imasu*. I'll be right back. I'm going to change into normal clothes."

Cain assumed Umiko was going to change into some casual clothes, but when she emerged from the locker room, she was dressed up and well put together.

"I know just the perfect place for us to get a drink," she said. "It's walking distance, too."

"I'm down."

After a couple of minutes of walking, they arrived at a popular beer garden with a bunch of outside seats. Umiko and Cain found an empty bench and plopped down.

"How did you enjoy the class tonight?" Umiko asked.

"You were amazing. Remind me to *never* get into a fight with you."

Umiko blushed. "Are you joking with me? You know we Japanese have a difficult time recognizing American sarcasm."

Cain laughed. "Not at all. You're a real badass.

If you ever wanna switch from executive assistant to being on my security detail, let me know. I'll be happy to have you."

She smiled. "Japan might be changing a little bit, but not enough for Sato-san to have a female on his security detail."

"That's too bad," Cain said. "The Secret Service uses women to protect the president."

"But probably not a lot, huh?"

"Women make up about 10 percent."

"Why did you decide to leave the Secret Service and move to Japan?"

"Because I was interested in studying kendo."

"Really?"

He laughed. "Nah, I'm just joking."

"See? I told you we don't get American sarcasm."

"But I would be interested in taking kendo with you."

"I can ask the sensei if that is okay. You would be the first gaijin in the class."

"I've heard *that* word a lot since I've been here."

Umiko smiled. "It would be fun to have you in the class."

"Are gaijin allowed?"

"I don't think the sensei would mind. He is also a Zen priest. He quotes Zen philosophy a lot. Like, 'If you light a candle for somebody else, it also brightens your path.' And my favorite: 'A rising tide lifts all boats.'"

"I like that one. I'll have to put that in the back pocket and meditate on it."

"You meditate?"

"Not really. It's just a saying. Speaking of sayings, what was it your sensei kept yelling in class?"

"Mushin."

"Moo-shin," Cain repeated. "What does it mean?"

"It means 'no mind.' Block out every distraction and focus only on the present."

"That's hard to do, especially in our rushed society," Cain said. "The past has a way of haunting us."

"I know," Umiko said. "That's why I love kendo. It has helped me out so much."

Cain leaned in. "What do you mean?"

Umiko opened her mouth and paused. She seemed sad. It was the first time Cain had seen this fun and energetic lady look mournful.

"I'm sorry. I shouldn't have asked," he said.

"No, it's okay. When I was eighteen years old, in high school, I was in love with my first real boyfriend. He was so studious before we met. He wanted to be a Japan Airlines pilot. But I took him away from his studies a lot. I always wanted to go to the movies, or to the mall, or to the park. College exams are very important here in Japan. The family places so much pressure on passing these exams, and he didn't pass his."

"Did he retake them?"

"No." Umiko looked down at the table. "He killed himself."

"Oh, God. I'm so sorry. My God. That is *just* horrible."

"I blamed myself for a long time."

"But it wasn't your fault."

"I thought, had I not taken him away from his studies, he would have learned more and made a better grade."

"You can't blame yourself."

"I did, though. For a long time. I lost ten kilograms and started hanging out with the wrong crowd. Kendo turned my life around. It taught me how to find inner peace by blending the mind and body with the spiritual."

"That's wonderful. You've sold me. Yes, please talk to the sensei and let him know I would consider it an honor to be accepted into his class."

Umiko clapped her hands together. "I will be happy to."

"But it'll have to be next week because until then I'm spending all my time making sure my team is prepared to make this press conference go off without a hitch."

"With you in charge, we have nothing to worry about."

CHAPTER 42

CAIN SPENT THE next several days at work interviewing and hiring three additional guards. In the States, these guards would have been more tactically inclined, but in Japan, they seemed to be more service oriented. *A little bit of something is better than a whole lot of nothing,* he reminded himself. *At least I have a few extra bodies that I can mold and eventually turn into executive protection specialists.*

He conducted self-defense courses, oversaw the implementation of new security cameras, and, in the lot behind the building, watched some of the security team learn how to operate and fly the new drone they had purchased.

"This is a hell of a lot harder than flying an actual plane," Cain said as he manipulated the drone's control module. "I should have hired some teenagers. Give 'em a bag of Doritos and some Mountain Dew and they'd fly this thing for free!"

After crashing the drone a few times, he let Tanaka try. Tanaka flew it well.

"How are you flying this so well? I'm the licensed pilot with over a thousand hours under my belt!"

"I am part of the Tokyo aero club," Tanaka said.

"I build and fly remote-controlled airplanes on the weekends."

"That's good to know," Cain said. "I'd like to go with you one weekend."

"I would be happy for you to come."

Cain directed everyone back into the building for another all-hands meeting.

"We have to be prepared for any type of attack," he warned once everyone was huddled into the break room. "But you're probably well aware that statistically, knife attacks are the most common in Japan. A few things to remember about knife attacks. Rule number one is don't get cut. Rule number two is, if you do get cut, don't freak out. Chances are slim that it's life-threatening. And most importantly, rule number three is always control the hand with the knife. If there are no questions, let's head outside and act out some scenarios."

One of the guards said something in Japanese that made Tanaka laugh.

"What did he say?" Cain asked.

Tanaka smiled. "He said this used to be an easy job before you showed up."

Cain chuckled. "It's still easier than digging ditches in Louisiana. Did I ever tell you about my first job?"

"No, but I'm interested."

"One evening over sake, I'll tell you all about it. But I'm not ever staying at a capsule hotel again!"

They laughed together. Their working partnership was forming well.

After practicing knife-disarming techniques with fake knives, Cain pulled aside Morita-san. "Normally, Secret Service agents who drive the American president receive months of specialized driver training. Everything from counter-ambush recognition, J-turns, bootleggers, other evasive maneuvers, and ramming techniques."

Mr. Morita looked at Cain in confusion.

"I realize all those terms have no meaning to you, and that tomorrow you will not be driving Sato-san to the press conference because we're taking a helicopter. But that doesn't mean you have the day off. You still have to drive the car to the conference just in case we have any problems with the helicopter. Murphy's Law."

"Mur-fee?" Morita-san asked.

"It means what can go wrong will go wrong. We're under the gun and simply don't have enough time to go over everything. So I just want to make sure you understand a few basics about driving a VIP."

"Driving what?"

"It's an acronym," Cain replied. "VIP. Very important person."

"What is *acronym*?"

"Never mind that. The protectee must be kept safe."

"Pro-tect-tee?" Mr. Morita pronounced each syllable as if it were a question.

Frustrated, Cain just replied, "Sato-san!"

"Hai!" Morita-san nodded his head vigorously up and down in recognition.

"Hai," Cain muttered under his breath.

CHAPTER 43

THE HELICOPTER PILOT was adamant that it was too dangerous to fly because of the marine layer that had formed over the water. A light ocean breeze had blown fog toward the city, and it hovered from about one hundred feet above the ground to at least one thousand feet.

"Any chopper pilot worth his salt could easily fly through this cloud layer," Cain told Tanaka. "That's what the instruments are for."

Tanaka sucked air through his teeth. "The pilot said the company policy requires at least one-mile visibility."

Cain shook his head in disbelief. He looked skyward, momentarily thinking back to his flying career, during which he'd flown countless missions referencing just the instruments in the cockpit. He turned to Mr. Morita. "Murphy's Law."

"*Hai!* Mur-fee." Morita smiled nonchalantly.

Cain looked back at Tanaka. "Our team isn't ready for a ground movement like this. I'm going to go talk with Sato-san." He walked into the main office and approached Sato, who was rehearsing his speech.

"The helicopter is not available today," Cain informed him.

"Then we will take my car," Mr. Sato replied, more concerned about his speech to the public than about how he would arrive there.

"That's what I wanted to talk to you about, sir. I don't recommend it. If we wait just a few hours, this fog will burn off and we can take the helicopter. My team is getting better every day, but they are not ready for a high-stakes movement like this yet."

"Our stock is dropping too fast. I must give this speech, even if it puts me in danger."

"Sir," Cain continued, pleading, "this is a high-profile event publicized in advance. Your picture is plastered all over the news. The vehicles are not bulletproof, the Japanese government doesn't authorize me to carry a firearm, and it's going to be at least a one-hour drive."

"I understand your concerns. That's why I hired you—to free me to concentrate on saving this business. We must go by car. End of discussion."

End of discussion, Cain thought. He had heard that phrase before, and he didn't like how that scenario had ultimately ended. "Copy that, sir. Give me ten minutes to activate the foul-weather plan, and my team will be in place to transport you."

Cain quickly arranged for the two-vehicle motorcade to stage outside the front doors of the main lobby. The engines were running, the gas tanks were full of premium fuel, and the drivers were in position. He was used to presidential motorcades, which included police motorcycles, decoy vehicles, heavily armed counterassault members, special radar-jamming equipment, extra vans for the press corps and support staff, and a fully stocked ambulance that carried a doctor and extra vials of the president's blood type.

"The danger and threat against Sato-san are real," Cain told his security team. "And we have fewer resources than I'd prefer. Don't drop your guard."

The elderly Mr. Morita smiled and lifted his white-gloved hand in the air, acknowledging that he understood his role as the primary driver. Cain had already talked to him about procedure in the event that they encountered any vehicle problems. They would pull over to the side of the road, and Sato would quickly get into the van that would be following behind them. "The show must go on," Cain had said. "That's why we always have at least one backup vehicle." He knew that statistically, a flat tire or a mechanical failure was more probable than an assassination attempt while commuting.

The main lobby's glass doors slid open, and Umiko, Mr. Sato, and his entourage of advisors flowed out toward the vehicles. With a slight bow, Cain opened the rear passenger door. Mr. Sato took his seat in the black Nissan President while Umiko gracefully slid onto the long back seat from the other rear passenger door. The President PGF50 was Nissan's finest sedan, and it had been used by Mr. Sato for the last three years. Mr. Morita took excellent care of it and had hand-washed and waxed it for this big event. Cain understood that appearances were important, especially in Japanese society.

Cain looked at Tanaka, who was standing outside the follow-up vehicle, a black Elgrand luxury passenger van. Tanaka made one last check to be sure the support staff was situated inside the van. Once this was confirmed, Tanaka gave Cain a thumbs-up. Cain returned the signal and took his position in the front seat of the Nissan President. Their handheld radio earpieces had not arrived yet, so Tanaka and Cain had to communicate by hand signals and text messages. Otherwise, their radio broadcasts would interrupt Sato's train of thought and any conversation he might be having in his car.

Because the Japanese drove on the opposite side of the road from Americans, Cain sat on the left side of the luxury sedan.

"The radio says traffic is very bad today," Mr. Morita announced as the motorcade pulled away from the lobby doors. "Too much Tokyo construction and bad weather," he told Cain.

"I must rely on your expertise, Morita-san. I've never driven in Tokyo." Cain hated that he hadn't had time to survey the routes and do a walk-through of the Tokyo International Forum himself, but he'd been busy overseeing all the physical security improvements at Sato's house and at the company's headquarters. He had, however, tasked Mr. Morita with doing the survey route the day prior.

Mr. Morita flashed his headlights and the guard pushed a button, opening the massive vehicle gate. Cain waved, and the uniformed guard bowed as the motorcade passed. The man did not rise from the bow until the motorcade had passed.

After a few moments of driving, the Nissan President turned onto the main street that would eventually connect them with the toll road. The motorcade slowed to a stop at a red light. Cain's eyes were drawn like a magnet to a black motorcycle that crept up beside them. The motorcyclist was wearing black boots, black pants, a black jacket, and a full-face helmet with a dark tinted visor. The operator turned left to look into the unarmored vehicle. An uneasy feeling moved over Cain. When he had protected POTUS and other VIPs, no motorcycles like this would have ever been allowed to get so close to the motorcade. He double-checked to make sure the vehicle's doors were locked. They were. He looked back at Mr. Sato, who was holding his speech with two hands, resting it in his lap. He was quietly reading his speech and was unaware of what was happening outside the car. The traffic signal turned green and Mr. Morita eased on the gas. The motorcycle turned right and fell out of sight.

Cain took a deep breath and let it out slowly. He texted Tanaka: DID NOT LIKE THAT MOTORCYCLE NEXT TO US. FOLLOW VEHICLE. MAKE SURE THAT DOESN'T HAPPEN.

Mr. Sato began talking to Umiko. They were speaking Japanese, so Cain couldn't understand them, but he assumed it was about Sato's speech. He saw Sato scribbling some last-minute notes in the margins of his sheets of paper.

Cain's attention zeroed in on the roadblock that was up ahead in the distance. Two Japanese construction workers wearing white helmets and dressed in the typical blue overalls with light-reflective jackets were in the road directing traffic. Close to them were several yellow road barrels with black stripes.

"What's going on?" Cain asked Mr. Morita. "What does that sign say?"

"Road repair," he replied.

"Were they doing construction yesterday when you ran the route?"

"No."

I don't like this, Cain thought. *Not at all. Has all the textbook signs of an ambush.* "The road looks perfect to me, Morita-san. Don't stop. Just keep driving."

"Cain-san," the driver replied, "we must obey all Japanese traffic rules. Or I lose my license."

Cain reached for his handheld radio and twisted the volume knob up. He pushed the mic and was about to talk to Tanaka when he heard a troubling sound in the distance.

The dull whine of two sport motorcycles had broken the silence. The high-pitched sounds of their exhausts were growing louder by the second as they drew closer. Cain whipped his head over his left shoulder. In the side-view mirror he saw two sport motorcycles quickly approaching from the rear. They were definitely a pair. Each had a passenger on the back, and the models matched the motorcycle from before.

One of the construction workers was waving a handheld flashlight with a blinking red light on the end. He was holding it in such a way as to ensure that the motorcade remained stopped while the other worker was repositioning one of the road barrels.

Cain pressed the mic on the handheld radio and shouted, "Two motorcycles coming in hot! *Ambush! Evacuate!*" Then Cain yelled to Morita-san, *"Drive!"*

Cain quickly turned to Sato. "Get down, sir!" Cain unbuckled his seat belt and was preparing to jump into the back to cover Mr. Sato with his own body when Mr. Morita stomped his dress shoe onto the gas pedal. The 278-horsepower V-8 engine roared to life. The fresh tires squealed before they gripped the concrete and thrusted everyone into their seat. The powerful 4.5-liter engine chewed the concrete and spat rocks as Mr. Morita weaved around the construction workers and blasted through traffic.

Umiko shrieked in terror.

"They have guns!" Tanaka's voice shrilled over the

radio as the rear passengers on the motorcycles pulled out Uzis and pointed them toward Tanaka's van.

Takka takka takka takka. The sound of high-velocity rounds being fired from the submachine guns at a rate of six hundred rounds per minute echoed off the high-rise buildings as the 9mm bullets sprayed the van.

Umiko screamed in horror and shock.

The motorcycles whined louder as the drivers rolled the throttle to max speed to close the gap. Morita-san was a completely different person than Cain had ever imagined. It was as if a trance had come over him and he was channeling Steve McQueen in the movie *Bullitt.*

"Stay down!" Cain shouted in Mr. Sato's ear as he used his own body as a shield to cover his protectee. He had been hired by Koichi Sato and was legally and morally bound to protect him, but Cain also wanted Umiko to comply to increase her chances of survival as well. "You, too, Umiko. *Stay down!*" He pulled her tiny body close to his.

The black motorcycles flanked Sato's car, approaching both sides of the rear passenger compartment. Mr. Morita jerked the steering wheel violently left and right to shake them off the car, but it didn't work. The drivers comfortably maneuvered their bikes at high speeds, and they would come right back alongside the car.

Takka takka takka takka. Bullets and smoke spewed from the Uzis. At least three rounds penetrated the rear window, and glass shattered throughout the passenger compartment. Umiko cried out as broken glass rained down onto her head. She wildly tossed her head left and right to shake the shards of glass out.

"Don't move!" Cain yelled. "Just stay down." He continued pushing Sato and Umiko as far into the floorboard as he could, placing his outstretched body on top of them both.

He grabbed Sato's briefcase from the rear seat and placed it over their heads. He figured it was a little protection—at least better than nothing.

Mr. Morita continued jerking the steering wheel from side to side. The motorcycles were swarming the car like angry bees. "Stick to one!" Cain yelled out to him.

"Hai!" Morita replied, and trained all his attention on the motorcycle to his right. He turned the steering wheel to the right and forced the motorcycle to veer right. When the motorcycle couldn't go any farther right without hitting the guardrail, the motorcyclist released the throttle and slowed down to get behind the sedan. At that very instant, Cain yelled out to Morita, "Hit the brakes now!" Morita listened to Cain, though it was a command that was completely counterintuitive in a situation where assassins were on the heels of their prey. Morita stomped his foot on the brake. Smoke billowed into the air from burnt rubber and overheated brakes as all the momentum transferred to the car's front chassis. Cain felt his body roll forward and abruptly stop against the back cushion of the front seats.

As Cain had predicted, the new Kawasaki sport bike had been going too fast. It couldn't stop in time. The motorcycle slammed into the trunk of the sedan and flipped the rider and passenger onto the roof, breaking the hood ornament off the car as they crashed onto the pavement and continued rolling.

"Great job, Morita-san! Now *go, go, go!*"

Mr. Morita lifted his foot off the brake and pushed the pedal to the floor. The sedan responded with raw power. The momentum snapped his head back into the headrest, and Cain watched as Morita ran over one of the attackers, causing two thuds as the tires rolled over the body. Cain peered through the shattered rear window as the two assassins lay still on the pavement.

"Find me a fire or police station!" Cain instructed the driver, his face now so close he was practically spitting on Morita. *"Shoubousho! Koban!"* Their car wasn't on fire, but fire and police stations were safe havens during protective missions because they were government buildings with medical equipment and emergency communications.

The remaining motorcycle sprinted forward and pulled alongside the battered Nissan President.

"Chotto mate!" Morita yelled.

"Hold on!" Umiko quickly translated as Morita blew through a red light at a busy intersection. Passing cars blared their horns and screeched to a halt. Morita swerved off the main road and squeezed the large sedan down an alley that led to a hidden labyrinth normally closed to cars because of pedestrian traffic. The Kawasaki Ninja 1000 followed close behind like a shadow. The narrow alleys were no obstacle for the bike or its operator.

Morita-san hit the horn with his palm and held it as he yelled out in Japanese. Shoppers and business-people scattered in every direction and leaped out of the way to avoid the massive car barreling through.

As the motorcycle pulled alongside the passenger compartment, Cain grabbed the handle of Sato's brief-case and swung the case all the way from his hip into the helmet of the motorcycle's passenger. The briefcase busted open and sent papers flying as the Samsonite case broke the face shield and catapulted the rider off the motorcycle and into the wall of the tight alley.

"Sato-san is bleeding!" Umiko cried out.

Cain looked down and grabbed Umiko's cherry blossom scarf from around her neck. He quickly untied it and placed it against Mr. Sato's neck.

"Keep pressure on it!" he yelled as the scarf continued soaking up blood. "And stay down!"

Police sirens wailed loudly as two Japanese police officers joined the pursuit. Red emergency lights flashed from the powerful white Honda motorcycles.

"It's about damn time!" Cain exclaimed. He grabbed the handheld radio and keyed the mic. "Tanaka, what's your status?"

The radio crackled. Cain twisted the squelch knob and turned up the volume so he could hear over the blaring sirens.

"Tanaka?" he repeated. "Report in."

There was no response. Cain's stomach seized. He feared the worst. "Dammit, Tanaka!" he yelled in anguish. "Report in!"

"Minor injuries from shattered glass," Tanaka said, his voice fading in and out over the airwaves. "But we are okay. Van is disabled on the side of the road. I gave your direction to the police. Is Sato-san okay?"

Cain emitted a huge sigh of relief, knowing that everyone in Tanaka's vehicle was safe. "We're all okay. The good guys are finally here," he announced over the radio. "Rendezvous back at base."

The police downshifted their transmission, maximizing every ounce of torque their V-4 engines could provide. The assassin and motorcycle police officers blew past Cain and his injured passengers. The police quickly caught up to the remaining assassin, who had to abort or risk arrest.

Morita-san let off the accelerator and stomped on the emergency brake. When the rear tires locked up, he swung the steering wheel to the left. The car slid 180 degrees around the weight of the heavy engine, coming to a dramatic stop.

Cain jumped off Mr. Sato and ran his fingers through the executive's hair and across his face and neck. He then inspected the man's fingers for blood and other signs of life-threatening wounds. He removed a golf ball–size piece of glass from Sato's neck. Cain held it up for Sato to see. "You're a lucky man. This missed your artery by half an inch."

Mr. Sato nodded, clearly shaken by the attempt on his life. "I'm okay, thanks to you and Morita-san."

Cain was on autopilot as the adrenaline raced through his body. He ripped open Sato's button-down shirt and was shocked by what he saw.

Sato forcibly removed Cain's bloody hands and buttoned up his shirt. "I told you: I am fine. Now get me back to the office. There are people everywhere taking photos!"

"Yes. You're right. Let's get you back to the office. We'll regroup there and have a medic look at your neck."

Cain turned to Mr. Morita, who was outside the car, inspecting the damage. "*Damn!* Morita-san, you are the shit!"

Mr. Morita lowered his head in shame. "I am sorry, Cain-san."

"Sorry for what?"

"You say I am shit."

Cain chuckled. "No, Morita-san. It's an expression. You were awesome! You are *the man*! Where did you learn to drive like that?"

Mr. Morita raised his head and beamed. *"The Fast and the Furious: Tokyo Drift."*

Cain laughed out loud. "Get us back to the office.

Too many onlookers gathering and snapping photos, and we gotta get Sato-san checked out."

"Hai!"

During the short drive back, Cain's thoughts bounced around in his mind—the ambush, the assassins, the automatic weapons, Mr. Morita's awesome driving—but one question kept nagging at him: *Why did Mr. Sato have a dragon tattoo on his chest?*

CHAPTER 44

MR. SATO'S PERSONAL PHYSICIAN, an accomplished doctor who had trained in Australia, examined him in the safety of his large office at the automotive headquarters.

"That was a close call," Sato said in English, for Cain's benefit.

"Yes, it was." The doctor continued attending to Sato's neck. "No stitches needed, though. Just some cuts from the glass. You're lucky you had your American security guard with you."

"They are the lucky ones! If they had been brave enough to face me hand to hand, I would have destroyed them."

"Who were they?" the doctor inquired.

"Trust me," Sato replied. "I will find out."

"Until we do," Cain said, "you're still in great danger. My team and I will continue to train hard to protect you."

"When will these threats stop?" the doctor asked. "Sato-san is not getting any younger."

"They won't," Cain replied. "Not until they get what they want."

"What do they want?" the doctor asked.

"They want me to resign," Sato said angrily. "And I will not! I've come too far. I was born in this world alone. Abandoned at an orphanage without any clothing on my back. I worked day and night to reach this position. I carry the sacred name of my adoptive parents. I will not give my attackers, nor my competition, the pleasure of seeing me resign in defeat and in disgrace. I will not do that to the Sato family name."

Cain was surprised by Mr. Sato's history, which he had never heard before. "Then we'll outlast them. The threats against the United States president never stop, either. I'm used to this kind of pressure. And obviously, you are, too."

Mr. Sato grabbed a pack of Marlboros from his desk drawer and lit an imported cigarette.

"Those things will kill you," the doctor said.

Sato took a drag and slowly exhaled the smoke. He looked Cain directly in his eyes and nodded. Cain could practically read his thoughts: *The gaijin was better than he had expected.*

CHAPTER 45

THE FOLLOWING MORNING, Cain was back at his office. He had been working steadily on improving security for Mr. Sato. At Cain's request, his team assembled in the break room to debrief the ambush from the previous day.

"I've got good news and bad news," Cain said. "Which do you want to hear first?"

"The bad news," one of the security officers said.

"Okay," Cain replied as he scanned the room. "The bad news is—wait! We're missing a team member. Where is Nakamura-san?"

Nakamura was one of the guards who had recently been hired. The room was silent. No one on the team said anything. Cain looked at Tanaka. "What's going on? Where is Nakamura?"

Tanaka stood and answered with his head hung low. "He has resigned."

There was an audible gasp in the cramped room.

"The attack scared him too much," Tanaka continued. "He said he is suffering nightmares from it."

Cain thought about his own nightmares, about how Nakamura was not alone. "This profession is dangerous. Each of us could lose our lives, and yesterday proved that. But there is honor in courage." He raised a clenched fist into the air to inspire his team. "Cowards die many times before their death, but the brave taste death only once."

The room filled with the sound of his team members clapping in admiration. When they stopped clapping and cheering, Cain asked, "What was I saying?"

"The good news and the bad news," Tanaka said.

"Yes! That's right. Well, the good news is that even with one member gone, this room is getting more cramped for us to meet in since we've increased our manpower."

"And the bad news?" Tanaka asked.

"Yesterday's coordinated attack on Sato-san was a reminder of the seriousness of our business. Now you can understand that there *is* a method to the gaijin's madness." Cain pointed to his chest. "We didn't prevent the attack, *but* we prevented our boss from getting killed. Now is not the time for overconfidence, though. We can't ease up and let our guard down. Yesterday's attack could have been much worse. Imagine if there would have been just one more motorcycle with an Uzi-wielding attacker. We might all be pushing up daisies right now."

Cain's audience had a collectively confused look, and one of the guards raised his hand and asked for clarification.

"*Pushing up daisies* means we'd be having this meeting in heaven."

"In Shinto, there is no heaven," the security guard said.

"But there is reincarnation in Buddhism," Tanaka-san said.

That started a religious discussion among the guards, who were normally much more reserved.

"Religion and politics," Cain muttered under his breath. He tolerated the discussion for a few more seconds, his eyes darting back and forth; he didn't understand a word the guards were saying. Then he continued, "Team, we're getting way off topic. The bottom line is that we should expect and be prepared for more attacks."

One of the guards stood and bowed before asking his question. "Who is responsible?"

"For the attack?" Cain asked.

"Hai."

"When the police tell me, I'll let you know." Cain was hesitant to express his belief that it was the yakuza. He understood that just muttering the word *yakuza* scared people throughout Japan. If the security guards felt they were up against the Japanese mafia, he'd have a hard time keeping them on the payroll. *A man will throw himself in the line of fire for his country's supreme leader,* Cain knew, *but finding people to do it for a businessman was a whole other struggle.*

Tanaka had brought in a copy of the *Japan Times,* an English-language publication.

"You're a hero," Tanaka announced in front of the group.

"Only in my mom's eyes," Cain replied, trying to diffuse any praise. "Hand me that paper."

The front page showed a picture of Cain, with bloodstained hands, with Mr. Sato in the back of the tattered Nissan President. The headline, in one-inch bold print, read THE GAIJIN!

"Seriously?" Cain said. "We saved his life, but that picture looks like I'm about to kill Sato-san." He began to read the story underneath the headline: "Exiled American Secret Service paid to protect Sato…" Cain rested his forehead in the palm of his hand. *I knew the scandal had made international news,* he thought, *but damn! It's like getting sprayed by a skunk: you just can't escape the stink.*

The guards laughed, to Cain's relief. *Hopefully I can keep them motivated and working as a team.* "Of course they would have to print *that* picture, and not the one of me helping get broken glass out of Umiko's hair," he said, and shook his head with embarrassment. "My sister already called me this morning to rub it in. She said I looked like a wild animal, and that I perfectly embodied the gaijin stereotype. I tried to explain to her that the blood was from providing lifesaving first aid to Sato-san."

"The media loves it," said Aito, a friend of Tanaka's who'd recently joined the security team. "This will be their best-selling paper of the year. Right, Tanaka-san?"

"Yes," Tanaka replied. "Bonnie-san is right. It makes the gaijin look like a real barbarian. I am happy to tell my friends I work for an American cowboy."

"Yes!" Aito agreed, and laughed.

"The good news," Tanaka said, "is that I don't think we have to worry about any more attacks on Sato-san. With your picture, everyone will surely be too scared to attack now."

"Thanks, guys," Cain said. "But we can't drop our guard. We have to stay vigilant. There is a high possibility of more attacks. A lot of people lost money, and people will do crazy things for money."

Cain was getting more comfortable with his team members every day, but he still didn't know enough about them to completely trust them. There just wasn't enough time to properly vet the security detail, especially since he had hired additional bodies at the last minute. Secret Service background checks for an agent took a year; investigators would go all the way back and interview an applicant's kindergarten teacher.

A female receptionist announced over the company-wide PA system, "Cain-san, you have a telephone call on line number two."

Who would be calling me at work? Cain thought. *Bonnie would just call my cell phone.*

CHAPTER 46

HE WALKED TO his office and picked up the phone. "This is Cain Lemaire speaking."

"I'm sorry, but I asked to speak to the gaijin." The male voice on the line had a distinctive Southern accent.

Cain smiled as he recognized the voice from what seemed like another lifetime. "This couldn't be the wet-behind-the-ears pup from Saint Augustine, Florida, who used to yelp in my David Clarks all those years ago, could it?"

"Holy shit! Hurricane, it is you!" Hurricane was Cain's navy call sign, but nobody had used that in years.

"SFB Alvarez. I can't believe it," Cain said.

"That's Chief Alvarez to you, buddy."

"Jesus Christ! The navy will promote anyone nowadays. They must have short memories," he teased his former flight engineer.

"Obviously someone has a memory like an elephant." The chief laughed.

"How could I forget that?" Cain asked incredulously. "You almost got us court-martialed."

Naval aviators rarely got nicknames for things

they did well; they were usually given when a service member screwed up. Alvarez was no different. SFB stood for "shit for brains." It had come from a time when Alvarez's dyslexia had caused him to transpose two grid digits on a map, causing him to mistakenly drop ordinance too close to an American submarine during a training exercise. Cain had recognized the error immediately and radioed the sub's captain to take emergency evasive maneuvers. After the disaster was narrowly avoided, the submarine's captain screamed furiously over the radio, "I want the name of that shit-for-brains son of a bitch who tried to sink my sub!" And so "shit for brains" was shortened to "SFB," and Alvarez had his new call sign.

"Chief, huh? Since when?"

"Yes, sir! Navy diagnosed me with sleep apnea. They booted me out of flying on P-3s. Got my promotion working on F-14 engines aboard the USS *George Washington*."

"Well, congratulations are certainly in order."

"Thank you, sir."

"How in the hell did you find me?"

"It's a crazy story. You see, the USS *Washington* is docked in Yokosuka, Japan. I was riding the train to base this morning and saw a bunch of people reading the *Japan Times*. This ugly, bloodied-up man was on the front page, and he looked *real* familiar to me. He looked a lot older so I couldn't be sure, though."

"Oh, God." Cain sighed. "I know where this is heading."

"Oh, yeah," Chief Alvarez said, chuckling. "I've already been telling everybody on board the ship that I used to fly with that gaijin who's all over the news."

"Talking with you brings back some great memories." Cain smiled.

"For me, too, Hurricane. Thousands of hours over the oceans looking for commie subs."

"Look, how about we get together for a drink this weekend and catch up? I'm at work right now and I gotta get back to it. You can imagine how intense things are at the moment."

"Why don't you come down to Yokosuka and I'll show you the base? If you're up for it, we can even take one of the sailboats out and cruise Tokyo Bay."

"As long as you don't read me poetry and try to hold my hand," Cain joked.

Chief Alvarez laughed. "I'm still trying to find true love"—he paused before disclosing the punch line—"at the bottom of a bottle."

Cain chuckled. "Then I'll bring an ice chest full of true love for you."

"Don't bring anything! I will take care of everything. If my shipmates found out that my old pilot—"

"Jeez," Cain said. "Easy on the old jokes. This old man can still whip your ass!"

"That's probably still true." The chief laughed. "I can't wait to smoke a stogie with you and talk about old times."

"And that's how sea stories are made up," Cain said.

"And you've got a lot of 'em," Chief Alvarez said before they hung up.

CHAPTER 47

CAIN THOROUGHLY ENJOYED his Sunday get-away with Chief Alvarez in the fishing village of Yokosuka. The navy base felt like a slice of small-town USA. They had a hearty brunch at the officers' club before renting *El Viento,* a sail-boat from the recreation department. Far away from the US embargo against Cuba, they smoked Cohiba cigars on board the eighteen-foot boat as they sailed around Tokyo Bay and caught up on each other's lives.

"It's nice to have someone I can really trust out here," Cain said.

"We go way back, Hurricane. I'll never forget you bailing my butt out in El Salvador. You saved my navy career."

Cain nodded as he puffed on his cigar. "I appreciate that you recognize that I stuck my neck out for you. I did a similar thing for a guy I worked with at the Secret Service, but he didn't give a damn."

"He sounds like a piece of shit."

"He's back in DC, and I'm over here. I'm not complaining, though. I'm starting to piece my life back together."

"Like I said, I'll never forget what you did for me. I'll always have your six."

Cain nodded. "Hooyah."

When he arrived at work on Monday morning, Cain was reenergized but sunburned. It was six thirty and he thought he'd be the first one in the office, but Tanaka was already at his desk going through personnel folders, looking for potential threats, and reading through the reports the guards had generated over the weekend.

"Good morning, Cain-san."

"Right back at you," Cain said. "You're here bright and early."

"Yes. I wanted to get a head start, as you might say."

Cain smiled. "I appreciate your work ethic. It would be difficult for me to get this job done without you."

Tanaka stood and bowed. *"Arigato gozaimasu."*

"So, what did you do this weekend?" Cain asked.

"Aito-san and I went near Tokyo to fly our RC planes."

"Very nice! I'd like to join you guys one weekend. I need help getting better at flying those things."

"Yes, that would be very fun. Maybe we can build you a navy plane."

"Make it a fast one, like an F-14 Tomcat." Cain smiled.

Tanaka gave him two thumbs-ups.

Cain headed to his desk to drop off his backpack.

"Before you settle in, I wanted you to know we received another death threat letter addressed to Sato-san. I translated it for you."

Before Cain could respond, Umiko appeared in the doorway. She softly knocked, even though they both saw her.

"Hi, Umiko," Cain said with a smile.

"Good morning, Cain-san. How was your Sunday?"

"Great. Got out yesterday and saw some of Japan."

"What did you think about what you saw?"

"I'm loving this place more every day."

Tanaka said something in Japanese, which prompted her to giggle and converse back and forth with him.

"Um, okay, guys. You know it's rude to talk about me in Japanese while I'm standing right here." Cain smiled.

"I have the solution," Umiko said.

"Yeah? What's that?"

"Tanaka-san should teach you Japanese."

"Well, I'm going to need *a lot* of help," Cain said. "Maybe I'll need *two* teachers." He held up two fingers and then pointed to both Tanaka and Umiko.

Umiko blushed and changed the subject. "Sato-san has asked for you, Tanaka-san, and Morita-san to come to his office. He would like to thank you for protecting him last week."

"That's very thoughtful of him, and I appreciate it. But I was just doing my job. His appreciation and support are thanks enough."

"Japanese business, just like kendo, is very ceremonial," Umiko explained. "And I also would like for you to be there. You saved my life, too."

"Those thugs wouldn't have had a chance against you if they were brave enough to meet you in the dojo," Cain said.

"Especially if I had a katana instead of a *shinai,*" Umiko said.

"I agree," Cain said as he nodded. "Okay. You've convinced me. Plus, I have a gift for both Sato-san and Morita-san. Tanaka and I will be honored to go."

"The honor is ours. I will escort you to Sato-san's office."

"*Merci,*" Cain said.

"It's time for you to start practicing your Japanese," Umiko playfully suggested.

"*Arigato,*" Cain said, and bowed.

Umiko clapped. "Very good. Soon you will speak perfect Japanese."

"Especially with a sensei like you." Cain smiled. "You see what I did there? I'm already piecing together Japanese words."

Tanaka cracked open his briefcase and pulled out a tie. He tossed it around his neck and started tying it.

"Is it a black-tie affair?" Cain asked. He pointed to his boots. "Had I known, I would have worn my gators instead of my cowhides."

They walked across the parking lot and Cain noticed a brand-new 2012 Nissan Fuga.

"Is this our new car for Sato-san?"

"*Hai,*" Umiko said. "Do you like it?"

"It's gorgeous. Is it armored?"

"*Hai,*" Umiko replied. "And it has three hundred and twenty-nine horsepower. Morita-san will be able to go even faster now."

Cain laughed out loud. "If he goes any faster, his passengers will have to clean their seats when they get out."

Umiko looked confused.

"Bad joke, I guess." Cain smiled and followed Umiko into the building.

Mr. Sato's bandage was gone and replaced by a tan Band-Aid. "Your neck has healed very well," Cain said.

"Yes, it has. Thank you again."

"I'm sorry about your briefcase." Cain presented

Mr. Sato with a new leather briefcase. "I bought this for you yesterday while I was at the navy base. It's American made. I thought you'd like it."

Sato inspected it. "It's fantastic. Thank you."

Cain then turned to Morita-san. "I also picked these up for you at the base."

Morita-san smiled as he saw his gift, a pair of black fingerless motorcycle gloves.

"No more white gloves for you," Cain said, and winked. "These are more your style."

Morita-san smiled wide but looked a little embarrassed by all the attention.

"Let us begin," Sato said, and presided over the celebration in his massive office.

"I am alive today because of the actions of Morita-san, Tanaka-san, Umiko-san, and Cain-san. The company would like to present each of you with a certificate to demonstrate its appreciation for your courage and dedication to duty." Mr. Sato presented each employee with an elaborate twenty-by-fifteen-inch frame, each of which contained a thick-bonded certificate written in Japanese calligraphy. Sato then turned to Tanaka.

"Tanaka-san, you have shown great wisdom in helping Cain-san. If it were not for your expertise in showing him our protocols and procedures here in Japan, I would not be alive today. The future of this company would be in great peril without strong leadership. As a token of my personal appreciation, I am giving you and Cain-san my table for a night at Hakugei."

"*Arigato gozaimashita,*" Tanaka said several times, bowing a full ninety degrees not once but twice. Tanaka then walked backward, which prompted Cain to follow his lead.

"Mr. Sato is giving us his private table at Hakugei," Tanaka whispered to Cain. "This is very cool. It's a very expensive restaurant."

"Expensive doesn't always mean good," Cain replied. He wasn't trying to be dismissive; he was just managing his expectations.

"*Hakugei* means 'white whale.' It's illegal now in Japan, but my father told me this restaurant secretly sells it. I've never had it before, but I'm told it's very tasty."

"Whale doesn't seem very appetizing to me, Tanaka. Sounds fatty and rubbery. How about a steak house?"

"There will be sake, too. Lots of it."

Cain thought it over. "Okay, but I ain't staying at a capsule hotel afterward again. Been there, done that."

"Got the T-shirt?" Tanaka smiled.

Cain laughed. "I love it when you get American humor."

"Hakugei—it's a deal." Tanaka shook Cain's hand. "When should I make the reservation?"

"Friday night's always a good time to blow off some steam."

CHAPTER 48

"LET'S SHUT IT DOWN," Cain said to Tanaka that Friday evening after they had been working for more than ten hours.

"I've been looking forward to Hakugei all week," Tanaka said with a big grin.

"This whale you keep droning on and on about must be the best in the world."

"Are you going to at least try it?" Tanaka asked.

"Which is better? Eel or whale?"

"Both are delicious," he said. "But I prefer whale."

"Well, I'm going to have to drink a lot of sake before I start eating raw whale," Cain said as they headed out of the office.

The restaurant was a stone building with bamboo and wooden accents. The entryway was illuminated by amber lighting. The hostess, who was dressed like a geisha, greeted them upon entry. She provided Cain and Tanaka with slippers. They quickly put them on and trailed the hostess as she led them to their table. It was an antique solid-wood table that sat about a foot above a traditional tatami mat. Cain and Tanaka kneeled on the soft but firm mat, which was made of rice straw.

A few moments later, a group of customers walked in. Cain saw the manager covertly slide his finger down his cheek to signal one of the other well-dressed staffers.

Tanaka was reading the menu and did not see the exchange, so Cain asked him what it meant.

"They are realtors," Tanaka said.

"Are you telling me those people sell houses?"

"No." Tanaka lowered his voice. "*Realtors* is a slang word for *yakuza* because they own so much real estate, and they use the property to hide their illegal money legitimately. Or so I'm told by my father."

"What's the mafia doing in here?"

"Same reason other Japanese come here: it's a place for rich people to eat expensive *and* illegal food. It is also a status symbol."

"And to think," Cain said, "our American mafia just likes spaghetti with meatballs."

Tanaka laughed. "I'm sure yakuza like spaghetti with meatballs, too. And they probably like the *Godfather* movie as well." Tanaka did his best Marlon Brando impression: "I'll make him an offer he can't refuse."

"If your house is as small as my apartment, a horse's head wouldn't even fit!" Cain said with a half smile. "On second thought, it wouldn't even fit on the mattress in my apartment!"

Cain's apartment, one of over four hundred located in an apartment complex that towered over downtown Yokohama, was furnished, but like most Japanese apartments, it was tiny. Cain reckoned it was only about five hundred square feet. His refrigerator resembled a college dorm fridge, and his single bed was so small his feet dangled off the end. So Cain had thrown his mattress on the floor and slept there. The stove and oven dials were all in Japanese, so he never used them. His favorite room was the bathroom. It was the most utilitarian. The toilet seat was heated, and the shower and a small washer-dryer combo were next to it. There were several complicated panels that controlled everything, but Cain didn't know what half the buttons did.

Tanaka raised his sake cup. "To Japanese life."

"*Kanpai*," Cain replied.

They drank warm sake as their elite meals were delivered on white plates with wasabi on the side.

Cain used his *hashi* to pick up a piece of food, dipped it in wasabi, and started chewing it. "What is this?" He continued chewing the fatty meat. "Is this the whale you've been talking about? It tastes like boiled beef!"

"It is the liver of the fugu."

"Come on, Tanaka. I'm not interested in experimenting with my taste buds tonight. I just want a good meal after all the hard work we've been doing."

"The liver of the fugu is the most poisonous—"

"The most poisonous!" Cain put his napkin to his mouth and subtly spit out his fugu.

"But it is also the tastiest," Tanaka said. "Before it was made illegal in Japan, my father used to enjoy it very much."

"Don't you find it odd?" Cain asked. "In a country where 99.9 percent of the population are rule followers, Sato-san sent us here—to a restaurant that serves illegal dishes?"

"Not really," Tanaka said. "I think he is part owner of this restaurant—or at least was before all the news about the company."

"Really?" Cain was always interested in learning more about the people he protected. "Tell me more."

"He used to come here a lot. But after the news of the company was published, I think he sold his partnership in the restaurant."

"Interesting." Cain ruminated on that for a moment. "Was that in the news?"

"No. Sato-san is a private man. He's normally not in the news, except when he builds a new orphanage."

"A new orphanage?"

"Hai, hai, hai." Tanaka's voice reflected his admiration. "Sato-san spends a lot of his money on helping kids without families. He also helps find them work at our factory. I think Morita-san was once an orphan."

"Is that why Morita-san is his driver?"

"Japanese culture places a high importance on loyalty—sometimes more than on talent. Sato-san will keep Morita-san as his driver until Morita-san can no longer do the job."

"Well, he certainly impressed me the other day. Gives credence to not judging a book by its cover."

"But Sato-san also realized he needed an expert to keep him alive. That's why you were chosen. As a Japanese CEO of one of the most powerful car companies in the world, he knew it was culturally important to highlight the good of Japan, especially because of the bad press he is receiving. That's why at the award ceremony he thanked *me* for helping you assimilate."

"Assimilate?" Cain chuckled. "I still feel like a bull in a china shop here."

"It will take time," Tanaka said. "Japanese culture goes back thousands of years. Only 2 percent of our population is non-Japanese. We all share the same language, the same religion, the same customs."

"How long, you think, before I start blending in?"

"Um, maybe twenty, twenty-five years," Tanaka said matter-of-factly.

Cain laughed out loud. "I like you, Tanaka-san. You keep it real."

"That's why," Tanaka continued, "I would like to take you to a *special* place—a fun place."

"Why do I get the impression you and I don't see eye to eye on *fun?*"

"We can sing karaoke!"

Cain laughed again. "If I'm singing, the customers are gonna scatter. The place won't make any business. They'll have to close down."

"Seriously, I would like to take you to the Angel Cloud. It's a popular hangout for expats and Japanese who want to sing with foreigners like yourself. It's a very short walk from here. It will help you become more like a Japanese man."

"I won't sing, but I'll join you for a cigar and American whiskey. I need something stronger than that sake to wash that fugu down! I can still taste that poison in my throat."

"Great!" Tanaka raised his wooden sake cup into the air.

Cain did the same. "Here's to turning Japanese in twenty-five years."

"Kanpai!" Tanaka said. "And to tonight—a night we will never forget."

CHAPTER 49

ABOVE THE SOLID-WOOD DOOR was a sign that said ANGEL CLOUD. Below that: WHERE DREAMS TAKE FLIGHT. Tanaka pushed open the door and held it for Cain.

"The party is upstairs," Tanaka said.

They ascended the twenty or so steps, which led to a large open-bay room filled with couches, tables, a bar, and an area for singing karaoke. The place was crowded, but the manager immediately escorted Cain and Tanaka to a large kidney-shaped booth in the far corner. They were seated for only a few seconds before an older Japanese woman in a traditional black cherry blossom kimono came over to their table.

"Welcome," she said with a slow and methodical bow. "We are very pleased you are here tonight."

Cain smiled and returned the bow. "Thank you for the welcome, and for the royal treatment. I don't know what we did to deserve one of your best tables on such a crowded night."

"Our manager recognized you from the *Japan Times*."

Cain turned to Tanaka. "I guess my fifteen minutes of fame is going to last a lot longer here."

"I would like to send over two of our most beautiful women to entertain you this evening," the woman said.

Cain opened his mouth to protest, but the petite lady had already bowed and shuffled away toward a group of women standing next to the bar.

"I realize she was speaking English, but I hope I misunderstood. What does 'entertain you this evening' mean?"

"This is a *kyabakura*," Tanaka said. "It's a hostess bar. She is a mama-san."

"You mean a madam?"

"No," Tanaka replied quickly. "More like a manager of the hostesses. It's not what you think, Cain-san. This is very popular in Japan. It's just fun conversation and drinking."

"Good. I'm down for good convo and drinking."

"Especially after this week, right?" Tanaka asked.

Cain smiled. "I'm down for it any day of the week, actually." His smile widened and he began laughing.

"Why are you laughing?"

"Tanaka-san, do you know what irony is?"

"I think so."

"Too much media attention here got me a 'lady of the evening,'" Cain said with air quotes. "But not so long ago, a lady of the evening got me too much media attention."

"Sounds like one of your stories for another time, as you often say."

Both laughed.

"I'm sorry," Cain said. "I can't help it. I grew up in a storytelling family."

"I know," Tanaka said. "When I worked with Bonnie, she used to tell marvelous stories, too."

"She and I get it from our pops. I'll introduce you if I can talk 'em into making the long flight out here."

"I would like that very much," Tanaka said. "My father is not a storyteller. He is very typical Japanese. Very serious and quiet."

"He must be very proud of you for saving our bacon during the attack."

"He's not proud. The van had two flat tires, and I could not protect Sato-san."

"That's simply not true. If you were not there to contact the police and give them our vehicle info and direction of travel, I'm not sure how much longer our car was gonna hold up. It was taking a real beating."

The mama-san returned with two stunning young Eastern European women who looked as though they should be on the cover of a fashion magazine. "May I introduce Sabrina and Natasha?"

"Hello," the girls said, smiling naturally.

Cain and Tanaka sprang from the booth, allowing the hostesses to take the center seats.

"Please enjoy your evening, gentlemen." The mama-san bowed and disappeared into the crowd, which seemed to be growing.

"Thank you." Sabrina smiled as she tossed her long, dark locks of hair off her shoulder. Her blue eyes sparkled against the stark contrast of her black hair.

"Where are you from?" Cain asked.

"Where do you think I'm from?" she asked with a flirtatious tone.

"Eastern Europe."

"You're getting warmer." She smiled.

"Romania," Cain blurted out.

"Yes!" She seemed genuinely surprised. "How did you guess that?"

"I recognized your accent. I've been to Romania a few times."

"Really? I never meet anybody in here who has been to my country before."

"Well, I'm not just anybody." The sake Cain had had at Hakugei made it even easier for him to banter back and forth with her.

Sabrina laughed. "True. You are somebody."

Cain and Sabrina laughed together and she touched his shoulder.

"Why were you in Romania?"

"I was on a mission," Cain said, lowering his voice.

Sabrina leaned in. "What kind of mission?"

Cain leaned in closer. "If I told you, I'd have to kill you."

She shook her head and smiled at him.

The bar manager stopped by their table. "It's a pleasure to meet you."

"You, too," Cain replied. "Thank you for the hospitality tonight."

"Thank *you* for protecting Sato-san. He used to be one of our favorite customers, but we have not seen him in several weeks."

Mr. Sato hangs out here? Cain thought. *The multi-million-dollar CEO? I can't see him singing, but I guess I can imagine him enjoying the company of these women.*

Tanaka stopped talking with the Russian hostess, Natasha, and turned to the manager. "Sato-san is very busy managing the company. He has been working day and night. But he is well, and I will let him know you have asked about him. I am sure that will please him."

"*Arigato,*" the manager gratefully responded. "Also, I would like to present you with a bottle of our finest champagne. On the house, of course." He motioned to a bartender, who brought over some glasses and a bottle of Dom Pérignon nestled in a silver bucket of ice.

Cain and Tanaka thanked the manager, and then toasted each other.

"I toast to Cain-san and his new life in Japan."

"To turning Japanese in twenty years—maybe only ten after tonight. *Kanpai!*"

Tanaka opened his blazer and reached into his inner pocket. He pulled out two cigars and held them in the air. "Here you go," he said as he handed one to Cain.

"First Sabrina, then Dom Pérignon, and now a Romeo y Julieta. I can't wait to see what's next," Cain exclaimed. He was having a fantastic time. Cain cut the tip off his cigar and placed it in his mouth. He reached into his pocket to grab whatever box of matches or Zippo he had that day. Before he could, Sabrina lit his cigar with a lighter she had hidden somewhere on her body.

"Wow!" Cain exclaimed. "You're quite resourceful."

"I take care of my favorite customers."

"Am I already a favorite customer?"

"Yes." She smiled.

"Well, then you should know I prefer to light my cigars with a match, instead of a cigarette lighter."

"I will remember that for next time."

Cain chuckled. "You're confident I'll be back, huh?"

"Oh, you'll come back to see me, or I'll have to kill you." They both laughed.

The four of them drank champagne and enjoyed lighthearted conversation. Music played in the background as various customers sang different American songs in the karaoke area.

"Shall we order another bottle of champagne?" Tanaka asked.

"Let's ask the ladies," Cain suggested.

They smiled and nodded yes, which didn't surprise Cain.

"Another bottle it is." Cain smiled.

Sabrina and Natasha stood and went to the bar to get another bottle of Dom Pérignon.

"Tanaka, this is actually more fun than I had imagined."

"I knew you would like *kyabakura*."

Through the noise of the crowd, Cain heard a man and a woman singing a Frank Sinatra and Sammy Davis Jr. duet. Cain swayed his head to the music and sang along: *"Walking down the av-e-nue. Me, and my shadow."*

"I like this song, too," Tanaka said.

"My mom and pops had this record. They played it all the time in our living room. My sister and I would perform this duet for our parents."

"You told me you couldn't sing."

"Well." Cain smirked. "Not good enough to get paid for it. I've gotta see who is singing this song. She's impressive, and definitely American."

He stood and walked through the smoke-filled lounge toward the karaoke area. Onstage was a very fit Japanese man who appeared to be in his late twenties or early thirties. Despite being inside the club, he wore a pair of rose-colored Matsuda sunglasses with gold frames. Cain noted that the man seemed different from other Japanese he had encountered— he didn't seem to adhere to Japan's strict societal norms. He wore a typical dark suit and white shirt but with a bright-purple tie. On his wrist was an expensive watch with an overexaggerated case and crown. The wristband was bright orange. It was easy for Cain to see, because the man's arm was draped over the American woman's shoulder, his hand close to her breast.

What the hell is Bonnie doing here? Cain thought as he tried to make sense of the situation. *She must be here with some of her American friends, right?*

But the way this man was touching his sister made him mad, so Cain walked onstage and removed the man's arm from Bonnie's shoulder, and instead put his own arm around her. Together, Bonnie and Cain finished crooning the song: *"Me, and my shadow. All alone and feeling blue."* They feigned taking cowboy hats off their heads, putting them on their feet, and kicking them into the air.

The crowd erupted in applause.

"Smile and give them a show," Bonnie said to her brother. They bowed to the cheering audience, but Cain observed two men at a nearby table who were not clapping. They stood and started walking toward the stage.

The Japanese man who had been singing with Bonnie warned Cain, "Get away from Bella."

"Bella?" Cain turned to his sister. "What the hell is going on?"

"This woman is taken," the Japanese customer said.

"It's okay, Watanabe-san," Bonnie said, trying to ease everyone's tension. "This is my—" Before she could say "brother," Watanabe told Cain, "Go find your own whore."

Instantly Cain smashed his fist into Watanabe's face, breaking his rose-colored sunglasses and sending him to the floor. Blood gushed from his broken nose.

Bonnie grabbed Cain and told him to stop as he was advancing toward Watanabe.

"Since when are you okay with being called a whore?" he asked his sister.

"We've got to get out of here," Tanaka frantically yelled.

Before Bonnie could respond, two of Watanabe's thugs who had been closely watching the ordeal from the crowd rushed toward Cain. One came behind him and put him in a bear hug. Cain was much bigger in height and bulk and his adrenaline was in overdrive, but this was two against one. He struggled to break free until he grabbed his attacker's index finger and bent it back until he heard it snap like a twig. The man hollered in pain and released his hold.

Free from the bear hug, Cain turned around and stepped back a few feet to gain distance from his attackers. The one holding his broken finger was trying desperately to ease the pain, with no success. The other attacker lunged toward Cain with both hands outstretched to choke him. Cain raised his arms in a V shape and deflected the man's momentum to the side, simultaneously jamming a knee into the advancing attacker's solar plexus. The air left the man's lungs and he bent forward and crumbled to the floor.

Watanabe was wiping blood from his face with his hand. "You broke my nose! You're dead, gaijin." He pulled back and launched a wild punch toward the left side of Cain's face. Cain instinctively crouched and ducked under the punch. He stood back up and shoved the heel of his palm into Watanabe's nose. The forceful strike propelled Watanabe backward. He crashed into a table and knocked over customers' drinks and snacks.

"He's got a knife!" Tanaka yelled out, and pointed.

Cain lifted both of his arms to protect his vital organs while he scanned the crowded bar area for the knife-wielding attacker.

The thug who had been kneed in the solar plexus had regained his breath and pulled out a shiny butter-fly knife. He flipped it open, exposing the sharp blade. He slashed it twice toward Cain's face, but Cain back-stepped twice, narrowly avoiding getting cut. The attacker became impatient and lunged at Cain, thrust-ing the four-inch blade toward Cain's heart. Cain sidestepped to the left and then propelled his right foot toward the attacker's knee. Cain's boot pushed through the attacker's kneecap, instantly sending the man to the ground.

"Aaaaaaaayyyyy!" The fallen assailant dropped the knife and gripped his knee. He continued yelling out in pain as he flopped around on the floor like a fish out of water.

Cain was breathing heavily and assessing the damage. He saw the butterfly knife on the floor so he kicked it. He was watching it slide across the floor and under a table when Watanabe surprised him from behind, wrapping his arm around Cain's throat. Cain tried to loosen Watanabe's choke hold but couldn't. Cain purposely dropped all his body weight like a sack of potatoes, forcing the men to collide on the ground. When they hit the floor, Watanabe lost his grip and Cain gulped for air.

In the struggle, Watanabe's bloodied white dress shirt got ripped off, exposing very detailed tattoos covering most of his body. Cain had seen artwork like that only once before, but these particular depictions were seared into his mind. Across Watanabe's chest was a fire-breathing dragon wrapping its tail around a white-faced geisha gasping for air. His back tattoo was of a falcon, wings spread out and talons clutching a bloodstained samurai sword.

They continued wrestling on the ground. Cain was

used to American boxing and the skills he had learned at the Secret Service academy, but Watanabe was clearly experienced in Japanese judo. He was getting the better of Cain. Watanabe was keeping Cain close to him so Cain couldn't use his strength or distance to pummel his assailant with powerful punches. As Watanabe wrapped his long, lean, and muscular arms around Cain's throat again, Cain noticed that he was missing the pinky finger on his hand. Watanabe began to squeeze tighter and tighter. Cain's face turned red and his eyes began watering as they bulged. The entire room started getting dark.

He had begun to black out when Watanabe's grip suddenly and unexpectedly released. Tanaka had grabbed their half-drunk bottle of Dom Pérignon off their table and swung it full force into the back of Watanabe's head. The glass shattered. Onlookers gasped as expensive champagne and blood sprayed them. Watanabe went limp.

Tanaka turned to Bonnie and Cain. "We have to leave now! Follow me, quickly!" Bonnie and Cain trailed Tanaka down the stairs and out of the building. They ran a few meters and took a turn down a back alley.

Once they finally stopped, Cain began questioning Bonnie. "What were you—" He tried to catch his breath. "What were you doing in there? Who's Watanabe? Why did he"—Cain continued breathing heavily—"call you a whore?"

"I sometimes work here. It's where I find a lot of my clients who want me to teach them English."

"What?" Cain said incredulously. "I thought you were a flight attendant."

"I have more than one job."

"I can't believe you'd be working at a place like that!"

"A place like what? Correct me if I'm wrong, but you and Tanaka were just in a place *like that*!"

"Hey, sis! It's not like that."

"Exactly! It's not like that. Japanese men work very hard and they just wanna talk to American girls. There's no sex involved."

"Do you date them?"

"That's none of your business."

"Who was that Watanabe piece of shit? He was tatted up like a lifer at Angola."

"I don't know," Bonnie said. "Tonight was the first night I met him."

"First night you met him?" Cain asked incredulously. "He had his arm all over you."

"He's yakuza," Tanaka interjected.

"Now you've done it! Beating up the yakuza will certainly piss them off," Bonnie complained with fear in her voice. "There's no way in hell I can even go back into the Angel Cloud now." She seemed to be panicking. "And my purse is in there."

Bonnie pulled her iPhone out of a small pocket on her dress. Cain could see that text messages were popping up on her screen. She turned and started walking away.

"Where are you going?" Cain asked, following her.

"Just leave me alone! You've caused enough problems tonight for the both of us!" Bonnie rounded the corner and called Sabrina. "I can't go back inside after what just happened. Would you mind grabbing my purse and bringing it to me?"

Cain heard Sabrina's raised voice when she responded. "Those men who fought the American. They took your purse."

CHAPTER 50

THE FOLLOWING MORNING Cain was already at his desk when Tanaka arrived at the office. It was a Saturday, and although both had the day off, their personalities were such that they wanted to occupy themselves with work.

"Good morning, boss," Tanaka said.

"Good morning, Tanaka-san. Just because last night went to shit doesn't mean you gotta go back to calling me 'boss.'"

"Okay," Tanaka replied.

Cain looked back at his computer and continued pounding on the keys to his keyboard.

"Would you like for me to turn the lights on?" Tanaka asked.

"Negative. I have a migraine. Feels like someone hit my head with an expensive bottle of champagne — even though it wasn't *my* head."

Tanaka lowered his head and spoke more softly. "I feel responsible for last night's fight. I should have never recommended we go there."

"No, Tanaka. It's not your fault. I got migraines before I ever moved to Japan. Doctors don't know what causes mine. But I know one thing: all these fluorescent lights that the Japanese love so much don't help prevent them." Cain dropped two Alka-Seltzer tablets into a drink he was putting together and watched it fizz for a few seconds. He stirred the drink with his index finger.

"What are you drinking?" Tanaka asked.

"Homemade concoction."

"Should I even ask?"

"To get rid of this pounding headache and hangover. Ice-brewed coffee, two shots of espresso, two Alka-Seltzer tablets, and ten drops of Tabasco sauce. Any flavor will work, but the habanero one works the best, I find."

"That does not sound very good," Tanaka said with a sour face.

"It's not, but you remember what ol' Frank Rogers would say?"

"In an emergency, even the Devil eats flies."

"That's right. The Devil is used to eating Kobe fillet steaks, but he'll eat flies in an emergency."

"I hope it helps," Tanaka said, not sounding very convinced of the drink's medicinal qualities.

Cain gulped it down. His eyes closed and his face scrunched up. "It's *gooood*."

"If there is anything I can do, please let me know." Tanaka turned to head to his cubicle.

"Wait. Before you leave, I do have a few questions."

"*Hai,*" Tanaka said, turning back around.

"I've been researching the yakuza more," Cain continued, "and there's very little information about them."

"More?" Tanaka asked, not realizing that Cain had already been looking into Japan's secret society of organized criminals.

"What did you think about that one guy's tattoo?"

"*Irezumi* are taboo in Japan. People with tattoos are prohibited from public beaches, fitness gyms, and *onsens*. Only yakuza and Westerners in Japan have *irezumi*."

"There's gotta be exceptions, right?" Cain was thinking about Sato but didn't want to mention anything yet.

"I don't know of any exceptions."

"So, just from the tattoo, you knew they were yakuza?"

"That. And also his pinky. It was cut off."

"Yeah," Cain said. "I saw that when I was wrestling with him."

"The yakuza's pinkies are cut off when they are punished, or to show their loyalty to the organization."

"I've seen that before in a movie. Eighties flick with Michael Douglas. You know what I can't quite understand?"

"Please tell me."

"Every single Japanese person I've met has been nothing but incredibly polite. You said it yourself: the nail that sticks out gets hammered down. But Watanabe called Bonnie a whore."

Tanaka nodded and looked away—perhaps from embarrassment or shame. "Yakuza view women as property. My father, the inspector, also tells me that the yakuza are very vindictive. They are also involved in drug smuggling, human trafficking, illegal gambling, and blackmailing politicians."

"I thought there was no corruption in this country," Cain said facetiously.

"It is very rare. I've never seen it. I've only heard about it."

"That's my point. Bonnie and I are in trouble,

especially if they have her purse. They'll know where she lives and works."

"You and Bonnie are gaijin. Yakuza will probably leave you alone."

"Probably?" Cain asked with raised eyebrows. "I don't like those odds."

"Yakuza will not want the international attention."

Cain scoffed. "You don't know the kind of luck I have. Trouble finds me no matter where I'm at."

CHAPTER 51

"I MISS MY iPhone," Cain told Tanaka as he was digging into his jacket pocket to answer the call on his Sharp Aquos smartphone. "That SoftBank woman told me this was supposed to be the best, but you just can't beat Apple."

"I prefer Android," Tanaka said. "It's more customizable."

"Says the man who wears a dark suit and white button-down to work every day," Cain quipped.

"I'm Japanese on the outside but *American* on the inside. Banana was my nickname at Embry-Riddle. You get it?"

"Yeah." Cain laughed along with Tanaka. "I get it. Yellow on the outside, white on the inside." His laughter was interrupted by the ringing of his phone. He answered it.

"Ohio gozaimasu," Cain heard Umiko say.

Without even thinking about it, Cain stood to talk to her. "Good morning, Umiko-san. How's your Saturday going?"

"I have some good news to share with you."

"That's wonderful. I can use some good news."

"Sensei said you can join our kendo class."

"That's better than good—that's fantastic news! When do I start?"

"We have a class this afternoon if you are not busy."

"I'll wrap up some things here at the office, and I'll be there."

"I look forward to seeing you," she said.

A few hours later, Cain caught the train and showed up for the afternoon kendo class. Umiko greeted him when he walked in the door.

"Oh, my God. Are you okay?" she asked, noticing the scratches on his face.

"I'm okay, but I obviously need this martial arts class," he said lightheartedly.

She smiled but continued to look concerned. "Well, I'm very glad you are now in the class."

"Me, too. But I gotta ask. Are you just glad because you're looking forward to using me as your personal punching bag?"

Umiko giggled. "Maybe, but you won't be the only new student for us to practice on. We have two new students from the university. But you will be the only foreigner."

"I'm getting used to being the only gaijin in my circles."

"Let me introduce you to my kendo friends. They speak English, but they are shy. So they may not talk too much. Please understand they are not being rude."

"That's fine. I'll just speak to 'em in Japanese."

"Really?" Umiko asked, looking surprised, as they neared a small group of students.

"I've been studying a language book my sister gave me."

"I'm impressed." She turned to a young woman. "Hiroko-san, this is my American friend. He's in charge of security at our company. His name is Cain-san."

Cain placed his arms by his side and bowed. *"Hajime mashita."*

Hiroko put her hand over her mouth as she giggled.

"Hey, now. If you're going to laugh at my Japanese, I'm not going to speak it anymore."

"I'm so sorry. I'm not laughing. Your Japanese is very good."

Cain smirked. "Remind me to never partner with you at the poker table. On the streets in a kendo fight? Yes. But never when you have to hide your true feelings."

Hiroko didn't seem to get the reference. "Have you studied kendo before?"

"I've never taken a formal kendo class, but I have watched a lot of Steven Seagal movies."

Umiko picked up on the joke and laughed. When Hiroko saw this, she followed suit.

"You should come to our retreat this weekend," Hiroko suggested.

"Retreat? Like a ladies' day at the spa?"

"Even better," Hiroko replied. "A Zen retreat for the weekend. We go every year. Our sensei takes us to the foot of Mount Fuji. We will meditate and practice kendo. One weekend of intense kendo training there is like a month of training here. It is a wonderful time."

"Sato-san has no engagements this weekend," Cain said. "I technically have off work." He looked at Umiko. "Are you going?"

"Yes. This will be my second year. I really liked it."

"Okay," Cain said. "I'll give it some thought. If I'm invited, that is."

"Yes," Hiroko said. "Everyone in the class is invited, even new students."

"We should get ready for class," Umiko said. "If we are late, sensei makes us do push-ups. I hate doing push-ups."

"I don't mind the push-ups," Cain said. "But I agree with you about not being late."

Umiko handed him the protective gear. "Since this is your first class, you can borrow this equipment. But you're going to want to buy your own soon. Unless you like putting on sweaty *bogu*."

Cain burst out laughing. "*Bogu?* I'm not sure if I like mine sweaty or not yet."

Umiko giggled.

"I'll buy my own—that is, if I make it past this class without getting killed."

"I've seen you in action. This class might be boring for you."

"I'm never bored when I'm with you." He smiled, and she blushed.

The class lasted an hour, and Cain enjoyed it. *It's more than just a workout,* he thought. *It requires strategy.*

Because the sensei was a Zen priest, at the end of class, he provided a Zen quote for the students to ponder until their next class. All the students bowed in unison and profusely thanked the instructor. They then bowed to one another and gave thanks to their classmates for allowing them to train with one another to get better.

"What did the sensei say?" Cain asked Umiko.

"He gave us a quote from Buddha. He said, 'Just as the snake sheds its skin over and over, we must shed our past.' Sensei said that is the secret to *mushin*."

"*Mushin,*" Cain repeated. "I remember that word. No mind. That's deep. I thought we were here to learn how to sword fight."

Umiko giggled again.

"Well, at least you get my sense of humor. Sometimes it goes over Tanaka's head."

"Tanaka needs a girlfriend," Umiko said with light humor.

"I think he found one last night," Cain joked.

"Really?"

"I'll tell you about it over dinner."

"It's not too late for you? You always work very early."

"I rarely sleep. So, no. It's not too late for me. Is it too late for you?"

"No, I would like to have dinner with you."

"Great! An old navy buddy told me about a place in Yokosuka called Nawlins. They have barbecue and other Louisiana foods."

"Louisiana foods?" Her eyes widened. "I've always wanted to go to New Orleans for that famous festival. Um. Um." She put her hand to her forehead as she thought. "What is it called?"

"Mardi Gras."

"*Oui. Le mardi gras.* It looks like so much fun."

Cain laughed. "It's a hoot! That's for sure. This restaurant should be a mild introduction for you."

"Do I look okay to go to this restaurant?"

"You look perfect, Umi," Cain said with a warm smile, using her nickname. *She always looks perfect,* he thought. He wasn't sure if she considered this a date, but he did.

CHAPTER 52

THE TRAIN RIDE from Yokohama Station to Yokosuka was about forty-five minutes. Talking on public transportation was frowned upon in Japanese culture, but Cain couldn't help it. They whispered back and forth to each other during the ride.

"Thank you for translating the kendo class for me," Cain said.

"There were some words the sensei said that I will need to look up in the dictionary. I don't know the English word for some of the kendo techniques."

"Nah," Cain replied. "Your English is remarkable. You learned in Canada, right?"

She smiled and nodded.

"I gotta ask. Why did you choose to study in Canada instead of the United States?"

"I *wanted* to study in California, but my parents are very traditional, and I'm an only child. The Japanese news says America has lots of problems with racism and gun violence. My parents were afraid to let me go to the United States. They thought I might get shot."

Cain knew from personal experience how the media could overdramatize a situation. "I was raised with guns and have carried one professionally for years. I've never shot anyone, and I've never been shot."

"Thank goodness," Umiko replied.

Nawlins BBQ was situated in a back alley, near the military base. Its storefront had a large window where customers walking by could see people inside enjoying Southern cuisine and drinking craft beer on tap at the tall wooden bar.

The restaurant's walls were lined with Mardi Gras masks and beads and pictures of the New Orleans Saints football team.

"I've never been to the United States," Umiko began. "I really only know what I've seen in movies."

"Well, what kind of movies have you been watching?"

Umiko placed her finger on her chin as she thought. "One of my favorite American movies is *Pretty Woman*. I also like *Rocky*."

Cain's jaw dropped. *"Rocky?"*

"Why is that so shocking?"

Cain closed his mouth and smiled. "That's one of my favorite movies, too. It's an American classic. I just didn't picture you as a *Rocky* fan."

"Yes. I like boxing. I like the music in the movie. And I like cheering for—um, I think you call it the below dog."

Cain smiled even bigger. "Yes, Americans love an underdog! But I'll have to show you some good Louisiana movies. Maybe something like *The Big Easy, The Green Mile,* or my mom's favorite, *Steel Magnolias.*"

The waitress stopped by their table. "Good evening, folks. What can I get y'all to drink?"

Cain looked to Umiko to answer first.

"I would like an American beer."

"Bottle or tap, sweetie?"

"Bottle."

The waitress committed the order to memory and then turned to Cain.

"I'll have some house wine of the South."

"You wanna lemon in that?"

"Ain't no other way to enjoy it." Cain smiled. The waitress left the table.

"I could not understand what you and she were talking about," Umiko said.

"We were just jabbering—speaking a little Southern. I asked for a sweet tea with lemon."

"Tanaka-san is right. You use a lot of slang."

Cain laughed. "It's good for him. He told me he's a banana."

Umiko wrinkled her face in confusion.

"Japanese on the outside and American on the inside," Cain explained.

Umiko smiled. "I can see that."

"What about you?" Cain asked.

"I'm 100 percent Japanese. But"—she stretched out the word—"I'm a little more progressive. I moved out of my parents' home in Osaka and took a job in Yokohama."

"That's not common, is it?"

"No. I don't know for sure, but I imagine Tanaka-san still lives with his parents."

"He told me he did," Cain said.

The waitress returned with their drinks. "Y'all ready to order?"

Cain looked at Umiko. "Have you decided what you'd like?"

Umiko quickly studied the menu. "What do you recommend?"

"Would you like for me to order a bunch of different stuff and we can share?"

"That sounds fun," she replied.

Cain ordered the chicken and sausage gumbo, the fried catfish, red beans and rice, and jalapeño corn bread.

When the food arrived, Umiko was shocked. "Wow! Look how big these plates are."

Cain nodded. "Yep, these are American sizes. That's why we have a little bit of a weight problem back home."

"It smells so good, though," Umiko said as she inhaled slowly. She then placed her hands together with a light clap and gave a quick blessing: *"Itadakimasu."*

Cain knew that it was a ritual for Japanese to express thanks for the food they were about to eat, just as in his family.

"Bon appétit," Cain replied.

They enjoyed eating and talking about everything from Zen to the cultural differences between the United States and Japan. Cain felt comfortable with Umiko. She was funny and respectful at the same time. He could tell she had a fiery spirit but a gentleness.

"You have an inner peace that I would like to find for myself," Cain said.

"Kendo helped me, and it will help you. The retreat will be good for you."

"I'm looking forward to it, and to getting outside the city and back into the countryside for a bit," he said.

After some time, the waitress returned to the table. "Looks like you guys didn't leave any room for dessert. Would you like the check now?"

"Why, we'd love some dessert," Cain said. "How's your bread pudding with bourbon sauce?"

"It's the best west of the Mississippi River," the lady replied, "and we make it fresh every day."

"Please bring us some."

"One plate?"

"One plate, two spoons."

The waitress left, then returned with the bread pudding.

Cain turned to Umiko. "This is my sister's favorite dessert. We're twins, so it's actually my favorite dessert, too."

"Twins?"

Cain nodded.

"That is very cool. I knew you had a sister, but I did not know you were twins. I only know one twins. When I was in school, two boys in my class were twins. They could read each other's minds."

"I can't really read Bonnie's mind, and I probably wouldn't want to. But we certainly have a unique connection. One that I don't have with anyone else in my family."

"I'd like to meet her."

"I'd like for you to meet her," Cain said.

Cain grabbed some yen from his wallet and paid for the meal. He and Umiko walked to a nearby park, where the main attraction was the imperial Japanese battleship *Mikasa*.

Cain sensed that Umiko's mood had changed a bit.

"Is everything okay?"

"My grandfather was in World War II," Umiko said.

"Is he still alive?"

"No. I never knew him. Most Japanese do not talk about the war, but my father is still very angry."

Cain listened patiently.

"My grandfather was killed by the Americans during the war. My father was not born yet. My grandmother was pregnant with my father during the war. So my father blames the Americans for his growing up without a father. He would be so mad if he knew I was having dinner with you."

Cain sighed. "The war was a long time ago, but I know some people who have a hard time letting go of the past."

"You would certainly be the first American I introduced to my parents."

"Would you ever do that?"

Umiko turned her glance elsewhere. "I'm the only child. It's my duty to take care of my parents. My father would never approve. My mother? Maybe. But it would break her heart if I married an American. She'd be afraid I'd move away from Japan."

"Well, it's just our first date. So, no reason for anyone to get their heart broken. I'm just glad you came out with me tonight. I always enjoy spending time with you."

Umiko smiled. "Me, too." Cain saw her glance at the gold band he still wore on his ring finger. "You wear a wedding ring, but Tanaka-san told me you are not married."

"You were asking about me?" Cain's stomach fluttered for a second.

"Maybe," she replied, concealing her true feelings.

"I'm not married, Umi. Not anymore." Cain changed the subject. "Look right there. That's the navy base. There's the sailboat my friend and I rented a while back. It's bobbing up against the dock."

The sailboat was illuminated beyond the navy's chain-link fence. "It looks very small," Umiko said. "I'd be scared to take that into Tokyo Bay."

"Ah, it was just fine for the chief and me." He pointed to a small island in the distance. "We sailed right past that island with all the monkeys."

Umiko laughed and laughed until her eyes watered. "No monkeys live there."

"What? My friend told me it was called Monkey Island."

Umiko continued laughing. "There are no monkeys there. Its nickname is Monkey Island, but its real name is Sarushima."

Cain changed the subject again. "Since you are my unofficial Japanese cultural expert," he joked, "what can you tell me about *kyabakura*?"

"*Kyabakura?*" Umiko repeated. "Hostess bar?"

"Yeah."

"Did Tanaka-san take you to one?"

"Maybe."

"Did you like it?"

"It was okay. Had a drink, a cigar, sang a little karaoke, and mingled with the locals."

"They are very popular with Japanese men. Girlfriends and wives accept the fact that their men will most likely go to *kyabakura*."

"Wives don't care?" Cain asked.

"They probably care about their men wasting money on it, but it's understood that Japanese men will visit *kyabakura*."

"Is it a brothel?"

Umiko shook her head. "No. Prostitution is illegal in Japan. A hostess bar is like a modern-day geisha who laughs at your jokes, lights your cigarette, and refills your glass. It's like a fake relationship."

"That sounds like typical Japanese duality," Cain said, and winked. "The expense of a relationship without the rewards. In America, we would call it friends *without* benefits."

CHAPTER 53

CAIN WASN'T SURE what to expect on the Zen retreat. He had never been to anything like it before, but he figured if Umiko was going to be there, then he'd also want to be there. Umiko had an innocence and cautious optimism about her. She was rooted in Japan's centuries-old traditions, but she was curious and open to the outside world.

All the kendo students met at the dojo in Yokohama at 5:00 a.m. It was still dark outside. Everyone arrived on time, if not early. All the students were cheerful, smiled a lot, and bowed to one another as their customary greeting.

"Umi," Cain said, "I'm always in awe at how polite the Japanese are."

"Arigato gozaimasu," she said with a bow.

"We Americans have to have our coffee first, and even then, it would be fifty-fifty."

Umiko nodded as she listened. "I'm excited about today. Are you?"

"I am," Cain replied. "A little nervous, though. Not sure what to expect."

"Mushin," Umiko said. "Go with an empty cup, so sensei can fill it with Zen."

The students loaded their kendo gear and luggage into the tour bus's baggage compartment. They climbed on the bus in an orderly fashion, and the uniformed bus driver, wearing white gloves and a chauffeur's hat, drove them the several hours it took to reach the foot of Mount Fuji. Cain sat next to Umiko, but like most of the other Japanese on the bus, she slept during the road trip. Instead, Cain enjoyed sightseeing. He snapped a few pictures through the window, but the early-morning sunrays created a glare and distorted most of his pictures.

When Cain exited the bus, he took a deep breath. The cool, crisp mountain air felt good in his lungs. He looked around and took notice of the sights and sounds. The wind rustled the leaves of the trees, and birds chirped nearby. *Nature is better experienced in the now anyway,* he thought, *instead of trying to capture it on film.* He turned to Umiko, but she spoke first.

"It's so beautiful here," she whispered, emitting steam with her breath.

"Amen," Cain said, getting into the spiritual mood. "Far from the distractions of city life."

She pointed. "That's Mount Fuji."

"Where's it at?" he asked.

She pointed again. "Over there. You can see people in the distance hiking."

He snickered. "That was a joke. You normally get my humor."

She smiled and looked relieved for a second.

"We ain't hiking, are we?" he asked. "I didn't bring my hiking boots."

"Not this trip. This retreat is for intense kendo training and meditation."

"I've never meditated before. Not sure how to," Cain confessed.

"This whole trip has been prepared to create the perfect environment for meditation. It will help us see things as they *are,* and not how we wish."

A large bell that hung in the center of the Zen retreat rang as two monks hit it with a large mallet. The sound echoed throughout the wilderness, and for a moment all the birds quit chirping. *It's as if even the birds respect the importance of this event,* Cain thought.

"It begins," Umiko said as if she was expecting a life-changing event at the retreat. "The monks are scaring away evil spirits with the bell."

The students took off their shoes and lined up on tatami mats, which would "make kneeling more comfortable during meditation," Umiko told Cain.

The monks walked down the line of students while holding a large bag. Students were directed to put their cell phones in the bag.

"When do we get our phones back?" Cain asked.

"When we leave," Umiko answered.

"Hopefully Sato-san won't need me," Cain said.

"You have trained Tanaka-san well," Umiko said. "Your confidence in him is important."

Cain dropped his phone in the bag, and one of the monks provided him with a white uniform that resembled pajamas. The monks also handed each student a pair of flip-flops.

"Thank you," Cain said, "but I brought my own. You wouldn't believe how hard it is to find a size twelve in this country."

Some of the students laughed at Cain's joke, especially Hiroko.

"I almost forgot," Umiko said as she faced Cain. "I brought something to help you. I have *jinko* incense candles. They will help your meditation."

Cain took the candles and sniffed them. "They smell like wood."

"We'll use them later, during meditation. But they are going to exercise us for a few hours first."

"For a few hours?" Cain asked, hoping he had misunderstood. "I thought this was a Zen retreat. A place to relax."

"The monks will make us tired first. It's easier for the mind to meditate when the body is tired."

The sensei called the class to attention, then announced *rei* — the command to bow. He led the group through a series of stretches for about twenty minutes. Then they did jumping jacks, push-ups, sit-ups, and forward rolls similar to somersaults, and they jogged in place to increase their heart rate and breathing.

The sensei said something in Japanese and then looked at Cain. "Ready for kendo now," he said in English.

"*Hai,*" Cain replied between labored breaths, and bowed.

The students picked up their shinai, and for the next two hours practiced their kendo footwork, strikes, and thrusts. Cain's cotton uniform felt heavy from his sweat. When he started to think that the grueling training would never end, the sensei finally yelled, "*Matte,*" indicating for them to stop.

Thank God, Cain thought. *I couldn't go anymore.* He looked over at Umiko and was impressed by her stamina. *Well, she's younger,* he reasoned. *And she's been training in kendo much longer than me.*

The sensei looked at Cain and spoke in Japanese. Umiko translated. "He said you are very good — that you must have trained in some type of martial art before in order to have kept up with us."

Cain smiled. "I had a lot of baton training in the

Secret Service. Some of the techniques are similar, just with a shorter weapon."

The sensei continued speaking, and Umiko translated again. "Now we will put the *shinai* away and work on holding our positions and strengthening our concentration."

The sensei ordered the students to squat into a *kiba dachi* stance, which made them look as if they were riding a horse.

Cain closed his eyes and felt his thighs burn as if they were on fire. The pain, intermixed with Japan's natural humidity, caused him to continue sweating profusely.

Whap! The sound of the bamboo training sword hitting the back of a nearby student's knee broke the silence.

Everybody but the sensei had stowed their *shinais,* Cain observed.

The sensei continued walking behind the students, analyzing their *kiba dachi* stance and ensuring that they were squatting as low as they could.

Cain's muscular thighs began to quiver and swell. He felt the lactic acid building up in his quadriceps. He was exhausted physically and mentally. Sweat dripped into his eyes and the salt burned. *Why the hell did I agree to this abuse?* he cried out internally. With the whack of each bamboo strike, a flashback popped into his thoughts. The sensei swung his forty-two-inch bamboo training sword at another student, and the flashback popped up again. Cain had depleted his sweat reserves. No more sweat dripped from his body. He was mentally exhausted, and he started to feel nauseous. His mind wandered in slow motion, as if he was seeing an old film clip on an eight-millimeter tape.

Christmas 2004, in Thailand. He's standing in four-foot-high water and furiously banging on his hotel door to break it open in order to rescue his family. He bangs harder and harder and collapses in the water, gasping for air but sucking in the contaminated salt water. His eyes are open, but he can't see through the muddy water. His lungs fill with water as he screams for help. He's drowning. Everything slowly goes black. Then complete silence. No more sounds of rushing water or banging.

Cain awakened, coughing for air. He was on the tatami mat looking up. Standing over him were two monks. The sensei continued swinging his bamboo staff, but the sound was inaudible. Cain saw one of the monks speaking but could not hear anything. Slowly the sounds came back into range. The monk had a set of kind eyes that sparkled. Cain sensed a humanity from this old man who comforted him. Then all the sound came back when the monk placed his hand on Cain's shoulder.

"Mountains exist for you to climb," the monk said slowly in English, "not for you to carry."

CHAPTER 54

UMIKO RAN UP to Cain and kneeled beside him. "Are you okay?"

She appeared blurry in his vision. "Yeah, I think so. I must be a little dehydrated." He massaged his right temple. "I got a migraine. It blurs my vision sometimes. Not sure if it's from the migraine or from the dehydration."

"Sensei just gave us one hour personal time for tea."

"That sounds great right now."

"I agree," Umiko said. "He was training us very hard today."

Umiko and Cain walked the flat stone path toward a more private area near the garden.

"Please sit and relax," she instructed. "I will be back with the tea."

As Cain waited for Umiko, he looked around the Zen retreat. Perfectly manicured bonsai trees, raked granite, and a man-made pond with koi fish were nearby. He had a panoramic view of Mount Fuji towering over Japan's sacred landscape. *This is such a tranquil place,* he thought. *I'll come back someday, without the sensei.*

Umiko returned, holding a wooden tray with the

tea-making essentials. She kneeled in a *seiza* position and began the ceremonial ritual of preparing the tea. She placed a spoonful of matcha green tea powder in his ornate bowl. She poured about four ounces of hot water into the bowl. She used a bamboo whisk brush to vigorously stir the powder and water together until the green tea became frothy.

Cain watched her closely, impressed by her level of perfection and attention to detail. He felt that she was honorable and someone who would never betray his trust.

She cupped the bowl with both hands and presented it to Cain.

Cain wanted to chug it, but it was too hot. So he sipped it as quickly as he could. He felt himself getting better with each gulp. "Thank you, Umi. Your tea is a lifesaver. My vision is getting sharper and I can tell my headache is fading."

Umiko smiled while performing a half bow. "Matcha green tea has special powers to heal the body," she said. "It's very good for you."

"The only tea we drink back home is sweet tea, loaded with the power of sugar." Cain smiled. "You remember that tea I had at Nawlins—the one you tasted?"

"Yes. Sweet tea is good"—Umiko paused—"for dessert."

Cain laughed, and Umiko covered her mouth and looked nervously around the Zen garden—mindful not to disturb the other retreaters.

"The garden, the landscape, the topography—it's all magical here," Cain said. "It looks exactly like it does in the magazines."

"I can't wait to show you this place in March or April, when the sakura—the cherry blossoms—bloom."

"Sakura," he repeated. "I look forward to coming back with you."

"*Sakura* also means to smile, because you always smile when you see the beauty of the cherry blossoms."

Cain smiled. "Then your parents should have named you Sakura."

Umiko blushed and turned away for a brief moment before looking back at Cain. "I'm sorry to be so nosy," she said.

"No," Cain replied. "Ask me anything."

"I heard you speak to the monk."

Cain sighed, embarrassed. "I'm sure I was rambling from the dehydration."

"We have a popular saying in Japan: *Au wa wakare no hajimari*."

"Does it mean to drink plenty of water before doing kendo for two hours in the wilderness with a stick-wielding sensei?" Cain asked, deflecting her question.

"It means 'Meeting is the beginning of parting.' We remember the past, but *live* for the present, because even the present will be the past someday." After a moment, she said, "Would you like to tell me about what happened?"

Cain paused for a beat. "Normally, I would say no. But if there were ever a time and place"—he inhaled and exhaled slowly—"and a person to share this with, it's now and with you."

Umiko prepared him another cup of tea, and one for her. She sipped hers as she listened to him talk.

"Ever since I was a child, I have loved the water. Year-round, after school, friends and I would swim the lakes near my home. They were a lot like the lakes here, but our lakes had catfish instead of koi." He smiled. "Instead of being lined with rocks, they were lined with dirt and mud.

"My freshman year at the university, I took a scuba diving class. My instructor, Mr. Terry, was a former Navy SEAL. He took a liking to me and became like a mentor. He would tell me exciting stories of scuba diving all over the world—and because he was in the military, the navy paid for it. His favorite spot to dive was off the coast of Thailand. He showed me pictures of him diving off the island of Krabi. The white sand beaches, the crystal clear waters—it all looked like paradise on earth."

Umiko listened intently as Cain slowly continued his story.

"Truth be told, he was the reason I joined the navy. I wanted to be just like him. But the day I tested to be a diver, I had a head cold. My sinuses wouldn't equalize. When I descended into the water, my ears burst and my goggles filled with my own blood."

"That's horrible!" Umiko closed her eyes and crinkled her face at the thought of blood flooding his mask.

"It was scary," Cain confessed. "I didn't know if I had lost my hearing, or what had really happened. But the navy was really good about it. They told me they had enough divers anyway, but what they *really* needed were pilots. I had already been flying for years. You see, my father is a pilot. Just like your family believes in tradition, mine does, too. My father believed that flying was a tradition that had to be passed down from generation to generation, or eventually it would become too expensive—a hobby just for the wealthy. When the navy learned about this, they sent me to flight school instead."

"So you were a military pilot?"

"Yes."

"Like Tom Cruise?"

Cain chuckled. "No. Not like Maverick at all. He flew fighter planes with jet engines. I flew airplanes with four propellers. I carried a crew of six people and we flew for long hours over the ocean looking for Russian submarines and ships carrying tons of drugs from Central America to our shores to poison our people."

Umiko nodded in acknowledgment.

"But I could never get that paradise image out of my mind. I wanted to scuba dive in Thailand like my instructor had done. Claire Bear—" Cain smiled at the sound and memory of her name. "That was my wife. She was pretty adventurous, but she didn't want to go. We had a one-year-old son, Christopher, and Claire thought it was too far to travel. I convinced her it would be a great getaway for the whole family. It was a resort and they had childcare services to help us enjoy the vacation. We spent Christmas of 2004 in Krabi." His thoughts seemed to trail off as he looked skyward. "It was the last Christmas our small family would spend together."

Umiko's eyes widened as the timeline started making sense to her. Cain could tell she now had an idea where this tragic story was going.

"I woke up super early on December twenty-sixth. I didn't want to wake her or the baby. I hopped on a scuba boat at the hotel and went out. The sun was coming out by the time we arrived at our first dive location. During my second dive, I was about forty feet below when I saw the boat's anchor dragging through the ocean floor. I knew something was wrong right away. I had never seen that before, and I couldn't hear the boat's motor. So I knew it wasn't just a hungover captain trying to move his boat while anchored.

"I had to ascend, but I had to go up really slowly. Otherwise, I risked getting decompression sickness.

My dive partner, a British traveler who was vacationing alone, surfaced with me. When we popped our heads out of the water, our boat was gone! We dropped our weight belts and inflated our BCDs. We swam for hours and hours to get back to the hotel. We eventually found the boat, but the hotel was practically gone. It looked like it had been bombed."

Cain's voice started to shake. "Dead bodies were floating in the water. Cars and roads were not visible anymore. Poisonous snakes were swimming in the water with us. I rushed to where our room had once been. I could barely move. My skin was wrinkled from being in the water for over five hours, and my muscles were failing me from swimming thousands of yards. I was operating on pure adrenaline to rescue my family. I went to our room—what was left of it. It was blocked by broken boards. I grabbed my scuba tank and banged it repeatedly until the boards broke and I was able to enter. Everything was gone."

Umiko's tears streamed down her soft face. "Did you find your wife and son?"

Cain lowered his head into his hand. He shook his head no. "Over the next several days, I saw relatives using cooking utensils to dig graves for their loved ones who had died. There were also some monks who were burning the bodies of those who had died. They didn't even know the names of who they were cremating."

Cain looked up into Umiko's eyes. "I cling to the hope they died quickly—even better if it was while they slept together in the hotel bed."

Umiko embraced Cain and they cried together.

"You will see them again," she assured him. "On the other side, they will be waiting for you."

"Do you really think so?" he asked.

"With all my heart."

CHAPTER 55

MONDAY MORNING APPROACHED quickly, but it felt like no other Monday Cain had experienced. He felt different because he *was* different. He had come to grips with the reality that he could not change the past. He had finally found peace with the tragedy in Thailand. *I will strive to live in the present,* he promised himself. *When it's my time to die, then I'll see my Claire Bear and little Christopher. But I will honor their deaths by living.*

The world took on a different form. The sky seemed a brighter blue, the grass beneath his feet softer, the air fresher, and the flowers smelled sweeter. And more importantly, Cain's connection with Umiko was deeper, and his fondness for her continued to grow. The two made sure to sit across from each other during the retreat's breakfast.

"No wonder everyone is so thin and fit in Japan," Cain commented to Umiko.

"Because of our diet?"

"*Diet* is certainly an appropriate word to use here. This has gotta be a first for me—grilled fish on a bed of lettuce for breakfast!"

"What do you normally eat for breakfast?"

"I enjoy cooking, so if I have time, I make a vegetable omelet with bacon. Or, if I'm feeling homesick, I'll fry beignets."

"Mm, that sounds delicious. I've only seen beignets on television."

"Oh, they are." He smiled mischievously. "But don't take my word for it. I'll cook for you sometime and you can be the judge."

"Okay," Umiko replied. "I will be the judge. But I must warn you: I'm very fair."

As they were grabbing their belongings in preparation for jumping on the bus and heading back to Yokohama, the monks wandered through the gathering to return the cell phones. Cain grabbed his and looked into the monk's eyes. They were the same eyes he'd peered into the day before, when he had awakened on the floor.

Cain rested his arms by his side and very slowly bowed. *"Domo arigato gozaimasu."*

The monk returned the bow.

"I will never forget you," Cain said. "You've given me something I haven't had in a very long time: forgiveness."

"The great Buddha reminds us," the monk said, "that to have anger is like holding a hot piece of coal to throw at another person. But whoever is holding the hot coal is the one who gets burned. Leave the coal here with nature."

"I have," Cain replied, and bowed again.

"Hai," the monk said as he nodded his head. "Go in peace."

Cain bowed again and then took his seat on the bus and powered on his phone. The Zen temple grounds were far from the city, so his phone searched for a cell tower. When the bus was on the main road, Cain's phone chimed and he saw that he'd gotten a voicemail from Bonnie.

"Oh, this is fantastic news," he said to Umiko. "My sister called. This means she most likely wants to bury the hatchet."

"Bury the what?"

"The hatchet. You know: like an ax. It's an expression. Maybe she wants to make up for the fight we had at the Angel Cloud. Even if she doesn't, I'll smooth things over with her. This retreat has been life-changing for me. It's given me a new take on life. And the fact that Bonnie is calling is just *lagniappe*."

"*Lagniappe?*"

Cain laughed. "That's a Louisiana word for something extra—like icing on the cake. I'll make lunch plans so we can all get together next weekend."

"That will be nice. I look forward to meeting her."

"It'll be great. We'll go out to that famous city you're always talking so fondly about. Kama...Kama..."

"Kura," Umiko said.

"Kamakura! That's it," Cain said.

Umiko's smile took up her whole face.

Cain's voicemail finally connected. "You have one message," the automated voice announced. "Saturday, 9:57 p.m." Cain put a finger in his opposite ear so he could hear the message. "Cain, why aren't you answering?" Bonnie's voice sounded worried. "I think I'm being followed. It's dark, so I'm not sure, but I think it might be one of those guys you fought at the Angel Cloud. He's got a limp. Call me back as soon as you get this. I'm almost home now."

Cain turned to Umiko. "Something's wrong!"

"What?" Umiko said, surprised.

Cain redialed Bonnie's number several times. The calls went straight to her voicemail.

"Umi, please call this number and see if you can get through." He waited impatiently as Umiko powered up her phone and dialed Bonnie's number.

"It's a Japanese recording. It says the voicemail is full."

"Bonnie's in trouble. Tell the driver to go faster."

Umiko stood to address the driver. *"Sumimasen,"* she said with a short bow.

The bus driver raised his voice to be heard over the hum of the engine and said something back to her in hurried Japanese.

Umiko quickly sat back down, and all her friends looked at her. "He asked me to please not stand while the bus is in motion."

"Good grief," Cain scoffed while shaking his head. "I'm going to call Tanaka-san. He should be able to shoot over to Bonnie's apartment and wait there until I get there."

"How is the retreat?" Tanaka asked when he answered the phone. "Did they make you climb Mount Fuji?"

"Are you in Tokyo?" Cain was speaking quickly. "Could you get to Bonnie's apartment as soon as possible?"

"I'm at my aero club—not too far away. What's wrong?"

"I think Bonnie is in trouble. She left me a voicemail. She said one of the guys from the bar the other night was following her."

"Text me the address, and I will go straight there. I will bring Aito-san with me."

"I'll see you there as soon as I can. It might be two or three hours given how slow this bus driver is going."

"I will call you as soon as I get there. We will leave now."

"Okay. Thanks. Oh, wait: one last thing. Don't disturb anything. Leave everything just as it is."

About an hour later, Tanaka telephoned Cain. "I'm here, but I don't see anything unusual. The door is locked. I rang the doorbell a few times, but nobody answered. Have you called her work?"

"Yes, of course. But United wouldn't give me her work schedule over the phone. They cited some company policy bullshit. Do you still have some contacts over there?"

"I'll call and see if they will give me that information," Tanaka said. "I still have a friend who works the ticket counter at Narita."

When Cain arrived at Bonnie's several hours later, Tanaka and Aito were waiting outside her door.

"Thanks for coming," Cain said, and pounded on the door with his closed fist. "Bonnie, open the door! It's your brother." He turned to Tanaka. "Any update?"

"Bonnie was scheduled to fly today," Tanaka said, and then lowered his head. "But she never showed up."

Cain pulled out his money clip. He grabbed a credit card and slid it between the doorframe and the door. He jiggled it for a bit until the latch popped open.

"Don't touch anything," he instructed Tanaka and Aito. "Something's wrong. I can feel it. There's definitely foul play here. Bonnie's not here, and she was supposed to be on a flight, but her airline badge is on the floor, by the couch." When he kneeled to pick it up using a tissue, he saw something small out of the corner of his eye. It was under the couch. He got on all fours and looked closer. He carefully pulled the object out from its hiding place. It was an empty syringe, and it had blood drops on the end of the needle.

"Is Bonnie a diabetic?" Aito asked.

"No," Cain said forcefully. "She was drugged. That would be the only way for someone to take her." He looked around the living room for more clues. "Help me find her phone."

The three of them searched the entire apartment, which was easy given its small size. But they could not find Bonnie's phone.

Cain turned to Tanaka. "Call your father. Have him get down here and start processing this scene."

"He's at my grandparents' farm near Yokota. It's his day off."

"I don't give a damn if it's Chinese New Year. We've got a kidnapped American! Tell him to start rolling some detectives this way. Have them bring a K9 and a fingerprint-dusting kit."

Half an hour later, two local patrol officers arrived. They appeared to be in their midforties and smelled of cigarettes. They were breathing heavily from the three flights of stairs.

Cain looked at Tanaka. "Where are the detectives?"

"This is procedure, Cain. The patrol officers come first to investigate and take a report. Then they make a determination about whether a detective needs to respond."

"Anyone with half a brain can see that a detective needs to be summoned!" Cain said with great frustration.

"This is how things are done in Japan," Aito replied, trying to calm Cain down.

"I'll play their bureaucratic game, but just for a few moments. Time is of the essence in these types of cases. If we don't find Bonnie within twenty-four hours, she's likely gone forever."

The uniformed officers spoke with Tanaka in Japanese.

"Cain, they want to know how you entered the apartment."

"What does that matter?"

"They want to know if an intruder had to break open the door."

"No. Tell them about how I used my credit card to open the door."

Tanaka inhaled through his teeth. "I don't think that is such a good idea. Technically, we were breaking and entering. That's a crime here."

"What?" Cain asked incredulously. "For Christ's sake! I'm her twin brother!" Cain's mood switched from defensive to offensive. "When they find Bonnie, they can ask *her* if she wants to press charges against me. Okay?"

"This is not like America. Japan has very many rules. There is no gray here. Only black and white."

"Then tell them the door was unlocked." He pointed his finger at Tanaka's chest. "Do whatever you have to do to get them to investigate this!"

Tanaka turned to the police and conversed with them in Japanese for several minutes.

The uniformed officers walked around the apartment. They opened the refrigerator and kitchen cabinets and looked through the bedroom and bathroom.

"They want to know how many people live here."

"Just Bonnie."

Tanaka translated. The two officers spoke with each other in Japanese for a bit and then turned to Tanaka.

"They said they do not have enough evidence to call a detective," Tanaka told Cain. "They said you can file a report at the station if you want, but missing persons only get assigned to a detective after twenty-four hours, or under suspicious circumstances."

"I'm telling them that these are suspicious circumstances. Have them listen to my voicemail. Or have 'em take a closer look at this." Cain raised the empty syringe into the air.

Tanaka pulled Cain aside. "Drugs are very taboo in Japan. If they think she is a drug user, they will not look for her."

Cain felt his blood boiling when one of the officers pointed to an Angel Cloud brochure on the table. The officer said in broken English, "Westerners come and go there. It is normal. Very safe here. Maybe vacation with customer. We will talk with the neighbors."

Cain stormed toward the door. "I'm not dealing with these Keystone Cops any longer."

Tanaka followed Cain to the door. "Where are you going?"

"To get some answers."

"Take Aito-san. He can translate for you."

"Where I'm going, I don't need a translator!"

PART THREE

"IN DER NOT FRISST DER TEUFEL FLIEGEN"

CHAPTER 56

THE BLACK TOYOTA CROWN rolled to a stop. With his white-gloved hand, the driver pointed toward the massive ten-story concrete building that took up an entire city block in Tokyo. *The taxi driver understood my poor Japanese after all,* Cain thought.

Cain handed the driver two one-thousand-yen bills, which more than covered the fare, and opened the rear passenger door. He folded out of the sedan and looked upon the embassy's black wrought-iron gates. *Yep, it's undeniably the American embassy. It's the most fortified building in the entire neighborhood.* Half a dozen uniformed police officers were patrolling on foot behind waist-high concrete barriers. Beyond the gate's walls, a lone American flag blew lightly in the wind.

"*Sumimasen,*" the driver said as he ran around the front of the car to hand Cain his change. Tipping was not customary in Japan, and it often made Japanese people feel uncomfortable. "*Sumimasen,*" he repeated as he handed Cain his change on a small plate. The driver seemed relieved when Cain took it.

Cain tossed the yennies, as he called the Japanese coins, into his pocket and marched through the crosswalk to approach the heavily guarded compound. The

Department of State crest was bolted to the bars of the gate. The American eagle, with its wings outstretched, was clutching arrows in one talon and an olive branch in the other. Cain read the sign: E PLURIBUS UNUM. "Out of many, one," he said softly to himself. *It's time to call in the backup.* He felt confident that the embassy would be able to light a fire under the Tokyo police.

Cain approached the security hut and punched the push-button intercom. "I'm an American citizen. I'd like to speak to the regional security officer," Cain said to one of the guards behind bulletproof glass that was at least two inches thick.

"Do you have an appointment?"

"No, but it's very important. Tell the duty agent that it's an emergency and that I'm a Secret Service agent. I need to discuss a kidnapping with him."

"Do you have any identification?"

Cain pushed his passport through a narrow opening in the partition.

The guard thumbed through a folder of names and numbers. He picked up a landline and punched a series of keys. The call lasted less than a minute, and Cain couldn't hear the conversation. The guard pushed the intercom button and instructed Cain to empty his pockets and walk through the metal detector. It was like going through airport security, although Cain didn't have to remove his boots. A different security guard escorted him up the hill to the main entrance of the embassy.

"Please sit here," he said. "Mr. Rose will meet you here as soon as he arrives."

"Mr. Rose?" Cain asked.

"The deputy regional security officer. He's the duty officer."

Cain glanced at his watch. "When will he be here?"

"I don't know the exact time, but he has been notified."

"Please tell him to hurry. This is a level-one priority."

The guard nodded, but Cain understood that the duty agent would arrive whenever he felt like it.

The guard directed Cain to sit in a chair in the lobby while he waited for Mr. Rose to arrive. But Cain couldn't sit still. He paced back and forth across the marble floor. "Mountains exist for you to climb, not for you to carry," he repeated to himself. He tried breathing exercises he had learned at the retreat. He continued inhaling air as many times as possible to stretch his lungs, and then he exhaled as slowly as he could without passing out. The monks had said that lungs are like rubber bands: they need to be stretched.

Cain quit pacing when the man he took to be Mr. Rose approached him about an hour later.

"Oh." Mr. Rose sighed and paused at the sight of Cain. "I recognize you from the *Japan Times*. You're a *former* Secret Service agent."

"I need your help."

"You sound just like a Secret Service agent." Mr. Rose chuckled. "They are always needing the RSO's help. What happened? You and your partner stiff a prostitute again, but this time in Japan?" Mr. Rose smirked.

"I'm gonna let that go, thanks to some recent Zen training I've been undergoing."

"Well, I appreciate your restraint," Mr. Rose replied with dry humor. He led Cain into his office and they sat down at the desk. "What's so important that made you tell the guard that it's a level-one priority?"

"My sister's been kidnapped."

"Have you told the local police?"

"Yes. They weren't interested."

"A gaijin getting kidnapped in Japan is big news. Why weren't they interested?"

"She worked at the Angel Cloud—"

"So, I was right. This story does involve a prostitute."

Cain's face flushed red. "My sister is *not* a prostitute. And if you say that again, your diplomatic immunity is not gonna help with your newfound hospital bills."

"Relax, man. I didn't mean anything by it. Just thought it might ease the tension."

"Let's not," Cain replied.

"Japan's a safe country—one of the safest. I'm sure there is a misunderstanding, and we'll find your sister."

"Everyone touts how safe this place is, but when I tried to report a genuine violent crime, the police didn't give a damn. They just cited policy and procedures." Cain's voice started to rise. "They're more concerned with appearances than with substance."

"I sympathize with you. I really do. The Japanese take perfection and bureaucracy to a level I've never seen before. Investigations here can take years."

"I've got hours, not years! I can't even get the police to start an investigation."

"I feel your pain. It's frustrating for me, too. Trust me. That's why I'm just biding my time here, and then, *inshallah,* I'll be back in the Middle East. That's where the real action is."

"The action is right here, in your backyard! But nobody is doing anything about it. The yakuza kidnapped my sister because I got into a fight with three of them at the Angel Cloud."

"Well, *now* this story is making a little more sense to me. The Japanese police, well, they're scared of the yakuza. Their congress implemented tough laws recently, yet when a yakuza warehouse was raided, they found pictures on the wall of police officers with their families. It was a loud message to stay clear, or else the yakuza would come after *their* families."

"There are over nine million people in Tokyo. I need some help here. There's no way I can find Bonnie by myself—even if she is a blond-haired gaijin."

"Do you have any leads?"

"One of the guys I fought at the Angel Cloud was named Watanabe."

"Watanabe?" Mr. Rose scoffed. "That's like Smith in America. I'm sorry, I can't help you, sir. I wish I could. I'd love taking some American justice and shoving it down the yakuza's throat. But my hands are tied up in the political and diplomatic sensitivity of being strategic guests in Japan. You know: with China and North Korea just next door." Mr. Rose opened his desk drawer and grabbed a stack of business cards. He flipped through them. "Here's the card of an American reporter. He comes by often to interview me and get information off the record. Not that I give information off the record."

"I don't need a reporter," said Cain. "They just sensationalize everything. What I need is someone who knows the yakuza organization, their safe houses, their command structure, even their clubhouses."

"Just take the card. Maybe it'll help, maybe it won't."

Cain plucked the card from Mr. Rose's fingertips.

"He's a pain in the ass, but very hungry. Works all the time, and doesn't mind getting his hands dirty. Someday we'll be seeing him on CNN."

Cain glanced down at the card. "'Champ Albright the Third,'" he said aloud. *I recognize that name. It's the* Stars and Stripes *reporter Bonnie mentioned before.*

This is a sign, he thought. For a brief moment, he felt hopeful—as though fate was helping him.

"If I worked here," Cain said with disgust, "there's no way I'd turn away helping an American." Cain pocketed the business card. "I'll show myself to the door."

"I'll have to escort you out. This is a secure building."

Cain stood to leave.

"Just remember," Mr. Rose said, moving from behind his cherrywood desk. "This is Japan. They have strict rules. They will not tolerate a rogue gaijin disrupting those rules. They will kick you out of this country so fast and never let you back in. *Never.* Their collective memory goes back thousands of years."

"I have no intention of being back in the news. Been there, done that. But I can't promise you those who took Bonnie won't be."

A worried look came upon Mr. Rose's face. "What do you plan on doing?"

"Cajun justice, Mr. Rose. Cajun justice!"

CHAPTER 57

CAIN WAS FURIOUS when he left the embassy. The lone American flag that had blown in the wind had been taken down for the night. Cain walked down a street he didn't recognize, passing the Spanish embassy on his way toward Roppongi. Compared with the fortified American embassy compound, the Spanish embassy looked more like a modest office building. Outside its gates was a framed poster highlighting a Picasso painting depicting a bullfight. The bright, multicolored artistry popped out among the otherwise gray and dull neighborhood. *I bet they would have done more to help one of their countrymen. Political and diplomatic sensitivity, my ass!*

Cain pulled out the Angel Cloud brochure he'd taken from Bonnie's apartment. He studied the map and found the entrance to the bar. It was in a crowded area known for its late-night activities, but it was relatively quiet that night.

He opened the door and ascended the stairs. He climbed faster and faster as he neared the top. A muscular Japanese man in a white tuxedo stopped Cain at the top.

"You are not welcome here," the bouncer said.

"I'm just looking for Bonnie—my sister."

"She is not here. She quit."

"Okay," Cain said as he raised his hands chest level. "I don't want trouble." He scanned the room. "She asked me to grab her purse. She said she left it in her locker."

"The purse is not here," the bouncer said gruffly.

Cain looked past the surly bouncer and saw Sabrina across the lounge, sitting at a table with some other hostess girls.

"Time to go." The bouncer put his hand on Cain's shoulder.

"Easy, Road House," Cain warned. "I'm leaving."

The bouncer escorted him down the stairs and outside. As Cain stood on the sidewalk, he looked around. Normally, he stood out in Japan because of his height and build, but this popular nightlife area was frequented by Westerners. A few strolled by, presumably on their way to various eateries and bars.

Cain walked into the Lawson convenience store across the street from the Angel Cloud. The book section was crowded with about seven Japanese men ranging in age from twenty to sixty; they were standing in the aisle and reading manga. *American cops would love this setup,* Cain thought. *Coffee, doughnuts, and pedophiles all in one convenient place.*

Cain grabbed a copy of the *Japan Times* and headed to the register. Checkout was taking a while because the customer in front of him was paying her monthly electric bill. The cashier took the money and then had to stamp the bills and receipts several times with an official rubber stamp. Cain felt his patience wearing thin. *All that Zen training and I'm about to blow my lid.*

While waiting, Cain could smell a corn dog resting in the heating container. It suddenly hit him that he was starving. *I haven't had anything to eat since breakfast with Umi.*

When Cain finally reached the counter, he said in a mix of Japanese and English, "*Ichi* corn dog, *kudesei.*" He lifted his newspaper in the air. "*Ichi* Japan Times."

"*Hai,*" the young Japanese cashier said with a friendly smile. "One American dog. One *Japan Times.*" She then gestured at the cash register, which displayed a price of three hundred yen.

Cain dug into his pocket and retrieved the yennies he still had from the taxi ride.

"Mustard and ketchup?" the cashier asked, holding up a small plastic package that contained both condiments.

"*Hai. Arigato,*" Cain said. He took his purchases and grabbed a seat by the window. He removed the corn dog's paper packaging and placed the dog on top of it. He grabbed the combo condiment and slathered it on the corn dog. He gobbled it up and read the paper while surveilling the entrance to the Angel Cloud.

Eventually, he saw the tall, slim, black-haired Romanian leave the Angel Cloud and start walking northbound. He crumpled all his trash together and tossed it in a bin as he hurried out the door to catch up with the Eastern European hostess.

"Sabrina!" he said. "It's me—your favorite customer."

"I can't talk to you. You will get me in trouble."

"I don't want any trouble for you. I need your help. Please. For Bonnie."

"Too many eyes are watching us in this neighborhood."

"I'll meet you anywhere."

She continued walking northbound, with Cain one pace behind her. "Meet me here, at Yoyogi Park, in thirty minutes," she said.

"Make it fifteen."

"What if I'm followed?" she asked nervously.

"I will worry about that. You just please be there, Sabrina."

"I have to worry," she said, clearly scared. "Or they might take me, too!"

"Give me a cigarette," he instructed. "If you see me smoking, that means you were followed and to just keep on walking past. Okay?"

She thought for a second and then pulled a cigarette from her Chanel purse—no doubt a gift from one of her wealthy clients.

Cain took the cigarette and reminded her, "Fifteen minutes."

"*Da,*" she replied in her native Romanian.

Cain circled the park and sat on a bench. He watched closely the few people who were out and about, walking through the park. Some were businesspeople just cutting through to save time, and others were sweethearts enjoying a romantic walk.

He looked at his watch—the dials emitted a soft glow. *It's been fifteen minutes. Where the hell is she?* His legs started to shake with anxious energy. Another ten minutes passed. Just when he thought of getting up to go search for her, her silhouette appeared in the distance. She didn't stick to the plan. Instead of walking toward Cain, she sat at a bench about fifty yards away.

What the hell is she doing? he wondered. He continued his scan, and when he felt confident she had not been followed, he stood and walked toward her.

"What the hell was that all about? You didn't stick to our plan," he said.

"I got nervous," she said. "I couldn't remember our plan. I almost didn't even come, so give me some credit!" She pulled out another cigarette from her purse.

He pulled out a matchbox. "Natural wood is better than butane." He struck the match. "Healthier, too."

She half laughed. "There's a lot of things healthier than smoking, I suppose."

"Yeah," Cain said. "Like doing the right thing. Where's Bonnie?"

"I don't know. I swear."

"You gotta know something! You're smart, and you're observant. You haven't survived in this business without being street-smart."

"They lured my friend Elena over here for a modeling job." Sabrina took a long drag and slowly exhaled it toward the night sky. "Then they took her passport."

"Who? The same people who kidnapped Bonnie?"

"They threatened to tell the police that she was prostituting and selling drugs in Japan."

"Bonnie? Or your friend Elena?"

"Elena. She was so scared. She had no identity. And then one day she disappeared. I'm afraid that is what has happened to Bonnie."

"Why would they do that to Bonnie? She's never hurt anyone."

"You shamed them. Saving face is everything here. You challenged them and fought three yakuza members in front of many prominent Japanese businessmen. They were always going to get their revenge."

"Why didn't they come after me, then? Why did they go after Bonnie? She wasn't involved."

"They'll *kill* you, but they'll *use* Bonnie. I've heard they will sell women to make money for their organization. You should have caught the next flight to America after the fight in the Angel Cloud."

"There's no way in hell I'm going back to America without my sister. Who were those men I fought?"

"I don't know. I had never seen them before."

"You sure?"

"Like I said, I've never seen them."

"One of them was named Watanabe," he said. "Does that ring a bell?"

She blew the smoke from her cigarette into the air. "I meet five guys a week who are named Watanabe."

"You don't know anything about them?" Cain repeated, feeling as though he was back at the Secret Service, interrogating suspects.

"I don't know who they are, but I saw them leave that night in a Nissan Skyline."

Cain scoffed. "There's gotta be hundreds of those in Tokyo—probably thousands."

"This one is easy to see. It's orange and very loud. Like a race car."

"Oh, that's good intel," he said. As he looked at her pretty face and striking blue eyes, he realized it could have just as easily been Sabrina who was kidnapped. "If you're so afraid of them, why are you helping me?"

"I like Bonnie. She isn't like us. She doesn't need the money. She just enjoys meeting different people. She's always very nice to us. She called me and asked if I would meet her at Starbucks the Saturday before I went on shift. I agreed, but she never showed up."

"What happened?"

"I don't know." Sabrina began to tear up. "She seemed fine when I talked to her."

"What else did she say?"

"She just said that she'd enjoyed working with me and the other girls, but that she had to quit. She said it wasn't safe for her to go back, especially after I had told her that the man with the bloody face had taken her purse that night."

Cain's heart sank.

"I wasn't sure, but I thought Bonnie would be okay because—"

"Because why?" Cain interrupted.

"Because Bonnie was protected by the manager. She was American. She didn't know about how they treated the Russian girls."

"But you're not Russian," Cain said.

"Romanian, Ukrainian, Hungarian—they call us all Russians."

Cain handed Sabrina a piece of paper. "This is my number. Please call me if you ever see them back at the Angel Cloud. I can protect you."

She scoffed. "You can't protect me from them."

"I *can* protect you. There was a time when I made my living protecting presidents and kings."

She took the paper and shoved it in her purse. She thanked him in her native Romanian: *"Multumesc."*

"Cu plăcere," he replied. He turned around and started walking away.

Before he disappeared into the darkness, Sabrina made one last quick request. "Please find her. Make those bastards pay—for Bonnie, and for Elena."

He looked back only briefly. "You can bet your life on it."

CHAPTER 58

CAIN HAILED A TAXI. He wanted to return to Bonnie's apartment. *Was there anything I missed?* He kept asking himself this question and replaying her voicemail message. *I shouldn't have gone to that retreat, just as I shouldn't have gone to Thailand.*

As Cain sat in the back of the taxi, he peered out the window. The high-rise buildings towered into the sky, some disappearing into the cloud cover. *Bonnie could be anywhere,* he worried. *How am I going to find her in Japan when I couldn't even find Claire and Christopher in Krabi?* He lowered his head into his hand. He felt the onset of a migraine. He rubbed his temples to ease the pressure.

When the taxi neared the apartment complex, Cain instructed the driver to stop right there and not go any closer to the main doors.

"This is good. Right here. Here! *Koko ni.*" Cain didn't want to be dropped off at the front doors because he wasn't yet sure if they were being watched by the yakuza.

Cain walked around the neighborhood and the building's parking lot. He looked intently at all the cars and made sure that none harbored a lookout.

Black was the most popular color in Japan. It didn't matter the make or model—almost all the sedans were black. Some were silver, but none were the orange Nissan Skyline that Sabrina had described.

Cain's phone buzzed in his hand. It was a text message.

IS EVERYTHING OKAY? Umiko wrote. IT'S REALLY LATE AND I HAVEN'T HEARD BACK FROM YOU.

He called her. "Bonnie has been kidnapped."

"Are you sure? This is unbelievable!" Umiko said.

"I'm trying to backtrack her steps. I'm at her apartment now. But I gotta be honest with you, Umi. I'm feeling overwhelmed right now. Everyone is right. I'm a gaijin—an outsider in this foreign place." His voice started to crack. "It's my fault. Now she has been taken. And I'm the *only* person Bonnie has looking for her."

"I will help you. I can go with you to the police station," Umiko offered.

Cain sighed. "That's not going to do any good. I spoke with some officers earlier at Bonnie's apartment. They were useless."

"That is why you need my help," Umiko said with confidence. "I have lived my whole life in Japan. I understand Japanese procedures, and I also know how to get around them."

"I didn't think navigating Japanese bureaucracy was even possible," Cain said. "That's how it feels around here, but maybe there's hope. My crew chief used to say that an officer knows the rules, but a chief knows the exceptions to those rules. If you're willing to help me, I'll take it. I can use any help I can get right about now."

"I will meet you at Tokyo police headquarters in one hour."

"There's a *koban* near Bonnie's apartment. Wouldn't that be quicker?"

"Quicker is not always better."

"That's a very Japanese thing to say."

"What can I say? I'm Japanese."

Cain let out a chuckle and realized it was the first time he had laughed since he shared breakfast with Umiko that very morning. But it seemed as though days had passed already.

About an hour later, Umiko showed up carrying a Dunkin' Donuts box. "I purchased these on my way here. They will help us. Japanese inspectors watch American police movies."

"And even if they don't, everybody loves doughnuts."

"*Hai,* and I have chocolate, glazed, and some with cute sprinkles." Umiko smiled.

Tokyo's metropolitan police headquarters was an enormous wedge-shaped building that ascended eighteen stories. It was the station responsible for overseeing more than forty thousand police officers. On the roof was a large red communications tower— undoubtedly for dispatching police and receiving 110 calls, the equivalent of America's 911.

About thirty civilians were lined up to speak with the officer on duty.

"I'm sorry for this long line," Umiko said.

"Are you kidding? New Orleans has a fraction of the population Tokyo does, and their line would snake out the door, all the way into the French Quarter."

Umiko and Cain took their place in line. The line was orderly, and everyone waited patiently except for Cain. He continued glancing at his Omega Seamaster. "I just need to find that orange Skyline."

Cain had been observing the people in line. After

about the fourth person had given money to the duty officer before leaving, Cain decided to say something.

"Why is everyone paying the duty officer? What's that all about?"

"They are turning in money," Umiko said.

"What?"

"Yes. They have found money, or someone's wallet or umbrella. Most likely on the train. And they are turning it in."

"You're kidding, right?"

"No. I think over one million dollars in yen gets turned in to the lost and found every year."

"The hell with umbrellas. Someone needs to turn in Bonnie," Cain exclaimed.

At about that time, they reached the front of the line. "I will talk to the police officer," Umiko said. "Please try to relax, and trust me."

It was as if Umiko was a different person. Instead of her normal appearance of stability, athleticism, and competence, she presented herself to the officer as very timid and shy.

"*Sumimasen,*" she said, and quasi bowed several times. The rest of what she said was in Japanese, and Cain didn't know what she was saying. At one point, she lifted the box of doughnuts into the air to show the officer. He smiled—perhaps for the first time during his shift that day.

A few moments later, an inspector came to the lobby and requested that Umiko and Cain follow him back to the detective bureau. It was an open-bay area illuminated by bright fluorescent lights. They walked past at least fifty desks at which sat uniformed and plainclothes detectives clacking on typewriters and computers and answering ringing phones. All the desks, chairs, and telephones looked identical.

The detective, who looked worn-out and had a loose tie around his neck, plopped himself down into his office chair and wheeled himself toward his desk. He picked up his Seven Stars cigarette from the ashtray where it had been resting. He inhaled and slowly blew out the smoke.

I'm just one problem out of a thousand for this man, Cain thought. *He's not going to be helpful.*

Umiko spoke to him in Japanese and presented the doughnuts. The inspector accepted the box and thanked her but didn't take a doughnut. Instead, he offered them to his colleagues nearby, who huddled around and picked their favorite flavors.

"He wants to know if the parents have been notified."

"God, no. This would crush my parents. They would be heartbroken beyond repair. They didn't even want Bonnie moving to Japan. And now she's missing because of me! There's no way I can tell my parents."

"Okay. I'll tell him yes."

"You sure that's a good idea?"

"Otherwise, they won't file the report until the family has been called."

Cain nodded.

The exchange between the inspector and Umiko lasted an agonizing eighty-three minutes. Cain knew the exact time because he had nervously kept checking his watch—feeling as if he was wasting his time dealing with the Japanese police and their lengthy protocols. They appeared much more interested in administration than in actual investigation, but Cain trusted Umiko.

When the inspector finished typing his forms and rubber-stamping them with his personal *honko,* he stood and bowed—first to Cain and then to Umiko.

She returned the inspector's bow. *"Domo arigato gozaimashita."* She bowed a second time, this time even lower. *"Domo arigato gozaimashita."*

"What's next?" Cain asked Umiko.

"They have filed the report in their computer, and if a police officer finds Bonnie, they will call you. I also gave him my number."

"That's exactly why I didn't want to come here. This was a complete waste of time! I could have been out there looking for Bonnie."

She placed her hand on his elbow and guided him toward the exit. "We never came here only to file a police report. I came with you to overhear what the police were saying. And I think I have what you need."

"What do you mean?" Cain asked as the sliding doors opened automatically when the motion sensor detected their movement.

"When I mentioned the orange Skyline to the inspector, I overheard another inspector say that it sounded like a yakuza member named Watanabe, who goes by the street name Hayabusa. That means 'falcon' in Japanese. I don't know who he is, but he must be important for the police to know him by name. You have at least a more specific name now to investigate. Do you still have friends in the government back in America who can help you? The United States has files on everybody. WikiLeaks is proof of that."

Cain caught himself nodding yes with each second as he grew more confident. "Yes, I still have a contact in the Secret Service who owes me a favor—a big one!"

"Have you eaten?" a worried Umiko asked.

"Just an American dog a few hours ago, but I don't have time to eat right now. Th—"

"I know a noodle place nearby. My treat."

"I don't have time to eat."

"You are not able to think clearly to help your sister. Please stop and eat. Do it so you can find Bonnie."

Cain paused before responding. "You're right. You're always right, Umi."

"You said yourself you are the only one looking for Bonnie. That means you must take care of your body and your mind first."

The restaurant reminded Cain of a Waffle House, but it served only drinks and soba, a broth with thick noodles. Umiko ordered for them.

Cain sat but was frantic. "I've gone to Bonnie's apartment. I didn't see anything tangible there. I went to the embassy, then the Angel Cloud. They wouldn't let me in. I've gotta find a way into the Angel Cloud, and I need to find out where—"

"Cain-san, you are going to find your sister. But first you have to eat something. You look exhausted." Umiko frowned.

"My body is starving, Umi, but I can't even think about that right now. My mind is racing. In the United States, there is only a small window of opportunity to find a missing person. It's about twenty-four hours."

"You are going to find your sister. I can feel it. She is very lucky to have you in her life."

"I'm the lucky one. To have her as my sister and you helping me."

Umiko smiled and then poured some green tea into her cup and sipped it.

Their food arrived, and both started eating.

"Oh, this is spicy," Cain said. "It's very tasty."

"I told her that you wanted yours extra spicy since you are from Louisiana."

Cain smiled and continued devouring his meal.

The broth and noodles, paired with tempura, cleared his head. "I'm too reliant on the trains and taxis here. I have to get a car. Do you know someone who can help me get a car? It can be anything."

"I don't have a car, but I have a motorcycle I never use."

"That's awesome! Where's it at?"

"My apartment."

CHAPTER 59

"I'VE GOTTA MAKE some calls," Cain said. "I'll just stay here in the lobby while you go upstairs."

"I'll be right back," Umiko said, and darted upstairs to her apartment to retrieve the keys to her bike.

Cain pulled out his cell phone and paced back and forth in the lobby.

"Tanaka, it's Cain," he blurted out before Tanaka could even answer with the standard *"Mushi, mushi"* greeting. "I'm calling because I need your help at the office."

"Yes. I will help you." Tanaka answered as if he had been asleep and suddenly awakened.

"I'm leaving you in charge of the team for the next few days. I don't have time to fill you in with all the details right now, but I'm going to be chasing down some leads. I need you to cover for me at work."

"*Hai.* Of course. It would be my honor."

"Thank you, Tanaka-san. I appreciate it."

"Mr. Cain, I am very sorry about what happened to Bonnie. I feel very responsible."

"There's no time for those feelings right now," Cain said. "That's not going to help us find Bonnie."

"You must be careful, Cain-san. You once told me that trouble finds you."

"I'm counting on it."

"Ganbatte!" Tanaka said to wish him good luck.

Cain hung up the phone and started dialing an American number. Right before the call connected, Umiko emerged from the elevator. He disconnected and shoved the phone into his pocket. He opened the lobby door for her and followed behind her, as she led the way through the parking garage. In the corner were a dozen scooters in each of several rows and twice as many bicycles.

Cain scanned the sea of black and silver scooters. "I don't see any motorcycles," he commented.

"Oh, I'm sorry. I think I used the wrong word. And I apologize about the color. It's not very discreet."

In the far corner was a scooter painted robin's-egg blue. "Well"—he searched for the right words—"it certainly fits you perfectly."

Umiko grinned. "It's custom paint. It's my way of being a rebel."

"A rebel." Cain smiled. "I love how having a greenish-blue scooter makes you look like a rebel in Japan."

"Will it work for you?" she asked. "It's more powerful than the forty-nine cc engines, so it's legal on the highway."

"It's no Harley, but beggars can't be choosy. It should do the job."

"Great! I'm thankful to be useful."

"I'm the thankful one." Cain exhaled deeply. "You've helped me out so much tonight. I'd be lost without you."

"I'm pleased to help you." Umiko's keys were secured on a small pink-and-gold cherry blossom key chain. "Here." She held the keys in the air, dangling from her fingertips.

"Sakura." Cain used the Japanese word for cherry blossom as he reached for the keys. When their hands touched, Umiko folded hers into his, and she blushed.

"Please let me know if you need anything else," she said.

"You've done so much for me, Umi. I don't know how I can ever repay you."

"Just find your sister, Cain-san."

Cain felt butterflies in his stomach as he got caught up in the moment. He stepped closer to her, placed his hands on the outside of her arms, and leaned in. His solid body pressed against her tiny frame. He felt her heart beating fast—like the fluttering wings of a hummingbird.

His lips touched her soft, full lips. He held the kiss for only a second.

Umiko slowly opened her eyes and smiled.

"That felt wonderful," he said. "It felt right. *You* felt right. I wish I could stay longer, but I've got to go."

"I understand," Umiko said. "Remember. *Mushin.* One mind."

Cain turned toward the scooter and Umiko spoke up. "One more thing. I almost forgot." She reached into the compartment underneath the seat and removed a helmet that matched the color of her scooter.

"No way!" he protested. "Ain't gonna happen!"

"It is the law. You can't afford to be stopped by the police," she warned. "A traffic stop in Japan would delay you for at least thirty minutes—maybe even longer."

Fuckin' Japan and its stupid laws! he thought as he snapped on the helmet. *They don't give a damn about the yakuza kidnapping an American, but don't be caught without a helmet!* He swung his leg easily over the scooter and started the 125cc engine. It purred quietly.

"I'll call you," Umiko said, "if I hear from the police about Bonnie."

He nodded to acknowledge her and said, "Sayonara."

"Not *sayonara,*" she replied. "That word has a certain finality to it. *Mata ne* — see you soon." She smiled.

Cain was on a mission — a mission that would have only one outcome, he promised himself. *Mushin,* he thought as he rolled the throttle and cruised off into the night to find Bonnie.

CHAPTER 60

THE SMALL SUZUKI Address V125G scooter was not conducive to Cain's six-foot frame. *At least it's quiet and reliable,* he thought. He cruised the backstreets of Yokohama's complicated maze of narrow streets and dark alleys. *Driving on the opposite side of the road is a lot harder than I thought it would be. Thank God this thing doesn't draw attention,* he thought. He then laughed at himself for even thinking that a six-foot gaijin on a robin's-egg-blue scooter with a helmet to match would go unnoticed. *I must look like one of those bears that ride around on a unicycle in a Russian circus.* But then he smiled, fondly remembering Frank Rogers. *Even the Devil eats flies when he has to.*

Cain navigated the roadways as best he could. His eyes darted from sign to sign. Traffic advisories, distances in kilometers, and directions were on the left, right, and above him. Eighty percent of the signs were written in a mixture of Japan's three alphabet systems: hiragana, katakana, and kanji. The other 20 percent were thankfully in English.

"Oh, there's Chinatown!" he said aloud. Yokohama's Chinatown had one of the world's largest concentrations of Chinese shops and culture outside

Beijing, and the neighborhood was a popular tourist destination. During the day, it was a grand area to be experienced with the senses—bright colors of red and yellow to stimulate the sight, and a variety of aromas to awaken the nose. Some smells were pleasant and inviting, others hideous and foul. The last time Cain had visited was at lunchtime on a weekday. Raw chickens had been hung upside down by sidewalk vendors who were eager to advertise their lunch specials consisting of kung pao chicken, chow mein, and Peking roasted duck. But at this witching hour, Chinatown reminded Cain of an abandoned town that had once been a thriving civilization. The bright-red columns and elongated fire-breathing-dragon murals offered a stark cultural difference from Japan's more subdued culture of bonsai trees, geishas, and the samurai warrior class. The black Chinese characters that were painted on the building made it look as though someone had just thrown black confetti against the brick and it had stuck. Cain didn't know what the writing meant—only that it was made up of Chinese characters.

The putrid odor of rotting trash in overstuffed bins followed Cain like a shadow as he rode through the heart of Chinatown. The only discernible activity was two rats scurrying along the dark alley, one chewing on a piece of what looked like the remains of a sliced carrot. The foul smells were replaced with the familiar odor of Tokyo Bay. *There's the sea! I've got my bearings now.*

Cain saw the large green sign that let him know the toll road was up ahead. He merged onto the toll road and saw the lighted booth. He stopped a couple of feet before the wooden barrier, and the uniformed toll employee greeted him with the kindness of a man who hadn't seen a friend in weeks. The elderly employee bowed and then extended both his hands, which were holding a plastic tray to collect the fare. The exact amount was displayed on a large screen in Cain's direct line of sight. He reached into his pocket and pulled out the yennies and placed them on the tray. The barricade arm lifted and Cain rolled the throttle.

The engine whined louder before the scooter started moving. The multilane toll road was well lit under the dark sky, but the cloud layer prevented any stars from shining through. The cool, humid air blew against Cain's face. The only sounds were the hum of the engine and the air rushing past his ears. *This is eerie,* he thought. *Where are all the other cars? How can everybody in a city of nine million be sleeping? What is Bonnie doing? Is she being tortured or sexually abused?* He couldn't stomach the thought.

Cain pushed those awful thoughts away and remembered his Zen retreat. *Mushin. Live in the moment.*

He rolled the throttle as much as he could, but the scooter wouldn't budge past eighty kilometers per hour. The big city was behind him—far behind him now. He passed the marina and gazed at all the sailboats and private yachts that were docked. Most displayed Japanese flags high on the bow, but there were a few luxury yachts with foreign flags. *There's an American, a New Zealand…Huh. That's some type of Middle Eastern flag. Wonder what they're doing all the way out here.*

Cain rode the last stretch of the road that led to Sato's company. He pulled up to the closed gate and the security guard cautiously approached. The guard's left hand gripped the Maglite flashlight that rested on his left shoulder, just as Cain had taught him. Before Cain had arrived, none of the security guards had been shown how to use their four-cell D-battery Maglite as a baton against a burglar if necessary.

"*Konnichiwa,*" Cain said in greeting, squinting his eyes to protect them from the flashlight's blinding beam.

"Cain-san," the guard replied with a big grin, and exhaled a sigh of relief. He bowed several times. "You surprise me at this hour."

"I like how prepared you were, though. Well done! *Yoku yattane!*"

"*Hai.*"

"How are you tonight?"

"Very good. It is very quiet."

"Quiet is good, especially in this business," Cain said. "I need to go to my office for a bit."

"*Hai!*" The guard rushed back to his shack and pushed the button to open the gate.

"*Arigato,*" Cain said. "Head on a swivel," he reminded the guard as he lifted his legs. Cain was about to throttle the scooter when he noticed that the guard looked confused. Cain instantly realized that the guard had interpreted his instruction literally. He immediately rephrased. "Be alert. *Ki o tsukete.*"

"*Hai,*" the guard said with visible relief.

Cain smiled at the visual the guard must have seen when Cain told him "Head on a swivel." He rolled through the gate and up to the main building.

Inside his office, Cain forwent the overhead fluorescent and instead opted for the small desk lamp he had purchased from IKEA. He yanked on its chain and collapsed into his black faux-leather roller chair. He exhaled deeply. *Bonnie, how in the hell did we get ourselves into this shit?* He leaned back into his chair and stared at the ceiling. *Where are you, Bonnie? Talk to me. Send me a message.*

He heard a familiar voice answer, but it wasn't Bonnie's. It was the calm, reassuring voice of his father. *No matter what's going on around you, son, always fly the airplane.* Cain had been only twelve years old when his father said it. *This is the most important thing in flying and in life: Take the controls.*

Cain straightened his legs to make it easier to retrieve his cell phone and money clip from his front pockets. He tossed all the contents on his desk. He saw the red-and-gold Old Ebbitt Grill matchbook staring at him. Cain was about to do what he never thought he would do. Even considering it ate at his core. There was nothing left; he was simply out of options. *Bonnie, you know how much anger I have toward the Service now, for ruining my career and reputation. But for you I'll make this call.*

He picked up the landline, momentarily stared at the phone, and started dialing the number.

CHAPTER 61

"HAYES SPEAKING," the familiar voice answered. The line was remarkably clear for an international call.

"LeRoy the King Hayes," Cain said slowly and methodically.

"I never thought I'd hear from you again, Cain," LeRoy said. "I thought the swamps had swallowed you up, but I guess you called to get the scoop, huh?"

"Sure did," Cain replied without having any idea what "scoop" LeRoy was talking about.

"Yep, it's true," the King offered.

"Okay," Cain replied. "I confess. I have no idea what you're talking about."

"You're joking, right?"

"Afraid not. Seriously. I have no idea what you're talking about."

"What rock have you been hiding under?" LeRoy asked.

"I'm in Japan. Been working here for a while now."

"Oh, shit! I thought you were calling because of the news."

Cain's patience was wearing thin. "What *news* are you talking about? The only news I have is bad news."

"Your old partner was fired."

"Tomcat?"

"Well, it wasn't Jill," LeRoy replied.

"It was about time Jackson's actions caught up to him."

"That idiot got drunk at the Hinckley Hotel and put his hands on the wrong woman. She was the daughter of a congressman. The hotel provided the surveillance video. Needless to say, it was no secret that his services were no longer needed, and I perp walked him off the premises myself."

Cain smiled, but for only a second. He didn't have time to revel in that satisfying news.

LeRoy continued. "I imagine he's fretting that the congressman will push for sexual-assault charges against him. If convicted, he'll be a registered sex offender and never get a job again."

The more Cain thought about it, the sadder he felt for Tom's wife and daughters and about the embarrassment suffered by the family.

"I thought you'd love hearing that," LeRoy said when Cain didn't respond.

"Under different circumstances, probably. How's Beth taking it?"

"She's already filed for divorce and hired the most ruthless divorce attorney. They'll go after Jackson's retirement. She'll probably be rich when all this is over."

"She was never interested in the money," Cain replied. "She just wanted a loving family. Jackson ruined his own life. But I've got more important fish to fry right now. I need your help, LeRoy. And you owe me one."

"I owe you? How do you figure that? I gave you your options and *you* chose, not me. Now, I admit the Service served you a shit sandwich. Matter of fact, you got yours without the bread, but that ain't my fault."

"Dammit, LeRoy! You know I wouldn't have called you unless I really needed your help."

LeRoy seemed unsettled by the unusual urgency and desperation in Cain's voice. "I will help you if I can. What do you need?"

"I need the Service files on a CEO named Koichi Sato and his company, and—"

"Say what?" LeRoy interrupted.

"And a yakuza member who goes by the moniker Hayabusa."

"Who the hell do you think you are? Jason Bourne? There ain't no way in hell I can give you that information! Jesus Christ, Cain! They would fire my ass just like they did that chickenshit Jackson."

"They won't fire you. They *can't* fire you. You have a discrimination lawsuit against them. It would look like retaliation."

"Boy, you better lay off the sake because you ain't thinking clear. This kind of shit is exactly what they're looking for. This could be the nail in my coffin they've been looking for. I'm sorry, Cain. I would help you if I could, but I've got way too much to lose."

"Like your sister?" Cain quietly replied.

"What are you talking about?"

"The yakuza kidnapped Bonnie. I've got nowhere else to turn," Cain said without emotion.

LeRoy knew and liked Bonnie. He had met her at the Secret Service's annual Christmas party at the White House and had told Cain he thought she was feisty.

"Bonnie is good people, and it sickens me to

think she is in danger. Are you sure it was yakuza?" LeRoy asked.

"Beyond a shadow of a doubt," Cain replied. "But if you ain't gonna help Bonnie, I gotta go now."

"Just hold on a sec," LeRoy said. "You know I can't help you like *that*. You know the rules and regulations almost better than anyone. It's illegal. Worse than getting fired, it could land my ass up in the pokey. But let's just say, hypothetically, of course, I wanted to mail you a Christmas card. Where would I send it?"

"Don't worry about it. I'll be long gone before Christmas."

"Okay, then." LeRoy coughed to clear his throat. He seemed to place his mouth closer to the phone's receiver. "Let's say I wanted to mail you a"—he paused for a moment—"an early Christmas gift. Something for you and Bonnie both. What's the address I'd use?"

Cain rummaged through his money clip, looking for Tanaka's business card. "Here, use this address." He read it over the phone.

"Got it," LeRoy said. "Happy fishing."

Cain disconnected from LeRoy and was putting Tanaka's pristine business card back into his money clip when he saw the business card that Rose from the embassy had given him for the *Stars and Stripes* reporter. CHAMP ALBRIGHT THE THIRD, it read. INVESTIGATIVE JOURNALIST FOR THE FAR EAST DIVISION.

Oh, God, I hate the press. Never thought in a million years there'd be a scenario where I'd need the help of your kind. But this must be a sign, because you keep turning up.

CHAPTER 62

"THIS IS CAT," the man answered with a Southern twang.

"Um." Cain was caught off guard by the nickname and twang. He was used to Southern accents, but this one had a rushed cadence to it. "I was looking for Champ Albright."

"You got the Cat—Champ Albright the Third. What can I do for ya?"

"Your business card was given to me at the American embassy."

"*Who* at the American embassy?"

"Mr. Rose."

"It's about time that old bureaucrat passed out my card. You must be in some kind of trouble, then. I've been working him for years, and he's never given my card to anyone."

"Well, I am—"

"In a bit of trouble?" Champ interjected. "Look, I'm really busy covering a story for the navy's Seventh Fleet. If you've got something worthwhile, just spit it out."

"My sister was kidnapped by the yakuza."

Champ cleared his throat. "What did you say your name was?"

"I didn't."

"I'm an *investigative journalist,* not a mind reader. So, if this is some kind of joke—"

"I don't joke about this kind of stuff."

"Me, either. So we got that in common."

"My name is Cain Lemaire."

"The only Cain Lemaire I know is the one who the Secret Service fired, and he found himself on the front page of the *Japan Times* bleeding all over one of the most important CEOs in this country."

"I figured this was a waste of my time, but I did it for Bonnie." Cain sighed.

"Bonnie Lemaire? Of course. Dammit. This case has me so busy I wasn't thinking straight. Who's Bonnie to you?"

"My twin sister. She said she knows you. I'm hoping that means you're her friend."

"Ha!" Champ snickered. "I wouldn't say we're friends. My friends help me."

"Look! I'm sleep-deprived, angry, and in an emergency situation. I'm not in the mood for your riddles."

"I know your sister, but she wasn't any help to me. She dated a navy lieutenant—a supply officer—who was embezzling ship funds and fabricating false contracts. I interviewed her in hopes that she could help me break the story."

"She never told me that."

"Yet you make it sound like you're not surprised."

"Nobody's perfect."

"I like to think I am," Champ quipped. "My wife would probably disagree, though." He chuckled. "It's hard—perhaps impossible—to live up to the expectations of Japanese in-laws."

"Bonnie's had bad luck with boyfriends, to say the least."

"Sounds like it—going from naval officers to yakuza members."

"Look, I don't want to talk about this over the phone. Can we—"

"Amen!" Champ exclaimed. "Neither do I. Damn NSA's been bugging my phone. I've always known it, but WikiLeaks has proven it. Reporters are not protected from espionage anymore. Even the damn CIA is now infiltrating nonprofit organizations. It's a different era we live in."

Oh, God, Cain thought. *A conspiracy nut.*

"I'm on a stakeout right now, but I'd be willing to meet up with you at four thirty p.m. Meet me at—"

"We gotta meet up earlier," Cain insisted. "I'll buy you breakfast. A good old-fashioned American breakfast, not fish and salad."

"No can do," Champ responded. "I'm tied up until then. Meet me at the pachinko club next to the Yokosuka Chuo Station."

"What's the name of it?"

"You read Japanese?"

"No."

"That's what I thought," Champ said with mild annoyance. "It's in Yokosuka—by the navy base. If you can't find it, you'll *never* find your sister. Oh, and one last thing."

"Yes?"

"Come alone," Champ instructed.

"I *am* alone," Cain replied.

CHAPTER 63

CAIN'S FATIGUE HAD caught up with him. He hadn't slept since Saturday night. He strained to keep his eyes open, and when they were, his vision blurred more and more. He folded his arms on top of his desk and rested his head on them. He fell into a deep sleep.

Cain shot awake when Tanaka shook his shoulders. It took Cain a few seconds to recall where he was. "I can't believe you were able to sneak up on me like that, Tanaka. I must be slipping."

"Cain-san, you look exhausted. Let me get you something to drink."

Cain's heart raced and his breathing matched that rapid pace.

"What time is it?"

"It's five o'clock," Tanaka answered as he headed to the break room, presumably to buy Cain a coffee from the vending machine.

Cain had been asleep for only a few hours, but it felt like half the day. He stood. "I'm late. I've gotta go."

Tanaka handed him the hot can of Suntory Boss coffee as Cain was leaving the office.

Cain popped the top and guzzled the coffee while Tanaka looked on with wide eyes.

"Thank you," Cain said, and tossed the can into the recycle bin. "Call me if you need anything." He left the office and sprinted across the empty parking lot toward Umiko's scooter. It dawned on him that it was five in the morning, not in the evening. When he stopped at Umiko's robin's-egg-blue scooter, which looked more pronounced when sparkling in the sun-rays, he heard her voice in his head telling him to take care of himself first, that he can't help Bonnie if he's not healthy. He thought, *She's right.* The wind picked up and he suddenly caught a musty whiff of himself. *I need to shower and get a fresh pair of clothes. I smell like sweat, BO, Zen retreat, Chinatown, and Tokyo Bay all bottled up.*

Cain rode to his apartment, showered, shaved his several days of stubble, and threw on a pair of cargo pants and a button-up short-sleeve shirt. He stood at his balcony door and overlooked Yokohama Bay. He could see the iconic Ferris wheel and tons of commuters starting their workday. The conversation with Champ Albright kept replaying itself in his mind. *I am alone,* he'd told Champ. But now Cain realized that while it was his fight, he still had a shipmate who could help. He grabbed his phone and called Chief Alvarez.

"Hurricane! It's great to hear from you. What's cooking?"

Cain skipped the pleasantries. "My sister, Bonnie, has been kidnapped by some Japanese criminals," he said. "They don't want ransom. They want to punish her for what I did."

"How can I help?"

"I'm meeting a reporter with the *Stars and Stripes* this afternoon."

"Who is it?" Chief Alvarez asked. "I might know 'em."

"Champ Albright. You know him?"

"Yeah, I know him. He's a weasel, but he's well connected. He's got a Japanese wife and he speaks the language. He's a strange cat, though."

"That's ironic," Cain said. "He goes by the nickname Cat. Look, I don't know how else to say this…"

"Just shoot it straight and level, Hurricane, like you always have."

"I don't want to involve you. That's the last thing I wanna do. You still have your career ahead of you, and you're drawing closer to either getting promoted to senior chief or retirement. But you remember those expeditionary bags the navy used to give us when we were flying on deployments?"

"*Affirm.*"

"Where could I *procure* one of those?"

"Um, hmm. I think I'm smelling what you're stepping in. Meet me at the bar on the southwest corner of Shiyakushomae Park in Yokosuka. I'll have one for you."

"I see the chiefs still run the navy," Cain said.

Alvarez shouted the navy's battle cry: *"Hooyah!"*

CHAPTER 64

CAIN RECOGNIZED YOKOSUKA from a distance. As he crossed the bridge that merged the toll road with Highway 16, he could see both the Japanese and American navy bases off to the left. In the water were several military ships. There were a few submarines with submariners walking on top of them. The officers appeared to be inspecting something. Behind them were the destroyer battleships, and in the greater distance was the lone USS *George Washington* aircraft carrier. It looked more like a skyscraper than a ship. Although aircraft carriers had been based in Yokosuka for several decades, this was the first nuclear-powered one. Many Japanese citizens had protested its arrival out of fear of nuclear contamination.

Cain continued into the heart of Yokosuka, passing the multilevel Daiei shopping mall. The heavily fortified entrance to the American Navy base was on his left. Outside the gates, standing alone on the sidewalk, was a lone uniformed Japanese police officer. He stood watch, holding his *keijo* alongside him. Umiko had previously told Cain that the *keijo*—a police stick— was used to fend off potential attackers. She said that the police often trained in kendo.

Cain parked Umiko's scooter at the foot of a three-story building on the opposite side of the military base. A nearby elementary school was dismissing students for the day. A flock of joyful kids, wearing stiff leather backpacks over their black-and-white school uniforms, flooded the congested area. Cain recalled a conversation he'd had with Umiko about children's backpacks.

"Back in Louisiana," Cain had explained, "they're called book bags. For obvious reasons, you store your textbooks in 'em."

"Here they are called *randoseru*," Umiko had replied. "They are very expensive. They can cost as much as sixty thousand yen!"

Cain did the math in his head. "That's a little more than seven hundred bucks!"

"*Hai.* That's why many times grandparents will buy them. But the child will keep the same one from first to sixth grade. It used to be that boys would get black and girls would get red, but Japan is changing a little bit. You'll see some girls get pink now, and some boys will choose brown or blue."

Thinking of Umiko warmed Cain's heart. *I need to call her soon,* he reminded himself.

Cain didn't know the name of the street, only that Chief Alvarez had said all the Americans referred to it as Blue Street since all the signs were in blue. When Cain crossed the side street where the Nawlins restaurant was, fond memories of his date with Umiko flashed in his memory. He felt lucky that she had come into his life when she did.

He approached the bar that Chief Alvarez had suggested. The front entrance and wall were completely made of glass, and a dim red light from within illuminated the small place. Through the glass

Cain could see a large wooden bar that formed an L shape and a familiar face sitting in the corner of the empty room.

Cain opened the door and joined Chief Alvarez at a back table. Alvarez handed him a heavy backpack. Cain unzipped it and carefully explored its contents without taking any of the items out.

The bartender, who wore a black vest over a white long-sleeve dress shirt, took their order.

"Two old-fashioneds," Chief Alvarez said before turning to Cain. "You gotta try these. You'll love 'em."

"That's fine," Cain replied.

After the bartender brought them the drinks, Cain leaned in and asked, "What do you know about the yakuza?"

"We had one sailor—naive kid from Kansas or Kentucky. Maybe even Iowa. I can't remember exactly where. But we called him Big Country. He got into a fight with one of them yakuza jokers at a bar in Tokyo. It was one of those places that was not friendly to the round eye, if you know what I mean. But Big Country thought *nobody* was going to tell him where he could and could not buy a drink."

"Well?" Cain asked, eager to hear the rest of the story.

"The yakuza slashed him up real bad. It was horrible. NCIS got involved and tried to work with the Tokyo police, but they could never make any headway without the assistance of the Japanese police."

"That seems to be a recurring theme," Cain said. "The American embassy told me practically the same thing. I just don't understand it. How can the yakuza operate with such impunity?"

"How in the hell would I know? I'm just a chief.

That yakuza realm is a whole separate world, and I'm not part of it."

"What happened to Big Country?"

"He wanted to cooperate with the investigation, but he was too afraid. They had stolen his ID and said they knew who he was, and that they'd come looking for him. They even said they had people in America that could find him."

"Yakuza in America?"

Alvarez nodded.

Cain looked at the time on his phone. "Thank you for the bag and the drink, but I gotta go. I'm meeting with Champ."

"You want me to go with you?" Alvarez asked.

Cain shook his head. "He was adamant about me going alone. If I can't handle a *Stars and Stripes* reporter, then going against the yakuza will be a disaster."

"Oh, it's gonna be a disaster. I promise you that."

Cain tilted his head and squinted his eyes, not quite sure how to take the chief's comment.

"For them, that is," Chief Alvarez remarked with confidence.

CHAPTER 65

CAIN WALKED TOWARD the white multilevel building with a huge red banner that went from one side of the structure to the other advertising PACHINKO. The motion-sensored double doors slid open. The sound inside was deafening, a stark contrast to Japan's normal adherence to tranquility. *Well, this is certainly different!* Cain thought. *This is like a mini Vegas.* Japanese men sat in endless rows of chairs that were arranged in front of brightly lit and multicolored machines. Through the heavy fog of cigarette smoke, Cain observed men furiously slapping the flippers and watching the metal balls flinging around inside the machine's glassed chamber.

It should be easy to spot Champ in here, he reckoned. *Yup, that's gotta be the Cat.* Cain walked toward the only non-Japanese in the place. Even if the man wasn't American, he would have stood out. He wasn't wearing a dark suit like the other patrons. Champ wore a fedora that matched the brown tweed waistcoat that he had on over his long-sleeve white button-up. Instead of a cigarette, a wooden pipe hung lazily from his mouth. Cain couldn't help but smirk as he thought, *The* New

York Times *called and they'd like their star reporter from the 1930s back*.

Cain sat in the empty chair next to Champ, put down his expeditionary bag, and started playing the machine in front of him. "What gives? You got a gambling addiction?"

"Every man has his vice." Champ spoke quickly, as if he was in a rush. "For some, it's alcohol and prostitutes." He turned to look at Cain; perhaps he was alluding to how Cain had gotten fired from the Secret Service. "Maybe even religion. My vices are simple. I call them the trifecta."

Cain leaned in toward Champ, straining to hear him over the tremendous noise of the metal balls bouncing around inside all the machines in the establishment.

"Pachinko, America, and—"

"America?" Cain interrupted. "America is a vice nowadays?"

"I'm a flag-waving American who serves my country—perhaps not in the military like you did, but I serve by keeping people in powerful positions honest to those they serve. I hate having to air out dirty laundry, but somebody's gotta take out the trash. It's a responsibility I shoulder. I don't expect you to understand. You took an oath of secrecy. I took mine to expose the secrets of corruption."

"My oath was to defend the Constitution," Cain said as he considered Champ's words. "Finish the third so we can move on with this story."

"I *was* telling you what my third vice was when you rudely cut me off."

"Gomen nosai," Cain said flatly.

"Ah, very good. Saying you're sorry might be the most important phrase for foreigners to learn here in Japan. Who taught you that? Japanese girlfriend?

They love Americans, you know. Mine tricked me years ago with foot massages and green tea served when I'd get off work. Then, before you know it, you've been married for seven years. If seven is lucky, I'd hate to see what year eight brings."

"I don't know how you endure it," Cain said with dry sarcasm.

"Ha!" Champ chuckled. "Don't let the stereotype fool you. You wanna know the difference between an American wife and a Japanese wife?"

"Look, I don't have time for all your damn games," Cain said.

Completely unfazed and without skipping a beat, Champ answered his own question. "An American wife will call you an asshole in public. A Japanese wife will wait till you're home." Champ let out a belly laugh.

"There are more serious issues at hand. Let's go somewhere quieter."

"The noise is safety. Keeps the NSA from hearing my conversations."

Oh, God. Not this conspiracy nonsense again. Cain's head fell backward and he looked at the billow of cigarette smoke that clouded the ceiling.

"My grandfather was a great reporter," Champ began. "I'm actually named after him. He earned a Pulitzer for his coverage of the Kennedy assassination in Dallas. Per your inquiry, that's my third vice: the relentless pursuit of getting a Pulitzer."

"You ain't gonna earn one in this broke-ass casino. The battlefield is a better place."

"Been there, done that." Champ grabbed his pipe from his mouth. He looked around the parlor and leaned in toward Cain. "What I'm about to expose out here is going to make international headlines. Heads will roll! All the way to PACFLEET in Hawaii, and maybe even into the halls of the Pentagon." Champ leaned back toward his machine and slapped the lever.

"Mr. Rose believed you'd be able to help me find Bonnie," said Cain. "He obviously overexaggerated your abilities."

That struck a nerve with the high-energy reporter. "You government functionaries are pretty dense at times."

Cain felt the blood rush to his head as he clenched his hand and hammer-fisted Champ's pachinko machine, cracking the glass and scaring Champ in the process.

The noisy casino went silent for a moment while all the patrons stared at Cain.

"They're going to make you pay for that," Champ said nervously.

"My family already has," Cain replied. He stood and yelled, "You're a waste of my time. I'm outta here."

"Wait!" Champ grabbed Cain's arm and tried to pull him to sit back down, but Cain was too strong to be budged by Champ. "I'll help you."

"So far I've gotten riddles and a history of your family tree, but no help."

"You wanna find the animals who kidnapped your sister? I know where to look."

Cain's ears perked up. "Where?"

"What makes the yakuza different from the everyday Japanese person?"

Cain rolled his eyes in frustration and then thought for just a second. "They commit crimes."

"Physically, I mean."

Cain thought again. "They have tattoos."

"Exactly! Tattoos are taboo here in Japanese culture.

You don't see any advertised around here. But who *does* get tattoos on the island?"

"The American military," Cain replied. It was as if a light bulb had turned on.

"You're batting two for two!" Champ removed his cocktail from the napkin it had been resting on. He pulled a pen from his vest's inner pocket and started scribbling something on the napkin. "This is the name of a tattoo place I'd check out if I were you. It's here in Yokosuka. It's"—he lifted his hands and used air quotes—"'rumored to be frequented by yakuza members.'" Champ put his drink down. "A rogue American, with nothing to lose and disrupting the *wa* in the process, will get the heat off *my* investigation into the Seventh Fleet. I'll use that to my advantage."

"Let's get two things straight," Cain fired back. "One: I'm not interested in your Seventh Fleet investigation. And riddle me this: what's thicker than water?"

"Blood?" Champ answered hesitantly.

"Good. You're batting one for one," Cain responded. "Two: I have *everything* to lose." He grabbed the napkin from Champ and headed for the exit.

"You're welcome," Champ shouted, and then, under his breath as he returned to his pachinko machine, "Unless they kill you tonight."

CHAPTER 66

CAIN LEFT THE pachinko parlor and marched toward the tattoo shop, Dragon's Ink. He referenced Champ's scribbled directions on the napkin. *That's convenient,* he thought as he saw that he'd parked Umiko's scooter right in front of the building before he had met with Chief Alvarez earlier that day.

Cain looked skyward. The building appeared to be only about three stories high, and it wasn't that wide. That type of construction was common in Japan because of the limited space. He pulled on the glass door and entered the tiny lobby. A directory was on the wall. Dragon's Ink was listed as the business on the third floor.

He ascended a narrow stairway. Each floor of the complex was occupied by only one door that led to the single business on that level.

With each step, Cain's legs moved faster and his heart beat harder. It felt as though an invisible magnet was pulling him. He reached the third floor and saw the only door. Elaborate stickers and artwork covered its entire surface. In the center was wording in both English and Japanese. The English said DRAGON'S INK, and below that was smaller text that said GI-FRIENDLY.

"Good," Cain muttered under his breath, "because I'm coming in." He took a deep breath and exhaled. He used the crook of his elbow to wipe the sweat from his forehead. A popular Japanese-model doorbell, which also had a video camera and a two-way audio intercom system, was next to the doorknob.

Cain tried the door but it was locked. He rang the buzzer and could hear its alert sounding from within the studio. A few moments later, a scantily clad Japanese woman in her early twenties opened the door. She wore a black silk dress that revealed her cleavage.

"I'm here for a tattoo."

"Do you have appointment?" she asked.

"No, but I have cash. Lots of it."

She nodded and gestured for him to come inside and follow her. When she turned forward he saw elaborate tattoos that started at the nape of her neck and went down her back and out of view because of the dress. His confidence grew. *Yep, I'm at the right place. That style of tattoo looks a lot like Hayabusa's.*

The woman escorted Cain to a nearby love seat and motioned for him to sit. He put his expeditionary bag down on the floor. She opened the clear door of a small fridge and took out a bottle of Kirin Lager. She used the ring on her finger to pop the top off the bottle in a single rehearsed move.

Cain's eyes widened. "Didn't see that coming," he told her. "That was impressive."

Gripping the bottle with one hand while resting its bottom on the palm of her other hand, she presented the beer to him.

"Arigato," Cain said as he grabbed the chilled drink. "I've only had Asahi before. This'll be my first time with Kirin Lager."

She half smiled.

He took a sip. "*Aaah.* That's refreshing. Hits the spot." He read the label aloud: "'The legendary Kirin is a symbol of good luck.'" He took another swig. "Good, because I can use all the luck I can get."

The woman walked toward a rice-paper wall that divided the waiting room from the tattoo room. When she slid open the door for a few moments to leave, Cain saw a muscular customer sitting in the hydraulic chair. The black man had his shirt off, and the artist was inking a tribal pattern on his shoulder.

Cain could see the man's other tattoos and knew he had to be a sailor: he recognized the star tattoo on the man's chest. The North Star was a popular tattoo in the navy. It was how a sailor found his way back home.

Cain took another sip of his beer when he heard the low-pitched rumble of a car's exhaust getting louder as it neared. *That sounds just like the modified exhaust that Sabrina described.* At that moment, he overheard the tattoo artist and the woman speaking in Japanese. He had no idea what they were saying, but he understood one word from their conversation: Hayabusa. He knew that the word *falcon* would not be spoken in casual conversation. And their conversation seemed hurried, almost panicky. The rice-paper door slid open, and the Japanese woman headed toward the mini fridge. She grabbed a bottle of beer and cracked it open. She poured it into a cold glass and placed it onto a tray.

That's not the same treatment I got, he thought. *They're afraid of whoever is coming in.*

He turned toward the artist, who had stopped inking and was now looking through the window at the ground below.

The American customer looked confused. "What's

going on? You gonna finish my tat or what? I got ship duty tonight."

"New appointment. So sorry," the artist replied.

Cain walked toward the window and peered outside, directing his gaze at the street below. He saw the orange Skyline parked curbside, near Umiko's scooter. The exhaust was rumbling, and loud techno music boomed from the car speakers. Then everything went quiet. Hayabusa got out of the Skyline and walked toward the building. Cain looked at the beer in his hand. *Maybe there is something to this Kirin luck.*

The sailor grew impatient. "I ain't got all day. I gotta get back to base soon."

Cain turned toward the American. "Shit's about to go down, sailor. I don't want you involved in this." He raised a handful of cash. "Here's ten thousand yen for the inconvenience. Find another place to go." Cain hoped that the intensity on his face conveyed the life-or-death seriousness of the situation. The sailor got up from the reclined chair, tossed on his T-shirt, and snatched the money out of Cain's hand.

"Good luck, bro," the young sailor said as he headed to the exit.

"Take that woman with you on your way out. It's gonna get ugly in here."

"I gotcha," he replied.

"And leave that door open," Cain instructed. "I'm going to welcome him Cajun-style."

CHAPTER 67

THE SOUND OF rushed footsteps in the stairwell echoed louder as Hayabusa approached the third floor. The steps slowed and approached more cautiously, though, as they drew closer to the studio's open door.

Cain noticed that the tattooist stayed still behind the paper screen, where he couldn't be seen.

Hayabusa, wearing a snug black leather jacket and jeans, appeared at the doorway, obviously completely surprised that Cain was there.

"Watanabe Hayabusa," Cain said slowly and deliberately as they locked eyes. Hayabusa was wearing a new pair of rose-colored sunglasses. "I see you have a new pair of sunglasses," Cain said with a smirk. "What do I owe you?"

"Your sister," he replied.

Cain felt the adrenaline flooding his body and his sight becoming sharper. He instinctively looked at his opponent's hands. *The hands are what kill,* he could hear his Secret Service instructors saying at the academy.

"That must have hurt." Cain nodded toward Hayabusa's hand, where the pinky was supposed to be. "But it's going to pale in comparison to the hurt I'm about to deliver."

"I would have killed you last time had your friend not intervened," Hayabusa said.

"This time's gonna be a lot different than the last. I'm not drunk, and there aren't three of you. I'm going to break more than your nose, you little piece of shit."

Hayabusa looked as though he could sense Cain's determination and his menace. He turned quickly and eyed the exit. He darted toward the door, but Cain had anticipated this and raced across the room. He kicked the door shut with such force that the walls shook. Hayabusa reached into his jacket pocket, pulled out a butterfly knife, and flipped it open. Without hesitation, Cain grabbed his wrist with both hands and pulled it down toward his hip to secure it. He used his own body to push Hayabusa against the wall and pin him. He headbutted Hayabusa, crushing the sunglasses and cracking his already busted nose again. Hayabusa screamed in pain and dropped the knife.

"Where's my sister?" Cain screamed into Hayabusa's face.

Hayabusa used his legs to kick off the wall and free himself. He tried to rush toward the exit again, but Cain grabbed the back of his jacket. Hayabusa squirmed out of it and Cain dropped the jacket on the floor. Hayabusa was at the door and twisted the knob as Cain pummeled him from behind, putting him in a bear hug. Cain lifted him a foot into the air and slammed him onto the coffee table, scattering tattoo magazines across the floor. Cain reached down to punch Hayabusa, but Hayabusa used his left arm to block the strike. He grabbed Cain's hair, simultaneously putting his foot into his chest, and propelled Cain forward in a classic judo technique. Cain crashed into one of the waiting room chairs.

Hayabusa grabbed the opened Kirin Lager bottle that was nearby and broke it on the floor. The sharp ragged edges now protruded. He slashed wildly at Cain. The glass tore into Cain's flesh on the side of his neck, right below his ear.

Cain growled in pain. He wiped the blood from his ear and neck with his hand and was relieved it was light red in color. He knew that meant there was no arterial bleeding, so he didn't panic.

With Cain bleeding, Hayabusa apparently felt more confident and began taunting him. "Fuck your sister! She's on a boat heading to the Middle East. We will get a good price for her. You'll never see her again."

Cain scanned the room, searching for an object to use against the bladed bottle. In movies, he'd seen Jason Bourne use a magazine and a Korean master use a T-shirt, but this was real life. He spotted a banquet chair against the wall.

Cain opened both hands, palms facing skyward, and motioned to Hayabusa. "Come get me, you coward!"

With the bottle held tightly in his hand, Hayabusa lunged toward Cain. At the same time, Cain side-stepped and quickly grabbed the chair and swung it like a baseball bat. It impacted Hayabusa's midsection and thrust his body through the rice-paper wall and onto the floor.

The difference was noticeable right away. The waiting room had been dimly lit, but the tattoo artist's work space was brightly lit under a fluorescent bulb to provide him with the best illumination possible for his artwork. The suddenly exposed tattoo artist was frantic, trying to maneuver away from the violence.

Cain jumped on top of Hayabusa, who then wrapped his legs around Cain's torso and locked his ankles. He began jabbing his thumb into Cain's neck wound. Blood splattered across Cain's face and neck. It mixed with sweat and started to impair his vision.

He was breathing harder every second. He was in the greatest fight of his life and there was still the threat of the tattoo artist and any others who might come to the yakuza member's aid. Cain mustered all the strength he could and pushed himself up from the ground. Hayabusa's legs were still wrapped around Cain's body. Although Hayabusa weighed only about 130 pounds, it felt like two hundred pounds of dead weight. Cain's legs burned as he grunted to his feet and pushed forward all the way across the room until Hayabusa's head hit the wall, momentarily stunning him. Cain slammed him onto the hard floor and grabbed the tattoo pen from the table. He then sat on top of Hayabusa and screamed into his face, "Where is Bonnie? Where is my sister?"

Cain flipped the switch on the pen and the tattoo machine started buzzing. He pressed the pen against Hayabusa's face and started scribbling like a child with a coloring book.

Hayabusa screamed in agony as the needle seared through his skin. He thrashed his body violently as he tried to escape the unbearable pain, but Cain's full weight was on top of him.

Cain caught movement out of the corner of his eye. *There's another threat!* his mind shouted with alarm. He shifted his weight and quickly turned his attention to the tattoo artist, who immediately put his arms in the air in a gesture of submission.

"No E-E-Engrish," he stuttered nervously. "No p-p-probrem here."

In that brief moment of distraction, Hayabusa squirmed free and jumped to his feet. He sprinted toward the closed window and jumped right into the glass. The window broke and shards of glass shattered everywhere. Hayabusa screamed as his momentum propelled him into the night sky. Cain reached out to grab him, but it all happened way too fast. Hayabusa's shouts ended only with the thud when he smashed into Umiko's scooter below.

Cain watched from the window as a crowd began to assemble around Hayabusa. The crowd looked up at Cain and started pointing at him. He stepped back from the window and sat in the tattoo client's chair. He looked in the large mirror that was bolted to the wall. His face was pale and bloody. He looked like a wild animal. He grabbed a towel off the table. He brushed the broken glass out of his hair and off his shoulders. He cleaned the blood from his face and neck and tied the towel around his neck to serve as a makeshift tourniquet.

Cain snatched the black address book off the counter and flipped through it. It was full of dates, addresses, names, and telephone numbers. He stuffed it in his expeditionary bag and raced down the stairs to Hayabusa.

The glass had cut his head in multiple locations, and a broken rib protruded from his shirt. Hayabusa was suffocating on his own blood.

Cain leaned in and stopped about four inches from his face. He could feel Hayabusa's hot, laboring breath.

"Where is Bonnie?"

Hayabusa tried to say something, but Cain couldn't

understand it. All he could hear was blood gurgling. Hayabusa's eyes rolled back, and he stopped breathing.

Cain yanked him off Umiko's scooter and tossed him aside. The headlight and turn signals were busted, and the handlebar was bent. The scooter was too badly damaged to ride.

"Shit!" Cain muttered under his breath. "Shit, shit, shit!"

A police whistle pierced the air. It sounded again. Cain looked up and could see a Japanese police officer running straight toward him from the military base. Several military guards were trailing behind. They would be on top of Cain in less than twenty seconds.

CHAPTER 68

CAIN REACHED INTO Hayabusa's jean pocket and found a set of keys. He ran toward the orange Skyline and opened the door. He fumbled with the keys until he found the right one. The car's exhaust rumbled to life, along with the techno music blaring through the speakers.

The Japanese police officer appeared at the driver's side window. He was yelling something in Japanese when the American military police arrived. They tried to open the door, but Cain had locked it. One of the guards drew his expandable baton and raised it in the air. He was about to break the driver's side window.

Cain pressed the clutch and shifted the stick into drive. His boot heel pushed the pedal to the floorboard. The tires squealed as they struggled to gain traction. The Skyline fishtailed as it fled the crime scene.

Cain's eyes darted wildly in every direction as he escaped capture. His heart thumped against his chest like a drum and his thoughts rambled, but his eye caught someone familiar. *I can't believe what I just saw. It can't be.* Down one of the alleys, Cain saw a man in the shadows wearing a fedora and smoking a pipe. He was leaning against a building and snapping photos. *That son of a bitch! Champ's reporting my murder!*

His rageful thoughts toward Champ were broken by the cawing of a bird in the back seat. The car swerved on the roadway as Cain twisted the steering wheel at the same time he turned his aching body to see behind him. *What the—?* A brown-and-gray hawk with yellow claws and matching eyes stared back at him. It flapped its wings from inside a custom-made wooden cage. *Of course,* Cain thought, *Hayabusa would have a live falcon as his mascot.*

Cain ditched the Skyline about a half mile from Umiko's apartment. *I can't leave this bird in here. The owner might be a piece of shit, but this is a helpless animal.* He grabbed the cage, along with his backpack, and walked the ten minutes to the high-rise apartment.

"Shh. Be quiet," he instructed the bird. "You're drawing too much attention." *And I'm not? An American with blood on his shirt, walking with a Japanese sparrow hawk and using a towel for a bandage?*

Cain took the stairs, hoping to avoid any residents who would have likely used the elevator. He reached the seventh floor and tapped on the door with his middle knuckle.

"Nande ya nen!" Umiko shrieked as she opened the door. "What happened to you?"

Cain quickly invited himself in and shut the door behind him.

"Why are you bloody?" She continued her rapid-fire questions. "Why do you have a falcon? What happened?"

He placed the birdcage on the floor and looked her straight in the eyes. "I'm in a lot of trouble, Umi. I found Hayabusa, the man who took Bonnie."

"Seiza kudesei," she replied. "Sit. I will get a towel."

Cain moaned from pain as he sat on the floor and propped his back against the sofa.

Umiko returned from the kitchen with a towel and a bowl of warm water. She soaked the towel in the water and wrung it out. She gently applied it to Cain's neck and face. She cared for him with tenderness as she cleaned away all the blood that had caked to his neck, face, and ear.

"You need to go to a doctor," she insisted as she looked into his eyes.

"Grab the expeditionary bag. There'll be emergency aid equipment inside."

She grabbed the bag and pulled out various types of medical equipment. "Your shirt is full of—" Umiko paused, clearly distressed by what she saw.

"Blood," Cain answered for her. "This shirt is ruined beyond repair." He looked at his hands, which were still bloody.

"What happened?"

"Doesn't matter. Hayabusa's dead now."

Umiko gasped and covered her mouth with her free hand.

"It was suicide. But it might as well have been murder."

"We have to go to the police," she said with conviction.

"No! No police."

"They will know what to do."

Her sense of morality and ability to see the best in people were two of the traits Cain found attractive about her. But he recognized the stakes. The danger of never seeing Bonnie again was increasing every second, and Japanese bureaucracy would tie him up for weeks—possibly even leading to his arrest for manslaughter. "I'm so sorry, Umiko." Cain teared up. "You are now in danger."

"Why am I in danger?" Her eyes widened. "Because you're here?"

"I had to leave your scooter at the scene. Eventually the police—maybe even the yakuza if they have the police on their payroll—will be able to trace the license plate back to you. They'll come here. They'll do to you what they've done to Bonnie."

"I didn't do anything wrong, though." She began to panic. "I let my friend borrow my scooter."

"I know you did nothing wrong. But you have to report your scooter stolen. And please promise me that you'll go tomorrow to stay with your parents in Osaka—at least until this blows over."

"I cannot leave my work tomorrow. Sato-san needs me."

"Don't worry about Sato-san. You are in danger. The yakuza can be here any minute. We must find a safe place and go there now."

"The only hotel nearby that would be private and not ask for ID would be a capsule hotel."

Cain shook his head. "No. I swore never to stay in one of those coffins again. There's gotta be another option. This is Yokohama, for crying out loud."

"Well," Umiko said, "there is *one* place." She told him there was an apartment owned by Mr. Sato's automotive company that was used to host visiting VIPs. It had been prepared for the marketing director from Germany, but he was not arriving until the following night.

"Let's go," said Cain.

CHAPTER 69

THE LUXURY CABIN on board the expensive yacht swayed with the rhythmic waves of the ocean. In almost any other scenario, this would be a dream vacation — except this was no vacation. It was a nightmare, yet Bonnie was wide-awake. The pain was a constant reminder of that.

The room was dark. She was nude, and her wrists throbbed with pain. The nylon rope that bound her was tight — too tight, but the yakuza guard knew she was a fighter. She had fought like a wild animal when they took her from her apartment. The chunk missing from his right ear served as a reminder of that.

Dried blood circled her wrists from the raw motion of trying to free her hands from the rope that tied them to the headboard of the queen-size bed. She was able to lie down but found sleeping too uncomfortable in that position. Gravity pulled the blood from her hands and it stung like a thousand needles jabbing her skin.

She peered through the small porthole. The waxing crescent moon provided a soft white glow over the ocean. That's how she kept track of the three days she'd been in captivity. *How many more nights will I be tied to this bed?* she worried. She reasoned that it was better than the alternative: death.

If only I can get Cain's attention. I've done it before.

She thought back to a childhood memory. *She had lost the coin toss with her brothers, and it had fallen on her to check the catfish traps in the middle of the lake. As she maneuvered her father's small boat close to the bobbing buoy, she saw her teenage brothers on the dock waving at her to come back to the shore.*

"Bonnie, it's not worth it. Just come back," Seth had yelled through cupped hands.

She'd looked skyward at the ominous clouds above. "I'd be done already if I had some help, but I don't need any help!" Hand over hand, she'd pulled the thick nylon rope to the trap until she felt its weight. It was heavy and caused the boat to tip as she hovered over the edge, pulling with all her might.

A clap of thunder and a gust of wind caused Bonnie to lose her footing. She toppled headfirst into the lake, inhaling a mouthful of muddy water. Bonnie kicked her legs furiously while trying to surface, but the rope ensnared her right leg above the knee, anchoring her underwater with the hefty fish trap.

She tried to untie the knot, but with every movement, it tightened more. She closed her stinging eyes.

Hurry, Cain! I'm drowning! *she'd messaged him telepathically.*

Bonnie's lungs had burned as she fought with the knotted rope. She could see through the murky water that the trap was not full of fish but lodged between an old stump and a large rock on the bottom of the lake.

Bonnie made one last effort to free herself, but it didn't work. Panic set in and she believed she was about to drown. Suddenly, she sensed she was not alone. Cain was in the water. She felt his presence before she ever saw him.

Her eyes opened to see her twin, calmly and carefully cutting the rope with his pocketknife. Cain grabbed Bonnie and pushed her up to the water's surface.

Bonnie gasped for air and coughed up dirty lake water.

"Is she okay?" Seth yelled, swimming toward them.

Cain was patting Bonnie's back to help her regain her breath.

"You got my message," Bonnie said with relief.

"Yes," Cain replied.

"I was hoping you would."

"I always do." Cain winked at his twin.

Bonnie smiled at that memory, and at the thought of how she and her brother were connected. She continued staring at the moon through the yacht's porthole, directing all her energy and thoughts toward her twin. *I'm on a yacht. I'm sure it's in Tokyo Bay, near land. I can hear seagulls and the constant arrival and departure of airplanes.*

She heard muffled voices from the hall. The door opened, backlighting the silhouette of a large man in a suit. The bald man in the doorway was Japanese and had a tattoo that covered his neck and head. He was carrying what looked like a small medical bag as he walked toward the edge of her bed. He gawked at Bonnie as she lay helpless on the bed. She felt violated by the way he looked her up and down. Her bound wrists did not allow her to cover herself. She crossed her legs tightly and turned away from him.

"You are very beautiful," he said. "It is a pity you will not be with us much longer. I would have enjoyed myself with you."

Bonnie heard him reach into his bag. She could not look. She felt cold metal touch her neck at the top of her spine and continue slowly down her back, stopping briefly at the bottom of her tailbone before continuing around her buttocks toward the inside of her thighs. Angered and repulsed, she kicked wildly at him. He laughed maniacally and slapped her hard on her thigh. It blossomed bright red and she tried to stifle her cry of pain and humiliation. She didn't want to give him the satisfaction. She turned to face her abuser and saw that he was holding a small pistol of some sort. It reminded her of something a television detective might carry around his ankle as a backup gun.

"Go ahead and shoot me, you chickenshit!" she exclaimed. "I'd rather die than give you any pleasure, you sick pervert!"

"Oh, I have no intention of shooting you, Bonnie. May I call you Bonnie?"

She was disgusted by him and spat in his face.

He was unfazed. "You are worth more to us alive than dead. Although from what I hear about our Saudi friends, you may wish that I had killed you."

Saudis? What is he talking about?

As if reading her mind, he said, "Yes, the Saudis will pay top dollar for a yellow-haired girl. And I can see that you are naturally blonde."

Bonnie knew that her face showed her anguish.

"They were very happy with Elena and the others. That is the beauty of the Japanese. We are very efficient, and because we are an island nation, we are experts at the sea trade. I'm sure they will be very pleased with you also." He was searching for something in his bag as he spoke. "Your brother has become quite a nuisance."

Bonnie immediately felt grateful: that meant Cain was looking for her. Tears of joy streamed down her face.

"First by saving Sato, and now by killing Hayabusa."

Hayabusa? Who the hell is that?

As if reading her mind again, the man continued. "Your brother caused Hayabusa, the only grandson of Yamamoto, to lose face in front of many people at the Angel Cloud. And in his quest to find you, he threw Hayabusa out of a third-story window. He has angered many people who should not have been angered."

"My brother can be a real pain in the ass." Bonnie smirked. "He's going to cause a lot more problems until he finds me."

"Yes, I believe you. He has proven to be quite the adversary, which is why we have chosen to expedite our shipment."

Bonnie gasped when she saw the man put his revolver into the medical bag and remove a large syringe. She thrashed wildly, and the bald man shouted for another guard to come into the room and hold her still. A guard rushed in, and a hand covered her mouth and nose, depriving her of air. She felt the sharp needle puncture her skin, and then the warm liquid flow through her veins. It gave her the strange sensation of being underwater. Her last thought before slipping into unconsciousness was, *Hurry, Cain! I'm drowning!*

CHAPTER 70

CAIN LAY AWAKE, Umiko's head resting on his chest. His body ached from the fight at the tattoo shop, and he was restless, worried about Bonnie. He carefully got up from the futon on the floor in the living room and walked toward the balcony. He quietly slid the door open and walked outside onto the balcony of the apartment.

It was still dark outside, and a slight cool breeze blew from Tokyo Bay. Red and green navigation lights bobbed up and down from all the ships in the bay. The waxing crescent moon provided a beam of light over the water. Cain reached out to touch it. No matter how big the world was, the moon gave him a connection to Bonnie. He *knew* they were staring at it together.

He continued staring at the moon until it disappeared with the sun rising over the horizon. He grabbed the birdcage and unhooked its door. The powerful flapping of wings as the falcon took flight woke Umiko. She joined Cain outside and put her arm around him.

I'm gonna free Bonnie like I freed that bird, he promised himself as the falcon soared into the distance.

Umiko kissed Cain's neck. "Did you get any sleep?"

He shook his head no.

"Would you like for me to make you some tea?" she asked. "They have my favorite inside: TWG."

"Yes, please," he replied. "If we had more time, I would have enjoyed making beignets for you."

"Next time," she said.

"I promise." He smiled.

They walked inside and Cain flipped on the television while Umiko prepared vanilla bourbon tea in the small kitchen.

"Enough already," Umiko said in frustration. "The Japanese media is obsessed with this emissions story. Sato-san is *not* going to resign. He uses his position for good. Every year he donates so much of his personal money toward orphanages. It is uncommon for a Japanese CEO to be so generous and donate so much of his money to help orphaned children."

"Sato-san might not be investing in a greener environment," Cain said, "but at least he's doing his part to invest in the future, I guess."

Umiko caught Cain's sarcasm. "Be nice. Sato-san has given you and me good jobs. Work is hard to find in Japan. There are more people than jobs." She returned to watching the television. "They're saying that the JR line is delayed. Someone committed suicide by jumping in front of the train."

"That's terrible," Cain said.

"Unfortunately, it happens often. It's most likely a man who has lost his job. The JR train company will now bill his family ten million yen."

Cain did the conversion in his head. "Isn't that almost one hundred thousand US dollars?"

"Something like that—maybe a little less. They call it 'obstruction of business.'"

The newscast switched to an interview, and Cain felt rage build up inside him as he saw who it was with.

"That son of a bitch!"

Umiko was startled. "You know this man?"

"He's a *Stars and Stripes* reporter I met last night. What's he saying?"

She listened intently and translated as quickly as she could. "He speaks really great Japanese," she commented. "He's saying that the yakuza have kidnapped an American woman, and her family is now demanding her return. The tattoo shop behind him was the scene of a violent killing last night of a prominent yakuza member. This place is believed to be a money laundering front for the yakuza, and many American sailors use it to get their tattoos. The Seventh Fleet commander is now issuing a ban for all American military personnel. Tattoo shops in Japan are now off-limits."

Cain's eyes were glued to the screen. The video transitioned to another scene: a dozen members of Tokyo's crime scene unit were huddled around the orange Skyline that Cain had abandoned. They were dusting for fingerprints and putting hair samples into plastic evidence bags.

"That's it!" Cain shouted. "I've gotta dig this weasel out of his hole before he puts Bonnie in a six-foot-deep one, and me in jail!" He then turned to Umiko and took her hand. "Go to Osaka now. Promise me you'll stay with your parents."

"I will," she replied.

She handed him a bento box. "I took this from the fridge for you. It'll give you strength. It's got rice, meat, and vegetables—and no eel." She smiled.

He laid his hands softly on her cheeks. Umiko

stood on her toes to meet him for a kiss. He held the kiss for a second longer.

As they left the apartment and went their separate ways, Cain looked at the gold band on his ring finger. It had been there since the day he'd promised Claire "I do." Now he removed the ring and placed it in his pocket. *Claire, there's nobody who can ever replace you. But I've found somebody who makes me feel loved again. Someone I get the feeling that you would approve of also.*

CHAPTER 71

CAIN HOPPED ONTO the train headed to Yokosuka. It was packed with commuters, so he leaned
against one of the poles to steady himself during the
one-hour ride. He found himself feeling more anxious
with each passing moment, thinking of how Champ
was potentially endangering Bonnie to promote his
career. Cain instinctively clenched his fists. *I'm gonna
punch the daylights out of Cat when I see him. If he
gets Bonnie killed…I can't think like that.* He pushed
those thoughts away and refocused on finding his
twin sister.

He habitually reached for his ring finger to fidget
with his wedding band but it was no longer there. It
felt strange. The only other time he had removed the
ring was when he was at the Secret Service academy
and had to remove all jewelry before they practiced
their defensive tactics training.

Chief Alvarez, as promised, was waiting outside
the military's perimeter fence, near the entrance to
the Enlisted Alliance Club. The bottom of his blue
camouflage uniform was tucked into his spit-shined
black boots. He greeted Cain with a bear hug.

"Hurricane, you look like shit!"

"I've been hearing that a lot lately," Cain said. "For a sailor trying to scam the navy out of an extra 5 percent disability for *navy-induced sleep apnea,* you look more rested than me," Cain teased his friend.

"Hey, it's a real thing," Alvarez replied defensively. "You see how wired I am? Imagine how calm I'd be if I slept well."

"You're wired because you keep drinking those energy drinks." Cain pointed to the sixteen-ounce aluminum can in Chief Alvarez's hand. "Those things will kill you."

"So will flying P-3s, but that never seemed to bother you." The chief looked at Cain with concern. "Seriously, when was the last time you slept?"

"Don't worry about that. Just take me to Sherlock Holmes. I'm getting angrier by the second thinking about him."

"Aye, aye." Chief Alvarez saluted.

The *Stars and Stripes* office was a single ten-by-ten-foot room next to the military's vehicle licensing office. Cain and the chief had to walk through an industrial hallway full of newly arrived military members who were trying to take their driving tests, register their cars, and purchase Japanese insurance.

Champ's office door had a small nameplate above an after-hours letter drop. Cain turned the knob and opened the door to a space with nondescript furnishings. He saw Champ sitting at his desk in the corner, blabbing on the telephone. A look of fear came over him when he saw Cain.

"Um, something's come up rather unexpectedly. I'll call you later." He dropped the phone's receiver on its cradle and stood.

Cain advanced toward the reporter and grabbed him by the collar. Cain slammed him against the wall, which was full of tacked newspaper articles with Champ's byline. When the back of his head hit the wall, something fell out of Champ's mouth.

"What was that?" Chief Alvarez asked, looking at the carpet by the reporter's feet. "You lose a tooth?"

Champ coughed for air. "It was my throat lozenge."

Cain turned to Chief Alvarez, who locked the door and guarded it with his back so nobody could enter.

"He's all yours," the chief said. "Show 'em why you were called Hurricane in the world's finest navy."

"Wh—wh—what do you mean by that?" Champ nervously stammered. "You can't treat me like this." His face was turning red from fear and embarrassment. "It's an assault on a member of the press."

"I saw you on television today—dramatizing the situation to get your ugly mug all over the news. You're not going to get your Pulitzer on *my* case!" Cain shouted. "Bonnie's not your pawn!"

"It's not what it appears." Champ's voice cracked. "I was *helping* you. I swear to God."

Cain loosened his grip slightly. "How in the hell is your reporting this all over the news helping me? I saw you taking pictures of me last night. What were you going to do? Sell them to the *Japan Times*?"

"Well, yes. But—"

Cain retightened his grip on Champ's collar.

"But only *after* you find Bonnie. I swear. I can prove it to you. Let go and I'll show you."

Cain let go, and Champ took a deep breath. He stepped toward his desk and opened one of the drawers. He pulled out a license plate. "You see? I was protecting you. This is the plate off your scooter. I took it before the police could trace it back to you."

"Wait—how did you know it was my scooter?"

"Let's just say it was my journalistic instinct.

Though quite frankly, I was surprised to see you on a scooter at all. But anyway, I took it to give you more time to find Bonnie. Nobody else is searching for her—they're all searching for you!"

Cain's heart sank. He felt the weight of guilt—his old familiar friend—once again. *Oh, God. It's not Champ. It's me who has put Bonnie in more danger.*

Champ's next words gave Cain a little encouragement.

"The Japanese are afraid of the yakuza. They'll never stand up against them, but you did! The more I publicize this in the news, the more of a hero you become."

Cain squeezed his temples to ease the pressure. "I'm not a hero. I'm just trying to find my sister. But surely with all this publicity, they'll kill her—or worse, ship her off to be a sex slave for the rest of her life."

Chief Alvarez left the door and put his arm around Cain's shoulders. "You can't think like that. You're her only chance right now. And you're not alone. You have me to help you."

"Even if you never find your sister—"

Chief Alvarez's glare shot darts at Champ for his insensitive comment, but the reporter continued. "The very least you can do is punish those who kidnapped her in the first place. Not only for Bonnie, but for all the others we suspect that they've kidnapped."

"I don't know where they're hiding," Cain replied. "Or I would."

Champ cleared his throat with a cough. "I know where you can find some more."

Cain looked up, hopeful that he still had a chance.

"The man you killed last night—"

"I didn't kill him. He jumped out the window," Cain interjected.

"Regardless, he was no ordinary yakuza member. Hayabusa was the grandson of the yakuza leader."

Cain's eyes widened.

"His wake is tonight." Champ seemed to get more excited every second he talked. "And I know where it's at. *Stars and Stripes*'s leadership has tasked me with covering the story. After all, the yakuza in Yokosuka impacts the Seventh Fleet. The navy doesn't want their sailors getting tangled up in this dark web of organized crime. We're talking sex trafficking, blackmail, illegal gambling—"

"Where's it at?" Cain interrupted. "The wake?"

"It's in Kamakura. But security will be massive. They're checking badges for everyone who attends. Let's just say you stick out."

"Like a nail?" Cain said, remembering the popular Japanese phrase.

"Oh, no," Champ replied. "This is on a whole different level. The nail that sticks out"—he pointed to Cain—"gets sliced up in a thousand pieces and fed to the fish in Tokyo Bay."

"That's why you've just volunteered to be my eyes on the inside, then."

"You make it sound like I don't have a choice."

"You don't. But if it makes you feel better, what would your grandfather choose to do?"

Champ thought about it for a second and nodded in agreement. "He'd earn a Pulitzer."

CHAPTER 72

THE GREAT BUDDHA, as the Americans called it, towered over everything else in the historic village of Kamakura. This bronze statue was over forty-three feet high and weighed more than 267,000 pounds. The sacred temple was a popular tourist destination, but police had blocked off the roads and diverted tour buses for Hayabusa's wake. Several hundred visitors had gathered to pay their respects to the fallen yakuza member. The men wore black suits and ties over white shirts, and the women wore traditional black kimonos or subdued dresses, a few with beautiful pearls around their necks. They carried envelopes wrapped in black and silver string, which contained yen to present to the family of the deceased.

Champ adhered to the ritual of wearing a black suit to a funeral, but his was a three-piece with a pocket watch attached to a gold chain. As Champ walked toward the gate of the Kotoku-in temple, he saw a female competitor from the *Japan Times*.

"Cat, I am surprised to see you here," the Osaka native said.

"You shouldn't be. You know I go where the action is."

"They let you leave the military base? I thought the *Stars and Stripes* put a leash on you."

"Nobody puts this Cat on a leash." Champ pointed to his chest. *God, that woman gets under my skin. She wouldn't be such a pain in the ass if she were from Tokyo.* Champ had learned that sarcasm and edginess were much more common in Osaka than in Tokyo.

"What's your story here?" She continued her probe. "Doesn't your jurisdiction end in Yokosuka?"

He scowled. "I guess you didn't see me on television this morning. Perhaps if they were paying you what I earn, you'd be able to afford cable."

"I'm too busy writing the news to be *in* the news," she quipped.

"We Americans have a little saying," Champ replied. "Have your cake and eat it, too. That's why I'm here."

"Bon appétit." She smiled.

A line of yakuza members serving as security guards blocked the entrance. They were checking everyone's invitations.

"No American press," a yakuza member said.

"Good, because I'm Canadian," Champ lied, but he was used to thinking on his feet.

"Canada. United States. It is all the same."

Champ reached into his inner jacket pocket and retrieved an ornately decorated piece of hard-stock paper the size of a postcard. "Here is my formal invitation." He presented the document with both hands. "I am honored to be here to show my respect." *Nobody needs to know how I got this,* he thought. *Let's just be thankful bribes work with the right people in Japan.*

The yakuza members conversed in dialect, which was quite different from typical Japanese. It was spoken in a harsher tone, and slang was used much more frequently. Regardless, Champ was able to pick up about 80 percent of what they were saying.

"You may enter," the guard said, and paused. "But you have to be escorted."

"This is a wake, not a middle school dance." Champ's humor was lost on the hardened criminal.

"You must be searched also," the guard ordered, and pointed to the messenger bag slung across Champ's shoulder.

"It's just my camera," Champ replied. "A good reporter always has a pen, a pad of paper, and a reliable camera."

The yakuza member gruffly pulled Champ's bag off his shoulder and began inspecting the contents.

"Easy," Champ cautioned. "That camera cost thousands of dollars. That's why I keep it protected in American buffalo skin."

The *Japan Times* reporter snickered as she passed easily through security. "Maybe I'll see you on the other side. If not, I'll send you a copy of my story."

Champ mumbled under his breath before he was allowed access. Flanked by one of the stout yakuza members, he approached the several-hundred-year-old temple. He was in awe of the religious grounds. Perfectly manicured bonsai trees surrounded the compound, and a forest on a hill provided the backdrop. Where there were no tiles to walk on, loose gravel coated the ground. There were also several wells for water to pour over one's hands to cleanse oneself.

The wake was attended predominantly by Japanese society, but a handful of prominent Western business owners were there. Champ, escorted by his chaperone, walked around trying to eavesdrop on the various conversations taking place among the guests. He overheard some of the yakuza members mention that the gang was going to an *izakaya* called Matchbox afterward to drink sake and celebrate Hayabusa's life.

Armed with that vital information, Champ walked toward the bathroom. He looked rearward at his chaperone, who was still following close behind. "Are you going to wipe my ass, too?"

The gangster's face turned red. He stopped at the bathroom doorway and ran his fingers through his slick hair. "Hurry up."

Champ entered the stall and latched the door. He fumbled for his phone. When he found it, he sat on the toilet and texted Cain.

OYABUN IS HERE.

WHO? Cain texted back.

THE HEAD BOSS OF THE YAMAMOTO-GUMI. THEY ARE GOING TO MATCHBOX BAR AFTER. WALKING DISTANCE FROM TRAIN STATION. STAKE IT OUT NOW BEFORE EVERYONE STARTS ARRIVING.

CHAPTER 73

CAIN WALKED THE BACKSTREETS for about ten minutes to avoid detection by any yakuza members not at the wake. When it seemed safe, he hopped a city bus going to the Kamakura train station. After a few stops, he arrived at the heart of Kamakura. Trains were arriving and departing, buses were zipping in and out, and taxis lined the parking lot for travelers who were in a hurry and didn't want to take public transportation.

Cain saw the *izakaya* and walked toward it. As he got closer, he saw a sign in the window that was in both Japanese and English: CLOSED FOR PRIVATE EVENT. MEMBERS ONLY. The curtains were drawn, and he couldn't see through the window.

Cain walked around the back of the building. Along the narrow alley he noticed a window cracked open. He peered through the opening and saw a lone sink and stall. He looked around to make sure nobody saw him, and he raised the window. He threw the backpack in, put both hands on the windowsill, and pulled himself up and through the frame. He closed the window behind him and then approached the closed bathroom door. He got down on one knee and peered through the latch hole.

This'll be a good place to keep an eye on 'em, he thought. *But what's my plan when I see them? I have no idea. Cain,* he told himself, *you better figure this out now, because you ain't getting a second chance. You've broken your own cardinal rule: you've given yourself only one way out—through a tight window.*

His concentration was broken by the vibration of his phone in his pocket. He saw that it was Tanaka. He sent the call to voicemail. *Not now, Tanaka.*

The phone vibrated again. This time it was a text message from Tanaka: SUSPICIOUS PACKAGE ARRIVED OVERNIGHT FOR YOU.

Suspicious, Cain thought. *Oh, God. Is it a ransom note? One of Bonnie's fingers as proof of life?* Then his Secret Service training for how to recognize mail bombs took over. IS IT TICKING? Cain texted back.

WHAT? Tanaka asked.

PUT YOUR EAR TO IT—THE ONE YOU DON'T MIND GETTING BLOWN OFF. HEAR ANYTHING?

IT'S QUIET.

DOES IT HAVE MORE POSTAGE STAMPS THAN NECESSARY? Cain's fingers were tiring from the texting. He preferred talking on the phone, but he couldn't risk being heard talking in the bathroom—right in the den of the yakuza's clubhouse.

I DON'T KNOW. NO POSTAGE STAMPS. ONLY SHIPPING LABEL. WAS SHIPPED OVERNIGHT—INTERNATIONALLY.

WHAT'S THE RETURN ADDRESS?

THAT IS SUSPICIOUS PART. HIS ROYAL HIGHNESS.

Cain exhaled with a huge sense of relief and grinned wide. *The King risked his career. He had a change of heart and did the right thing after all.*

?? Tanaka waited for a response.

IT'S OK. I KNOW HIM. NEED PACKAGE ASAP!

WANT ME TO GIVE TO UMIKO-SAN? Tanaka asked.

SHE'S OUT OF TOWN.

NO. SHE'S AT WORK.

WHAT? Cain wasn't sure whether to feel worried or angry that Umiko hadn't listened to him about leaving town.

CLOSED-DOOR MEETING WITH SATO-SAN FOR 1 HOUR.

Why would she be at work—in a private meeting with Sato? She knows the danger she's in. She promised me she'd go straightaway to her parents in Osaka.

OPEN THE PACKAGE.

OK. About thirty seconds later Tanaka texted Cain back. LOTS OF ENGLISH DOCUMENTS.

IT'S IMPORTANT INFORMATION. LOOKING FOR CLUES TO HELP FIND BONNIE. NAMES OF BOATS, EXPORT COMPANIES, OR SHIPPING CONTAINERS.

OK. I WILL DO MY BEST.

I BELIEVE BONNIE WILL BE SHIPPED TO MIDDLE EAST AS SEX SLAVE.

CHAPTER 74

CHAMP ALBRIGHT LEFT the immaculate bathroom and walked to the temple. He sat on the tatami mat when the ceremony officially began. The Buddhist monk who was presiding over the wake kneeled in front of the coffin to chant a sutra. The coffin was open, and Hayabusa lay in eternal rest. The deceased yakuza member was dressed in a white kimono. His coffin was filled with flowers, and on top of his chest rested a shiny *tanto* — to protect him from evil spirits in the afterlife.

Damn! Champ thought. *They should have chosen a closed casket. This dude had the shit beat out of him.*

The immediate family, which was about twenty individuals, including several high-ranking yakuza members, approached the coffin one by one to honor their fallen brother. The head boss of the Yamamoto-gumi was a physically fit businessman in his sixties who controlled some of Tokyo's most expensive real estate. He'd also invested heavily in Japan's automotive industry as a way to expand his influence in other countries.

From his research, Champ knew that Yamamoto, Hayabusa's grandfather, had been orphaned as a child when his parents and sister died in the blast from Little Boy, dropped from the Enola Gay on August 6, 1945. Their bodies were never found. Growing up in a poor orphanage in Hiroshima, young Yamamoto was recruited into the yakuza and became known as one of the most vengeful. For instance, when he learned that a real estate agent had cheated him out of 1 percent on a business deal, Yamamoto had killed him with a katana. Yamamoto served six years in prison, and when he was released, he climbed his way to the top and eventually took over the yakuza clan in Tokyo and Yokohama.

Champ watched Yamamoto open the incense bowl and grab a piece of incense. He put it in the burning bowl, placed his hands together at chest level, and bowed at a forty-five-degree angle. Each of the family members repeated this process until they had all performed this sacred ritual.

Before the other guests were afforded the opportunity to pay their respects to Hayabusa, Yamamoto turned toward the crowd and addressed them in Japanese.

"Hayabusa was my own flesh and blood. I raised my grandson as my own son. He learned the yakuza way, and he brought us great honor. He was destined to take over and carry on my legacy. His death will be avenged."

Yamamoto looked toward a group of four teenage yakuza members, each holding a birdcage.

"Hai!" Yamamoto yelled with a quick head bow.

The yakuza opened the cages, and four falcons flapped their wings and took flight into the evening sky.

"We pay homage to Hayabusa's spirit. He will be our eyes in the sky."

Although four was an unlucky number in Japanese culture, Champ thought this made sense in a strange way. The number four, *shi,* also meant "death." The yakuza would not forget the death of the *oyabun*'s grandson.

The ceremony concluded, and as Champ reached for his phone, the female reporter he'd run into earlier asked, "What's your angle going to be on this one?"

Champ ignored her. He texted Cain, YAMAMOTO IS SAYING HIS GOOD-BYES.

"Cat got your tongue?" the reporter asked Champ. "I've never seen you this nervous before."

"Don't worry about me," he replied without looking up from his phone. He finished the message. HEAD BOSS HEADING YOUR WAY SOON.

COPY, Cain replied. I'M IN POSITION.

CHAPTER 75

CAIN SQUINTED THROUGH the keyhole. He saw the solemn yakuza members filing into the restaurant. Sake was waiting for them at the bar in traditional small wooden boxes. They reached for the drinks and downed the room-temperature sake. They unbuttoned their shirts and let them fall off their backs, showcasing their full-body tattoos. Some gathered around a table and began playing a card game. Cain didn't recognize the game, only that the deck of cards looked smaller than American playing cards.

Cain felt a jolt of excitement as he saw one of the members limping across the room. It was the same punk he'd fought at the Angel Cloud. He had thrust his boot against the man's kneecap, permanently injuring the yakuza member. Cain continued scanning the room from the limited viewing angle provided by the keyhole. *Where is Yamamoto? He'll know where Bonnie is.*

Cain's phone vibrated. He looked down and saw the low-battery indicator flashing. *Murphy's Law!* He didn't have a charger on him. The phone vibrated again. "Stop vibrating," he muttered to his phone. But this time it was a text from Champ.

YAMAMOTO IS GETTING INTO HIS MERCEDES.

FOLLOW HIM, Cain instructed.

WHY? HE'S GOING TO THE IZAKAYA, Champ replied.

BATTERY IS DYING. NO TIME FOR BACK AND FORTH. FOLLOW HIM!

Suddenly the bathroom doorknob turned. Cain had been so preoccupied with his phone that he hadn't been looking through the peephole. A surge of adrenaline shot through his body. He stood quickly and made himself as slim as possible against the wall as the door slowly opened.

What is taking so long?

Then it was clear. The man entering the bathroom had an injured knee and was walking with great difficulty.

Cain smiled. *Perfect,* he thought. *We meet again, shithead.*

When the yakuza cleared the threshold of the bathroom, Cain closed the door and locked it. The sound of the bolt sliding into place caught the yakuza member's attention, and he turned rearward. Cain glided across the clean floor and used his hand to cup the gangster's mouth to prevent him from screaming out for his associates. As Cain's momentum drove forward, the thug stumbled backward and banged his head on the tile wall. Fresh blood splattered against the white tile. Cain swept his leg powerfully against the yakuza's calf and sent him crashing to the floor. Cain quickly squatted on top of the dazed and disoriented kidnapper in judo's popular mount position.

"Where is Bonnie? *Bonnie wa doko desuka?*" Cain removed his hand from the thug's mouth so the man could speak.

"*Tasukete!*" he screamed, hoping to summon help.

Cain quickly threw an elbow strike to the gangster's

face. "Where is she? Tell me or I'll kill you like Hayabusa."

"She is dead," he gurgled through blood and broken teeth.

"Bullshit!" Cain could sense that his sister was still alive, but he did not have enough time to get any information out of this yakuza member.

Cain reached for the backpack that Chief Alvarez had given him. He quickly duct-taped the thug's mouth so he couldn't scream out again, and then Cain tied the man's hands and feet together, anchoring them to the toilet. He searched the gangster and took his keys and cell phone. He tried to call Champ, but the phone was password protected.

Cain punched in the numbers 1, 2, 3, 4. An incorrect password notification popped up. He tried 0, 1, 2, 3, but that was also wrong. *Lucky number seven,* he thought. He input 7, 7, 7, 7. A message appeared saying that he had three more attempts before the phone was wiped clean. Cain took a deep breath and slowly exhaled. *Quit thinking like an American!*

Cain's phone buzzed with a call from Champ. He had to answer it.

"Something strange is going on." Champ was speaking rapidly. "I'm tailing Yamamoto's Mercedes and we're not going to your location. We're heading toward the Yokohama seaport."

"Keep following him. Let me know where you land, and I'll meet up. He's the key to finding Bonnie."

"Okay. Talk to you soon."

"*Wait!* Before you hang up, I got one of their cell phones. I'm trying to unlock it. But I'm thinking like an American, and I need to be thinking like a yakuza. What would the combination be?"

"How would I know that? It could be his anniversary, his birthday. It could be *anything*."

Cain looked at the battered thug. "This dirtbag ain't married, and these guys don't look like the birthday-celebrating kind of people."

"Damn!" Champ thought out loud. "Okay, try four, six, four, nine. It's a popular phone code in Japanese because the numbers—*yo, ro, shi, ku*—mean hello."

"*Hello*? Are you shittin' me?" Cain asked.

"How have you done so far?" Champ replied defiantly.

"Hold on a second." Cain tried those numbers. "Nope, that ain't it. What else you got? I've only got two tries left before the phone freezes up."

"Pressure is my middle name. I operate best against the clock," Champ said arrogantly. "Um, let me see. What would a yakuza member use? Six, six, six, six? Nah, that's too American. Oh, I got it! Of course, it was there all along. Try eight, nine, three, zero."

"Why that number?" Cain asked.

"*Ya-ku-za* is Japanese for eight, nine, three. It's based on a card game called *oicho-kabu*. The worst hand to be dealt is eight, nine, three because it's good for nothing."

"Good for nothing, huh? That sums up the yakuza perfectly." Cain punched in the digits. "It worked! I'm in now! You're the man, Champ!"

There were two loud knocks at the bathroom door, followed by some shouting. Cain couldn't understand the Japanese, but he knew there was another man trying to use the bathroom, and that man was in a hurry.

"Where are you?" Cain asked Champ.

"Getting closer to the Yokohama marina. I can smell the sea."

"I'll head that way right now," Cain said as he slid the gangster's phone into his front pocket.

He managed to give one last command before his battery died. "Don't lose that son of a bitch! You're our only hope right now." His phone's screen shut off. Cain grabbed the tactical backpack and squeezed himself through the window as the yakuza shoved the bathroom door open.

Cain saw several yakuza members rushing outside, filling the alleys as they searched for him. The sight of the bare-chested tattooed yakuza shocked the town's commuters, who froze in fear. Cain hurried toward the taxi stand in front of the Kamakura train station. One of the yakuza noticed the tall American in the crowd, pointed, and alerted the others.

Cain sprinted to the closest taxi. The cabdriver casually pushed a button to open the rear passenger door, but Cain threw open the front door and jumped in. The startled driver began speaking in Japanese and motioning for Cain to get into the back seat. Through the windshield, Cain noticed one of the yakuza pointing frantically toward the cab. Several yakuza began rushing toward him.

"Go! Go! Go!" Cain commanded the driver.

Oblivious to the immediate danger, the stubborn driver continued ordering Cain to move to the back seat. His demand was interrupted by the shattering of the driver's side window. Glass flew into the car as a pair of tattooed arms reached into the broken window and seized the slender driver by his dress shirt.

The terrified driver screamed and desperately grabbed the door to prevent himself from being dragged out. The broken glass cut through his white gloves and skin, and the bleeding caused him to lose his grip.

As the cabdriver and his attacker fell away, Cain slid into the driver's seat. Shifting the car into drive, he grabbed the steering wheel and stomped on the gas pedal. The taxi accelerated toward the angry mob of yakuza, colliding with two and hurtling them onto the hood and over the top of the fleeing vehicle. The car fishtailed as Cain skidded left onto the main road, which was divided by a pedestrian median. In the distance, he recognized the red wooden torii, Kamakura's shrine gate, and sped in that direction. Once clear of the danger, he plugged his phone into the cigarette lighter and called Chief Alvarez.

"I need a big favor," Cain said.

"Name it," Alvarez replied, shouting over loud music playing in the background.

"Get the boat and a set of scuba gear and meet me at the Yokohama marina," Cain instructed. "Apply full military power."

"Roger that, Hurricane. See you in thirty."

Upon arriving at the seaport, Cain saw Champ looking toward the ocean through the lens of his camera and adjusting the detachable telescope. Champ heard the car approach and no doubt clocked the cracked windshield and broken driver's side window. He peered curiously into the battered taxi. "You left the meter running," Champ observed.

CHAPTER 76

"*OYABUN* HOPPED ONTO a small boat with two of his henchmen," Champ said as he and Cain walked toward the floating pier. "They went out to a yacht near the commercial shipping lanes. You can barely see it from here, but with the zoom on this Nikon you can make out the red and green navigation lights." Champ turned the camera so Cain could inspect the photos he had taken.

"The yacht's black," Cain said. He dropped his backpack onto the pier and retrieved a pair of marine binoculars. He put them to his eyes and adjusted the focus with his finger. "It's big—gotta be about fifty meters. The name is on the side in white lettering. *Mi-na-shi-go*. What's that mean?"

The choppy sound of an approaching helicopter muffled Champ's reply.

"*What?*" Cain said, turning his ear toward Champ.

"*Orphan!*" Champ shouted through cupped hands. "*Minashigo* means 'orphan'!"

The helicopter swooped down to just fifty feet above the pier and hovered overhead. Its downwash disturbed the water and caused the anchored boats to bob and crash against the docks. Cain plugged his ears with his fingertips to dull the piercing sounds of the rotor blades and turbine engine. He strained to keep his eyes squinted against the downwash. The helicopter's nose dipped and raced toward the yacht.

"Who was *that*?" Champ asked.

"I don't know, but I intend to find out," Cain replied.

Chief Alvarez motored *El Viento* into the marina and tossed the rope to Cain. "Tie us up."

"We're not staying," Cain replied. He pointed into the darkness. "We're going out there."

Cain stepped onto the hull, and Champ followed behind. "Hey!" Cain pushed his palm into Champ's chest. "Where do you think you're going?"

"With you guys. That's where the story is."

"No way in hell. It's way too dangerous, Champ. You've gotta stay behind to tell our story in case we don't make it."

"I'll cover it from this rust bucket," he said as he studied *El Viento,* noting the boat's dings and scratches from years of recreational use.

"I had my doubts about you at first, Champ, but you've proved me wrong. You did great tonight. Take this." Cain handed him the phone he had ripped from the yakuza gangster at Matchbox. "You brilliantly guessed the code to unlock it, and I'm sure there's another story in there somewhere. But this is where we part ways." Cain kicked off the dock.

Chief Alvarez twisted the throttle of the outboard engine to full power and navigated out of the harbor toward Tokyo's busy shipping lanes. Cain peered over the bow and the port and starboard sides of the keelboat. The moon illuminated the murky waters.

He noticed floating trash, plastic bottles, and other debris—an unusual sight for Japan's notoriously clean society.

I guess the sea is where Japan hides its trash and dirty secrets, Cain thought as the smallest hint of the *Minashigo* appeared through the darkness like a modern-day pirate ship.

Cain's impatience grew as the sailboat did its best to wade through the rocky waters and avoid the various fishing vessels anchored throughout the bay. Fishing was a popular industry in Japan, and many locals were hoping to find their dinner at sea.

"Hold on, Bonnie, I'm almost there," Cain whispered, believing she would receive his message.

The yakuza's yacht slowly came into focus, and Chief Alvarez killed *El Viento'*s engine and hoisted its sails. Cain began assembling the scuba gear. He spit into the round mask and dipped it into the salt water. He hooked the hose to the nitrogen tank and snapped the gear into place. Then he froze, paralyzed by his thoughts. He felt petrified as he stared at the scuba equipment.

The chief noticed the sudden change in his friend's demeanor. "Is everything okay, Hurricane?"

Cain didn't respond.

"Hurricane!" the chief repeated. "Cain, are you okay?"

Cain snapped out of it and wiped the sweat from his brow. He took a couple of deep breaths. "I'm okay. I just realized the last time I dived was that Christmas in Thailand."

The chief understood. He nodded. "I'll go for you."

"No! This is something I have to do. I will not lose another one to the sea." Cain cinched the weight belt around his waist and tied the dive knife around his calf. He threw the oxygen tank over his back, put the regulator into his mouth, held his mask in place, and tipped backward into the ocean. The cold water sent a chill down his spine, and then everything suddenly went quiet and black.

CHAPTER 77

CAIN'S UPPER TORSO SURFACED to the top of the water. He signaled that he was okay, and the chief handed him an underwater flashlight and fifty feet of coiled three-eighths-inch-thick polypropylene rope. The navy preferred this type of rope because it was water-resistant and it floated.

Cain hooked the rope to a D-shaped aluminum carabiner and tugged on it to make sure it was secured. He turned to face the *Minashigo*. He got his bearings and mentally calculated the distance. The boat was approximately one hundred yards away.

"Good luck," Chief Alvarez whispered, and gave Cain a thumbs-up. "I'll be waiting right here for you when you're done."

Cain stared through his mask while the water slowly engulfed him as he submerged. He caught himself sucking in too much oxygen as he tried to perfectly buoy himself—that sweet spot where he could dangle between the two worlds without surfacing or sinking to the ocean floor. He was out of practice, and he had never thought he would be diving again. After a few moments, he found himself getting back into the swing of it. *Just like riding a bike,* he thought before calmly and rhythmically kicking his rubber fins to propel himself toward the yacht's two massive diesel engines. It took only about ten minutes, but it felt more like an hour. He knew from his training that the time warp was caused by the adrenaline flowing through his veins. Tonight he was either going to rescue Bonnie or die in the process. His father's words to Cain's adolescent self came to mind. Cain had been in the seventh grade when he told his dad about wanting to fight a bully at school who was picking on Bonnie. "Nobody messes wit da Lemaire family," his dad had declared. "Even eef you don't win da fight, make sure he walks away dinkin' eet wasn't worth tanglin' wit a Lemaire. Dat's da Lemaire brand of Cajun justice."

Cain unhooked the rope and began tying a bowline knot to the propellers. *If they try to flee,* he reasoned, *this'll stop the props and burn up the transmission. I can't keep chasing 'em all around Japan. It ends tonight.*

When Cain finished, he ascended to the surface. He wasn't worried about decompression sickness— he hadn't gone deep for long enough. He saw a man in a dark suit standing guard on board and another man standing near the helicopter on the second deck— most likely the pilot. He was clad in a blue flight suit with patches and was smoking a cigarette.

I guess the visibility was at least one mile, Cain thought, harking back to that day when assassins had ambushed Sato's motorcade.

Cain moved silently, careful to go unnoticed. He inflated his BCD with a few presses of a button. The short bursts of air filled his BCD and were not heard over the yacht's massive generator, which was providing electricity and hot water to the luxury boat. Once buoyant, Cain pulled the quick-release buckle and his ten-pound weight belt sank to the bottom of the ocean. He unsnapped the clips of his BCD and removed it from his shoulders. Under the moonlight, the ocean looked like a smooth velvet sheet—a place of comfort and relaxation. But Cain knew better. The sea was mysterious and merciless, indifferent to whose lives she claimed.

He used the remaining rope to hold the BCD and tied it to one of the cleats on the yacht's aft. He stretched out his arm and latched onto the yacht for stability as the vessel rose and dipped with the ocean's current. He removed his flippers one at a time, turning them upside down to pour out the salt water before quietly laying them on the deck, and then pulled himself onto the *Minashigo*. He was trespassing into the dragon's lair; all he could think about was Hayabusa's tattoo and how the dragon's tail wrapped around the geisha, suffocating the life out of her. This war between the Lemaire family and the yakuza began that night at the Angel Cloud, and Cain was going to end it now.

He saw an orange box bolted to a bulkhead. He walked toward it and opened the metal container. It contained a flare gun and two extra cartridges. Cain grabbed the gun and pocketed the two extra flares. He began exploring the deck, peeking into each window, searching for clues to Bonnie's whereabouts. The fourth window he came upon was different. It was a large rectangle, and he soon realized why. It belonged to the yacht's luxurious grand room—it was at least three times larger than the average Japanese home's living room. Glass cabinets stretched to the ceiling, displaying treasures of antique Japanese pottery and expensive bottles of alcohol from around the world. His heart pounded against his chest like a drum when he recognized the two men he saw talking to each other. One of them was Yamamoto.

Cain felt a gut-wrenching knot form in the pit of his stomach. Betrayal was the worst type of pain. *I would have given my life for him, and he crossed me like this. He betrayed me and Bonnie. Koichi Sato was behind her kidnapping the whole time!*

CHAPTER 78

CAIN METHODICALLY SCANNED the grand room, searching for any other yakuza members he would have to fight. *I can't just go blasting in there,* he thought. *That'll be certain suicide. Can't rescue Bonnie if I'm dead.* Self-preservation was one of the tenets the Secret Service taught at its academy in Maryland. Rookie agents thought they were issued bulletproof vests for *their* protection, but in reality, the point was merely to keep the agents alive long enough to protect the VIP until backup arrived.

Cain noticed a gruff-looking Japanese man in the corner of the room. A tattoo sprawled across his neck and covered his bald head. Cain leaned his face against the window to gain a better view and to size him up. He could tell from the man's visible scars and how his suit looked—custom-tailored in order to accommodate his bulging biceps—that he was going to be a tough opponent. And then there was something odd about his ear—as if a piece of it was missing.

Movement in the corner of the room caught Cain's eye. He pressed his face against the window even harder. *Bonnie!* His heart fluttered with joy but just as quickly sank when he realized she was tied to a chair in the far corner, her hands and feet bound by rope. Her nude body was bruised; there was no hiding that she had been punished for Cain's actions.

Yamamoto shouted something in Japanese, and the bald guard walked toward the middle of the room and retrieved two swords from their traditional stands. He bowed and extended the swords with both hands. Yamamoto ceremonially received one, and then Sato received his. They unsheathed them; the razor-sharp blades reflected the overhead light.

Are they gonna kill Bonnie? Cain's mind swarmed with emotion. He envisioned them slicing her head off with a single proficient swipe of the samurai sword. *No!* he reminded himself. *She's worth more alive to them than dead.* The mere thought of her being forced into sexual slavery sickened him. He counted three men—Yamamoto, Sato, and the bald guard—plus Bonnie in the room. He readied himself to burst through the door and run into the room. He felt tunnel vision setting in, and he reminded himself to combat-breathe and continue to look around in order to make as many observations as possible. He inhaled and slowly exhaled in a calculated manner. He put his hand on the doorknob and began turning it when suddenly the yacht's diesel engines roared to life. The motors whined as they struggled to break the rope and spin the propellers. The odor of burnt transmission fluid permeated the air. Black and gray smoke bellowed into the night sky and was carried away with the breeze.

Cain let go of the doorknob and hid himself in the shadows as two guards sprinted to inspect the engines. Each carried an Uzi and had it pointed toward the stars. Cain studied how the guards held and moved with their machine guns. He knew that most Japanese were unfamiliar with guns, especially since the law in 1965 that prohibited civilians from owning small arms. But the yakuza didn't fear the law. And they owned the seaports—importing and exporting whatever black-market goods they desired.

Cain put the flare gun down and quickly and quietly grabbed the yacht's aluminum gaff pole, which was attached to the wall. Cain expanded the telescopic pole and tightened the fasteners. He held the gaff just like a *shinai*—the bamboo staff he'd trained with during his kendo classes. He lowered his center of gravity and shuffled toward the taller of his targets. Cain thrust the *shinai* into the man's midsection with such force that the fasteners couldn't sustain the impact. The gaff collapsed but not without first propelling the gangster off the yacht and into the abyss.

The other man, who had been inspecting the engine, glanced up and was shocked to come face-to-face with the gaijin. He pointed the Uzi's ten-inch barrel at Cain's head. Cain dropped the gaff and lunged toward the gunman with arms outstretched, attempting to grab the Uzi and redirect its aim. He arrived a millisecond too late. The yakuza pulled the trigger. Cain was sure he was dead. He had failed to save Bonnie, just as he had failed to save his wife and son.

In a surreal moment of recognition, Cain realized that he was *not* dead. The gangster had pulled the trigger, but the Uzi hadn't fired. Cain wrestled the muzzle away with his left hand while simultaneously reaching down toward his calf with his other hand. He depressed the safety button and released the ten-inch knife from its protective case. He gripped the knife and thrust it upward with such force that the blade tore into the man's solar plexus, stopping only when the hilt had struck his ribs. The mortally wounded yakuza went wide-eyed and dropped the Uzi onto the deck. He fell to his knees, clutching at his wound. Cain looked down at the dying yakuza without pity. He grabbed the handle of his knife, placed his foot against the man's chest, and yanked out the knife as he kicked the man off the yacht and into the black water.

El Viento slowly approached in the darkness. The other yakuza member was treading water and swimming back toward the *Minashigo*. Alvarez stood on the sailboat, widened his stance for balance and strength, and swung a baseball bat. The knocked-out yakuza submerged slowly like a crocodile.

Cain gave Chief Alvarez the thumbs-up.

"Behind you, Hurricane!" Chief Alvarez shouted, and pointed from his sailboat. "Check your six!"

Cain turned his head and saw the brawny yakuza man running full speed toward him while firing his revolver like a cornered soldier. Cain fell to the deck, making his body the smallest target he could, and retrieved the Uzi that only moments before had almost blown his head off. He cycled the bolt, which ejected the dud round, and inserted a fresh bullet into the chamber. While still lying on his back, he pointed the Uzi at the advancing yakuza. He put his left hand over his right wrist to control the recoil and pulled the trigger. At a firing rate of six hundred rounds per minute, the Uzi sprayed thirty-two bullets in three seconds. The slide locked to the rear when it ran out of bullets to spit out. The barrel and chamber were smoking, but all the bullets had hit the muscle-bound kidnapper. He fell flat on his face and his revolver slid across the deck. Cain grabbed it and opened the cylinder. All the bullets except one had been fired. *I better make this one count,* he told himself. He took the revolver and ran toward the cabin where Bonnie was tied up.

CHAPTER 79

CAIN HAD ONLY one bullet left in the revolver, and it was reserved for Yamamoto—he was going to personally take care of Sato with his bare hands. The betrayal he felt seethed through his body as he envisioned tearing Sato apart limb from limb.

Cain's elbow was bent at waist level, his pistol leading the way. He opened the door and entered the grand room unnoticed. He was confused to see Sato and Yamamoto sword fighting.

Although both men were in their sixties, they were strong and agile, and it was apparent that they were in a fight to the death as they swung their katanas with raw power and technique. With each potentially deadly swing, the air made a swooshing sound. With each contact, the swords' forged steel clanged loudly—a constant reminder of imminent death. Yamamoto gripped his sword tightly, brought it to his waist, and lunged toward Sato with a straight-in strike.

Sato stepped to the side, raised his arms in a clockwise direction, and swung his sword down like a lumberjack chopping wood. The downward swing was so powerful that the sword fell out of Yamamoto's hands and bounced on the floor. Sato swung his body 360 degrees, like a tornado. His out-stretched sword trailed him like a shadow. He stopped precisely below Yamamoto's head, the blade nicking his neck.

"You are defeated," Sato said between panting breaths. "You tried to take my life, yet I have spared yours. Leave me and my company alone."

Yamamoto touched his neck and looked at his hand. Fresh blood was on the tips of his fingers. He lowered his head in shame, a gesture ceremoniously acknowledging his defeat.

"Watashi wa haiboku o mitomemasu." Yamamoto had admitted defeat.

"Hai," Sato acknowledged, and turned toward Bonnie, his sword still in his hand.

Cain aimed his snub-nosed revolver at Sato and placed his finger on the trigger.

"I'm so sorry this happened to you, Bonnie-san." Sato untied the knots on the rope that bound her.

When Cain saw this, he lowered his pistol.

Sato took off his shirt, and Bonnie emitted a slight gasp at the sight of the tattoos on his chest.

"That was from a past life," he said as he covered her nude body with his shirt.

Yamamoto quickly picked up his sword from the floor and rushed toward the unarmed and now kneeling Sato.

"Watch out!" Bonnie yelled.

Sato looked at Yamamoto, but there was nothing he could do from his position. He turned and placed himself in front of Bonnie. At that very instant, Cain straightened his arms and pointed the revolver at Yamamoto. He squeezed the trigger and fired the remaining bullet. The single .38 full-metal-jacket bullet tore into Yamamoto's shoulder, causing him to drop the sword and fall to the floor a mere foot from Sato and Bonnie.

Cain ran toward Yamamoto, who was reaching for the sword, refusing to give up. Cain stepped on his hand clutching the katana and felt the man's bones break against the weight. He grabbed the sword out of Yamamoto's mangled fingers and stared into the emotionless eyes of the yakuza's head boss. Cain gripped the sword with both hands, just as he had learned to do at his kendo classes. He positioned his right foot in front of him and raised the samurai sword into the air.

"Cain!" Bonnie shouted. "Don't kill him."

He turned to Bonnie, still holding the sword at the ready.

"I'm safe now. Don't kill him. He's not worth it."

Cain was looking at his sister when he heard the swooshing sound of disturbed air. He quickly turned to Yamamoto and realized he was dead. With one powerful swing of the blade, Sato had decapitated Yamamoto, sending his head rolling across the carpet.

"You're right, Bonnie-san," Sato said. "He's not worth it."

Cain dropped the sword and rushed to Bonnie.

"I always knew you'd find me," she said. Tears of joy streamed down her face. "I never doubted."

"Well, that makes one of us, because I certainly had my doubts." After a moment of embracing his sister, Cain turned to Sato. "How do I know that this wasn't just some internal rivalry, and now you're taking over the yakuza as the new *oyabun*?"

"Cain, he risked his life to save me!" Bonnie exclaimed. "And he just killed the head of the Yamamoto-gumi."

"You must believe me, Cain-san," said Sato. "Had

I known that Bonnie-san was taken and held like this, I would have corrected this much sooner."

"How can I believe you after all I've seen?"

"*I* believe him," Bonnie said. "Sato-san is a good man."

"Yamamoto and I met as young boys in the orphanage," Sato explained. "The yakuza became our family. As I grew older, I became disheartened by the violence. I was more interested in making my money legitimately and giving back to the communities."

Sato turned to Bonnie. He reached out to shake her hand. She pushed it aside and tightly embraced him. "Thank you for coming for me. I will never forget you."

Sato's hardened eyes softened and he nodded his head briskly. He turned to Cain. "I have a helicopter here. I will take you and Bonnie-san wherever you want to go."

"Thank you, but I already have transportation waiting outside."

"I've never met a gaijin more resourceful than you," Sato said. "You have saved my life twice, and I am forever in your debt." He bowed in respect.

"*Arigato gozaimasu.*" Cain returned the bow. "You go ahead and hop in your chopper and get out of here. I'll make sure none of this gets tied back to you."

"*Arigato,*" Sato said. Before he left the room, he grabbed the *noren,* the yakuza's brotherhood banner, from the wall and ripped it. He used it to wipe off Yamamoto's blood from his sword and then tossed the blood-soaked *noren* onto Yamamoto's headless body.

Cain wrapped his arm around Bonnie's waist to support her. "Sis, how about getting the hell out of here?" On their way out, Cain turned back to look once more into the unblinking eyes of Yamamoto's severed head. "Sayonara."

CHAPTER 80

BONNIE WAS EXHAUSTED, and Cain supported her weight with his arm around her waist. "I kept sending you messages," she said. "I *knew* you'd get 'em."

"I always do." He picked up the flare gun outside the room and walked alongside her as they made their way aft.

"Yep." She smiled. "Ever since that day I fell overboard when we were just kids—that's when I was convinced."

"We're connected," he replied. "At the hip," he added for levity.

Chief Alvarez, who was still bobbing up and down on *El Viento,* saw them staggering toward the rear of the yacht. He pulled the rope that started the outboard engine and met them at the *Minashigo.*

"Give me your hand, Bonnie." Chief Alvarez helped her onto the small sailboat. Bonnie was still shaking.

"Alan Alvarez? Are my eyes deceiving me?" Bonnie said. "How many years has it been?"

"Hurricane and Claire's wedding." He embraced her. "You're safe now. Just relax."

"Where are we going?" she asked.

"I'm taking us to the American Navy base."

She nodded.

"I've got one last thing to do," said Cain, who was still on the *Minashigo*. He grabbed the fuel lines on the outboard motors and ripped them off with his hand. Diesel fuel started pouring onto the deck of the yacht and spreading. He then stepped on board *El Viento* and kicked the sailboat away from the yacht.

Chief Alvarez twisted the throttle and reversed the sailboat away from the yacht. When they were about ten yards away, Cain instructed the chief to stop.

Cain balanced himself on the rocking sailboat and retrieved the flare gun. He cocked the hammer and pointed the gun toward the yacht's outboard engines. He squeezed the trigger and an orange fireball rocketed across the ocean, lighting the darkness, until it hit the engines and they caught fire. The blaze grew, consuming more and more of the yacht until the entire *Minashigo* was on fire. Dark smoke billowed into the sky.

They could feel the heat and smell burning plastic and diesel from the sailboat. Cain turned to Chief Alvarez. "RTB."

"Roger," Alvarez acknowledged.

"What's RTB?" Bonnie asked.

"Return to base," Cain said. He sat on the deck next to her, his arm around her shoulder, and watched the *Minashigo* start to disintegrate.

Bonnie looked at him. "I gotta go to my apartment. I've got nothing with me. No clothes, no jewelry." She paused. "My life is there."

"We can't go back to your apartment. We can probably never even return to Japan. We'll both always be on the yakuza's hit list. Forever. Or at least until the yakuza is disbanded."

Bonnie started crying. "I feel so guilty," she said.

"Guilty?" Cain asked. "Why?"

"There are more women, just like me," she said. "They're being held somewhere else. I overheard them talking about how they were going to send them on a cargo ship that goes from Japan to Italy before heading to the Middle East."

"Where in Italy?"

"Naples," she said.

Dismantling the yakuza's global influence would require attacking the organization from multiple angles. Cain called Tanaka to follow up on the information that LeRoy Hayes had mailed.

"We did the impossible," Cain said with relief.

"You rescued Bonnie-san?"

"You guessed it. She's safe now."

"That is wonderful news!" Tanaka said.

"I need to get that package from you—the one His Royal Highness sent. Can you meet us at the base in Yokosuka?"

"You cannot come near me," Tanaka warned. "The police are looking everywhere for you. Your picture is all over the news. You're wanted for the murder of Hayabusa. My father even interrogated me about your whereabouts. The inspectors have been following me. I detected them using the countersurveillance techniques you taught us."

Cain's realization that he would never be free from this chase started to set in. He doubted that the Japanese would understand that a gaijin was a victim of circumstances. They would always look at him as a cold-blooded murderer.

"Then can you do me one last favor, Tanaka-san?"

"Hai."

"Please mail that package to the *Stars and Stripes*

office in Yokosuka. Address it to the attention of Champ Albright the Third. He'll know what to do with it."

"I thought you hated the press."

Cain smirked. "That journalist has grown on me. Kind of like an ugly birthmark you learn to accept."

Tanaka started laughing. "You have a certain way with words."

Cain laughed back. "You've always gotten my sense of humor, Tanaka-san. I'll miss you. You're always welcome at my home, *partner.*"

"Partner?" Tanaka repeated. "You've never called me *partner* before."

"You've earned it, Tanaka-san. Before I go, someone else here wants to talk to you." He handed the phone to Bonnie.

"I'll miss you, too, Tanaka-san," she said. "You're one of the good guys." She listened and smiled. "Thank you for being there for my brother." Following Tanaka's response, she replied with tears in her eyes, "*Genki de,* Tanaka-san."

After Bonnie handed the phone back to her brother, she asked, "Where is your wedding ring? Did you lose it on the yacht?" She knew what his ring meant to him, what it symbolized.

Cain looked down at his bare finger. "I stopped wearing it."

"What? After all these years?"

"I found a special woman who helped me find inner peace."

"That's wonderful." Bonnie smiled. "A little shocking, and way overdue, but still wonderful news. Who is she? Where is she?"

"Safe," he replied. "But we're not. The yakuza

must have stolen your passport at your apartment. It wasn't there when I searched the place."

"They must have," she replied. "I certainly don't have it."

"I was able to grab your flight attendant ID, though," he said. "The police are surely watching for us at Narita and Haneda. They'd be foolish not to."

"Do you have any suggestions?" Bonnie asked.

Cain shook his head.

"I might have an idea," Chief Alvarez suggested.

Bonnie and Cain turned to face him.

"It's a wild, crazy idea, and it's a long shot, but it might work."

"Well," Cain said. "We ain't got any other ideas. And beggars can't be choosers."

"The USS *George Washington* departs Yokosuka tomorrow for exercise Valiant Shield. What if I were able to smuggle y'all on board? There's over five thousand sailors. What's another two?"

"What's Valiant Shield?" Bonnie asked. "And how is being smuggled on board another ship gonna help us get back to America?"

"Valiant Shield is the largest military exercise in the Pacific. There'll be tons of ships, submarines, and other countries participating. We'll have a rest and relaxation port call in Guam."

Cain started nodding in agreement. "That might just work. Guam is American territory."

"And United Airlines has a hub there," Bonnie said. "If we can get to their counter, we can deadhead to America."

"Well then," Chief Alvarez began, "I just need to make a call and get two flight suits ready for you guys."

Cain felt a sense of relief as *El Viento* rounded

Monkey Island and headed toward the dock at the Yokosuka American Navy base. At that moment, nothing symbolized the United States more than the McDonald's right next to the boat launch. Its golden arches illuminated the night sky and served as a lighthouse calling the Lemaires home—or at least one step closer to being back in Louisiana.

But then it hit him. There was one big problem with Chief Alvarez's plan, Cain realized. It meant he'd be leaving behind what he had come to love most about Japan.

Umiko.

He stood up and walked toward the front of the sailboat for privacy. He pulled out his phone. He wanted to call her, but he couldn't. The police would be tracing his calls. He looked down at the phone. *If they're searching for me by this device, then they can look for me here.* He tossed his phone into the water and watched it get swallowed up by the ocean.

CHAPTER 81

"CAN I BORROW some yen from you?" Cain asked Alvarez. "I need to make a call before we board the *Washington*."

"Just use my phone," the chief offered, and patted his pockets in search of it.

"Thanks, but I don't want any of this being tied back to you. And I'm worried the police may be tracing my phone, so I'm gonna use the pay phone outside the Mickey D's."

"Okay, but make it fast. I have a petty officer bringing me the flight suits now." Alvarez gave him a handful of coins.

Cain went to the phone booth and lifted the handset, dropped in a few coins, and dialed Umiko's number from memory.

The phone rang a few times before her voicemail answered.

"Umi, this is Cain. I was hoping to talk to you one last time before I left. I'm not even really sure what to say, though." He paused for a moment. "I just wish things could have turned out differently for us."

Chief Alvarez and Bonnie were tying *El Viento* to the dock when three Japanese police cars lined up at the nearby gate. Their signature red emergency lights were on and rotating as the police officers talked to the military guards about gaining access.

Cain knew that he and Bonnie had to get on the USS *Washington* quickly. Even though this was an American base, the Japanese had concurrent jurisdiction. They'd be allowed on the base to look for him and arrest him. Besides the embassy, the ship was the only true American sovereignty in Japan.

Cain saw one of the police cars rolling through the gate. He made eye contact with Alvarez and nodded to his friend, acknowledging the urgency. He turned back to the phone and lowered his voice as he spoke into the handset.

"I've gotta run, Umi. Thank you for everything. I'm sorry it ended like this, but I don't think I'll ever be able to come back to Japan." Before he hung up, he said one last thing to her. It was what she had told him at their Zen retreat. "*Au wa wakare no hajimari.* I guess all good things come to an end, and you are a good thing, Umi."

CHAPTER 82

THE MILITARY POLICE OFFICER standing watch on the deck next to a wooden podium looked intimidating. The athletically built policeman had a Beretta 9mm handgun strapped to his hip and an M4 assault rifle slung across the body armor that hugged his torso. He inspected every sailor who requested to come aboard the USS *George Washington*.

"That military cop looks really serious," Bonnie said nervously. "We're going to get caught and arrested!"

"Relax, Lieutenant," Chief Alvarez said, trying to calm her. "You've already come this far. Plus, that watch stander is looking for terrorists, not two Cajuns in flight suits."

Cain and Bonnie headed to the gangway.

"Jesus, this boat is way bigger than I would have ever imagined," Bonnie said.

Alvarez put his arm around Bonnie. "This is not a boat. It's a ship, and not just any ship. It's a nuclear-powered super aircraft carrier. It's the might of the American military and what keeps us free."

Cain smiled with pride. He felt as though he was reliving his navy days. He and Bonnie were just two military pilots out of hundreds of aviators on board. And as pilots, they were commissioned officers, with a set of parallel silver bars displayed on each shoulder of their flight suits. *The chief really delivered. Bravo, Zulu,* Cain thought as they approached the gruff military police officer.

"Permission to come aboard," Chief Alvarez asked while simultaneously saluting.

The military policeman returned the salute. "Welcome aboard, Chief."

"Permission to come aboard," Bonnie requested.

The guard saluted Bonnie. "Welcome aboard, Lieutenant."

Cain stepped onto the deck of the USS *George Washington* and was overcome with emotion. The ship's motto was engraved on a large wooden plaque attached to the wall. "The Spirit of Freedom," he said aloud, feeling euphoric as goose bumps formed on his forearms. In the corner, near the wooden podium, was the bust of President George Washington — America's first president. Behind the bust was the American flag with a gold-plated eagle on top. *Despite all our flaws, we're still the greatest country in the world,* Cain thought.

Tears formed in his eyes as he requested "permission to come aboard."

The guard snapped a crisp salute. "Permission granted. Welcome aboard, sir!"

Cain returned the salute with the same vigor and precision. He turned toward Alvarez, who noticed that Cain's eyes had welled up with tears.

"Are you okay?" Chief Alvarez asked.

"Never better," Cain replied.

They ducked their heads and entered the ship's hatch. The chief escorted them through the large hangar bay, which was crowded with various F-18 fighter jets and H-60 Seahawk helicopters.

"Where's the plane y'all used to fly?" Bonnie asked.

"The Mighty War Pig wouldn't be on this ship," Cain said. "It was a land-based submarine hunter."

"How many missions you figure we flew together?" Chief Alvarez asked, obviously feeling nostalgic. "At least the ones we can talk about."

"Counting tonight?" Cain smiled wearily.

Chief Alvarez returned the smile. "I reckon tonight's mission will stay top secret, unless that Champ Albright has anything to do with it."

"Champ Albright?" Bonnie joined their conversation. "The reporter I meant to introduce you to?"

"One and the same," Cain said. "He actually helped me find you. I'll tell you about it on our way to Guam."

"This ought to be good. I can't wait to hear all about it," she said.

Cain and Alvarez laughed as the chief continued escorting them through the ship to their sleeping berth. Even though it was technically a VIP room, it was still on board a military ship designed for combat. The USS *George Washington*'s mattresses were prison-thin, the pillows hard as rocks, and the wool blankets scratchy as sandpaper. Cain didn't care, though. As far as he was concerned, the mighty ship was the Ritz-Carlton.

"How did you score this room?" he asked Alvarez.

"It may seem like a new navy with the new generation joining nowadays, but chiefs still take care of each other. Let's just say I owe the supply officer a drink when we reach Guam."

"A room like this, I'm sure it's a lot of drinks," Cain replied.

"You guys are worth it."

Cain felt an enormous sense of gratitude. He wrapped one arm around Alvarez and the other around Bonnie and pulled them close.

"I'm just glad I could help you out in your time of need," the chief said. "Nobody is assigned this room until we pick up an admiral in Guam. So you and Bonnie can rest easy. You're safe now. When you wake up tomorrow, we'll be preparing to get under way."

Cain was used to pushing his body to its limits, but this had been different. He had gone days without rest or peace of mind, having been fueled by sheer determination to rescue Bonnie. As soon as Chief Alvarez shut the door on his way out, Cain lay in the bottom bunk, staring at the bunk above him. His mind drifted toward wonderful thoughts of Umiko. He thought of how special she was. How she'd gently cared for him, and of their life-changing kendo trip to the base of Mount Fuji. He would never forget that trip: the retreat had helped him overcome his feelings of guilt. Feeling a sense of newfound peace, he crashed into a dreamless sleep.

Hours later, what seemed like chaotic activity woke him. Hatches were opening and slamming shut. Senior enlisted sailors were shouting instructions and junior sailors were replying with the same level of intensity. The intercom bellowed commands from various military officers, but it was the command from the boatswain's mate that caught Cain's attention.

"Prepare to shift colors."

That was the command for sailors to stand at attention on the side of the ship in their dress white uniforms.

Cain and Bonnie stayed put in their room, competing for a view from the porthole. The pier was full of hundreds of family members waving good-bye to their military spouses and parents. It felt as if they were waving good-bye to Cain and Bonnie.

The sun was peeking over the mountain, slowly rising with each minute. The island nation was getting smaller as the massive aircraft carrier cut through the water and sailed on its own power.

"Take one last look, sis. The land of the rising sun."

"Sayonara," she whispered, peering through the small porthole.

"Soon we'll be in Guam, and then back on the bayou."

"Home sweet home," she said.

EPILOGUE

Ten months later

NEW ORLEANS WAS celebrating Mardi Gras, and the French Quarter was bursting at the seams with excitement. More than a million visitors had gathered near Café du Monde, Cain's favorite place to relax and enjoy coffee and beignets. The rowdy tourists lined Decatur Street, hooting and hollering as masked kings and queens threw beads and doubloons from atop ornate purple, green, and yellow floats.

Cain sat under one of the café's rotating wooden ceiling fans, sipping his chicory coffee from a white mug and wiping the beignets' powdered sugar off his lips. He loved the Big Easy's energy during this special time of year. He double-checked the time. *I have time for another round of coffee,* he told himself. He pulled out his copy of the *Times-Picayune* newspaper. The news was predominantly about sports, Louisiana politics, and Mardi Gras, but a headline caught his attention: a story reprinted from *USA Today* by none other than Champ Albright the Third.

Cain was snickering as he read Champ's story but was interrupted by the buzzing cell phone in his shirt pocket.

"Hello?"

"Hi, twin brother."

"You gotta talk much louder," Cain shouted into his phone. "It's a wonderful madhouse down here. I wish you could have joined me."

"Me, too! Are you at Café du Monde?"

"You know it, sis."

"I don't know anyone who loves that chicory coffee as much as you and Pops," Bonnie said. "By the way, have you checked out today's paper? Our old friend Cat has a big story. Looks like Japanese prosecutors have indicted seven senior-level yakuza members and seized over ten of their businesses—including the Angel Cloud and Hakugei."

"Hooyah!" Cain said. "*That* is how you take down an enterprise. You gotta hit 'em where it hurts: in their pocketbook. We can thank LeRoy for sending that information that helped track their assets."

"No, we can thank *you*. None of this would have ever happened if you were not in the equation."

"You're just biased, sis."

"Maybe. You are my favorite twin. That's why I did something special for you."

"Oh, no." Cain feigned worry. "I'm afraid to ask. What did you do this time?"

"Relax," Bonnie said. "You'll like this one. It should be arriving any minute now."

"Thank you, sis. I'll call as soon as I get it." He placed his phone back in his pocket and took a few more swigs of his coffee. To his left, the Mardi Gras parade was crawling through the French Quarter. He took a break from the spectacle and turned to the right. He looked at the boats cruising the Mississippi River. It was a sight that always calmed him and connected him to his South Louisiana roots.

"Is this seat taken?"

Her voice was faint, but he would have recognized it anywhere in the world. He turned to face her. It was Umiko.

Cain was shocked but stood and embraced her. "What are you doing here?"

"I've always wanted to see Mardi Gras," she said with that disarming smile. "Plus, you promised me beignets."

"That I did, Umi." Cain smiled wide. "That I did."

ABOUT THE AUTHORS

JAMES PATTERSON is the world's bestselling author and most trusted storyteller. He has created many enduring fictional characters and series, including Alex Cross, the Women's Murder Club, Michael Bennett, Maximum Ride, Middle School, and I Funny. Among his notable literary collaborations are *The President Is Missing*, with President Bill Clinton, and the Max Einstein series, produced in partnership with the Albert Einstein estate. Patterson's writing career is characterized by a single mission: to prove that there is no such thing as a person who "doesn't like to read," only people who haven't found the right book. He's given over three million books to schoolkids and the military, donated more than seventy million dollars to support education, and endowed over five thousand college scholarships for teachers. For his prodigious imagination and championship of literacy in America, Patterson was awarded the 2019 National Humanities Medal. The National Book Foundation recently presented him with the Literarian Award for Outstanding Service to the American Literary Community, and he is also the recipient of an Edgar Award and nine Emmy Awards. He lives in Florida with his family.

* * *

TUCKER AXUM III is a career law enforcement professional who has served as a special agent in the United States, Europe, Africa, Asia, and Australia. His first novel, *The Reawakening of Mage Axum*, was inspired by the mysterious disappearance of his uncle in Germany during World War II.

READ ON FOR A
SNEAK PEEK OF
*THE PRESIDENT'S
DAUGHTER*
BY JAMES PATTERSON
AND BILL CLINTON.

COMING IN JUNE
2021.

LAKE MARIE

New Hampshire

An hour or so after my daughter, Mel, leaves, I've showered, had my second cup of coffee, and read the newspapers—just skimming them, really, for it's a sad state of affairs when you eventually realize just how wrong journalists can be in covering stories. With a handsaw and a set of pruning shears, I head off to the south side of our property.

It's a special place, even though my wife, Samantha, has spent less than a month here in all her visits. Most of the land in the area is conservation land, never to be built upon, and of the people who do live here, almost all follow the old New Hampshire tradition of never bothering their neighbors or gossiping about them to visitors or news reporters.

Out on the lake is a white Boston Whaler with two men supposedly fishing, although they are Secret

Service. Last year the *Union Leader* newspaper did a little piece about the agents stationed aboard the boat—calling them the unluckiest fishermen in the state—but since then, they've been pretty much left alone.

As I'm chopping, cutting, and piling brush, I think back to two famed fellow POTUS brush cutters—Ronald Reagan and George W. Bush—and how their exertions never quite made sense to a lot of people. They thought, *Hey, you've been at the pinnacle of fame and power, why go out and get your hands dirty?*

I saw at a stubborn pine sapling that's near an old stone wall on the property, and think, *Because it helps. It keeps your mind occupied, your thoughts busy, so you don't continually flash back to memories of your presidential term.*

The long and fruitless meetings with Congressional leaders from both sides of the aisle, talking with them, arguing with them, and sometimes pleading with them, at one point saying, "Damn it, we're all Americans here—isn't there anything we can work on to move our country forward?"

And constantly getting the same smug, superior answers. "Don't blame us, Mr. President. Blame *them*."

The late nights in the Oval Office, signing letters of condolence to the families of the best of us, men and women who had died for the idea of America, not the squabbling and revenge-minded nation we have become. And three times running across the names of men I knew and fought with, back when I was younger, fitter, and with the teams.

And other late nights as well, reviewing what was called—in typical innocuous, bureaucratic fashion—the Disposition Matrix database, prepared by the National Counterterrorism Center, but was really known as the "kill list." Months of work, research, surveillance, and intelligence intercepts resulting in a list of known terrorists who were a clear and present danger to the United States. And there I was, sitting by myself, and like a Roman emperor of old, I put a check mark next to those I decided were going to be killed in the next few days.

The sapling finally comes down.

Mission accomplished.

I look up and see something odd flying in the distance.

I stop, shade my eyes. Since moving here, I've gotten used to the different kinds of birds moving in and around Lake Marie, including the loons, whose night calls sound like someone's being throttled, but I don't recognize what's flying over there now.

I watch for a few seconds, and then it disappears behind the far tree line.

And I get back to work, something suddenly bothering me, something I can't quite figure out.

BASE OF THE HUNTSMEN TRAIL

Mount Rollins, New Hampshire

In the front seat of a black Cadillac Escalade, the older man rubs at his clean-shaven chin and looks at the video display from the laptop set up on top of the center console. Sitting next to him in the passenger seat, the younger man has a rectangular control system in his hand, with two small joysticks and other switches. He is controlling a drone with a video system, and they've just watched the home of former president Matthew Keating disappear from view.

It pleases the older man to see the West's famed drone technology turned against them. For years he's done the same thing with their wireless networks and cell phones, triggering devices and creating the bombs that shattered so many bodies and sowed so much terror.

And the Internet—which promised so much when

it came out to bind the world as one—ended up turning into a well-used and safe communications network for him and his warriors.

The Cadillac they're sitting in was stolen this morning from a young couple and their infant in northern Vermont, after the two men abandoned their stolen pickup truck. There's still a bit of blood spatter and brain matter on the dashboard in front of them. An empty baby's seat is in the rear, along with a flowered cloth bag stuffed with toys and other childish things.

"Next?" the older man asks.

"We find the girl," he says. "It shouldn't take long."

"Do it," the older man says, watching with quiet envy and fascination as the younger man manipulates the controls of the complex machine while the drone's camera-made images appear on the computer screen.

"There. There she is."

From a bird's-eye view, he thinks, staring at the screen. A red sedan moves along the narrow paved roads.

He says, "And you are sure that the Americans, that they are not tracking you?"

"Impossible," the younger man next to him says in confidence. "There are thousands of such drones at play across this country right now. The officials who control the airspace, they have rules about where drones can go, and how high and low they can go, but most people ignore the rules."

"But their Secret Service…"

"Once President Matthew Keating left office, his daughter was no longer due the Secret Service protection. It's the law, if you can believe it. Under special circumstances, it can be requested, but no, not with her. The daughter wants to be on her own, going to school, without armed guards near her."

He murmurs, "A brave girl, then."

"And foolish," comes the reply.

And a stupid father, he thinks, to let his daughter roam at will like this, with no guards, no security.

The camera in the air follows the vehicle with no difficulty, and the older man shakes his head, again looking around him at the rich land and forests. Such an impossibly plentiful and gifted country, but why in Allah's name do they persist in meddling and interfering and being colonialists around the world?

A flash of anger sears through him.

If only they would stay home, how many innocents would still be alive?

"There," his companion says. "As I earlier learned...they are stopping here. At the beginning of the trail called Sherman's Path."

The vehicle on screen pulls into a dirt lot still visible from the air. Again, the older man is stunned at how easy it was to find the girl's schedule by looking at websites and bulletin boards from her college, from something called the Dartmouth Outing Club. Less than an hour's work and research has brought him here, looking down at her, like some blessed, all-seeing spirit.

He stares at the screen once more. Other vehicles are parked in the lot, and the girl and the boy get out. Both retrieve knapsacks from the rear of the vehicle. There's an embrace, a kiss, and then they walk away from the vehicles and disappear into the woods.

"Satisfied?" his companion asks.

For years, he thinks in satisfaction, the West has used these drones to rain down hellfire upon his friends, his fighters, and, yes, his family and other families. Fat and comfortable men (and women!) sipping their sugary drinks in comfortable chairs in safety, killing from thousands of kilometers away, seeing the silent explosions but not once hearing them, or hearing the shrieking and crying of the wounded and dying, and then driving home without a care in the world.

Now, it's his turn.

His turn to look from the sky.

Like a falcon on the hunt, he thinks.

Patiently and quietly waiting to strike.

SHERMAN'S PATH

Mount Rollins, New Hampshire

It's a clear, cool, and gorgeous day on Sherman's Path, and Mel Keating is enjoying this climb up to Mount Rollins, where she and her boyfriend, Nick Kenyon, will spend the night with other members of the Dartmouth Outing Club at a small hut the club owns near the summit. She stops for a moment on a granite outcropping and puts her thumbs through her knapsack's straps.

Nick emerges from the trail and surrounding scrub brush, smiling, face a bit sweaty, bright blue knapsack on his back, and he takes her extended hand as he reaches her. "Damn nice view, Mel," he says.

She kisses him. "I've got a better view ahead."

"Where?"

"Just you wait."

She lets go of his hand and gazes at the rolling peaks of the White Mountains and the deep green of the forests, and notices the way some of the trees look a darker shade of green from the overhead clouds gently scudding by. Out beyond the trees is the Connecticut River and the mountains of Vermont.

Mel takes a deep, cleansing breath.

Just her and Nick and nobody else.

She lowers her glasses, and everything instantly turns to muddled shapes of green and blue. Nothing to see, nothing to spot. She remembers the boring times at state dinners back at the White House, when she'd be sitting with Mom and Dad, and she'd lower her glasses so all she could see were colored blobs. That made the time pass, when she really didn't want to be there, didn't really want to see all those well-dressed men and women pretending to like Dad and be his friend so they could get something in return.

Mel slides the glasses back up, and everything comes into view.

That's what she likes.

Being ignored and seeing only what she wants to see.

Nick reaches between the knapsack and rubs her neck. "What are you looking at?"

"Nothing."

"Oh, that doesn't sound good."

Mel laughs. "Silly man, it's the best! No staff, no news reporters, no cameras, no television correspondents, no Secret Service agents standing like dark-suited statues in the corner. Nobody! Just you and me."

"Sounds lonely," Nick says.

She slaps his butt. "Don't you get it? There's nobody

keeping an eye on me, and I'm loving every second of it. Come along, let's get moving."

Some minutes later, Nick is sitting at the edge of a small mountainside pool, ringed with boulders and saplings and shrubs, letting his feet soak, enjoying the sun on his back, thinking of how damn lucky he is.

He had been shy at first when meeting Mel last semester in an African history seminar—everyone on the Dartmouth campus knew who she was, so that was no secret—and he had no interest in trying to even talk to her until Mel started getting crap thrown at her one day in class. She had said something about the importance of microloans in Africa, and a few loudmouths started hammering her about being ignorant of the real world, being privileged, and not having an authentic life.

When the loudmouths took a moment to catch their respective breaths, Nick surprised himself by saying, "I grew up in a third-floor apartment in Southie. My Dad was a lineman for the electric company, my Mom worked cleaning other people's homes and clipped coupons to go grocery shopping, and man, I'd trade that authentic life for privilege any day of the week."

A bunch of the students laughed. Mel caught his eye with a smile and he asked her after class to get a coffee or something at Lou's Bakery, and that's how it started.

Him, a scholarship student, dating the daughter of President Matt Keating.

What a world.

What a life.

Sitting on a moss-colored boulder, Mel nudges him and says, "How's your feet?"

"Feeling cold and fine."

"Then let's do the whole thing," she says, standing up, tugging off her gray Dartmouth sweatshirt. "Feel like a swim?"

He smiles. "Mel…someone could see us!"

She smiles right back, wearing just a tan sports bra under the sweatshirt, as she starts lowering her shorts. "Here? In the middle of a national forest? Lighten up, sweetie. Nobody's around for miles."

After she strips, Mel yelps out as she jumps into the pool, keeping her head and glasses above water. The water is cold and sharp. Poor Nick takes his time, wading in, shifting his weight as he tries to keep his footing on the slippery rocks, and he yowls like a hurt puppy when the cold mountain water reaches just below his waist.

The pond is small, and Mel reaches the other side with three strong strokes, and she swims back, the cold water now bracing, making her heart race, everything tingling. She tilts her head back, looking up past the tall pines and seeing the bright, bare blue patch of sky. Nothing. Nobody watching her, following her, recording her.

Bliss.

Another yelp from Nick, and she turns her head to him. Nick had wanted to go Navy ROTC, but a bad set of lungs prevented him from doing so, and even though she knows Dad wishes he'd get a haircut, his Southie background and interest in the Navy scored Nick in the plus side of the boyfriend column with Dad.

Nick lowers himself farther into the water, until it reaches his strong shoulders. "Did you see the sign-up list for the overnight at the cabin?" he asks. "Sorry to say, Cam Carlucci is coming."

"I know," she says, treading water, leaning back, letting her hair soak, looking up at the sharp blue and empty sky.

"You know he's going to want you to—"

Mel looks back at Nick. "Yeah. He and his buds want to go to the Seabrook nuclear plant this Labor Day weekend, occupy it, and shut it down."

Poor Nick's lips seem to be turning blue. "They sure want you there."

In a mocking tone, Mel imitates Cam and says, "'Oh, Mel, you can make such an impact if you get arrested. Think of the headlines. Think of your influence.' To hell with him. They don't want me there as me. They want a puppet they can prop up to get coverage."

Nick laughs. "You going to tell him that tonight?"

"Nah," she says. "He's not worth it. I'll tell him I have plans for Labor Day weekend instead."

Her boyfriend looks puzzled. "You do?"

She swims to him and gives him a kiss, hands on his shoulders. "Dopey boy, yes, with you."

His hands move through the water to her waist, and she's enjoying the touch—just as she hears voices and looks up.

For the first time in a long time she's frightened.

LAKE MARIE

New Hampshire

After getting out of the shower for the second time today (the first after taking a spectacular tumble in a muddy patch of dirt) and drying off, I idly play the which-body-scar-goes-to-which-op when my iPhone rings. I wrap a towel around me, picking up the phone, knowing only about twenty people in the world have this number. Occasionally, though, a call comes in from "John" in Mumbai pretending to be a Microsoft employee in Redmond, Washington. I've been tempted to tell John who he's really talking to, but I've resisted the urge.

This time, however, the number is blocked, and puzzled, I answer the phone.

"Keating," I say.

A strong woman's voice comes through. "Mr. President? This is Sarah Palumbo, calling from the NSC."

The name quickly pops up in my mind. Sarah's been the deputy national security advisor for the National Security Council since my term, and she should have gotten the director's position when Melissa Powell retired to go back to academia. But someone to whom President Barnes owed a favor got the position. A former Army brigadier general and deputy director at the CIA, Sarah knows her stuff, from the annual output of Russian oilfields to the status of Colombian cartel smuggling submarines.

"Sarah, good to hear from you," I say, still dripping some water onto the bathroom's tile floor. "How're your mom and dad doing? Enjoying the snowbird life in Florida?"

Sarah and her family grew up in Buffalo, where lake effect winter storms can dump up to four feet of snow in an afternoon. She chuckles and says, "They're loving every warm second of it. Sir, do you have a moment?"

"My day is full of moments," I reply. "What's going on?"

"Sir...," and the tone of her voice instantly changes, worrying me. "Sir, this is unofficial, but I wanted to let you know what I learned this morning. Sometimes the bureaucracy takes too long to respond to emerging developments, and I don't want that to happen here. It's too important."

I say, "Go on."

She says, "I was sitting in for the director at today's threat-assessment meeting, going over the President's Daily Brief and other interagency reports."

With those words of jargon, I'm instantly transported back to being POTUS, and I'm not sure I like it.

"What's going on, Sarah?"

The briefest of pauses. "Sir, we've noticed an uptick in chatter from various terrorist cells in the Mideast, Europe, and Canada. Nothing we can specifically attach a name or a date to, but something is on the horizon, something bad, something that will generate a lot of attention."

Shit, I think. "All right," I say. "Terrorists are keying themselves up to strike. Why are you calling me? Who are they after?"

"Mr. President," she says, "they're coming after you."

JAMES
PATTERSON
RECOMMENDS

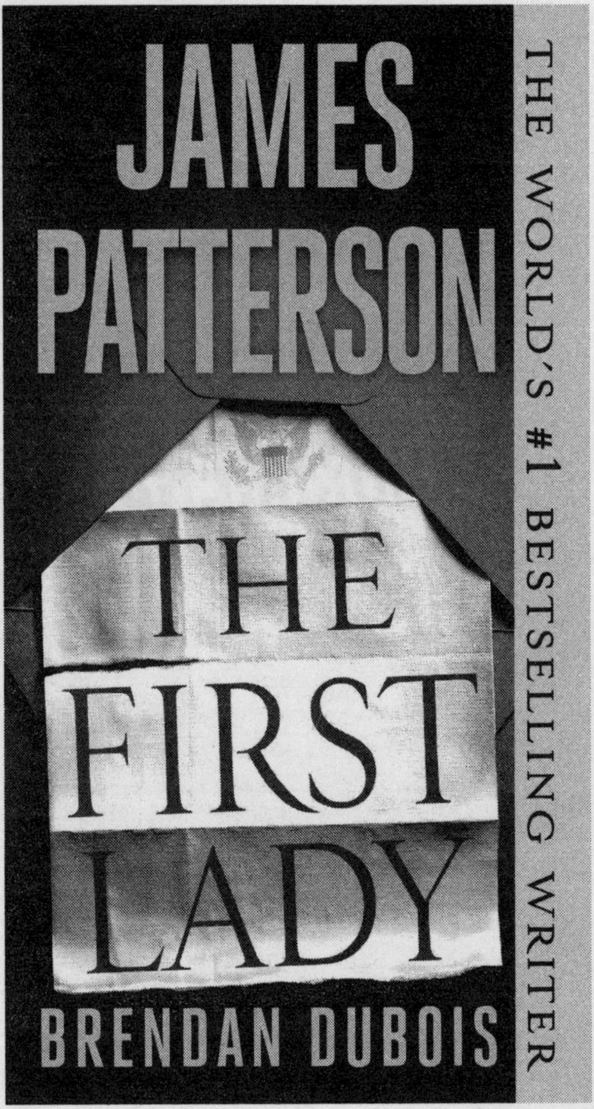
JAMES PATTERSON
THE FIRST LADY
BRENDAN DUBOIS
THE WORLD'S #1 BESTSELLING WRITER

THE FIRST LADY

The US government is at the forefront of everyone's mind these days, and I've become incredibly fascinated by the idea that one secret can bring it all down. What if that secret is a US president's affair that results in a nightmarish outcome?

Sally Grissom, leader of the Presidential Protection Division, is summoned to a private meeting with the president and his chief of staff to discuss the disappearance of the first lady. What at first seemed an escape to a safe haven turns into a kidnapping when a ransom note arrives along with what could be the first lady's finger.

It's a race against the clock to collect the evidence that all leads to one troubling question: could the kidnappers be people working inside the White House?

JAMES PATTERSON

TEXAS RANGER

& ANDREW BOURELLE

TEXAS RANGER

So many of my detectives are dark and gritty and deal with crimes in some of our grimmest cities. That's why I'm thrilled to bring you Detective Rory Yates, my most honorable detective yet.

As a Texas Ranger, he has a code that he lives and works by. But when he comes home for a much-needed break, he walks into a crime scene where the victim is none other than his ex-wife—and he's the prime suspect. Yates has to risk everything in order to clear his name, and he dives into the inferno of the most twisted mind I've ever created. Can his code bring him back out alive?

THE
WORLD'S
#1
BEST-
SELLING
WRITER

JAMES
PATTERSON
JUROR #3

AND NANCY ALLEN

A YOUNG
ATTORNEY
TRIES HER
FIRST
MAJOR
CASE...

AND IT'S
MURDER
ONE.

JUROR #3

In the Deep South of Mississippi, Ruby Bozarth is a newcomer, both to Rosedale and to the bar. And now she's tapped as a defense counsel in a racially charged felony. The murder of a woman from an old family has Rosedale's upper crust howling for blood, and the prosecutor is counting on Ruby's inexperience to help him deliver a swift conviction.

Ruby is determined to build a defense that sticks for her college football star client. While she's looking for help in unexpected quarters, her case is rattled as news of a second murder breaks. As intertwining investigations unfold, no one can be trusted, especially the twelve men and women on the jury. They may be hiding the most incendiary secret of all.

For a complete list of books by

JAMES PATTERSON

VISIT
JamesPatterson.com

 Follow James Patterson on Facebook
@JamesPatterson

 Follow James Patterson on Twitter
@JP_Books

 Follow James Patterson on Instagram
@jamespattersonbooks